IN GLITTERING SHANGHAI, A MONSTER AWAKENS. . . .

★ "A must-read with a conclusion that will leave readers craving more."—*Kirkus Reviews*, starred review

★ "Gong's debut is not to be missed. With a dazzling setting, a mysterious series of murders, and diverse, unapologetically criminal characters, this novel ranks with the greatest YA retellings."
—*SLJ* starred review

★ "A lush, wholly original debut that will satiate Shakespeare aficionados and draw those seeking an engrossing, multifaceted historical fantasy."
—*Publishers Weekly*, starred review

★ "The gripping stakes, diverse and compelling characters, and all-consuming mystery make this a particularly rich and rewarding debut."
—*Shelf Awareness*, starred review

★ "A high-energy novel about how people can be monsters, too."
—*Booklist*, starred review

"A thrilling blend of political intrigue, gruesome horror, race-against-the-clock mystery, and, yes, romance, set against a city that becomes a character in its own right."
—*BCCB*

"A deliciously dark twist on *Romeo and Juliet* that feels vibrant, modern, and wholly exciting. Gong's writing brims with energy. I was swept away to her dark Shanghai from the first page and never wanted to leave!"
—NATASHA NGAN, *New York Times* bestselling author of *Girls of Paper and Fire*

THESE

VIOLENT

DELIGHTS

CHLOE GONG

MARGARET K. McELDERRY BOOKS
New York London Toronto Sydney New Delhi

MARGARET K. McELDERRY BOOKS

An imprint of Simon & Schuster Children's Publishing Division

1230 Avenue of the Americas, New York, New York 10020

For information about special discounts for bulk purchases, please contact Simon & Schuster Special Sales at 1-866-506-1949 or business@simonandschuster.com.

The Simon & Schuster Speakers Bureau can bring authors to your live event.

For more information or to book an event contact the Simon & Schuster Speakers Bureau at 1-866-248-3049 or visit our website at www.simonspeakers.com.

Interior designed by Mike Rosamilia

The text of this book was set in ITC Galliard Std.

Manufactured in the United States of America

First Edition

2 4 6 8 10 9 7 5 3 1

Library of Congress Cataloging-in-Publication Data

Names: Gong, Chloe, author.

Title: These violent delights / by Chloe Gong.

Description: New York : Simon Pulse, 2020. | Series: These violent delights ; 1 | Audience: Ages 14 up. | Summary: In 1926 Shanghai, eighteen-year-old Juliette Cai, heir of the Scarlet Gang, and her first love-turned-rival Roma Montagov, leader of the White Flowers, must work together when mysterious deaths threaten their city.

Identifiers: LCCN 2019055326 (print) | LCCN 2019055327 (ebook) | ISBN 9781534457690 (hardcover) | ISBN 9781665921763 (paperback) | | ISBN 9781534457713 (ebook)

Subjects: CYAC: Monsters—Fiction. | Death—Fiction. | Gangs—Fiction. | Shanghai (China)—History—20th century—Fiction. | China—History—1912-1928—Fiction.

Classification: LCC PZ7.1.G65218 The 220 (print) | LCC PZ7.1.G65218 (ebook) | DDC [Fic]—dc23

LC record available at https://lccn.loc.gov/2019055326

LC ebook record available at https://lccn.loc.gov/2019055327

ISBN 9781665948623 (B&N Proprietary Edition)

FOR YOU,
DEAREST READER

These violent delights have violent ends
And in their triumph die, like fire and powder,
Which, as they kiss, consume.
                        —Shakespeare, *Romeo and Juliet*

THESE

VIOLENT

DELIGHTS

Prologue

In glittering Shanghai, a monster awakens.

Its eyes snap open in the belly of the Huangpu River, jaws unhinging at once to taste the foul blood seeping into the waters. Lines of red slither through this ancient city's modern streets: lines that draw webs in the cobblestones like a network of veins, and drip by drip these veins surge into the waters, pouring the city's life essence into the mouth of another.

As the night grows dark, the monster pushes itself up, eventually emerging from the waves with the leisure of a forgotten god. When it turns its head up, all that can be seen is the low-hanging, plump moon.

It breathes in. It slinks closer.

Its first breath transforms into a cold breeze, hurtling into the streets and brushing the ankles of those unfortunate enough to be stumbling home during the devil's hour. This place hums to the tune of debauchery. This city is filthy and deep in the thrall of unending sin, so saturated with the kiss of decadence that the sky threatens to buckle and crush all those living vivaciously beneath it in punishment.

But no punishment comes—not yet. The decade is loose and the morals are looser. As the West throws its arms up in unending party, as the rest of the Middle Kingdom remains splintered among aging warlords and the remnants of imperial rule, Shanghai sits in its own little bubble of power: *the Paris of the East, the New York of the West.*

Despite the toxin trickling from every dead-ended alleyway, this place is so, so very *alive*. And the monster, too, is birthed anew.

Unknowingly, the people of this divided city carry on. Two men stumble out from their favorite brothel's open doors, their laughter piercing and loud. The silence of the late hour stands in sudden contrast to the roaring activity they have emerged from, and their ears struggle to adjust, ringing loudly with the transition.

One is short and stout, as if he could lie on the ground and begin rolling down the sidewalk in the manner of a marble; the other is tall and gawky, his limbs drawn in right angles. With their arms swung around each other's shoulders, they stumble toward the waterfront, toward the river that runs in from the sea where merchants arrive with commodities—day in, day out.

The two men are familiar with these ports; after all, when they're not frequenting jazz clubs or downing the newest shipments of wine from some foreign country, they run messages here, guard merchants here, haul stock back and forth here—all for the Scarlet Gang. They know this boardwalk like the back of their hands, even when it is presently quiet of the usual thousand different languages hollered under a thousand different flags.

At this hour, there is only the muffled music from nearby bars and the large shop banners overhead ruffling with every gust of wind.

And the five White Flowers talking animatedly in Russian.

It is the fault of the two Scarlet men for not hearing the racket sooner, but their brains are clogged with alcohol and their senses are buzzing pleasantly. By the time the White Flowers are in sight, by the time the men see their rivals standing around one of the ports, passing a bottle, shoving shoulders with uproarious laughter, neither party can back away without losing face.

The White Flowers straighten up, heads tilting into the wind.

"We should continue walking," the short Scarlet man whispers to his companion. "You know what Lord Cai said about getting into another fight with the White Flowers."

The gawkier one only bites down on the inside of his cheeks, sucking his face in until he looks like a smug, drunk ghoul.

"He said we shouldn't initiate anything. He never said we *couldn't* get into a fight."

The Scarlet men speak in the dialect of their city, their tongues laid flat and their sounds pressed tight. Even as they raise their voices with the confidence of being on home turf, they are uneasy, because it is rare now for a White Flower to not know the language—sometimes their accents are indistinguishable from a Shanghai native.

A fact that proves correct when one of the White Flowers, grinning, bellows, "Well, are you trying to pick a fight?"

The taller Scarlet man makes a low sound at the base of his throat and aims a wad of spit at the White Flowers. It lands by the shoe of the nearest.

In a blink: guns upon guns, each arm raised and steady and trigger-happy, ready to pull. This is a scene that no soul bats an eye toward any longer; this is a scene that is more commonplace in heady Shanghai than the smoke of opium wafting from a thick pipe.

"Hey! Hey!"

A whistle blows into the terse silence. The policeman who runs on site only expresses annoyance at the standstill before him. He has seen this exact scene three times already within the week. He has forced rivals into jail cells and called for cleanup when the members left one another dead and pierced with bullets instead. Weary with the day, all he wants to do is go home, soak his feet in hot water, and eat the meal his wife would have left cold on the table. His hand is already itching for his baton, itching to beat some sense into these men, itching to remind these people that they have no personal grudge against the other. All that fuels them is reckless, baseless loyalty to the Cais and the Montagovs, and it would be their ruin.

"Do we want to break this up and go home?" the policeman asks. "Or do we want to come with me and—"

He stops abruptly.

A *growl* is echoing from the waters.

The warning that radiates from such a sound is not a deniable sensation. It is not the sort of paranoia one feels when they think they are being followed down an abandoned junction; nor is it the sort of panic that ensues when a floorboard creaks in a house thought empty. It is solid, tangible—it almost exudes a moisture into the air, a weight pressing down on bare skin. It is a threat as obvious as a gun to the face, and yet there is a moment of inaction, a moment of hesitation. The short and stout Scarlet man wavers first, his eyes darting to the edge of the boardwalk. He ducks his head, peering into the murky depths, squinting to follow the choppy, rolling motions of the water's small ripples.

He is just at the right height for his companion to scream and knock him down with a brutal elbow to the temple when something bursts from the river.

Little black specks.

As the short man falls to the ground and slams down hard, the world is raining down on him in dots—strange things he cannot quite see as his vision spins and his throat gags in nausea. He can only feel pinpricks landing on him, itching his arms, his legs, his neck; he hears his companion screaming, the White Flowers roaring at one another in indecipherable Russian, then finally, the policeman shrieking in English, "Get it off! Get them off!"

The man on the ground has a thudding, thunderous heartbeat. With his forehead pressed to the boardwalk, unwilling to behold whatever is causing these terrible howls, his own pulse consumes him. It overtakes every one of his senses, and only when something thick and wet splashes against his leg does he scramble upright in horror, flailing so extremely that he kicks free a shoe and doesn't bother to fetch it.

He doesn't look back as he runs. He scrubs himself free of the debris that had rained down on him, hiccuping in his desperation to breathe in, breathe in, breathe in.

He doesn't look back to check what had been lurking in the waters. He doesn't look back to see if his companion needs help, and he certainly doesn't look back to determine what had landed on his leg with a viscous, sticky sensation. The man only runs and runs, past the neon delight of the theaters as the last of their lights wink off, past the whispers crawling under the front doors of brothels, past the sweet dreams of merchants who sleep with piles of money underneath their mattresses.

And he is long gone by the time there are only dead men lying along the ports of Shanghai, their throats torn out and their eyes staring up at the night sky, glassy with the reflection of the moon.

One

I n the heart of Scarlet Gang territory, a burlesque club was the place to be.

The calendar was rolling closer and closer to the end of the season, the pages of each date ripping free and blowing away quicker than the browning tree leaves. Time was both hurried and unhurried at once, the days becoming scarce yet dragging on for far too long. Workers were always hurrying somewhere, never mind whether they truly had a destination to pursue. There was always a whistle blowing in the background; there was always the constant chugging noise of trams dragging themselves along the worn tracks grooved into the streets; there was always the stench of resentment stinking up the neighborhoods and burrowing deep into the laundry that waved with the wind, like shop banners outside cramped apartment windows.

Today was an exception.

The clock had paused on the Mid-Autumn Festival—the twenty-second of the month, according to Western methods of day-keeping this year. Once, it was customary to light lanterns and whisper tales of tragedy, to worship what the ancestors revered with moonlight cupped in their palms. Now it was a new age—one that thought itself above its ancestors. Regardless of which territory they stood upon, the people of Shanghai had been bustling about with the spirit of modern celebration since sunrise, and at present, with the bells ringing nine times for the hour, the festivities were only getting started.

Juliette Cai was surveying the club, her eyes searching for the first signs of trouble. It was dimly lit despite the abundance of twinkling chandeliers hanging from the ceiling, the atmosphere dark and murky and wet. There was also a strange, sodden smell wafting under Juliette's nose in waves, but the poor renovations seemed not to bother the mood of those seated at various round tables scattered throughout the club. The people here would hardly take notice of a small leak in the corner when constant activity consumed their attention instead. Couples were whispering over decks of tarot cards, men were shaking one another with vigor, women were inclining their heads to gasp and shriek in recollection of whatever story was being told over the flickering gaslight.

"You look rather woeful."

Juliette didn't immediately turn in haste to identify the voice. She didn't have to. There were very few people who would approach her speaking English to begin with, never mind English with the flat tones of a Chinese mother tongue and the accent of a French upbringing.

"I am. I am perpetually filled with woe." Only then did she crane her head, her lips curling up and her eyes narrowing at her cousin. "Aren't you supposed to be onstage next?"

Rosalind Lang shrugged and crossed her arms, the jade bangles on her slender brown wrists clinking together.

"They cannot begin the show without me," Rosalind scoffed, "so I am not worried."

Juliette scanned the crowd again, this time with a target in mind. She found Kathleen, Rosalind's fraternal twin, near a table at the back of the club. Her other cousin was patiently balancing a tray full of plates, staring at a British merchant while he tried to order a drink with exaggerated gesticulations. Rosalind was under contract here to dance; Kathleen showed up to wait tables when she got bored, and took a measly wage for the fun of it.

Sighing, Juliette dug out a lighter to keep her hands occupied, releasing the flame, then quenching it to the rhythm of the music gliding around the room. She waved the small silver rectangle under her cousin's nose. "Want?"

Rosalind responded by pulling out a cigarette tucked within the folds of her clothing.

"You don't even smoke," she said as Juliette angled the lighter down. "Why do you carry that thing around?"

Straight-faced, Juliette replied, "You know me. Running around. Living life. Committing arson."

Rosalind inhaled her first puff of smoke, then rolled her eyes. "Right."

A better mystery would have been where Juliette even kept the lighter. Most girls in the burlesque club—dancer or patron alike—were dressed as Rosalind was: in the fashionable qipao sweeping through Shanghai like a wildfire. With the outrageous slit down the side revealing ankle to thigh and the high collar acting like a choke hold, the design was a blend of Western flamboyance with Eastern roots, and in a city of divided worlds, the women were walking metaphors. But Juliette—Juliette had been transformed through and through, the little beads of her pocketless flapper dress swishing with every movement. She stood out here, that much was certain. She was a bright, burning star, a symbolic figurehead for the vitality of the Scarlet Gang.

Juliette and Rosalind both quietly turned their attention to the stage, where a woman was crooning a song in a language that neither were familiar with. The singer's voice was lovely, her dress shimmering against dark skin, but this was not the sort of show that this sort of cabaret was known for, and so no one save the two girls at the back was listening.

"You didn't tell me you would be here tonight," Rosalind said after a while, smoke escaping her mouth in a quick stream. There was betrayal in her voice, like the omission of information was out of character. The Juliette who had returned last week was not the same Juliette that her cousins had waved goodbye to four years ago, but the changes were mutual. Upon Juliette's return, before she had even set foot back into the house, she had heard talk of Rosalind's honey-coated tongue and effortless class. After four years away, Juliette's memories of the people she had left behind no longer aligned with who they had become. Nothing of her memory had withstood the test of time. This city had reshaped itself and everyone in it had continued moving forward without her, especially Rosalind.

"It was very last minute." Over at the back of the club, the British merchant had started pantomiming to Kathleen. Juliette gestured toward the scene with her chin. "Bàba is getting tired of some merchant called Walter Dexter pushing for a meeting, so I'm to hear what he wants."

"Sounds boring," Rosalind intoned. Her cousin always had a bite to her words, even when speaking with the driest intonation. A small smile perked at Juliette's lips. At the very least, even if Rosalind felt like a stranger—albeit a familiar one—she would always sound the same. Juliette could close her eyes and pretend they were children again, sniping at each other about the most offensive topics.

She sniffed haughtily, feigning offense. "We can't all be Parisian-trained dancers."

"Tell you what, you take over my routine and *I'll* be the heir to this city's underground empire."

A laugh burst from Juliette, short and loud in her amusement. Her cousin was different. Everything was different. But Juliette was a fast learner.

With a soft sigh, she pushed away from the wall she was leaning upon. "All right," she said, her gaze latched on Kathleen. "Duty calls. I'll see you at home."

Rosalind let her leave with a wave, dropping the cigarette to the ground and crushing it under her high-heeled shoe. Juliette really ought to have admonished her for doing so, but the floor couldn't have gotten any dirtier than its current state, so what was the point? From the moment she stepped into this place, five different sorts of opium had probably smeared into her soles. All she could do was push through the club as gingerly as possible, hoping the maids wouldn't damage the leather of her shoes when they scrubbed them clean later tonight.

"I'll take it from here."

Kathleen's chin jerked up in surprise, the jade pendant at her throat gleaming under the light. Rosalind used to tell her that someone was going to snatch such a precious stone if she wore it so obviously, but Kathleen liked it there. If people were to stare her throat, she always said she would rather it be because of the pendant than the bump of her Adam's apple underneath.

Her startled expression quickly smoothed into a smile, realizing it was Juliette sliding into the seat opposite the British merchant.

"Let me know if I can get anything for you," Kathleen said sweetly, in perfect, French-accented English.

As she walked away, Walter Dexter's jaw dropped slack. "She could understand me this whole time?"

"You'll learn, Mr. Dexter," Juliette began, swiping the candle from the center of the table and taking a sniff of the scented wax, "that when you assume someone cannot speak English right off the bat, they tend to make fun of you."

Walter blinked at her, then cocked his head. He took in her dress, her American accent, and her knowledge of his name.

"Juliette Cai," he concluded. "I was expecting your father."

The Scarlet Gang called itself a family business, but it did not stop there. The Cais were the pulsing heart, but the gang itself was a network of gangsters and smugglers and merchants and middlemen of all sorts, each and every single one of them answering to Lord Cai.

Less-enthused foreigners would call the Scarlets a secret society.

"My father has no time for merchants with no credible history," Juliette replied. "If it's important, I will pass along the message."

Unfortunately, it appeared that Walter Dexter was far more interested in small talk than actual business.

"Last I heard, you had moved to become a New Yorker."

Juliette dropped the candle back onto the table. The flame flickered, casting eerie shadows over the middle-aged merchant. The lighting only deepened the wrinkles in his perpetually scrunched forehead.

"I was only sent to the West for education, regrettably," Juliette said, leaning back into the curved couch seat. "Now I'm old enough to start contributing to the family business and whatnot, so they dragged me back kicking and screaming."

The merchant didn't laugh along to her joke, as Juliette had intended. Instead, he tapped his temple, ruffling his silver-patched hair.

"Hadn't you also returned for a brief period of time a few years ago?"

Juliette stiffened, her grin faltering. Behind her, a table of patrons erupted with uproarious laughter, collapsing in mirth over some comment made among themselves. The sound prickled at her neck, sweeping a hot sweat over her skin. She waited for the noise to die down, using the interruption to think fast and scramble hard.

"Just once," Juliette replied carefully. "New York City wasn't too safe during the Great War. My family was worried."

The merchant still didn't drop the subject. He made a noise of consideration. "The war ended eight years ago. You were here a mere four previous."

Juliette's smile dropped entirely. She pushed her bobbed hair back.

"Mr. Dexter, are we here to discuss your extensive knowledge of my personal life, or did this meeting actually have a purpose?"

Walter blanched. "I apologize, Miss Cai. My son, he's your age, so I happened to know—"

He cut himself off upon noting Juliette's glare. He cleared his throat.

"I requested to meet with your father regarding a new *product*."

Immediately, despite the vague word choice, it was quite clear what Walter Dexter was referring to. The Scarlet Gang was, first and foremost, a network of gangsters, and there was seldom a time when gangsters weren't heavily involved with the black market. If the Scarlets dominated Shanghai, it was hardly surprising that they dominated the black market, too—decided the comings and goings, decided the men who were allowed to thrive and the men who needed to drop dead. In the parts of the city that still belonged to the Chinese, the Scarlet Gang was not simply above the law; they *were* the law. Without the gangsters, the merchants were unprotected. Without the merchants, the gangsters would have little purpose or work. It was an ideal partnership—and one being threatened continually by the growing power of the White Flowers, the one other gang in Shanghai that actually had a chance at defeating the Scarlets in black market monopoly. After all, they had been working at it for generations.

"A product, hmm?" Juliette repeated. Her eyes swiveled up absently. The performers had switched, the spotlight dimming as the first opening notes from a saxophone played. Adorned in a brilliant new costume, Rosalind sashayed into view. "Remember what happened the last time the British wanted to introduce *a new product* into Shanghai?"

Walter frowned. "Are you referring to the Opium Wars?"

Juliette examined her fingernails. "Am I?"

"You cannot possibly blame me for something that was the fault of my country."

"Oh, that's not how it works?"

It was Walter's turn to look unimpressed. He folded his hands together as skirts swished and skin flashed on the stage behind him.

"Nevertheless, I require the help of the Scarlet Gang. I have bulk amounts of *lernicrom* to be rid of, and it is certain to be the next most desired opiate on the market." Walter cleared his throat. "I believe you are seeking an upper hand right now."

Juliette leaned forward. In that sudden motion, the beads on her dress clinked together frantically, clashing with the jazz in the background. "And do you really think *you* can give us an upper hand?"

The constant grappling between the Scarlet Gang and the White Flowers wasn't a secret. Far from it, in fact, because the blood feud was not something that raged only between those with Cai and Montagov to their name. It was a cause that ordinary members loyal to either faction took on personally, with a fervor that could almost be supernatural. Foreigners arriving in Shanghai to do business for the first time received one warning before learning of anything else: pick a side and pick it fast. If they traded once with the Scarlet Gang, they were a Scarlet through and through. They would be embraced in Scarlet territory and killed if they wandered into the areas where the White Flowers reigned.

"I think," Walter said softly, "that the Scarlet Gang is losing control of its own city."

Juliette sat back. Underneath the table, her fists tightened until the skin over her knuckles became bloodless. Four years ago, she had looked at Shanghai with glitter in her eyes, blinking at the Scarlet Gang with hope. She hadn't understood that Shanghai was a foreign city in its own country. Now she did. The British ruled a chunk. The French ruled a chunk. The Russian White Flowers were taking over the only parts that technically remained under Chinese governance. This loss of control was a long time coming—but Juliette would rather bite off her own tongue than admit it freely to a merchant who understood nothing.

"We will get back to you regarding your product, Mr. Dexter," she said after a long moment, flashing an easy smile. She let out her exhale imperceptibly, releasing the tension that had tightened her stomach to the point of pain. "Now, if you'll excuse me—"

The entire club fell into a hush, and suddenly Juliette was speaking too loudly. Walter's eyes bugged, latching on to a sight over Juliette's shoulder.

"I'll be," he remarked. "If it isn't one of the Bolshies."

At the merchant's words, Juliette felt herself go ice-cold. Slowly, ever so slowly, she turned around to seek Walter Dexter's line of sight, searching through the smoke and shadows dancing at the entranceway of the burlesque club.

Please, don't let it be, she pleaded. *Anyone but—*

Her vision turned hazy. For a terrifying second, the world was tilting on its axis and Juliette was barely clinging to its edge, moments away from taking a tumble. Then the floor righted itself and Juliette could breathe again. She stood and cleared her throat, concentrating all her might on sounding as bored as possible when she stated, "The Montagovs emigrated far before the Bolshevik Revolution, Mr. Dexter."

Before anybody could take note of her, Juliette slinked into the shadows, where the dark walls dimmed the sparkling of her dress and the soggy floorboards muffled the clicking of her heels. Her precautions were unnecessary. Everyone's gaze was firmly latched on Roma Montagov as he wound his way through the club. For once Rosalind was carrying out a performance that not a soul was paying attention to.

At first glance it could have seemed like the shock emanating from the round tables was because a foreigner had walked in. But this club had many foreigners scattered throughout the crowd, and Roma, with his dark hair, dark eyes, and pale skin could have blended in among the Chinese as naturally as a white rose painted red amid poppies. It wasn't because Roma Montagov was a foreigner. It was because the heir of the White Flowers was wholly recognizable as an enemy on Scarlet Gang territory. From the corner of her eye, Juliette was already catching sight of movement: guns pulled from pockets and knives pointed outward, bodies stirring with animosity.

Juliette stepped out of the shadows and lifted a hand to the closest table. The motion was simple: *wait.*

The gangsters stilled, each group watching those nearby in example. They waited, pretending to go on with their conversations while Roma Montagov passed table after table, his eyes narrowed in concentration.

Juliette started to creep closer. She pressed a hand to her throat and forced the lump there down, forced her breath to become even until she wasn't on the verge of panic, until she could wipe on a dazzling smile. Once, Roma would have been able to see right through her. But four years had gone by now. He had changed. So had she.

Juliette reached out and touched the back of his suit jacket. "Hello, stranger."

Roma turned around. For a moment it seemed as if he hadn't registered the sight before him. He stared, his gaze as blank as clear glass, utterly uncomprehending.

Then the sight of the Scarlet heiress washed over him like a bucket of ice. Roma's lips parted with a small puff of air.

The last time he'd seen her, they had been fifteen.

"Juliette," he exclaimed automatically, but they were no longer familiar enough to use each other's first names. They hadn't been for a long while.

Roma cleared his throat. "Miss Cai. When did you return to Shanghai?"

I never left, Juliette wanted to say, but that wasn't true. Her mind had remained here—her thoughts had constantly revolved around the chaos and the injustice and the burning fury that broiled in these streets—but her physical body had been shipped across the ocean a second time for safekeeping. She had hated it, hated being away so intensely that she felt the force of it burn into a fever each night when she left the parties and speakeasies. The weight of Shanghai was a steel crown nailed to her head. In another world, if she had been given a choice, perhaps she would have walked away, rejected herself as the heir to an empire of mobsters and merchants. But she never had a choice. This was her life, this was her city, these were her people, and because she loved them, she had sworn to herself a long time ago that she would do a damn good job of being who she was because she could be no one else.

It's all your fault, she wanted to say. *You're the reason I was forced away from my city. My people. My blood.*

"I returned a while ago," Juliette lied easily, checking her hip against the vacant table to her left. "Mr. Montagov, you'll have to forgive me for asking, but what are you doing *here?*"

She watched Roma move his hand ever so slightly and guessed that he was checking for the presence of his hidden weapons. She watched him take her in, slow to form words. Juliette had had time to brace herself—seven days and seven nights to enter this city and scrub her mind free of everything that had happened here between them. But whatever Roma had expected to find in this club when he walked in tonight, it certainly hadn't been *Juliette.*

"I need to speak to Lord Cai," Roma finally said, placing his hands behind his back. "It's important."

Juliette took a step closer. Her fingers had happened upon the lighter from within the folds of her dress again, thumbing the spark wheel while she hummed in thought. Roma said *Cai* like a foreign merchant, his mouth pulled wide. The Chinese and the Russians shared the same sound for Cai: *tsai*, like the sound of a match being struck. His butchering was intentional, an observation of the situation. She was fluent in Russian, he was fluent in Shanghai's unique dialect, and yet here they were, both speaking English with different accents like a couple of casual merchants. Switching to either of their native tongues would have been like taking a side, so they settled for a middle ground.

"I imagine it must be important, if you've come all the way here." Juliette shrugged, letting go of the lighter. "Speak to me instead, and I'll pass along the message. One heir to another, Mr. Montagov. You can trust me, can't you?"

It was a laughable question. Her words said one thing, but her cold, flat stare said another—*One misstep while you're in my territory, and I'll kill you with my bare hands.* She was the last person he would trust, and the same went the other way.

But whatever it was that Roma needed, it must have been serious. He didn't argue.

"Can we . . . ?"

He gestured to the side, into the shadows and the dim corners, where there would be less of an audience turned toward them like a second show, waiting for the moment Juliette walked away so they could pounce. Thinning her lips, Juliette pivoted and waved him along to the back of the club instead. He was fast to follow, his measured steps coming closely enough that the beads of Juliette's dress clinked angrily in disturbance. She didn't know why she was bothering. She should have thrown him to the Scarlets, let them deal with him.

No, she decided. *He is mine to deal with. He is mine to destroy.*

Juliette stopped. Now it was just her and Roma Montagov in the shadows, other sounds muffled and other sights dimmed. She rubbed her wrist, demanding her pulse slow down, as if that were within her control.

"Jump to it, then," she said.

Roma looked around. He ducked his head before speaking, lowering his voice until Juliette had to strain to hear him. And indeed she strained—she refused to lean any closer to him than she had to.

"Last night, five White Flowers died at the ports. Their throats had been torn out."

Juliette blinked at him.

"And?"

She didn't mean to be callous, but members of both their gangs killed each other on the weekly. Juliette herself had already added to the death toll. If he was going to put the blame on her Scarlets, then he was wasting his time.

"*And*," Roma said tightly, clearly biting back *if you would let me finish*, "one of yours. As well as a municipal police officer. British."

Now Juliette frowned a little, trying to recall if she had overheard anyone in the household last night muttering about a Scarlet death. It was strange for *both* gangs to have victims on scene, given that larger killings usually happened in ambushes, and stranger still for a police officer to have been pulled down too, but she wouldn't go so far as to say it was bizarre. She only raised an eyebrow at Roma, disinterested.

Until, continuing onward, he said, "All their wounds were self-inflicted. This wasn't a territory dispute."

Juliette shook her head repeatedly to one side, making sure she hadn't misheard him. When she was certain there was nothing jammed in her ear, she exclaimed, "Seven dead bodies with *self-inflicted* wounds?"

Roma nodded. He placed another look over his shoulder, as if merely keeping an eye on the gangsters around the tables would prevent them from attacking him. Or perhaps he didn't care to keep an eye on them at all. Perhaps he was trying to avoid looking straight ahead at Juliette.

"I'm here to find an explanation. Does your father know anything of this?"

Juliette scoffed, the noise deep and resentful. Did he mean to tell her that five White Flowers, one Scarlet, and a police officer had met up at the ports, then torn out their own throats? It sounded like the setup of a terrible joke without a punch line.

"We cannot help you," Juliette stated.

"Any information could be crucial to discovering what happened, Miss Cai," Roma persisted. A little notch between his eyebrows always appeared like a crescent moon whenever he was irritated. It was present now. There was more to these deaths than he was letting on; he wouldn't get this worked up for an ordinary ambush. "One of the dead was yours—"

"We're not going to cooperate with the White Flowers," Juliette cut in. Any false humor on her face had long disappeared. "Let me make that clear before you proceed. Regardless of whether my father knows anything about last night's deaths, we will not be sharing it with you and we will not be furthering any contact that could endanger our own business endeavors. Now, *good day*, sir."

Roma had clearly been dismissed, and yet he remained where he stood, glaring at Juliette like there was a sour taste in his mouth. She had already turned on her heel, preparing to make her exit, when she heard Roma whisper viciously, "What *happened* to you?"

She could have said anything in response. She could have chosen her words with the deathly venom she had acquired in her years away and spat it all out. She could have reminded him of what he did four years ago, pushed the blade of guilt in until he was bleeding. But before she could open her mouth, a scream was piercing through the club, interrupting every other noise as if it operated on another frequency.

The dancers onstage froze; the music was brought to a halt.

"What's going on?" Juliette muttered. Just as she moved to investigate, Roma hissed out sharply and caught her elbow.

"Juliette, don't."

His touch seared through her skin like a painful burn. Juliette jerked her arm away faster than if she had truly been set alight, her eyes blazing. He didn't have the right. He had lost the right to pretend he had ever wanted to protect her.

Juliette marched toward the other end of the club, ignoring Roma as he followed after her. Rumbles of panic grew louder and louder, though she couldn't comprehend *what* was inciting such a reaction until she nudged aside the gathering crowd with an assertive push.

Then she saw the man thrashing on the ground, his own fingers clawing at his thick neck.

"What is he doing?" Juliette shrieked, lunging forward. "Somebody stop him!"

But most of his nails were already buried deep into muscle. The man was digging with an animal-like intensity—as if there was something *there*, something no one else could see crawling under his skin. Deeper, deeper, deeper, until his fingers were wholly buried and he was pulling free tendons and veins and arteries.

In the next second, the club had fallen silent completely. Nothing was audible save the labored breathing of the short and stout man who had collapsed on the floor, his throat torn into pieces and his hands dripping with blood.

Two

The silence turned to screams, the screams turned to chaos, and Juliette rolled up her shiny sleeves, her lips thinned and her brow furrowed.

"Mr. Montagov," she said over the uproar, "you need to leave."

Juliette marched forward, waving for two nearby Scarlet men to come close. They obliged, but not without a strange expression, which Juliette almost took offense at, until—two beats later—she blinked and looked over her shoulder to find Roma still standing there, very much not leaving. Instead, he surged past her, acting like he owned the place, then dropped to a crouch near the dying man, squinting at the man's *shoes*, of all things.

"For crying out loud," Juliette muttered under her breath. She pointed the two Scarlets at Roma. "Escort him out."

It was what they had been waiting for. One of the Scarlets immediately pushed the heir of the White Flowers roughly, forcing Roma to spring to his feet with a hiss so he wouldn't tumble onto the bloody floor.

"I said *escort* him," Juliette snapped at the Scarlet. "It's the Mid-Autumn Festival. Don't be a *brute*."

"But, Miss Cai—"

"Don't you see?" Roma cut in coldly, pointing a finger at the dying man. He turned to face Juliette, his jaw tight, eyes level on her—only her. He acted like nobody else was present in his line of sight save for Juliette, like the two men weren't glaring daggers at him, like the whole club wasn't screaming in havoc, running in circles about the growing puddle of blood. "This is exactly what happened last night. It is not a one-off incident; it is *madness*—"

Juliette sighed, waving a floppy wrist. The two Scarlet men took a proper hold of Roma's shoulders, and Roma swallowed his words with an audible snap from his jaw. He wouldn't make a scene in Scarlet territory. He was already lucky to be leaving without a bullet hole in his back. He knew this. It was the only reason why he tolerated being manhandled by men he might have killed on the streets.

"Thank you for being so understanding," she simpered.

Roma said nothing as he was hauled from her sight. Juliette watched him, eyes narrowed, and only when she was certain he had been pushed out the door of the burlesque club did she focus on the mess in front of her, stepping forward with a sigh and kneeling gingerly beside the dying man.

There was no saving with a wound like this. It was still spurting blood, pulsating red puddles onto the floor. Blood was certainly seeping into the fabric of her dress, but Juliette hardly felt it. The man was trying to say something. Juliette couldn't hear what.

"You'd do well to put him out of his misery."

Walter Dexter had found his way near the scene and was now peering over Juliette's shoulder with an almost quizzical expression. He remained unmoving even when the waitresses started pushing the crowd back and cordoning the area off, yelling for the onlookers to scatter. Irritatingly, none of the Scarlet men bothered to haul Walter away—he had a look to him that made it seem like he needed to be here. Juliette had met plenty of men like him in America: men who assumed they had the right to go wherever they wished because the world had been built to favor their *civilized* etiquette. That sort of confidence knew no bounds.

"Hush," Juliette snapped, leaning her ear closer to the dying man. If he had last words, he deserved to be heard—

"I've seen this before; it's the lunacy of an addict. Perhaps methamphetamine or—"

"Hush!"

Juliette focused until she could hear the sounds coming from the dying man's mouth, focused until the hysteria around her faded to background noise.

"Guài. Guài. Guài."

Guài?

Head spinning, Juliette ran through every word that resembled what the man was chanting. The only one that made sense was—

"Monster?" she asked him, gripping his shoulder. "Is that what you mean to say?"

The man stilled. His gaze was startlingly clear for the briefest second. Then, in a fast garble, he said, "Huò bù dān xíng." After that one breath, one exhale, one warning, his eyes glazed over.

Juliette reached out, numb, and brushed his eyelids closed. Before she could quite register the dead man's words, Kathleen had already stepped forward to cover him with a tablecloth. Only his feet were sticking out, in those tattered shoes that Roma had been staring at.

They're mismatched, Juliette noted suddenly. One shoe was sleek and shined, still glinting with its last polish; the other was far too small and a different color entirely, the fabric held together by a thin piece of string wrapped thrice around the toes.

Strange.

"What was that? What did he say?"

Walter was still lurking at her elbow. He didn't seem to understand that this was his cue to remove himself. He didn't seem to care that Juliette was staring forward in a state of stupefaction, wondering how Roma had timed his visit to coincide with this death.

"Misfortunes tend to come all at once," Juliette translated when she finally jolted back to the frenzy of the situation. Walter Dexter only looked at her blankly, trying to understand why a dying man would say something so convoluted. He didn't understand the Chinese and their love for proverbs. His mouth was opening, likely to give another spiel about his extensive knowledge regarding the world of drugs, another plug about the dangers of purchasing products from those he deemed untrustworthy, but Juliette held up a finger to stop him. If she was certain of anything, it was that these weren't the last words of a man who took too many drugs. This was the final warning of a man who had seen something he shouldn't have.

"Let me correct myself. You British already have an appropriate translation," she said. "When it rains, it pours."

High above the leaky pipes and moldy carpeting of the White Flower house, Alisa Montagova was perched upon a wooden beam in the ceiling rafters, her chin pressed against the flat of her knees as she eavesdropped on the meeting below.

The Montagovs didn't live in a big, flashy residence like their money bags could afford. They preferred to stay in the heart of it all, one and the same with the dirt-smeared faces picking up trash on the streets. From the outside, their living space looked identical to the row of apartments along this bustling city street. On the inside, they had transformed what used to be an apartment complex into one big jigsaw puzzle of rooms and offices and staircases, maintaining the place not with servants or maids but with hierarchy. It wasn't just the Montagovs who lived here, but any White Flower who held some role in the gang, and among the assortment of people coming and going in this house, within the walls and outside them, there was an order. Lord Montagov reigned at the top and Roma—at least in name—stood second, but below, roles were constantly changing, determined by will rather than blood. Where the Scarlet Gang depended on relationships—on which family went the farthest back before this country crumbled from its imperial throne— the White Flowers operated on chaos, on constant movement. But the climb to power was one of choice, and those who remained low within the gang did so by their own desire. The point of becoming a White Flower wasn't power and riches. It was the knowing that they could walk at any point if they didn't like the orders given by the Montagovs. It was a fist to the chest, a lock of eyes, a nod of understanding—like that, the Russian refugees filing into Shanghai would do anything to join the ranks of the White Flowers, anything to reunite with the sense of belonging they had left behind when the Bolsheviks came knocking.

For the men, at least. The Russian women unfortunate enough not to be born into the White Flowers picked up jobs as dancers and mistresses. Just last week, Alisa had overheard a British woman crying about a state of emergency in the International Settlement—of families being broken up by pretty faces from Siberia who had no fortune, only face and figure and a will to live. The refugees had to do what they must. Moral compasses meant nothing in the face of starvation.

Alisa jolted. The man she had been eavesdropping on had suddenly started whispering. The abrupt change in volume drew her attention back to the meeting below.

"The political factions have made one too many snide remarks," a gruff voice muttered. "It is almost certain that the politicians are engineering the madness, but it's hard to say at this point in time whether the Kuomintang or the Communists are responsible. Many sources say Zhang Gutai, though . . . well, *I* hesitate to believe it."

Another voice added wryly, "Please, Zhang Gutai is so bad at being Secretary-General of the Communist Party that he printed the wrong date on one of their meeting posters."

Alisa could see three men seated opposite her father through the thin mesh that lined the ceiling space. Without risking a fall from the rafters, she couldn't quite pick out their features, but the accented Russian gave away enough. They were Chinese spies.

"What do we know of their methods? How does this madness spread?"

That was her father now, his slow voice as distinctive as nails against a chalkboard. Lord Montagov spoke in such a commandeering manner that it felt like a sin to deny him your full attention.

One of the Chinese men cleared his throat. He was wringing his hands on his shirt so aggressively that Alisa leaned forward into the rafters, squinting through the mesh to see if she was mistaking the motion.

"A monster."

Alisa almost toppled over. Her hands came down on the beam just in time to right herself, letting out a small exhale in relief.

"I beg your pardon?"

"We cannot confirm anything regarding the source of the madness except for one thing," the third and final man said. "It is linked to sightings of a monster. I saw it myself. I saw silver eyes in the Huangpu River, blinking in a way no man could—"

"Enough, enough," Lord Montagov interrupted. His tone was rough, impatient with the turn this information briefing had taken. "I have no interest in hearing nonsense on a monster. If that is all, I look forward to reconvening at our next meeting."

Frowning, Alisa scuttled along the beams, following the men as they left. She was already twelve years old, but she was tiny, always darting from shadow to shadow in the manner of a wild rodent. As the door shut below, she hopped from one ceiling beam to another until she was pressed flat directly above the men.

"He looked afraid," one remarked quietly.

The man in the middle hushed him, except the words had already been said and birthed into the world, becoming sharp arrows tearing through the room with no target in mind, only destruction. The men pulled their coats tightly around their bodies and left the broiling, chaotic mess of the Montagov house behind them. Alisa, however, remained in her little nook up in the ceiling.

Fear. That was something she didn't think her father knew how to feel anymore. Fear was a concept for the men without guns. Fear was reserved for people like Alisa, small and slight and always looking over her shoulder.

If Lord Montagov was afraid, the rules were changing.

Alisa leaped from the ceiling and sprinted off.

Three

The moment Juliette barreled into the hallway, shoving the last pin into her hair, she already knew she was too late.

It was partly the maid's fault for not waking her when she was supposed to and partly Juliette's own fault for failing to get up with the sunrise, as she had been attempting since her arrival back in Shanghai. Those sparse moments just as the sky was brightening—and before the rest of the household rumbled to life—were the most peaceful few minutes one could get in this house. The days she started early enough to snatch a breath of cold air and a gulp of utter, complete silence on her balcony were her favorites. She could trail through the house with no one to bother her, skipping into the kitchen and snatching whatever she liked from the cooks, then taking whichever seat she pleased on the empty dining table. Depending on how fast she chewed, she might even have a while to spend in the living room, the windows thrown open to let in the tunes of early birdsong. The days when she failed to scramble out of her covers fast enough, on other the hand, meant grumpily sitting through the morning meals with the rest of the household.

Juliette stopped outside her father's office door now, cursing under her breath. Today hadn't only been a matter of avoiding her distant relatives. She had wanted to poke her nose into one of Lord Cai's meetings.

The door opened swiftly. Juliette took a step back, trying to look natural. *Definitely too late.*

"Juliette." Lord Cai peered at her, frowning. "It's so early. Why are you awake?"

Juliette placed her hands under her chin, the picture of innocence. "I heard we had an esteemed visitor. I thought I'd come offer my greetings."

The aforementioned visitor raised a wry brow. He was a Nationalist, but whether or not he was truly esteemed was hard to determine when he was dressed merely in a Western suit, void of the decorations his Kuomintang military uniform might bear on the collar. The Scarlet Gang had been friendly with the Nationalists—the Kuomintang—ever since the Kuomintang's founding as a political party. Of late, relations had become even friendlier to combat the rise of their Communist "allies." Juliette had been home for only a week, and she had already watched her father take at least five different meetings with the harried Nationalists who wanted gangster support. Each time she had been just too late to slip in without acting like an embarrassment, and settled for idling outside the door instead to catch whatever bits and pieces she could.

The Nationalists were afraid, that much she knew. The budding Communist Party of China was encouraging its members to join the Kuomintang in a show of cooperation with the Nationalists, only instead of demonstrating cooperation, the growing influence of Communist numbers within the Kuomintang was starting to threaten the Nationalists. Such scandal was the talk of the country, but especially in Shanghai, a lawless place where governments came both to be born and to die.

"That's very kind of you, Juliette, but Mr. Qiao has another meeting to hurry to."

Lord Cai gestured for a servant to lead the Nationalist out. Mr. Qiao politely tipped his hat, and Juliette smiled tightly, swallowing back her sigh.

"It wouldn't hurt to let me sit in on one meeting, Bàba," she said as soon as Mr. Qiao was out of sight. "You're supposed to be teaching me."

"I can teach you slowly," Lord Cai replied, shaking his head. "You don't want to get involved in politics yet. It's boring business."

But it was relevant business, especially if the Scarlet Gang spent so much damn time entertaining these factions. Especially if Lord Cai had hardly blinked an eye last night when Juliette told him the heir of the White Flowers had pranced into their most central burlesque club, telling her that he had been made aware already and they would speak of it in the morning.

"Let's go to the breakfast table, hmm?" her father said. He placed his hand on the back of Juliette's neck, guiding her down the stairs as if she were at risk of running off. "We can talk about last night, too."

"Breakfast would be delightful," Juliette muttered. In truth, the clamor of morning meals gave her a headache. There was something about mornings in this household particularly that made Juliette uneasy. No matter what it was that her relatives discussed, no matter how mundane—like their speculation on the rising prices of rice— their words dripped with scheming and relentless wit. Everything they discussed seemed more fitting for the late night, when the maids retired to their rooms and the dark crawled in on the polished wood floors.

"Juliette, darling," an aunt crowed the moment she and her father approached the table. "Did you sleep well?"

"Yes, Ā yí," Juliette replied tightly, taking a seat. "I slept very well—"

"Did you cut your hair again? You must have. I don't remember it being this short."

As if her relatives weren't vexing enough, there were also so many of them coming in and out of the Cai household for Juliette to *care* very much about any of them. Rosalind and Kathleen were dually her closest cousins and only friends, and that was all she needed. Everybody else was merely a name and a relation she had to remember in case she needed something from them one day. This aunt jabbering in her ear now was far too distant to be useful at any point in the future, so distant that Juliette had to stop for a second to wonder why she was even at the breakfast table.

"Dà jiě, for God's sake, let the kid breathe."

Juliette's head jerked up, grinning at the voice who had chimed in from the end of the table. On second thought, there was only one exception to her apathy: Mr. Li, her favorite uncle.

Xiè xiè, she mouthed.

Mr. Li merely raised his teacup to her thanks, a twinkle in his eye. Her aunt huffed, but she ceased talking. Juliette turned in her father's direction.

"So, Bàba, last night," she started. "If talk is to be believed, one of our men met up with five White Flowers at the ports, then ripped his own throat out. What do you make of it?"

Lord Cai made a thoughtful noise from the head of the long rectangular table, then rubbed the bridge of his nose, sighing deeply. Juliette wondered when her father had last gotten a full night's sleep, uninterrupted by worrying and meetings. His exhaustion was invisible to the untrained eye, but Juliette knew. Juliette always knew.

Or maybe he was just tired of having to sit at the head of this table, hearing everyone's gossip first thing in the morning. Before Juliette left, their dining table had been round, as Chinese tables rightfully should be. She suspected they had switched it up only to appeal to the Western visitors who came through the Cai house for meetings, but the result was messy: family members unable to talk to who they wished, as they could if everybody was seated around a circle.

"Bàba," Juliette prompted, though she knew he was still thinking. It was only that her father was a man of few words and Juliette was a girl who couldn't stand silence. Even while it was hectic all around them, with staff bustling in and out of the kitchen, a meal underway, and the table accommodating various conversations at oscillating volumes, she couldn't stand it when her father let her question draw out in lieu of answering immediately.

The matter was, even if he indulged her now, Lord Cai was only pretending to be concerned about an alleged madness. Juliette could tell—this was child's play atop the already monstrous list plaguing her father's attention. After all, who would care for rumors of strange *creatures* rising from the waters of this city when the Nationalists and Communists were rising too, guns poised and armies ready to march?

"And that was all Roma Montagov revealed?" Lord Cai finally asked.

Juliette flinched. She couldn't help it. She had spent four years recoiling at the mere thought of Roma that hearing his name aloud—spoken from her own father, no less—felt like something improper.

"Yes."

Her father tapped his fingers on the table slowly.

"I suspect he knows more," Juliette continued, "but he was careful."

Lord Cai fell into silence once again, allowing the noise around him to lull and pick up and fall. Juliette wondered whether his mind was elsewhere at this very moment. He had been terribly blasé at news of the White Flower heir on their territory, after all. Given how important the blood feud was to the Scarlet Gang, it only showed how much more consequential politics had become if Lord Cai was barely giving Roma Montagov's infraction any serious consideration.

Before her father had the chance to resume speaking, however, the swinging doors to the kitchen slammed open, the sound ricocheting so loudly that the aunt seated next to Juliette knocked her cup of tea over.

"If we suspect the White Flowers have more information than we do, what are we doing sitting around *discussing* it?"

Juliette gritted her teeth, mopping the tea from her dress. It was only Tyler Cai who entered, the most irritating among her first cousins. Despite their shared age, in her four years away, it was as if he hadn't grown up at all. He still made crude jokes and expected others to kneel before him. If he could, he would demand the globe turn in the other direction simply because he thought it was a more efficient way to turn, no matter how unrealistic.

"Do you make a habit out of eavesdropping at doors instead of coming in?" Juliette sneered, but her scathing remark went unappreciated. Their relatives jumped to their feet at the sight of Tyler, hurrying to fetch a chair, to fetch more tea, to fetch another plate—probably one engraved with gold and crusted with crystal. Despite Juliette's position as the heir to the Scarlet Gang, they would never simper after her in such a manner. She was a girl. In their eyes, no matter how legitimate, she would never be good enough.

"It seems simple to me," Tyler continued. He slid into a seat, leaning back like it was a throne. "It's about time we show the White Flowers who really holds the power in this city. Let's demand they hand over what they know."

"We have the numbers, the weaponry," an obscure uncle chimed in, nodding and stroking his beard.

"The politicians will side with us," the aunt beside Juliette added. "They have to. They cannot tolerate the White Flowers."

"A territory battle is not wise—"

Finally, Juliette thought, turning toward the older second cousin who had spoken up, *a sensible voice at this table.*

"—but with your expertise, Tyler, who knows how much farther we could advance our turf lines."

Juliette's fists tightened. *Never mind.*

"Here is what we shall do," Tyler started excitedly. Juliette cast a glance at her father, but he seemed content to merely consume his food. Since her return, Tyler had been finding every opportunity to upstage her, whether in conversation or through sidelong remarks.

But each time, Lord Cai had stepped in to shut him down, to remind these aunts and uncles in as few words as possible to remember who the true heir was, to remember that this favoritism they were showing for Tyler would take them nowhere.

Only this time Lord Cai remained silent. Juliette didn't know if he was abstaining because he found his nephew's tactics to be laughable, or because he was actually taking Tyler seriously. Her stomach twisted, broiling with acid at the thought.

"—and it's not as if the foreign powers can complain," Tyler was saying. "If these deaths have been self-inflicted, it is a matter that could affect anyone. It is a matter of *our* people, who require *our* help to defend them. If we do not act now and take back the city for their sake, then what good are we? Are we to suffer another century of humiliation?"

The voices at the table sounded their approval. Grunts of praise; wrinkled, scarred thumbs stuck into the air; claps of esteem against Tyler's shoulder. Only Mr. Li and her father were quiet, their faces held neutral, but that wasn't enough. Juliette threw her utensils down, shattering her fine porcelain chopsticks into four pieces.

"You want to deliver yourself into White Flower territory?" She stood up, smoothed down her dress. "Be my guest. I'll have a maid untangle your guts when they send them back in a box."

With her relatives too shocked to protest, Juliette marched out of the kitchen. Her heart was thudding despite her calm demeanor, afraid that maybe this time she really had pushed it too far. As soon as she was in the hallway, she paused and glanced over her shoulder, watching the kitchen doors settle. The wood of those doors, imported from some distant nation, was carved with traditional Chinese calligraphy: poems that Juliette had memorized a long time ago. This house was a mirror of their city. It was a fusion of East and West, unable to let go of the old but desperate to mimic the new, and just like the city, the architecture of this house didn't quite meld well with itself.

The beautiful but ill-fitted kitchen doors flew open again. Juliette barely flinched. She had expected this.

"Juliette. A word."

It was only Tyler who had followed her out, a frown etched onto his face. He had the same pointed chin that Juliette had, the same single dimple at the lower-left corner of his lip that appeared in times of distress. How they looked so alike was beyond her. In every family portrait, Juliette and Tyler were always placed together, cooed at as if they were twins instead of cousins. But Juliette and Tyler had never gotten along. Not even in the cot, when they played with toy guns instead of real ones, and Tyler never missed a single wooden pellet aimed at Juliette's head.

"What is it?"

Tyler stopped. He folded his arms. "What is your problem?"

Juliette rolled her eyes. "My problem?"

"Yes, *your* problem. It's not amusing when you shut down my every idea—"

"You're not stupid, Tyler, so stop acting like it," Juliette interrupted. "I hate the Montagovs just as you do. We all hate them, so much that we bleed from it. But now is not the time to be waging a territory war. Not with our city already carved up by the foreigners."

A beat passed.

"Stupid?"

Tyler had missed the point entirely, and yet he was offended. Her cousin was a boy with steel skin and a heart of glass. Ever since he lost both his parents too young, he had become this faux Scarlet anarchist, pretentious for the sake of it, wild within the gang for no reason, and because like called to like, his only friends were those who hung around hoping to shortcut a connection with the Cais. Everyone tiptoed around him, happy to throw choreographed punches and let him think himself powerful when each hit bounced off, but give him one sudden kick down his middle and he would shatter.

"I hardly think defending our livelihood is stupid," Tyler went on. "I hardly think that reclaiming our country from those *Russians*—"

The problem was that Tyler thought his way was the only correct way. She wished she could find it in herself to not fault him. After all, Tyler was just like her; he wanted what was best for the Scarlet Gang. Only in his mind, *he* was what was best for the Scarlet Gang.

Juliette didn't want to continue listening. She turned on her heel and started to leave.

Until her cousin snagged her by the wrist.

"What kind of an heir *are* you?"

Quick as a flash, Tyler slammed her into the wall. He kept one hand scrunched against her left sleeve and the rest of his arm splayed against her clavicle, pushing just enough to make a threat.

"Let me go," Juliette hissed, jerking against his hold, "right now."

Tyler did not. "The Scarlet Gang is supposed to be your first priority. Our people should be your first priority."

"Watch yourself—"

"You know what I think it is?" Tyler breathed in, his nostrils flaring, deep wrinkles marring his face into absolute disgust. "I've heard the rumors. I don't think you hate the Montagovs at all. I think you're trying to protect Roma Montagov."

Juliette became utterly still. It was not fear that overtook her, nor any sort of intimidation that Tyler had sought to incite. It was indignation, and then hot, hot anger. She would tear Roma Montagov apart before she ever protected him again.

Her right hand jerked up—fist clenched, wrist hard, knuckles braced—and made centered, perfect contact with her cousin's cheek. There was a moment when he could not react. A moment when Tyler was only blinking, the lines of his pale face trembling in shock. Then he stumbled, letting go of Juliette and whipping his head to look at her, hatred stamped into the hollows of his eyes. A red slash bruised the line of his cheekbone, the result of Juliette's glittering ring scraping through skin.

It wasn't enough.

"Protecting Roma Montagov?" she echoed.

Tyler froze. He hadn't had a chance to move, hardly had a chance to take the slightest step back, before Juliette had pulled forth a knife from her pocket. She pressed it right to his cut and hissed, "We are not kids anymore, Tyler. And if you are to threaten me with outrageous accusations, then you will answer for them."

A soft laugh. "How so?" Tyler rasped. "Will you kill me right here in the hallway? Ten paces away from the breakfast table?"

Juliette pressed the knife in deeper. A stream of blood started down her cousin's cheek, trailed into the lines of her palm, dripped along her arm.

Tyler had stopped laughing.

"I am the heir of the Scarlet Gang," Juliette said. Her voice had grown just as sharp as her weapon. "And believe me, tángdì, I will kill you before I let you take it from me."

She shoved Tyler off the blade of her knife then, the metal flashing red. He said nothing more, offered no response save a blank stare.

Juliette turned, her heeled shoes twisting grooves into the carpeting, and walked off.

Four

There's nothing here."

Bristling, Roma Montagov continued his search, prodding his fingers into the cracks along the boardwalk.

"Shut up. Keep looking."

They had yet to find anything of note, that much was true, but the sun was still high in the sky. White-hot rays reflected off the waves quietly knocking against the boardwalk, blinding anyone who looked out for too long. Roma kept his back turned to the murky, green-yellow waters. While it was easy to keep the bright sun out of his field of vision, it was much harder to keep at bay the incessant, annoying voice jabbering on behind him.

"Roma. Roma-*ah*. Roma—"

"By God, mudak. What? What is it?"

The hours left in the day were aplenty, and Roma wasn't particularly fond of stepping foot back into his house without finding something for his father. He shuddered at the thought, imagining the thunderous disappointment that would pockmark his father's every word.

"You can take care of this one, can't you?" Lord Montagov had asked this morning, clapping a hand over Roma's shoulder. To a casual observer, it may have looked like Lord Montagov had applied a fatherly gesture of reassurance. In reality, the clap had been so forceful that Roma still bore a red mark on his shoulder.

"Don't let me down this time, *son*," Lord Montagov whispered.

It was always that word. *Son.* As if it even meant anything. As if Roma hadn't been replaced by Dimitri Voronin—not in name but in favoritism—relegated to the roles that Dimitri was too busy to take. Roma hadn't been given this task because his father trusted him greatly. He was given it because the Scarlet Gang was no longer the only problem plaguing their business, because the foreigners in Shanghai were trying to replace the White Flowers as the new force against the Scarlets, because the Communists were being a constant nuisance trying to recruit within White Flower ranks. While Roma scoured the ground for a few bloodstains, Lord Montagov and Dimitri were busy dealing with politicians. They were fending back the tireless British and Americans and French, all of whom were drooling for a slice of the cake that was the Middle Kingdom—most hungry for Shanghai, the city above the sea.

When was the last time his father had actually ordered him to go near the Scarlet Gang as he had last night, like a proper heir who was to know the enemy? It wasn't because Lord Montagov wanted to protect him from the blood feud. That had long passed. It was because his father didn't trust him one bit. Giving Roma this task was a last resort.

A long, irritated groan brought Roma's attention back to the present.

"You know," he snapped, turning around and shielding his eyes from the light reflecting off the river, "you *chose* to come today."

Marshall Seo only grinned, finally satisfied now that he had drawn Roma's attention. Rather than shooting back a quip, Marshall stuck his hands into the pockets of his neatly pressed slacks and casually changed the topic, jumping from Russian to rapid, ranting Korean. Roma managed to pick up a few words here and there: "*blood*," and "*unpleasant*," and "*police*," but the rest were lost, adrift in the void of lessons he had skipped when he was young.

"Mars," Roma interrupted. "You're going to have to switch. I don't have the brain for translation today."

In response, Marshall only continued with his tirade. His hands were gesticulating with his usual vigor and enthusiasm, moving at the same pace as he was speaking, syllable stacked upon syllable until Roma wasn't quite certain if Marshall was still using his native tongue, or merely making noises to express his frustration.

"The general gist is that it smells like fish here," a third, quieter, wearier voice sighed from a few paces away, "but you don't want to know the sort of analogies he's spouting to make the comparison."

The translation came from Benedikt Montagov, Roma's cousin and the third person who closed off their trio within the White Flowers. His blond head could usually be found bent toward Marshall's dark one, a matching pair conspiring some move to aid Roma's next task. Presently it was inclined downward, his attention focused on examining a stack of crates as tall as he was. He was so focused that he was unmoving, only his eyes scanning left and right.

Roma folded his arms. "Let's be thankful it smells like fish and not dead bodies."

His cousin snorted, but otherwise did not react. Benedikt was like that. He always seemed to be simmering over something right below the surface, but nothing ever came through, no matter how close he came to it. Those on the streets described him as the watered-down version of Roma, which Benedikt embraced only because such an association with Roma, no matter how disparaging, gave him power. Those who knew him better thought him to have two brains and two hearts. He was always feeling too much but thinking twice as fast—a modestly loaded grenade, putting its own pin in anytime someone tried to pull it out.

Marshall did not have the same control. Marshall Seo was a raging, two-ton explosive.

He had finally stopped with his fishy comparisons, at least, dropping to a sudden crouch by the water. Marshall always moved like this—like the world was on the verge of ending and he needed to jam as many movements in as possible. Ever since Marshall had been embroiled in a scandal involving another boy and a dark storage closet, he had learned to hit first and hit fast, countering the talk that followed him around with a Cheshire-cat grin on his face. If he was tougher, then he could not be beat down. If he was more vicious, then nobody could drop their judgment upon him without fearing a knife pressed to their throat.

"Roma."

Benedikt waved his hand, and Roma strode over to his cousin, hoping that he had found something. After last night, the bodies had been removed and sent to the local hospital for storage, but the blood-splattered crime scene remained. Roma, Marshall, and Benedikt needed to put together why five of their men, a Scarlet, and a British police officer would tear out their own throats, only the crime scene was so sparse of clues that obtaining answers felt like a lost cause.

"What is it?" Roma asked. "Did you find something?"

Benedikt looked up. "No."

Roma deflated.

"This is the second time we have searched the scene from corner to corner," Benedikt went on. "I think we've done all we can—there cannot be anything we have missed."

But other than examining the crime scene, what else could they do to understand this madness? There was nobody to question, no witnesses to interrogate, no backstories to piece together. When there was no perpetrator to a crime, when the victims did such a terrible thing to *themselves*, how were answers supposed to be found?

Over by the water, Marshall sighed loudly in exasperation, resting his elbow on his knee, his head on his fist. "Did you hear about an alleged second incident last night?" he asked, switching to Chinese now. "There are whispers, but I received nothing conclusive."

Roma pretended to find something of particular interest in the cracks along the ground. He couldn't hold back his grimace when he remarked, "The whispers are true. I happened to be there."

"Oh, excellent!" Marshall bolted upright, clapped his hands together. "Well, not quite excellent for the dead victim, but excellent! Let us go search the new scene instead and hope it will offer more information than this foul-smelling—"

"We cannot," Roma cut in. "It occurred within Scarlet territory."

Marshall stopped pumping his fists, disheartened. Benedikt, on the other hand, was watching his cousin curiously.

"And how did you *happen to be* on Scarlet territory?" he asked. *Without bringing us, no less* was the unspoken addition tacked to the end of his question.

"My father sent me to obtain answers from the Scarlets," Roma replied. That was half a truth. Lord Montagov had indeed waved Roma off with the order to determine what the Scarlets knew. Walking up to the burlesque club had been Roma's own doing.

Benedikt arched an eyebrow. "And did you obtain answers?"

"No." Roma's gaze wandered off. "Juliette knew nothing."

A sudden bang echoed loudly into the relative calm of the waterfront. Benedikt had accidentally elbowed the crates in disbelief, sending the one at the top of the stack hurtling onto the ground and splintering into dozens of wooden slabs.

"Juliette?" Benedikt exclaimed.

"Juliette is back?" Marshall echoed.

Roma remained silent, his eyes still tracing the edge of the river. An ache was building in his head, a sharp tension that throbbed each time he probed into his memories. It hurt him just to say her name. *Juliette.*

This was where he had known her. As workers bustled back and forth with dirty rag cloths tucked in their pockets, grabbed at periodically to wipe away the grime that collected on their fingers, two heirs had hidden here in plain sight almost every day, laughing over a common game of marbles.

Roma forced away the images. His two friends didn't know what had happened, but they knew *something* had. They knew that one day Roma had been trusted by his father as closely as one should expect from a son, and the next, regarded suspiciously as if Roma were the enemy. Roma remembered the stares, the glances exchanged between observers when Lord Montagov spoke over him, insulted him, smacked him over the head for the littlest infraction. All the White Flowers could sense the change, yet not a soul dared voice it aloud. It became something quietly accepted, something to wonder about but never discuss. Roma never brought it up, either. He was to accept this new strain, or risk shaking it even further upon confrontation. Four years had passed now on a careful tightrope. So long as he did not run any faster than what was asked of him, he would not lose his balance above the rest of the White Flowers.

"Juliette is back," Roma confirmed quietly. His fists tightened. His throat constricted. He breathed in, barely able to exhale through the shudder that consumed his chest.

All the abominable stories he had heard, all the stories that blanketed Shanghai like a heavy mist of terror, injected directly into the hearts of those outside Scarlet protection—he had hoped them to be lies, hoped them to be nothing but propaganda that sought to poison the willpower of men who were out to harm Juliette Cai. But he had faced her last night for the first time in four years. He had looked into Juliette's eyes and, in that instant, felt the truth of those stories as if a higher power had opened his head and nestled the thoughts neatly into his mind.

Killer. Violent. Ruthless. All those and more—that was who she was now.

And he mourned for her. He didn't wish to, but he did—he ached with the knowledge that the softness of their youth was gone forever, that the Juliette he remembered was long dead. He ached even more to think that though he was the one who had dealt the killing blow, he had still dreamed of her in these four years, of the Juliette whose laughter had rung along the riverside. It was a haunting. He had buried Juliette like a corpse beneath the floorboards, content to live with the ghosts that whispered to him in his sleep. Seeing her again was like finding the corpse beneath the floorboards to not only have resurrected, but to be pointing a gun right at his head.

"Hey, what is this?"

Benedikt nudged aside a piece of the crate he had broken, cupping something from the ground into his hands. He brought his hands up to his nose and took one look before yelping in disgust, shaking a dustlike substance from his palms. Attention captured, Roma dropped to one knee and Marshall hurried over, both squinting at what Benedikt had found with heavy confusion. A minute passed before anyone spoke.

"Are those . . . dead insects?" Marshall asked. He scratched his chin, unable to explain the presence of such small creatures scattered in the crate. They didn't resemble any insect that the three boys had seen before. Each creature certainly had three segments to its body and six legs, but they were weirdly misshapen—the size of a child's fingernail and pitch-black.

"Mars, check the other crates," Roma demanded. "Benedikt, give me your bag."

With a grimace, Benedikt handed over his shoulder bag, watching in disgust as Roma scooped up a few of the insects and put them with Benedikt's notebooks and pencils. There was no alternative: Roma needed to take these away for further inspection.

"Nothing in here," Marshall reported, having broken the lid off the second crate. They watched him work through the rest. Each crate was shaken thoroughly and smacked a few times, but there were no more insects.

Roma looked skyward.

"That crate at the very top," he said. "It was open before you touched it, was it not?"

Benedikt frowned. "I suppose so," he replied. "The insects could have crawled in—"

A sudden burst of Chinese voices came around the corner then, startling Roma badly enough to drop Benedikt's bag. He swiveled on his heel and met his cousin's wide gaze, then looked to the combative stance Marshall had immediately shifted into.

"Scarlets?" Marshall asked.

"We don't need to stick around to check," Benedikt said immediately. Faster than Marshall could react, he gave the other boy a rough push. It was only Marshall's surprise that allowed him to stumble to the edge of the boardwalk, teetering and teetering before tipping over, dropping into the water with a quiet *plink!* Roma had not managed one word of protest before his cousin was also charging at *him*, throwing them both into the Huangpu River before the merry voices could bend around the corner and come upon the boardwalk.

Murky darkness and blips of liquid sunlight closed around Roma. He had dropped into the water quietly with Benedikt's guidance, but now he was as loud as his raging heartbeat, his arms thrashing wildly in his haste to find his bearings amid the waves. Was he sinking lower or rising to the surface? Was he right-side up or upside down, swimming closer to the soil until his entire body was buried within the river, never to be seen again?

A hand jabbed his face. Roma's eyes flew open.

Benedikt was hovering before him, his hair flying in short locks all around his face. He pressed an angry finger to his lips, then dragged Roma by the arm, swimming until they were under the boardwalk. Marshall was already floating there, having poked his head into the few inches of breathable space between the underside of the boardwalk and the rippling river. Roma and Benedikt did the same, inhaling as silently as possible to catch their breaths, then pressing their ears close to the boardwalk panels. They could hear the Scarlet voices above, talking about a White Flower they had just beat to near death, running away only because a group of police officers had come by. The Scarlets did not stop nor notice the shoulder bag that Roma had dropped. They were too caught up in their high, caught up in the aftereffects of the feud's bloodlust. Their voices merely became terribly loud before fading again, heading onward in obliviousness to the three White Flowers hiding in the very water beneath them.

As soon as they were gone, Marshall reached over and thumped Benedikt over the head.

"You didn't have to *push* me," Marshall grumbled angrily. "Did you hear what they were saying? We could have fought them. Now I'm soggy in places no man should be soggy."

While Benedikt and Marshall started to argue back and forth, Roma's eyes wandered, scanning the underside of the boardwalk. With the sun beaming brightly through the slits of the platform, the light revealed all sorts of mold and dirt that collected in clumps under the space. It also immediately directed Roma's gaze toward . . . what looked like a shoe, floating in the water and knocking against the inner side of the boardwalk.

Roma recognized it.

"By God," Roma exclaimed. He swam for the shoe and plucked it out of the water, holding it up like a trophy. "Do you know what this means?"

Marshall stared at the shoe, supplying Roma with a look that was somehow vocal without saying any words. "That the Huangpu River is becoming increasingly polluted?"

At this point, Benedikt was getting fed up with floating in the grime under the boardwalk, and swam out. Marshall was fast to follow, and Roma—remembering with a start that it was indeed safe to surface now—hurriedly did the same, slapping his hands against the dry side of the floating boardwalk and shaking the water out of his trousers when he was back on his feet.

"This," Roma said, gesturing to the shoe, "belonged to the man who died on Scarlet territory. He was *here*, too." Roma grabbed Benedikt's shoulder bag and shoved the shoe in. "Let's go. I know where—"

"Hey," Marshall cut in. Still dripping wet, he squinted into the water. "Did you . . . ? Did you see that?"

When Roma looked out into the river, all he saw was blistering sunlight.

"Uh . . . ," he said. "Are you trying to be funny?"

Marshall turned to face him. There was something in his dead-serious expression then that stopped Roma's teasing remark, stilled it with a sour flavor on his tongue.

"I thought I saw eyes in the water."

The sourness spread. The whole air around them suddenly grew coppery with apprehension, and Roma tightened his grip on his cousin's bag until he was practically hugging it to himself.

"Where?" he asked.

"It was only a flash," Marshall said, scrubbing his hands through his hair in an effort to wring the water out. "Honestly, it might have just been the sunlight in the river."

"You sounded certain about the eyes."

"But why would there have been *eyes*—"

Benedikt cleared his throat, having finished stomping the water out of his trousers. Roma and Marshall both turned to him.

"You've heard what the people are saying, no?"

Their responses were immediate.

"Goe-mul," Marshall whispered, at the same time Roma intoned, "Chudovishche."

Benedikt made an affirming noise. It was that which finally shook

Roma out of his stupor, waving for his friends to hurry up and move away from the water.

"Oh, please, don't buy into the monster talk running through the city," he said. "Just come with me."

Roma hurried off. He whipped through the city streets, winding through the open market stalls and barely sparing the passing vendors a second glance, even when they reached out to catch him by the arm, hoping to advertise a strange new fruit sailed in from some other world. Benedikt and Marshall huffed and puffed to stay at his pace, trading occasional frowns and wondering where Roma was taking them so fervently with a bag full of dead insects clutched in his arms.

"Here," Roma declared finally, skidding to a stop outside the White Flower labs, panting heavily while he caught his breath. Benedikt and Marshall collided with each other behind him, both almost toppling over in their haste to stop when Roma did. By then, they were practically dried from their dip into the river.

"Ouch," Marshall complained.

"Sorry," Benedikt said. "I almost slipped on this." He lifted his foot and salvaged a thin piece of paper, a poster that had fallen off a signpost. They usually advertised transportation services or apartment vacancies, but this one had giant text at the top heralding AVOID THE MADNESS. GET VACCINATED!

"Give me that," Roma demanded. Benedikt passed the sheet and Roma folded it, slipping the small square into his pocket for later examination. "Follow me."

Roma barged into the building and wound through the long hallway, entering the labs without knocking. He was supposed to don a lab coat every time he entered the building, but no one had ever dared tell him off, and the various young scientists that the White Flowers employed at these workstations barely looked up when Roma visited once a month. They were familiar enough with his presence to let him be, and the head scientist, Lourens, was familiar enough with Roma not to say anything about his misconduct. Besides, who would ever bother protesting the behavior of the White Flower heir? As far as these scientists were concerned, Roma was practically the one distributing their wages.

"Lourens?" Roma called, scanning the labs. "Lourens, where are you?"

"Up here," Lourens's deep voice boomed in accented Russian, his hand waving from the second landing. Roma took the staircase up two at a time, with Marshall and Benedikt bounding behind him like eager puppies.

Lourens looked up at their arrival, then furrowed his bushy white brows. He wasn't used to seeing guests. Roma's lab visits tended to be solo trips, made with his head ducked into his shoulders. Roma always slinked into this lab like the physical act of shrinking could act as a shield against the greasy nature of their underground trade. Perhaps if he didn't walk with his usual good posture, he could absolve himself of blame when he came asking for the monthly progress reports of the products that came in and out of this lab.

This place was supposed to be a White Flower research facility at the cutting edge of pharmaceutical advancements, perfecting modern medicines for the hospitals operating on their territory. That was, at least, the facade they maintained. In truth, the tables at the back were smeared with opium, smelling like heaviness and tar while the scientists added their own unique toxins into the mixture, until the drugs were modified into the epitome of addiction.

Then the White Flowers would send them back out, take the money in, and life went on. This was not a humanitarian venture. This was a business that made poor lives even poorer and allowed the wealthy to burst at their seams.

"I wasn't expecting you today," Lourens said, stroking his straggly beard. He was leaning up against the railing to look onto the first floor, but his hunched back made the gesture appear terribly dangerous. "We haven't finished with the current batch yet."

Roma winced. Sooner or later he would get used to the blasé manner the people here treated their work. Work was work, after all. "I'm not here about the drugs. I need your expertise."

As Roma hurried to Lourens's worktable and brushed the papers aside to clear the space, Marshall sprang forward, taking the opportunity to make an extravagant introduction. His whole face lit up, as it always did when he could add another name to the eternally long list of people he had rubbed shoulders with.

"Marshall Seo, pleased to make your acquaintance." Marshall extended his hand, making a small bow.

Lourens, his joints slow and creaky, shook Marshall's outstretched fingers warily. His eyes turned to Benedikt next out of expectance, and with an imperceptible sigh, Benedikt extended his hand too, his wrist floppy.

"Benedikt Ivanovich Montagov," he said. If his impatience wasn't already oozing from his speech, his wandering eyes certainly proved where his attention was: the insects Roma was spreading out on Lourens's worktable. Roma's face was stuck in a grimace as he used his sleeve to cover his fingers and separate each little creature from the other.

Lourens made a thoughtful noise. He pointed his finger at Roma. "Isn't *your* patronymic Ivanovich?"

Roma turned away from the creatures. He squinted at the scientist. "Lourens, *my* father's name is not Ivan. You know this."

"For the life of me, my memory is worsening with my age if I can't remember yours," Lourens muttered. "Nikolaevich? Sergeyevich? Mik—"

"Can we take a look at this instead?" Roma interrupted.

"Ah." Lourens turned to face his worktable. Without caring about the crucial matter of hygiene, he reached out with his fingers and prodded at the insects, his weary eyes blinking in confusion. "What am I looking at?"

"We found them at a crime scene"—Roma folded his arms, tucking his shaking fingers into the fabric of his suit jacket—"where seven men lost their minds and tore out their own throats."

Lourens did not react to the aggravation of such a statement. He only pulled at his beard a few more times, knitting his eyebrows together until they became one long furry shape on his forehead.

"Is it that you think these insects caused the men to rip out their own throats?"

Roma exchanged a glance with Benedikt and Marshall. They shrugged.

"I don't know," Roma admitted. "I was hoping you could tell me. I confess I can't imagine why else we would find *insects* at the crime scene. The only other working theory is that a monster might have risen up from the Huangpu River and induced the madness."

Lourens sighed. If it had come from anybody else, Roma may have felt a prickling of irritation, an indication that he was not being taken seriously despite the severity of his request. But Lourens sighed when he was making his tea and he sighed when he was cutting open his letters. Roma had witnessed enough of Lourens Van Dijk's temper to know this was merely his neutral state.

Lourens prodded an insect again. This time he drew his finger back quickly.

"Ah—*oh*. That's interesting."

"What?" Roma demanded. "What's interesting?"

Lourens walked away without replying, his feet shuffling on the floor. He scanned his shelf, then muttered something under his breath in Dutch. Only when he had retrieved a lighter, a small thing red in color, did he respond, "I will show you."

Benedikt pulled a face, silently waving an arm through the air.

Why is he like this? he mouthed.

Let him have his fun, Marshall mouthed in return.

Lourens came hobbling back. He retrieved a petri dish from a drawer underneath the worktable and delicately picked up three of the dead insects, dropping them upon the dish one after the other.

"You should probably wear gloves," Benedikt said.

"Hush," Lourens said. "You did not notice, did you?"

Benedikt pulled another face, this one looking like he was chewing on a lemon. Roma stifled the slightest hint of a smile that threatened his lips and quickly placed a hand on his cousin's elbow in warning.

"Notice what?" he asked, when he was assured that Benedikt would remain quiet.

Lourens stepped away from the worktable, walking until he was at least ten paces away. "Come here."

Roma, Benedikt, and Marshall followed. They watched Lourens pull a flame free from the lighter, watched as he brought it to the insect in the center of the petri dish, holding the burning yellow light to the insect until it started to shrivel, the exoskeleton reacting to stimuli even past death.

But the strangest thing was happening: the *other* two insects on either side of the burning insect were burning up too, shriveling and glowing with heat. As the insect in the middle curled further and further inward, burning with the fire, those to either side of it did the exact same.

"That's a mighty strong lighter you have there," Marshall remarked.

Lourens quashed the flame. He strode toward the worktable then, with a pace that Roma didn't think him capable of, and hovered the petri dish over the rest of the dozens of insects that remained on the wooden surface.

"It is not the lighter's doing, dear boy."

He pushed down on the lighter. This time, as the insect under the flame turned fiery red and curled inward, so too did all the insects laid out on the table—viciously, suddenly, in a manner that almost gave Roma a fright in believing they had come alive.

Benedikt took a step back. Marshall pressed his hand to his mouth.

"How can that be?" Roma demanded. "How is this possible?"

"Distance is the determinant here," Lourens said. "Even in death, one insect's action is determined by the others nearby. It is possible that they do not have their own mind. It is possible they act as one—every single one of these insects that remain alive."

"What does this mean?" Roma pressed. "Are they responsible for the dead men?"

"Perhaps, but it is hard to say." Lourens set the petri dish down, then rubbed at his eyes. He seemed to hesitate, which was terribly unexpected and, for whatever reason, prompted a pit to begin growing in Roma's stomach. In the years that Roma had known the old scientist, Lourens was always saying whatever came to mind with no concern for propriety.

"Spit it out," Benedikt prodded.

A great, great sigh. "These are not organic creatures," Lourens said. "Whatever these things are, God did not make them."

And when Lourens crossed himself, Roma finally realized the unearthliness of what they were dealing with.

Five

Midday sunlight streamed through Juliette's bedroom window. Despite the shine, it was brisk out today, chilly in the sort of way that drew the roses in the garden a little straighter, as if they couldn't afford to lose a single second of the warmth filtering through the clouds.

"Can you believe Tyler?" Juliette fumed, pacing her room. "Who does he think he is? Has he been bullying his way around for the past four years?"

Rosalind and Kathleen both pulled a face from upon Juliette's bed, where Rosalind was braiding Kathleen's hair. That look was as good as confirmation.

"You know Tyler doesn't have any real influence in this gang," Kathleen tried. "Don't worry—*ow*, Rosalind!"

"Stop moving and maybe I wouldn't have to pull so hard," Rosalind replied evenly. "Do you want two even braids or two lop-sided braids?"

Kathleen folded her arms, huffing. Whatever point she had been raising to Juliette seemed completely forgotten. "Just wait until I learn how to braid my own hair. Then you'll have power over me no longer."

"You've been growing your hair long for five years, mèimei. Just admit you think my braiding is superior."

A smattering of sound came from right outside Juliette's bedroom door then. Juliette frowned, listening while Kathleen and Rosalind continued on, with no indication they had heard the same noise.

"Of course your braiding is superior. While *you* were learning how to style yourself and be ladylike, *I* was being taught how to swing a golf club and shake hands aggressively."

"I *know* the tutors were bigoted assholes about your education. I'm only saying right now to stop *squirming*—"

"Hey, hey, hush," Juliette whispered quickly, pressing a finger to her lips. It had been footsteps. Footsteps that stopped, probably in hopes of catching a floating piece of gossip.

While most mansions of big-name bosses sat along Bubbling Well Road in the city center, the Cai house resided quietly at the very edge of Shanghai; it was an effort to avoid the watchful eyes of the foreigners governing the city, yet despite its strange location, it was the hotspot of the Scarlet Gang. Anybody who was anybody in the network would come knocking when they had free time, even though the Cais owned countless smaller residences in the heart of the city.

In the silence, the footsteps sounded again, moving on. It probably mattered little if the maids and aunts and uncles passing by every minute tried to eavesdrop—Juliette, Rosalind, and Kathleen were always speaking in rapid English when it was only the three of them, and very few people in the house had the linguistic ability to act as eavesdroppers. Still, it was irritating.

"I think they're gone," Kathleen said after a while. "Anyway, before Rosalind *distracted me*"—she shot her sister a feigned dirty look for emphasis—"my point was that Tyler is merely a nuisance. Let him say what he wants to say. The Scarlet Gang is strong enough to deflect him."

Juliette sighed heavily. "But I worry." She wandered to her balcony doors. When she pressed her fingers to the glass, the heat of her skin misted up the surface immediately in little dots: five identical spots where she left her mark. "We don't take note of it, but the blood feud casualties keep rising. Now, with this strange madness, how long will it be before we don't have the numbers to be operating anymore?"

"That won't happen," Rosalind reassured her, finishing the braids. "Shanghai is under our fist—"

"Shanghai *was* under our fist," her sister cut in. Kathleen sniffed, and pointed to a map of the city that Juliette had unfurled on her desk. "Now the French control the French Concession. The British, the Americans, and the Japanese have the International Settlement. And we're battling the White Flowers for a stable grasp on everywhere else, which is a feat in itself considering how few Chinese-owned zones are left—"

"Oh, *stop*." Rosalind groaned, pretending to have a fainting spell. Juliette had to stifle a giggle as Rosalind splayed an arm across her forehead and flopped back onto the bed. "You've been listening to too much Communist propaganda."

Kathleen frowned. "I have not."

"At least admit you have Communist sympathies, come on."

"They're not wrong," Kathleen retorted. "This city is no longer Chinese."

"Who *cares*." Rosalind kicked out with her foot suddenly, using the momentum to push her body upright, sitting so fast that her coiffed hair whipped into her eyes. "Every armed force in this city either has an allegiance to the Scarlet Gang or the White Flowers. That is where the power is. No matter how much land we lose to the foreigners, gangsters are the most powerful force in this city, not foreign white men."

"Until the foreign white men start rolling in their own artilleries," Juliette muttered. She walked away from the balcony doors and trailed back toward her vanity table, hovering by the long seat. Almost absently, she reached out, trailing her finger along the lip of the ceramic vase that sat by her cosmetics. There used to be a blue-and-white Chinese vase here, but red roses did not match the whorls of porcelain, and so the swap had been made for a Western design instead.

It would have been so much easier if the Scarlets had run the foreigners out, had chased them away with bullets and threats the moment their ships and their fancy goods docked in the Bund. Even now the gangsters could still join forces with the tired factory workers and their boycotts. Together, if only the Scarlet Gang wanted to, they could overrun the foreigners . . . but they wouldn't. The Scarlet Gang was profiting far too much. They needed this investment, this economy, these stacks and stacks of money flooding into their ranks and holding them afloat.

It pained Juliette to think about. On her first day back, she had paused outside the Public Garden, spotted a sign that read NO CHINESE ALLOWED, and burst out laughing. Who in their right mind would forbid the Chinese from entering a space in their own country? Only later did she realize it hadn't been a joke. The foreigners truly thought themselves mighty enough to enforce spaces that were *reserved for the Foreign Community*, reasoning that the foreign funds they poured into their newly constructed parks and newly opened speakeasies justified their takeover.

For temporary riches, the Chinese were letting the foreigners make permanent marks upon their land, and the foreigners were growing cozy. Juliette feared the tables would turn suddenly one day, leaving the Scarlet Gang to realize they had found themselves standing on the outside.

"What's wrong with you?"

Juliette jerked to attention, using the vanity mirror to peer at Rosalind. "What?"

"You looked like you were plotting murder."

A knock came on Juliette's bedroom door before she could respond, forcing her to turn around properly. Ali, one of the maids, opened the door and shuffled through, but remained hovering over the threshold, unwilling to step too far in. None of the household staff knew how to deal with Juliette. She was too bold, too brazen, too Western, while they were too new, too uncertain, never comfortable. The household staff rotated every month as a matter of practicality. It prevented the Cais from learning their stories, their lives, their histories. In no time, their month was up and they were being shoved out the door for their own safety, cutting the ties that would bind Lord and Lady Cai to more and more people.

"Xiǎojiě, there's a visitor downstairs," Ali said softly.

It hadn't always been like this. Once, they had had a set of household staff that lasted through Juliette's first fifteen years of life. Once, Juliette had Nurse, and Nurse would tuck Juliette in and tell her the most heart-aching tales of desert lands and lush forests.

Juliette reached out, plucked a red rose from the vase. The moment she closed her hands around the stem, the thorns pricked her palm, but she hardly felt the sting past the calluses protecting her skin, past the years she had spent chasing away every part of her that qualified for *delicate*.

Juliette hadn't understood at first. Four years ago, while she knelt in the gardens, trimming their rosebushes with thick gloves on, she hadn't realized why the temperature around her had risen so intently, why it sounded almost as if the entire grounds of the Cai mansion were shuddering with . . . an *explosion*.

Her ears were screeching—first with the remnants of that awful, loud sound, then with the shouting, the panic, the cries wafting over from the back, where the servants' house was. When she hurried over, she saw rubble. She saw a leg. A pool of blood. Someone had been standing right at the threshold of the front door when the ceiling caved in. Someone in a dress that looked like the sort Nurse wore, with the same fabric that Juliette had always tugged on as a child, because it was all she could reach to get Nurse's attention.

There had been a single white flower lying on the path into the servants' house. When Juliette shook off her gloves and picked it up, her ears ringing and her whole mind dazed, her fingers came upon a pinned note, one written in Russian, in cursive, bleeding with ink when she unfolded it.

My son sends his regards.

They had wheeled so many bodies into the hospital that day. Corpses upon corpses. The Cais had been playing nice, had decided to ease up on an age-old hatred whose cause had been forgotten to time—and look where it had gotten them: death delivered directly to their doorstep. From that incident onward, the Scarlet Gang and White Flowers shot at each other on sight, guarding and defending territory lines as if their honor and reputation depended on it.

"Xiǎojiě?"

Juliette squeezed her eyes shut, dropping the rose and smoothing a cold hand over her face until she could swallow back every memory that threatened to erupt. When she opened her eyes again, her gaze was dull, uninterested as she inspected her fingernails.

"So?" she said. "*I* don't deal with the visitors. Get my parents."

Ali cleared her throat, then twisted her hands through the rough hem of her button shirt. "Your parents are out. I could fetch Cai Tailei—"

"No," Juliette snapped. She regretted her tone immediately when the maid's expression turned stricken. Out of all their household staff, Ali was the one who treated Juliette with the least amount of caution. She didn't deserve to be barked at.

Juliette tried for a smile. "Let Tyler be. It's probably just Walter Dexter downstairs. I'll go."

Ali inclined her chin respectfully, then hurried away before Juliette's temper came back. Juliette supposed she gave the household staff the wrong impression. She would do anything for the Scarlet Gang. She cared for their welfare and their politics, their coalitions and alliances with the merchant firms and investors.

But she did not care about little men like Walter Dexter, who thought themselves mightily important without the capacity to back such a claim. She had no desire to be running the errands that her father didn't want to do. This was far from the cutthroat business she had expected to be welcomed into when she was finally summoned back. If she had known that Lord Cai would leave her out of the blood feud, out of the same paralleled sniping occurring on the political stage, maybe she wouldn't have rushed to pack her bags and pour out the entire contents of her alcohol stash when she left New York behind.

After the attack that killed Nurse, Juliette had been shipped back to New York for her own safety, had had to simmer on her resentment for four long years. It wasn't who she was. She would have rather stayed and braced herself on her own two feet, fight with her chin held up. Juliette Cai had been taught not to run, but her parents—as parents tended to be—were hypocrites, and they had forced her to run, forced her out of the thick of the blood feud, forced her to become someone far removed from the danger.

And now she was back.

Rosalind made a throaty noise as Juliette shrugged a jacket over her beaded dress. "There it is again."

"What?"

"The murder face," Kathleen supplied without looking up from her magazine.

Juliette rolled her eyes. "I think this is simply my resting expression."

"No, your resting expression is this." Rosalind imitated the most scatterbrained expression she could manage, eyes wide and mouth open, swaying in circles on the bed. In response, Juliette threw a slipper at her, drawing giggles from Kathleen.

"Shoo," Rosalind chided, smacking the slipper away and biting down on her laugh. "Go attend to your duties."

Juliette was already walking out, making a rude gesture over her shoulder. As she trudged down the hallway of the second floor, picking at her chipping nails, she paused in front of her father's office to shake out her shoe, which hadn't fit right ever since it had gotten caught on a drain covering.

Then she froze, her hand on her ankle. She could hear voices coming from the office.

"Ah, *excuse me*," Juliette hollered, kicking the door open with her high-heeled shoe. "The maid said you were both *out*."

Her parents lifted their heads at once, blinking plainly. Her mother was standing over her father's shoulder, one hand rested on the desk and the other placed upon a document in front of them.

"The staff say what we want them to say, qīn'ài de," Lady Cai said. She made a flicking motion with her fingers at Juliette. "Don't you have a visitor to entertain downstairs?"

Huffing, Juliette pulled the door closed again, glaring daggers at her parents. They hardly paid her heed. They simply went back to their conversation, assuming Juliette would run along.

"We have lost two men to it already, and if the whispers are true, more will fall before we can determine exactly what is causing it," her mother said, voice low as she resumed speaking. Lady Cai always sounded different in Shanghainese than any other language or dialect. It was hard to verbalize exactly what it was except a feeling of calm, even if the subject matter carried a terrible squall of emotion. That was what it meant to speak your native tongue, Juliette supposed.

Juliette wasn't really sure what *her* native tongue was.

"The Communists are beside themselves with joy. Zhang Gutai won't even need a megaphone for recruitment anymore." Her father was the opposite. He was quick and sharp. Though the tones of Shanghainese came completely from the mouth instead of the tongue or throat, he somehow managed to make it reverberate tenfold within himself first before releasing the sound. "With people dropping like flies, capitalist ventures cease to grow, factories become ripe for revolution. Shanghai's commercial development comes to an abrupt stop."

Juliette grimaced, then hurried away from her father's office door. No matter how hard her father had tried through his letters, Juliette had never cared much about who was who in the government, not unless their ongoings had some direct effect on Scarlet business. All she cared about was the Scarlet Gang, about whatever immediate dangers and tribulations they were facing on a day-to-day basis. Which meant that in scheming, Juliette's mind liked to gravitate to the White Flowers, not to the Communists. But if the Communists had indeed unleashed madness onto this city as her father seemed to suspect, then they, too, were killing her people, and she had a bone to pick with them. Her father hadn't been overlooking the deaths in favor of politics this morning after all. Perhaps they were one and the same.

It does make sense that the Communists could be responsible for the madness, Juliette thought as she started down the staircase toward the first floor.

Only how could they possibly manage such a feat? Civil war was no novelty. This country was in political turmoil more than it was at peace. But something that caused innocent people to gouge their own throats out was certainly far from any biological warfare Juliette had studied.

Juliette bounded onto the last step of the staircase.

"Hello!" she shouted. "I am here! You may bow!" She entered the living room and, with a start, found a stranger primly seated on one of the couches. It was not the annoying British merchant, but it was indeed someone who looked very similar, only younger, around her age.

"I'll refrain from bowing if that's okay," the stranger said, an upward tilt to his mouth. He rose to his feet and stuck out his hand. "I'm Paul. Paul Dexter. My father couldn't make it today, so he sent me."

Juliette ignored the outstretched hand. *Poor etiquette,* she noted immediately. By the rules of British society, a lady was always to have the privilege of offering the handshake. Not that she cared about British etiquette, nor how their high society defined what a *lady* was, but such minuscule details pointed to a lack of training, and so Juliette filed that away in her head.

And he *really* should have bowed.

"I assume you're here for the same request still?" Juliette asked, smoothing her sleeves down.

"Indeed." Paul Dexter took back his hand without any malice. His smile was a cross between that of a Hollywood star and a desperate clown. "My father promises you that we have more *lernicrom* than any other merchant sailing into this city. You will not find better prices elsewhere."

Juliette sighed as a few cousins and uncles filtered through the living room, waiting for them to pass. As the group walked by, Mr. Li clapped a hand over her shoulder good-naturedly.

"Good luck, kid."

Juliette stuck out her tongue. Mr. Li grinned, wrinkling his entire face, then produced a small wrapped candy from his palm for Juliette to take. She was no longer an overeager four-year-old who would eat until she gave herself a toothache, but she took it anyway, popping the candy into her mouth while her uncle strolled away.

"Please sit, Mr. Dexter—"

"Call me Paul," he interrupted, perching again on the long couch. "We're a new generation of modern people and Mr. Dexter is my father."

Juliette barely refrained from gagging. She bit down on the hard candy instead, then collapsed onto an armchair perpendicular to Paul.

"We have been admiring the Scarlets for some time now," Paul continued. "My father has high hopes of a partnership."

A visible shudder swept through Juliette's body at the familiarity Paul had with the term "Scarlets." As a name, the Scarlet Gang sounded a lot nicer in Chinese. They called themselves hóng bāng, the two syllables twirled together in a quick snap of vowels. Such a name curled in and out through Scarlet tongues like a whip, and those who didn't know how to handle it properly ended up lashed.

This was Paul Dexter's lashing.

"I'll give you the same answer we gave your father," Juliette said. She drew her legs up onto the armrest, the layers of her dress falling back. Paul's eyes followed the motion. She watched his eyebrow twitch with the scandal of her long, pale thigh on show. "We're not taking on any new endeavors. We're busy enough with our current clients."

Paul feigned disappointment. He leaned forward, like he could persuade her with mere eye contact. All it did was show Juliette that he hadn't quite brushed out a clump of pomade in his sweep of dark-blond hair. "Don't be like that," he said. "I hear there's a rival business who might be more enthusiastic about the offer. . . ."

"So perhaps you should try them," Juliette suggested. She straightened up suddenly. He was trying to entice her into listening by suggesting he would take his business to the White Flowers, but it mattered little. Walter Dexter was a client they *wanted* to lose. "I'm glad we could resolve this matter so promptly."

"Wait, no—"

"Goodbye now . . ." Juliette pretended to think. "Peter? Paris?"

"Paul," he supplied, frowning.

Juliette summoned a smile, not unlike the scatterbrained one Rosalind had been mimicking earlier. "Right. Bye!"

She hopped to her feet and pranced across the living room, toward the front entrance. In a blink, her fingers were on the heavy handle and she was pulling the door open, eager to get rid of the British visitor.

Paul, to his credit, was fast to recover. He came up to the door and bowed. *Finally, some manners.*

"Very well."

He stepped out, onto the front stoop, then pivoted again to face Juliette. "May I make a request, Miss Cai?"

"I already told you—"

Paul smiled. "Can I see you again?"

Juliette slammed the door shut. "Absolutely not."

Six

Roma wasn't having a pleasant day.

Within his first hour awake, he had tripped going up the stairs, smashed his favorite mug with his favorite herbal tea, and checked his hip against the kitchen table so roughly that there was a giant purple splotch forming on his torso. Then he had been forced to inspect a crime scene. *Then* he had had to face the possibility that this was a crime scene of supernatural proportions.

As Roma trudged back into the city's central hub under the early-afternoon sun, he could feel his patience wearing incredibly thin. Every blow of whistling steam sounded like the noise his father made from his mouth when he got angry, and every *crack* of a butcher bringing his cleaver down reminded Roma of gunfire.

Usually, Roma adored the busyness that surrounded his home. He would deliberately take the long routes to skirt in and out of the stalls, peering at the bundles of farm-grown vegetables piled higher than their seller. He would make faces at the fish, inspecting the conditions of their small, dirty tanks. If he had time to kill, he would pick up sweets from every vendor selling them, popping them into his mouth as he went along and emerging from the markets with aching teeth and empty pockets.

The open market was one of his greatest loves. But today it was nothing but an irritant atop an already viral rash.

Roma ducked under the laundry lines pulled along the narrow alleyway leading into the Montagovs' central housing block. Both clean and dirty water dripped furious puddles onto the pavement: transparent if it was under a sopping-wet dress, black and sludgy if it was under a half-installed pipe.

That was a feature that became more prominent as one ventured deeper in Shanghai. It was as if a lazy artist had been in charge of building everything—rooftops and window ledges would curve and stretch with the most glorious angles and archways, only to abruptly end or cut into the neighboring block. There was never enough *space* in the poorest parts of this city. Resources were always running out just before the builders were ready. Pipes were always a smidgen too short, drains only had half a covering, sidewalks seemed to slope into themselves. If Roma wanted to, he could stretch his arms out from his bedroom window on the fourth floor and easily reach the outward-folding window shades of a bedroom in the building next to his. If he stretched with his legs instead, he could hop over without struggle to scare the old man who lived there.

It wasn't like they were short on space. There was an abundance of land outside the city for expansion—land untouched by the influence of the International Settlement and the French Concession. But the White Flowers' lodgings were nestled right beside the French Concession, and there they were resolute to stay. The Montagovs had been located here since Roma's grandfather emigrated. The foreigners had only claimed the nearby land in these recent years as they became more brash with their legal power. Every once in a while it gave the White Flowers great trouble whenever the French tried to control the gang's ongoings, but the state of affairs always blew in favor of the Russians. The French needed them; they did not need the French. The White Flowers would let the foreigners continue practicing their laws over a space that didn't seem to belong to either of them, and the pomp-ous merchants with their floral coats and polished shoes stepped aside when the gangsters ran amok on the streets.

It was a compromise, but it was one that would become more tense as more time drew out. Places like these were already suffocat-ing. It did naught to add more weight upon the pillow pressed to their faces.

Roma shrugged Benedikt's bag higher up his shoulder. Bene-dikt hadn't been very pleased that Roma was taking his art supplies away from him, but then Roma had pretended to offer it back, and his cousin had only needed one look—at all the dead bugs Lourens didn't want to keep and the dead man's shoe that Roma had shoved in there—before promptly pushing it back, asking Roma to return it after he gave it a good wash.

Roma unlocked his front door and slipped in. Just as he dragged himself into the living room, a door slammed to his right, and Dimitri Voronin was strolling in too.

Roma's already unpleasant day turned even worse.

"Roma!" Dimitri shouted. "Where have you been all morning?"

Despite being only a few years older, Dimitri acted as if he were legions superior to Roma. As Roma passed him, Dimitri grinned and reached out to ruffle Roma's hair.

Roma jerked away, narrowing his eyes. He was nineteen, heir to one of the two most powerful underground empires in the city, but whenever Dimitri was in the same room as him, he was reduced to a child again.

"Out," Roma replied vaguely. If he said it was anything related to White Flower business, Dimitri would pry and pry until he was in the know too. While Dimitri wasn't unintelligent enough to ever openly insult Roma, Roma could hear it in every reference to his youth, every quasi-sympathetic *tut* whenever he spoke up. It was because of Dimitri that Roma wasn't allowed to be soft. It was because of Dimitri that

Roma had crafted a cold and brutal face that he hated seeing every time he looked into a mirror.

"What do you want?" Roma asked now, pouring himself a glass of water.

"Don't worry." Dimitri wandered into the kitchen after him, grabbing a nearby chopping knife. He stabbed at a plate on the table, picked up a piece of cooked meat, and chomped down around the thick blade without regard for who had left the plate there or how long the food had been sitting out. "I was on my way out too."

Roma frowned, but Dimitri was already walking off, taking with him the heavy scent of musk and smoke. Left alone, Roma heaved a long exhale and turned to put his glass in the sink.

Only, as he turned, he found himself being watched by wide brown eyes on a small, pixie-like face.

He almost yelped.

"Alisa," Roma hissed at his sister, throwing open the doors of the kitchen cupboard. He couldn't figure out how she had been watching him from up there without his notice, or how she had even managed to fit in among the spices and sugars, but by now he had learned not to ask.

"Careful," she whined when Roma lifted her out of the cupboard. When he set her down on the floor, she gestured at the sleeve Roma had clenched in his fist. "This is new."

It was very much not new. In fact, the cloth-and-wrap shirt that went around her petite shoulders resembled the sort of clothing the peasantry wore before the royal dynasties in China ended, ripped in a sort of manner that could be caused only by slipping in and out of the tightest corners. Alisa simply spoke outrageous things on occasion for no reason other than to incite confusion, leading people to believe she skated a thin line between insane and overly immature.

"Hush," Roma told her. He smoothed down her collar, then froze, his hand stilling when it touched a chain Alisa had looped around her neck. It was their mother's, an heirloom from Moscow. The last time he'd seen it, it had been on her corpse after she was murdered by the Scarlet Gang, a bright silver chain that stood stark against the blood seeping from her slit throat.

Lady Montagova had gotten sick shortly after Alisa was born. Roma would see her once a month, when Lord Montagov took him to a secret location, a safe house tucked in the unknown nooks of Shanghai. In his mind, she had been gray and gaunt, but always alert, always ready to smile when Roma walked up to her bed.

The point of a safe house was so Lady Montagova didn't need guards. She was supposed to have been *safe*. But four years ago, the Scarlet Gang had found her anyway, had slashed her throat in response to an attack earlier that week, and left one wilted red rose clutched in her hands. When they buried her corpse, her palms were still embedded with the thorns.

Roma should have hated the Scarlet Gang long before they killed his mother, and he should have hated them even more—with a burning passion—after they killed Lady Montagova. But he didn't. After all, it was lex talionis: an eye for an eye—that was how the blood feud worked. If he hadn't launched that first attack, they wouldn't have retaliated against his mother. There was no way to spread blame in a feud of such scale. If there was anyone to blame, it was himself. If there was anybody to hate for his mother's death, it was himself.

Alisa waved a hand in front of Roma's face. "I see eyes, but I see no brain."

Roma snapped back into the present. He placed a gentle finger under the chain, shaking it about. "Where did you get this?" he asked softly.

"It was in the attic," Alisa replied. Her eyes lit up. "It's pretty, isn't it?"

Alisa had been only eight years old. She had not been told about the murder, only that Lady Montagova had at last succumbed to illness.

"Very pretty," Roma said, his voice hoarse. His eyes flicked up then, hearing footsteps on the second floor. Their father was in his office. "Run along now. I'll call you down when it's time for dinner."

Giving a mock salute, Alisa skittered out of the kitchen and up the stairs, her wispy blond hair trailing after her. When he heard her bedroom door close on the fourth floor, Roma started up the stairs too, going up to his father's office. He shook his head roughly, clearing his thoughts, and knocked.

"Enter."

Roma filled his lungs with air. He pulled the door open.

"Well?" Lord Montagov said in lieu of a greeting. He did not raise his eyes. His attention was on the letter in his hand, which he scanned quickly before tossing it away and picking up the next one in his stack. "I hope you found something."

Cautiously, Roma walked in and set the bag down on the floor. He reached into it, hesitating for a moment before pulling out the shoe and setting it down on his father's desk. Roma held his breath, clasping his hands behind his back.

Lord Montagov looked upon the shoe like Roma had presented him with a rabid dog. He made that expression at Roma rather frequently. "What is this?"

"I found it where the first seven men died," Roma explained carefully, "but it belongs to the man who died in the Scarlet club. I think he was present at the scene of the first crime, and if so, then this is a matter of contagion—"

Lord Montagov slammed his hands down on his desk. Roma flinched hard but forced himself not to close his eyes, forced himself to stare forward evenly.

"Contagion! Madness! Monsters! What is wrong with this city?" Lord Montagov bellowed. "I ask you to find answers and you bring me *this*?"

"I found exactly what you asked for," Roma replied, but quietly, barely audible. For the last four years, he was always doing what was asked of him, be it a little task or a terrible one. If he didn't, he would have the consequences to fear, and though he hated being a White Flower, he hated the thought of *not* being one even more. His title gave him power. Power kept him safe. It gave him authority, it held his threateners back, and it let him keep Alisa safe, let him keep all his friends within his circle of protection.

"Get this out of my face," Lord Montagov ordered, waving at the shoe.

Roma thinned his lips, but he pulled the shoe away and shoved it back into the bag. "The point remains, Papa." He shook the bag, letting the fabric swallow up the shoe. "Eight men clash on the ports of Shanghai—seven rip out their own throats, one escapes. If that one then proceeds to rip out his throat too the next day, does that not sound like a disease of contagion to you?"

Lord Montagov did not respond for a long while. Instead, he spun on his chair until he was facing the small window that overlooked a busy alleyway outside. Roma watched his father, watched his hands tighten on the arms of the large chair, his closely shaven head prickle with the faintest hint of sweat. The stack of letters had been momentarily abandoned. The names signed in Chinese at the base of many were familiar: Chen Duxiu, Li Dazhao, Zhang Gutai. *Communists.*

After the Bolshevik Revolution swept through Moscow, the tide of that political wave had blown down here, to Shanghai. The new factions that rumbled to life some few years ago had been persistently trying to recruit the White Flowers as allies, ignoring the fact that the last thing the White Flowers would want was *social redistribution*. Not after the Montagovs had spent generations climbing to the top. Not when most of their common gang members had *fled* the Bolsheviks.

Even if the Communists saw the White Flowers as potential allies, the White Flowers saw them as enemies.

Lord Montagov finally made a disgusted noise, turning away from the window.

"I wish not to be involved in this business of a *madness*," he decided. "Such shall be your task now. Figure out what is occurring."

Slowly Roma nodded. He wondered if the tightness of his father's voice was a sign that he thought this madness business beneath him, or if it was because his father was afraid of catching the madness himself. Roma was not afraid. He only feared the power of others. Monsters and things that walked the night were *strong*, but they were not *powerful*. There was a difference.

"I'll find what I can on this man," Roma decided, referring to the most recent victim.

Lord Montagov wheeled his chair back an inch, then lifted his feet onto his desk. "Don't act in haste, Roma. You must confirm that this shoe truly belongs to the man who died last night first."

Roma furrowed his brow. "The last victim is being kept in a Scarlet hospital. I'll be shot on sight."

"Find a way in," Lord Montagov responded simply. "When I gave you the order to obtain Scarlet information, you seemed to approach them with ease."

Roma stiffened. That was unfair. The only reason why his father had sent him into Scarlet territory in the first place was because lord against lord was too severe of an interaction. If Lord Cai and his father had met and had their encounter end peacefully, both would have lost face. Roma, on the other hand, could defer to the Scarlet Gang without consequence to the White Flowers. He was merely the heir, sent out on an important mission.

"What are you saying?" Roma asked. "Just because I had reason to enter their burlesque club does not mean I can gallivant through their hospital—"

"Find someone to take you in. I have heard rumors that the Scarlet heir has returned."

A clamp fixed itself onto Roma's chest. He did not dare react. "Papa, don't make me laugh."

Lord Montagov shrugged flippantly, but there was something in his eyes that Roma didn't like.

"It is not so absurd an idea," his father said. "Surely you can ask one favor. She was your lover once, after all."

Seven

In the span of a few short days, talk had started in the city. At first nothing except rumors: a suspicion that it was not an enemy nor a natural force bringing about this madness but the devil himself, knocking on doors in the dead of night and with one look, utter insanity was wrought on the victim.

Then the sightings began.

Housewives who hung their washing by the ports claimed to see tentacles skittering away when they ventured outside at nightfall to collect their things. A few Scarlet workers who showed up late to their shifts were scared away by growling, then flashes of silver eyes staring them down from the other end of the alleyway. The most horrific account was the story spread by the owner of a riverside brothel, speaking of a creature curled amid the trash bags outside his brothel as he closed up. He had described it panting, as if in pain, as if struggling against itself, half-cast in shadow but doubtlessly an unnatural, strange thing.

"It has a spine studded with *blades*," Juliette heard whispered in front of her now, the story presently being passed from son to mother as they waited for food from the window of a fast-serving restaurant. The little boy was bobbing up and down in excitement, echoing words heard from a schoolmate or a neighborhood friend. The more deaths there were—and there had been multiple since the man in the burlesque club—the more the people speculated, as if just by speaking the possibilities they could stumble upon the truth. But the more people talked, the further truth slipped.

Juliette would have shaken the stories off as rumors, but the fear seeping into the streets was very, very real, and she doubted such a feeling would reach these heights without substantial backing to the claims. So what was it, then? *Monsters* weren't real, no matter what Chinese fairy tales had once been taken as truth. This was a new age of science, of evolution. The so-called monster had to be a creature of someone's creation—but whose?

"Hush," the mother tried, the fingers of her left hand nervously twining through the beads on her right wrist. They were Buddhist prayer beads, used to track mantra, but whatever mantra the woman recited now couldn't compete with the limitless enthusiasm of her son.

"They say he has claws the size of forearms!" the boy continued. "He prowls the night for gangsters, and when he smells the taint of their blood, he pounces."

"It is not only the gangsters dying, qīn'ài de," his mother said quietly. Her hand tightened on the back of his neck, keeping him steady in the slow-moving line.

The little boy stopped. A tremor entered his sweet voice. "Māma, am *I* going to die?"

"What?" his mother exclaimed. "Of course not. Don't be ridiculous." She looked up, having reached the front of the line. "Two."

The shopkeeper passed a paper bag over the window and the mother-son pair hurried off. Juliette stared after them and thought about the sudden fear in the boy's voice. In that brief moment, the boy—barely older than five—had comprehended that he too could die with the rest of the corpses in Shanghai, because who could be safe from madness?

"On the house, miss."

Juliette looked up suddenly, finding a paper bag already hovering in front of her face.

"Only the best for the princess of Shanghai," the old shopkeeper said, his elbows resting on the perch of the serving window.

Juliette summoned her most dazzling smile. "Thank you," she said, taking the bag. Those two words would give the shopkeeper plenty of material to brag about when he met up with his friends for mahjong tomorrow.

Juliette turned around and left the line, reaching into the bag and ripping a chunk of the bun to chew on. Her smile fell as soon as she was out of sight. It was getting late and she would be expected at home soon, but still she dawdled among the shops and the bustle of Chenghuangmiao, one slow-moving girl in a crowd of havoc. She didn't have a lot of opportunities to wander about in places like these, but today she did. Lord Cai had sent her over to check on an opium distribution center, which unfortunately, hadn't been as exciting as she'd thought. It had merely smelled bad, and upon finally locating the owner with the papers her father wanted, the owner had passed them to her looking half-asleep. He hadn't even offered a greeting first nor verified Juliette's right to be asking for such confidential supply information. Juliette didn't understand how someone like that could be given management over fifty workers.

"Excuse me," she muttered, pushing through a particularly thick crowd gathered in front of a pencil sketch shop. Despite the darkness seeping into the pink skies, Chenghuangmiao was still bustling with visitors—lovers taking slow strolls through the chaos, grandparents purchasing xiǎolóngbāo for the children to slurp on, foreigners simply taking in the sights. The name Chenghuangmiao itself referred to the temple, but to the people of Shanghai, it had come to encompass all the busy surrounding markets and the cloisters of activity in the area. The British army had set up its head office here almost a century ago, in the Yuyuan Gardens, which Juliette was passing now. Since then, even after their departure, the foreigners had taken a liking to this place. It was always full of their faces, cast in wonder and amusement.

"This is the end! Get the cure now! There is only one cure!"

And sometimes it was full of native eccentrics too.

Juliette grimaced, tucking her chin in so as not to make eye contact with the ranting old man on the Jiuqu Bridge. However, despite her best efforts to pass unnoticed, the old man straightened at the sight of her and darted along the zigzag bridge—the thuds of his footsteps making sounds that were rather concerning to hear from such an old structure. He skittered to a stop in front of her before she could put enough distance between them.

"Salvation!" he screeched. His wrinkles deepened until his eyes were wholly swallowed by sagging skin. He could barely lift his back past a perpetual hunch, yet he moved as fast as a scurrying rodent on the hunt for food. "You must spread the message of salvation. The lā-gespu will give it to us!"

Juliette blinked rapidly, her eyebrows raised. She knew she shouldn't entertain ranting men on the streets, but there was something about him that pricked the little hairs on her neck straight up. Despite his rural accent, she had understood almost all of the man's croaky Shanghainese—all except that little pocket of gibberish.

Lā-gespu? Was the 's' sound merely a lisp of his generational upbringing?

"Lā gē bō?" Juliette tried to guess in correction. "A *toad* will give us salvation?"

The old man looked mightily offended. He shook his head from side to side, throwing around his thin, wispy white hairs and rustling up the flimsy braid he wore. He was one of those few people who still dressed like the country hadn't left the imperial era.

"My mother told me a wise proverb when I was young," Juliette continued, amusing herself now. "Lā gē bō xiāng qiē tī u ny."

The old man merely stared at her. Did he not understand her

Shanghainese? Abroad, she had constantly feared that she would lose her accent, feared she would forget how to pronounce those persistently flat tones found in no other dialect across this country.

"Bad joke?" Juliette asked. In the more common dialect, she repeated herself, this time more hesitantly. "Lài háma xiǎng chī tiān é ròu? Yes? I deserve at least a little chuckle, come on."

The old man stomped his foot down, shaking in his exertion to be taken seriously. Perhaps Juliette had chosen the wrong proverb to joke around with. *The ugly toad wants a bite of swan meat.* Maybe the old man hadn't been raised on fairy tales about the Frog Prince and his ugly toad stepbrother. Maybe he didn't like that her joke implied his lā-gespu savior—whatever that meant—was the equivalent of a proverbial, scheming, ugly creature who lusted after the swan, his Frog Prince brother's beloved.

"The lā-gespu is a *man*," he snapped right into Juliette's face, his voice a reedy hiss. "A man of great might. He gave me a cure. An injection! I should have died when my neighbor collapsed on me, tearing at his throat. Oh! So much blood! Blood in my eyes and blood running down my chest! But I did not die. I was saved. The lā-gespu saved me."

Juliette took a great step back, one she should have taken five minutes ago, before this conversation began.

"Uh, this has been fun," she said, "but I really should be going."

Before the old man could make a grab at her, she sidestepped him and hurried off.

"Salvation!" he screamed after her. "Only the lā-gespu can bring salvation now!"

Juliette took a sharp turn, moving out of view completely. Now that she was in a less crowded area, she let out a long breath and took her time weaving through the shops, casting glances over her shoulder to ensure she wasn't being followed. Once she was certain there was nobody on her tail, she sighed in sorrow to be leaving Chenghuangmiao behind and wove out from the collection of closely congregated shops, stepping back onto the city streets to begin her walk home. She could have flagged a rickshaw or stopped any one of the Scarlets loitering outside these cabarets, to have them fetch her a car. Any other girl her age would have, especially with a necklace as shiny as the one around her neck, especially if their footsteps reverberated with an echo that stretched two streets over. Kidnapping was a lucrative business. Human trafficking was thriving at an all-time high, and the economy was booming with crime.

But Juliette walked on. She passed men in large groups and men who squatted in front of brothels, leering like it was their second job. She passed gangsters throwing knives outside the casinos they had been hired to guard, passed shady merchants cleaning their guns and chewing on toothpicks. Juliette did not falter. The sky grew redder and her eyes grew brighter. Wherever she went, no matter how far into the darkest underbelly of the city she wandered, as long as she stayed within her territory, *she* was the reigning supreme.

Juliette paused, rolling out her ankle to ease the tightness of her shoe. In response, five nearby Scarlet gangsters who were waiting around a restaurant also stilled, waiting to see if they would be summoned. They were killers and extortionists and raging forces of violence, but as the rumors went, Juliette Cai was the girl who had strangled and killed her American lover with a string of pearls. Juliette Cai was the heiress who, on her second day back in Shanghai, had stepped into a brawl between four White Flowers and two Scarlets and killed all four White Flowers with only three bullets.

Only one of those rumors was true.

Juliette smiled and waved to the Scarlet men. In response, one waved back, and the other four nervously laughed among themselves. They feared Lord Cai's wrath if anything were to happen to her, but they feared her wrath more if they were to test the truth of the rumors.

It was her reputation that kept her safe. Without it, she was nothing.

Which meant that when Juliette wandered into an alleyway and was stopped by the sudden pressure of what felt like a gun pressed to the small of her back, she knew it wasn't a Scarlet who had dared stop her.

Juliette froze. In a split second, she ran through all the possibilities: an affronted merchant wanting comeuppance, a greedy foreigner wanting ransom, a confused addict on the streets who hadn't recognized her by the sparkly beads of her foreign dress. . . .

Then a familiar voice said, in English, of all languages: "Don't shout for help. Keep moving forward, follow my instructions, and I won't shoot."

The ice in her veins thawed in an instant and instead roared into a fiery rage. Had he waited for her to enter an isolated area, until no one was around to give aid, thinking she would be too afraid to react? Had he thought it would actually work?

"You really don't know me anymore," Juliette said quietly. Or maybe Roma Montagov thought he knew her too well. Maybe he thought himself an expert and had brushed off the rumors she spread about herself, thinking there was no way she had become the killer she claimed to be.

The first time she killed someone, she had been fourteen.

She had known Roma for only a month, but she had sworn to herself that she wouldn't follow the blood feud, that she would be better. Then, one night on their way to a restaurant, their car had been ambushed by White Flowers. Her mother had yelled for her to stay down, to hide behind the car with Tyler, to use the guns that had been placed in their hands only if absolutely necessary. The fight had almost ended. The Scarlets had killed almost every White Flower.

Then the last White Flower remaining dove in Juliette and Tyler's direction. There was a last-ditch fury burning in his eyes, and in that moment, though there was no doubt that it was a time of absolute necessity, Juliette had frozen. Tyler had been the one to shoot. His bullet had studded into the White Flower's stomach and the man had gone down, and in horror, Juliette had looked to the side, where her parents were watching.

It wasn't relief that she saw. It was confusion. Confusion over why Juliette had frozen. Confusion over why Tyler had been more capable. So Juliette had raised her gun and fired too, finishing the job.

Juliette Cai feared disapproval more than she feared grime on her soul. That killing was one of the few secrets she had kept from Roma. Now she knew she should have told him, if only to prove that she was just as nefarious as Shanghai always said she was.

"Walk," Roma demanded.

Juliette remained still. As she intended, he misread her inaction as fear, for ever so slightly, he hesitated and eased up the press of his gun just a smidgen.

She whirled around. Before Roma could so much as blink, her right hand came down hard on his right wrist, twisting his gun-wielding hand outward until his fingers were unnaturally bent. She slapped down at the gun with her left hand. The weapon skittered to the ground. Her jaw gritted to brace for impact, Juliette twisted her foot out behind Roma's and jerked it against his ankles—until he was falling backward and she followed, one hand locked on his neck and the other reaching into her dress pocket to retrieve a needle-thin knife.

"Okay," Juliette heaved, breathing hard. She had him pinned flat on his back, her knees on either side of his hips and her blade pressed to his throat. "Let's try this again like civilized people."

Roma's pulse jumped under her fingertips, his throat straining to move away from the blade. His eyes were dilated as he stared at her, adjusting to the shadows of the sunset while the alleyway faded into a dusky violet. They were close enough to be sharing quick, short breaths, despite both of their best efforts to appear unbothered by the exertion of the struggle.

"Civilized?" Roma echoed. His voice was scratchy. "You have me at knifepoint."

"*You* had me at gunpoint."

"I'm on *your* territory—I had no choice."

Juliette frowned, then pressed the knife in until a bead of blood appeared on its tip.

"Okay, stop, stop." Roma winced. "I get it."

One small slip of her hand now would cut his neck right open. She was almost tempted to give it a try. Everything between them felt far too familiar, too automatically intimate. She itched to be rid of that feeling, to slice it off like it was a malevolent tumor.

Roma still smelled as he used to: like gunmetal and mint and the softness of a gentle zephyr. This close, she could determine that everything and yet nothing had changed.

"Go on," Juliette prompted, wrinkling her nose. "Explain yourself."

Roma's eyes flickered up in vexation. He acted flippant, but Juliette was tracking his erratic pulse as it thudded away beneath her fingers. She could feel every jump and stutter of fear as she leaned in with her blade.

"I need information," Roma managed.

"Shocking."

His eyebrows rose. "If you let me go, I can explain."

"I'd prefer if you explain like this."

"Oh, Juliette."

Click.

The echo of the safety being pulled on a handgun sounded into the alley. Surprised, Juliette looked to her left, where the gun she had disarmed was still lying, untouched. She turned her gaze back to Roma and found him smiling, his beautiful, wicked lips quirked in mockery.

"What?" Roma asked. He sounded almost teasing. "You thought I only had one?"

The cold press of metal touched her waist. Its chill seeped through the fabric of her dress, printed its shape into her skin. Begrudgingly, slowly, Juliette removed her knife from Roma's throat and raised her hands high. She released her deathly grip on him, each step as prolonged as possible until she was standing up, striding backward to put herself two paces away from the pistol.

In unison, with no other way to avoid a deadlock, they put their weapons away.

"The man who died at your club last night," Roma began. "Do you remember his mismatched shoes?"

Juliette bit down on the insides of her cheeks, then nodded.

"I found the other half of one of the pairs in the Huangpu River, right where the rest of the men died the night of the Mid-Autumn Festival," Roma went on. "I think he escaped the first bloodshed. But he took the madness with him, took it to your club a day later and then succumbed to it."

"Impossible," Juliette snapped immediately. "What sort of *science*—"

"We are *past* science, Juliette."

Her indignation hot in her throat, Juliette brought her shoulders up to her ears and clutched her hands into fists. She entertained the idea of calling Roma paranoid, irrational, but unfortunately she knew how diligent he was when he found something to focus on. If he thought this a possibility, it was very likely a possibility.

"What are you saying?"

Roma folded his arms. "I'm saying that I need to know for certain if it was indeed the same man. I need to see the other shoe on his corpse. And if the shoes match up, then this madness—it could be contagious."

Juliette felt denial lay thick and heavy in her bones. The victim had died in *her* club, spraying blood onto a room full of *her* Scarlets, coughing spittle into a gathering full of *her* people. If this was indeed a disease of the mind—a *contagious* disease of the mind—the Scarlet Gang was in big trouble.

"It could have been a suicide pact," she suggested without much conviction. "Perhaps the man backed out, only to act later." But

Juliette had looked into the dying man's eyes. In there, terror had been the only emotion that existed.

God. She had looked into the dying man's eyes. If this was contagious, what was *her* risk of catching it?

"You sense it just as I do," Roma said. "Something is not right here. By the time this goes through official channels to be investigated, more innocent people will have died from this peculiar madness. I need to know if it is spreading."

Roma was looking right at Juliette when he fell silent. Juliette stared back, a deep coldness unfurling in her stomach.

"As if you care," she said softly, refusing to blink in case her eyes started watering, "about innocent people dying."

Every muscle along Roma's jaw tightened.

"Fine," he said sharply. "*My* people."

Juliette looked away. Two long seconds passed. Then she pivoted on her heel and started to walk.

"Hurry up," she called back. Just this once she would help him, and never again. Only because she, too, needed to know the answers he sought. "The morgue will be closing soon."

Eight

They walked in tense, palpable silence.

It was not that it was awkward—in honesty, that would have been preferable. It was rather that their proximity to each other, with Juliette walking ahead and Roma trailing three paces behind so they weren't seen together, was horrifyingly familiar and, quite frankly, the last thing Juliette wanted to feel for Roma Montagov was *nostalgia*.

Juliette dared a glance back as they worked through the long, winding streets of the French Concession. Because there were so many foreigners here clambering for a piece of the city, the roads of the French Concession reflected their greed, their scramble. Houses within each sector turned inward in a manner that—if viewed from the skies—almost appeared circular, huddling in on themselves to protect their underbelly.

The streets here were just as busy as the Chinese parts of the city, but everything was somewhat more orderly. Barbers performed their duties on the pavement like usual, only every few seconds they would reach down with their feet and neatly brush the discarded tufts of hair closer to the gutters. Vendors sold their wares at moderate volumes, rather than the usual screaming Juliette would hear in the western parts of Shanghai. It was not only the adaptations of the people that made the French Concession peculiar—the buildings seem to sit a little straighter, the water seemed to run a little clearer, the birds seemed to chirp a little louder.

Perhaps they all sensed Roma Montagov's presence and were bristling in warning.

And Roma was bristling right back, inspecting the houses with his eyes narrowed into the twilight.

It hurt to look at him like this: unaware, curious.

"Careful that you don't trip," Roma intoned.

Juliette glared at him, though he was still looking at the houses, then forced her gaze back onto the sidewalk before her. She should have known any sort of obliviousness from Roma Montagov was merely an act. She had once known him better than she knew herself. She used to be able to predict his every move . . . except the one time when it really mattered.

Roma and Juliette met on an evening like this four years ago, right before this city imploded with the bustle of its new reputation.

The year was 1922, and nothing was impossible. Planes dove and swooped in the sky and the last remnants of the Great War were being scrubbed clean. Humanity seemed to be on an upward turn from the fighting and the hatred and the warfare that had once spilled over the edges, allowing the good things at the bottom to slowly rise. Even the blood feud in Shanghai had reached an unspoken sort of equilibrium, where instead of fighting, a Scarlet and a White Flower might nod coldly at one another if they were to pass on the streets.

It was an atmosphere of hope that had welcomed Juliette when she stepped off the steamboat then, her legs unsteady after a month at sea. Mid-October, the air warm but becoming brisk, workers bantering by the port-side as they volleyed packages into waiting boats.

At fifteen, Juliette had come back with dreams. She was going to do something worthy of remembrance, be someone worthy of commemoration, ignite lives worth fighting for. It was a feeling she hadn't known when she left at the age of five, sent away with little more than some clothes, an elaborate fountain pen, and a photograph so she wouldn't forget what her parents looked like.

It was the high of that feeling that had sent her chasing after Roma Montagov.

Juliette's whole chest shuddered as she exhaled into the night. Her eyes burned, and quickly she wiped the sole tear that had fallen down her cheek, her teeth gritted hard.

"Are we almost there?"

"Relax," Juliette said without turning around. She didn't dare, in case her eyes were glimmering under the dimly burning streetlamps. "I'm not leading you astray."

Back then, she hadn't known who he was, but Roma had known *her*. He would reveal months later that he had rolled that marble at her on purpose, testing to see how she would react while she waited by the ports. The marble had come to a stop near her shoe—American shoes, shoes that wouldn't blend in with the cloth and heavy soles stomping down around her.

"That's mine."

She remembered her head jerking up upon picking up the marble, thinking the voice belonged to a rough Chinese merchant. Instead, she had been looking into a pale, young face with the features of a foreigner—a smorgasbord of sharp lines and wide, concerned eyes. The accent with which he spoke the local dialect was even better than hers, and her tutor had refused to speak anything except Shanghainese in case she forgot it.

Juliette had rolled the marble into her palm, closing her fingers around it tightly.

"It's *mine* now."

It was almost funny now, how Roma had startled upon hearing her Russian—flawless, if a little stilted from a lack of practice. His brow furrowed.

"That's not fair." He stayed in the Shanghai dialect.

"Finders keepers." Juliette refused to switch out of Russian.

"Fine," Roma said, finally returning to his native tongue so they spoke the same language. "Play a game with me. If you win, you may keep the marble. If I win, I get it back."

Juliette had lost, and rather grudgingly, returned the marble. But Roma had not started the game for the fun of it, and he wouldn't let her slip away that easily. When she turned to leave, he reached for her hand.

"I'm here every week at this time," he said sincerely. "We can play again."

Juliette was laughing as she slid her fingers out of his hold. "Just you wait," she called back. "I'll win them all from you."

She would find out later that the boy was Roma Montagov, the son of her greatest enemy. But she would return to find him anyway, thinking herself shrewd, thinking herself clever. For months they flirted and pretended and toed the line between enemy and friend, both knowing who the other was but neither admitting to it, both trying to gain something from this friendship but being uncareful, falling too deep without knowing.

When they were launching marbles along the uneven ground, they were just Roma and Juliette, not Roma Montagov and Juliette Cai, the heirs of rival gangs. They were laughing kids who had found a confidant, a friend who understood the need to be someone else if only for a while each day.

They fell in love.

At least—Juliette *thought* they had.

"Juliette!"

Juliette gasped, coming to a quick stop. In her daze, she had been two heartbeats away from walking right into a parked rickshaw. Roma yanked her back, and instinctively, she looked up at him, at his certainty and cautiousness and clear, cold eyes.

"Let me go," Juliette hissed, yanking her arm away. "We're almost to the hospital. Keep up."

She hurried ahead, her elbow stinging where he had touched her. Roma was fast to follow, as he always was, as he had always known how, trailing after her in a way that seemed natural to the untrained eye, so that anybody looking upon them would think it to be a coincidence Roma Montagov and Juliette Cai were walking near each other, if the prying eye recognized them at all.

The grandiose building ahead loomed into view. Number 17, Arsenal Road.

"We're here," Juliette announced coldly.

The same hospital where they had brought all the bodies after the explosion.

"Keep your head down."

Just to defy her, Roma squinted up at the hospital. He frowned like he could sense the familiarity of such a place merely by the shakiness of Juliette's voice. But of course he didn't—he couldn't. She watched him stand there, easy in his own skin, and felt her palms burn with fury. She supposed he knew exactly how deeply this city felt the weight of what he had done. The blood feud had never been as bloody in those first few months after his attack. If she had leaned in to smell the letters that Rosalind and Kathleen sent across the Pacific Ocean, breathed in the ink that they scrawled messily onto thick, white paper to describe the casualties, she imagined that she would have been able to smell the gore and violence that slicked the streets red.

She had believed Roma to be on the same side as her. She had believed that they could forge their own world, one free of the blood feud.

Nothing but *lies*. The explosion in the servants' house was the most serious hit that the White Flowers could ever get away with. They would have been spotted trying to blow the main mansion, but the servants' house was unwatched, dismissed, an afterthought.

So many Scarlet lives, gone in an instant. It had been a declaration of war.

And it could not have been achieved without Roma's help. The way the men had snuck in, the way the gate had been left open—it was all intel that only Roma could have known from the weeks and weeks spent with Juliette.

Juliette had been betrayed, and here she was, still reeling from it four years later. Here she was, harboring this pulsating lump of hatred burning in her stomach that had only gotten hotter and hotter in the years she had been robbed of a confrontation, an explanation, and yet *still* she did not have the courage to sink her knife right into Roma's chest, to get revenge in the only way she knew how.

I am weak, she thought. Even as this hate consumed her, it was not enough to burn away every instinct she had to reach for Roma, to keep him from harm.

Perhaps the strength to destroy him would come with time. Juliette simply needed to bide it.

"Head *down*," she prompted again, pushing through the double doors to enter the hospital foyer.

"Miss Cai," a doctor greeted as soon as Juliette approached the front desk. "Can I help you with anything?"

"Help me like this—" With one hand, Juliette mimed her lips zipping shut. With the other, she leaned over the desk and swiped the key to the morgue. The doctor's eyes widened, but he looked away. The key cold in her palm, Juliette kept moving through the hospital, trying to breathe as shallowly as possible. It always smelled like decay here.

Before long, they had reached the back of the hospital, and Juliette stopped in front of the door to the morgue with a huff. She turned around to face Roma, who had been walking while staring at his shoes, as commanded. Even with his best effort, his shrinking-violet act wasn't convincing. Poor posture was ill suited on him. He was born with pride stitched to his spine.

"In here?" he asked. He sounded hesitant, like Juliette was leading him into a trap.

Without speaking, Juliette slid the key in, unlocked the door, and flipped on the light switch, revealing the single corpse inside. It was lying on a metal table that took up half the floor space. Underneath the white-blue lighting, the dead man looked to have already wasted away, mostly covered by a sheet.

Roma stepped in after her and took one look at the tiny room. He started toward the corpse, rolling up his sleeves. Only before he could lift the sheet, he paused, hesitating.

"This is a small hospital and someone else is probably going to die within the hour," Juliette prompted. "Get a move on before they decide to transfer this man to a funeral home."

Roma threw a glance back at Juliette, eyeing the impatient stance she had adopted.

"Do you have somewhere better to be?"

"Yes," Juliette said without hesitation. "Get on with it."

Visibly prickled, Roma yanked the sheet off. He appeared to be surprised when he found bare feet on the man.

Juliette pushed off from the wall. "For crying out loud." She marched over and dropped to a crouch by the shelves beneath the metal table, retrieving a large box of bagged items and dumping out its contents. After tossing aside the slightly bloody wedding ring, the very bloody necklace, and the toupee, Juliette found the mismatched pair of shoes that had been on his feet that day. She peeled the bag open and shook the nicer one out.

"Yes?"

Roma's lips were thinned, his jaw pulled tight. "Yes."

"Can we agree that this man was indeed at the scene, then?" Juliette asked.

Roma nodded.

That was that. They didn't speak while Juliette put everything into the box again, her fingers working nimbly. Roma was somber, his eyes fixed to a random point on the wall. She figured that he couldn't wait to get out of here, to stretch the distance between their bodies as far as possible and pretend the other didn't exist—at least until the next corpse of the blood feud got thrown over the territory lines.

Juliette pushed the box back in and found her hands to be trembling. She scrunched them into fists, squeezing as hard as she could manage when she stood and met Roma's gaze.

"After you," he said, gesturing to the door.

Four years. It should have been enough. As the seasons blew by and all this time crawled forward, he should have become a stranger. He should have grown to smile differently, as Rosalind had, or walk differently, as Kathleen did. He should have turned more brash, like Tyler, or even adopted a wearier air, like Juliette's own mother. Only he looked at her now and all he had become was . . . older. He looked at her and Juliette still saw the exact same eyes wearing the exact same stare—unreadable unless he let her through, unshakable unless he allowed himself to let go.

Roma Montagov had not changed. The Roma who had loved her. The Roma who had betrayed her.

Juliette forced herself to release her fists, her fingers aching from the tension she had squeezed into them. With the briefest nod in Roma's direction, allowing him to follow her back out, she reached for the door and waved him through, shutting the morgue after herself with a heavy finality and opening her mouth to bid Roma a cold, firm farewell.

Only before she even had the chance to speak, she was interrupted by absolute, world-ending pandemonium within the hospital. At the far end of the corridor, doctors and nurses were wheeling gurneys, screaming at one another for an update on a situation or the location of a free room. Roma and Juliette ran forward immediately, returning to the lobby of the hospital. They were already expecting tragedy, but somehow, what they found was even worse.

The floor was slick with crimson. The air was heavy.

Everywhere they looked: dying Scarlet Gang members, gushing blood from their throats and screeching in agony. There had to be twenty, thirty, forty, either dying or already dead, either motionless or presently still trying to dig their fingers into their own veins.

"Oh God," Roma whispered. "It's started."

Nine

When I peeked into his room, he was sleeping so soundly that I was a little afraid he had died in the night," Marshall said, nudging the dead man with his foot. "I think he was faking it."

Benedikt rolled his eyes, then swatted Marshall's foot away from the corpse. "Could you give Roma some credit?"

"I think Roma is a pathological liar," Marshall replied, shrugging. "He merely did not want to come out with us to look at dead bodies."

Daylight had broken only an hour ago, but the streets were already roaring with activity. The sound of waves crashing onto the nearby boardwalk was barely audible from this alleyway, not with the chatter streaming in from the inner city. The early-morning glow encased the cold streets like an aura. Steam at the ports and the smoke from the factories pumped steadily upward, thick, sooty, and heavy.

"Oh, hush," Benedikt said. "You're distracting me from said task of inspecting dead bodies." Frowning deeply, he was kneeling over the corpse that Marshall had nudged into the wall. Again, Benedikt and Marshall had been assigned cleanup duty, which not only encompassed the cleanup of the bloody corpses, but also the cleanup of the municipal officers involved, paying off any and every legal force that tried to install themselves upon these dead gangsters.

"Distracting you?" Marshall dropped to a squat so that he was level with Benedikt. "If that is so, you should thank me for relieving the morbidity."

"I would thank you if you helped me out," Benedikt muttered. "We need these men identified before noon. At this rate, the only thing we will have identified is the number of bodies here—" He rolled his eyes when Marshall looked around and started counting. "Six, Mars."

"Six," Marshall repeated. "Six dead bodies. Six-digit contracts. Six moons circling the world." Marshall adored the sound of his own voice. In any circumstance where there was silence, he took it upon himself as a favor to the world to fill it.

"Don't start—"

Benedikt's protest went unheard.

"Shall I compare him to a winter's night?" Marshall proclaimed. *"More breathtaking and more rugged: tempest breezes do tremble with less might—"*

"You saw a stranger for two seconds on the street," Benedikt interrupted dully. "Please calm down."

"With eyes like deadly nightshade, lips like fresh fruit. A freckle atop his left cheek like" —Marshall paused, then suddenly shot to his feet— "like this strangely shaped spot on the ground."

Benedikt stopped short, frowning. He stood too, squinting at the culpable object on the ground. It was much more than just a strangely shaped spot.

"It's another insect."

Marshall lifted a leg onto a jutting brick in the wall. "Oh, *please* no."

Between the cracks in the pavement, a black speck dotted the cement, ordinary upon a mere, cursory glance. But just as an artist could pick out one accidental jerk of the paintbrush amid a smorgasbord of intentional slashes, the moment Benedikt's eye landed on the speck, a shudder swept down his spine and told him that the canvas of the world had made a mistake. This creature wasn't supposed to be here.

"It's the same," he said, gingerly pinching his fingers around the insect. "It's the same sort of insect as the ones we found at the port and took to the laboratory."

When Benedikt picked up the single dead thing and showed it to his wayward friend, he expected Marshall to make some crude comment or construct a song about the fragility of life. Instead, Marshall furrowed his brows.

"Do you remember Tsarina?" he asked suddenly.

Even for Marshall's usual tangents and long-winded stories, this abrupt topic switch was odd. Still, Benedikt entertained him and replied, "Of course."

Their golden retriever had passed away only last year. It had been a strange, mournful day, both in respect for their furry companion and in peculiarity over a death that for once hadn't occurred with the press of a bullet and a spray of blood.

"Do you remember when Lord Montagov first got her?" Marshall continued. "Do you remember her bounding through the streets and rubbing noses with every other animal she encountered, be it a cat or a wild rat?"

Marshall was trying to get at something, but Benedikt could not yet determine what. He would never understand the way people like Marshall talked, in circles upon circles until his speech was the ouroboros swallowing itself.

"Yes, of course," Benedikt answered, frowning. "She caught so many fleas that they were jumping in and out of her fur—"

The ouroboros finally spat out its own tail.

"Knife." Benedikt motioned for Marshall to rummage through his pockets. "Give me your knife."

Without missing a beat, Marshall flicked a blade free and tossed. The handle glided into Benedikt's palm cleanly, and Benedikt sliced the point down, shearing a strip through the corpse's hair as thoroughly as he could. When the loose hair fell to the ground, Benedikt and Marshall leaned in at once to examine the dead man's scalp.

Only then did Benedikt nearly throw up inside his mouth.

"That," Marshall deadpanned, "is disgusting."

There was only an inch of skin on show, an inch of gray-white between two crops of thick black hair. But in this space, a dozen pinky-nail-size bumps bulged forth, dotted homes for dead insects that had taken up residence just below the first layer of skin. Benedikt's scalp itched with phantom crawling at the sight, at the curled exoskeletons thinly visible under the membrane, at the legs and antennae and thoraxes trapped and frozen in time.

Benedikt tightened his grip on the knife. Cursing himself for his curiosity, he slowly flattened the tufts of the dead man's hair so it wasn't blocking his view of the exposed skin. Then, with his teeth gritted together and a wince dancing on the edge of his tongue, he pushed the tip of the blade into one of the bumps.

There was no sound of release nor any fluid discharge, as Benedikt had been expecting from a sight so disgusting. In tense silence, interspersed only by the occasional toot of a car chugging along the nearby street, Benedikt used the knife to slit the thin skin atop one of the dead insects.

"Go on," Benedikt said when one formerly buried insect became semi-exposed. "Give it a pull."

Marshall looked at him as if he had suggested that they both slaughter a baby and eat it. "You must be joking."

"My hands are both occupied, Mars."

"I hate you."

Marshall inhaled a deep breath. He stuck two fingers gingerly into the slit. He pulled out the dead insect.

It came into the world with veins and vessels and capillaries attached to its belly. It was as if the insect were an entity unto itself and the dead man grew out of it, when really, the paper-thin lines of pink and white sprouting from the insect were being pulled from the man's *brain*. Benedikt could have been fooled.

The veins trembled as a stray gust of wind blew in from the waterfront.

"What do you know?" Benedikt said. "I think we just discovered what's causing the madness."

Ten

A few days later, Juliette was on a warpath for leads.

"Stay alert," she told Rosalind and Kathleen quietly outside the squat building of an opium den. Across the street, there were two doors with red roses taped to them—a Scarlet calling card in theory, but a loud, clear threat in reality. Rumor had it that the Scarlets started using red roses only in mockery of the White Flowers, who would paste any old white flower to the doors of the buildings they took in territory disputes. But the use of the red rose had begun so long ago that Juliette wasn't sure if there was any truth to the claim. All that was certain was that having a red rose taped to one's door was a last warning: to pay up, give in, cash out, or do whatever it was that the Scarlet Gang had demanded of you, else face the consequences.

This entire street was under Scarlet control, but every territory had its problem areas.

"Stick close to me," Juliette continued, waving her cousins forward. The moment they entered the opium den and stepped upon damp, uneven floorboards, the three girls were instinctively pressing their hands to the line of their hips or the band of their waists, comforted only by the presence of the weapons hiding under the rich fabric of their clothing. "There may be active assassins working here."

"Assassins?" Kathleen echoed, her voice pitching high. "I thought we came here to shake unpaid rent money for your father."

"We are." Juliette parted the beaded curtains, stepping through the partition and into the main den, where the smells of distorted histories and forced addictions floated freely. The scents wafting into her nose reminded her of a rose on fire, of perfume mixed with gasoline and set aflame until the remaining ash could be used as thick, heady cosmetics. "But the Scarlet grapevine tells me this is also a socializing ground for Communists."

They paused in the middle of the den. The remnants of old China were stronger here, amid the various paraphernalia—the pipes and the oil lamps—that had been brought over from before the turn of the century. The decor lagged well behind the times too, for while the chandeliers on the ceiling looked like the ones hanging golden and glittering in every Shanghai burlesque club, the bulbs were covered in a thin layer of grime, oily in appearance.

"Be careful," Juliette warned. She eyed the bodies slumped against the walls of the den. "I doubt these people are as docile as they look."

A few centuries ago, when this place was still the home estate of a royal or a general, it might have been opulent and lush. Now it was a husked-out building of missing floorboards and a ceiling sagging with the weight of itself. Now the couches bore holes where patrons extended their legs, and the armrests were worn down where patrons rubbed their grubby hands before tossing up a few cents and hurrying out—that is, if they weren't enticed into the back rooms first. As Juliette craned her neck and searched the den for the madame in charge, she heard giggling echo from the corridors. In the next few seconds, a group of young women skittered out, each dressed in a different pale-colored hanfu, which Juliette supposed was an attempt to invoke the nostalgia of China's previous eras. If only the skirts of their hanfu weren't caked with dirt and their hairpins weren't one sharp motion from falling out. If only their giggles weren't incredulously fake even to the untrained ear, their red smiles curved vivaciously but their eyes dull.

Juliette sighed. In Shanghai, it was easier to count the establishments that *didn't* double as brothels than the ones that did.

"How can I help you?"

Juliette turned around, searching for the voice who had spoken cheerily from behind. Madame, as she called herself, was inclined upon one of the couches, a lamp burning away beside her and a pipe tossed carelessly across her torso. When Juliette wrinkled her nose, Madame rose, inspecting Juliette just as closely as Juliette was inspecting the black stains on the older woman's hands.

"I'll be," Madame said. "Juliette Cai. I haven't seen you since you were four years old."

Juliette raised an eyebrow. "I wasn't aware we had ever met."

Madame pursed her pale lips. "You wouldn't remember, of course. In my mind, you'll always be a little thing toddling around the gardens, oblivious to everything else in the world."

"Uh-huh," Juliette said. She shrugged flippantly. "My father failed to mention this."

Madame's eyes stayed level, but her shoulders hitched with the slightest signal of offense. "I was rather good friends with your mother for some time"—she harrumphed—"until . . . well, I'm sure you heard that somebody accused me of being too friendly with the White Flowers a decade ago. It was all hogwash, of course. You know I hate them as much as you do."

"I don't hate the White Flowers," Juliette shot back immediately. "I hate those who harm the people I love. Most often they tend to be the White Flowers. There's a difference."

Madame sniffed. With every attempt she was making to relate to Juliette, she was getting pushed away. Juliette could keep at this all day. She loved picking holes in other people.

"Indeed, but don't let them hear you say that," Madame muttered.

She shifted her attention away from Juliette then, changing tactics and grabbing Rosalind's wrist, crooning, "Oh, I know *you*. Rosalind Lang. I knew your father, too, of course. Such precious children. I was so upset when you were sent to France. You won't believe how much your father crowed on about the excellence of a Western education." Her eyes turned to Kathleen. A beat passed.

Juliette cleared her throat.

"Bàba sent us here to collect," she explained, hoping it would direct Madame's attention back to her. "You owe—"

"But who are *you*?" Madame asked, interrupting Juliette to address Kathleen.

Kathleen narrowed her eyes. Rather tightly, she replied, "I'm Kathleen."

Madame made a performance out of searching her memory.

"Oh, Kathleen. I remember now," she gushed, clicking her fingers. "You used to be so rude, always sticking your tongue out at me."

"I *was* a child, so you will have to forgive my past misdeeds," Kathleen replied dryly.

Madame pointed at Kathleen's forehead. "You have the Sagittarius constellation birthmark too. I thought I remembered—"

"Who?" Kathleen interrupted. It sounded like a dare. "Who do you remember having it?"

"Well," Madame said, embarrassed now. "There used to be three of you Lang siblings, right? You had a brother, too."

Juliette thinned her lips. Rosalind hissed through her teeth. But Kathleen—Kathleen only stared at Madame with the flattest look in her eyes and said, "Our brother is dead. I'm sure you heard."

"Yes, well, I'm very sorry," Madame said, sounding not sorry at all. "I also lost a brother. Sometimes I think—"

"Enough," Juliette interrupted. This had gone on long enough. "Can we speak elsewhere?"

Madame crossed her arms tightly and pivoted on her heel. She did not ask for the three Scarlets to follow her, but they did so anyway, trotting along and pressing up against the walls when they had to pass the pastel girls flittering about the narrow hallways. Madame led them into a bedroom decorated in various shades of red. There was another door here, one that led straight out onto the streets. Juliette wondered if it was for easy escape or easy entrance.

"I have your rent money." They watched Madame wade through the discarded clothes on her floor, reaching under the slab of a mattress she called a bed to retrieve her money. Muttering beneath her breath, Madame counted the coins, each clinking into her palm to the tune of the groaning ceiling beams.

Madame extended her arm, offering Juliette the money in her fist.

"Actually—" Juliette closed her hand around Madame's and pushed the money back. "Keep it. There is something else I would prefer."

Madame's pleasant expression faltered. Her eyes swiveled to the side, to the other door.

"And what would that be?"

Juliette smiled. "Information. I want your knowledge regarding the Communists."

The pleasant expression on Madame's face dropped entirely. "I beg your pardon?"

"I know you let them frequent this place for their meetings." Juliette cocked her head, once at Kathleen and once at Rosalind. The two sisters broke away from their positions beside her and fanned into the room, each planting themselves in front of an exit. "I know one of these back rooms isn't holding a girl and her eternal pleasure ride—it holds a table and a fireplace to keep the members of the Communist Party of China warm. So tell me, what have you heard about their role in this madness sweeping through the city?"

Madame barked out a sudden laugh. She lifted her lips too wide. Juliette could see the thick gap between her two front teeth.

"I haven't a clue what you mean," Madame said. "I keep out of their business."

Is it fear or loyalty preventing her from talking? Juliette wondered. Madame was Scarlet-associated but not a gangster, loyal to the cause but not quite willing to die for it.

"Of course. How rude of me to assume," Juliette said. She rifled through her pocket, then grinned brighter than the thin, diamond necklace she had retrieved, now dangling between her fingers. "Will you accept a gift from me to make up for my insolence?"

Juliette skittered behind Madame before Madame could protest, and Madame did not move, either, for what was the harm in taking a diamond necklace?

It was not a diamond necklace.

Madame squawked when Juliette pulled the garrote wire tight, her fingers flying up to scrabble at the pressure digging into her skin. By then the wire was already wrapped around her neck, the micro-blades piercing in.

"Those who are loyal to the Scarlet Gang are dropping dead in droves," Juliette hissed. "Those who dirty their hands for us are falling victim to the madness, while people like you remain tight-lipped, unable to decide whether you bleed scarlet or fight for the workers' red rags." Thin beads of blood bubbled to the surface of Madame's smooth skin, enough to stain the hues of her neck. If Juliette pulled the wire only a hairsbreadth further, the blades would dig deep enough to scar upon healing. "Which shade do you bleed, Madame? Scarlet or red?"

"Stop, stop!" She wheezed. "I speak! I speak!"

Juliette loosened the wire a minuscule fraction. "Then *speak*. What role do the Communists play in this madness?"

"They do not claim responsibility for the madness," Madame managed. "As a group, they remain resolute that this is not of their political doing. Privately, however, they speculate."

"Regarding what?" Juliette demanded.

"They think one genius within the Party schemed it up." Madame's fingers tried to claw at the wire again, but the wire was too thin for her to secure a grip. All she achieved was scratching, her nails grazing at skin as if she were mocking the madness's victims. "They whisper of having seen one man's notes, planning it all."

"Who?"

When Madame seemed to hesitate, her tongue gagging forward, Juliette pulled the wire tighter in threat. By the door, Rosalind cleared her throat, an unspoken recommendation for Juliette to ease up and watch herself, but Juliette did not falter. She only said, her voice as calm as the morning tide, "I want a name."

"Zhang Gutai," Madame spat out. "The Secretary-General of the Communists."

Immediately, Juliette let go of the wire, bringing it back to her side and giving it a shake. She retrieved a handkerchief from her pocket, giving the chain a wipe down until it was sparkly and silver once again. When she tucked the wire away, she offered Madame the handkerchief with the same bright smile she reserved for working flapper parties and charming old men.

Madame was pale and shaking. She did not protest when Juliette tied the handkerchief around her neck, carefully adjusting the fabric until it soaked up the line of blood.

"I apologize for your troubles," Juliette said. "You'll keep this between us, won't you?"

Madame nodded blankly. She did not move when Juliette summoned Rosalind and Kathleen back to her side; nor did she protest when Juliette tossed all the cash she had in her pocket onto the table to belatedly pay Madame for the information.

Juliette marched out of the room, her heels echoing loudly as she exited the den with her cousins. She was already forgetting how steady her grip had been upon the wire, how willing she had been to hurt

Madame for what she wanted to hear. All she could think about was the name she had received—Zhang Gutai—and how she was to proceed next.

Kathleen watched her the entire car ride back. Juliette could feel it like a slick sweep of grease across her forehead: something that was bothering her without doing any harm.

"What?" Juliette finally demanded when the car stopped to let Rosalind out. As soon as Rosalind slammed the door after herself, shrugging her fur throw over her shoulders and strutting into the burlesque club to do her noon shift, Juliette slid across the backseat until she was directly before Kathleen, who was slouched across the seats facing her. "Why do you keep giving me that funny look?"

Kathleen blinked. "Oh. I wasn't aware you had noticed."

Juliette rolled her eyes, raising her legs to rest on the soft cushion beside Kathleen. The car started back up, the crunch of gravel beneath its wheels loud. "Biǎojiě, you underestimate the eyes I have"—she gestured all over her face—"everywhere. Did I cause offense?"

"No, of course not," Kathleen said quickly. Slowly, she sat up straight, then gestured to Juliette's hands. Juliette looked down. There was a smear of blood that she hadn't managed to clean in the soft space between her thumb and index finger. "I guess I was expecting you to just wave a gun around or something. I didn't think you would actually threaten her."

Kathleen had always been the pacifist. In the letters that she and Rosalind had sent to America while Juliette was away—always tucked within the same envelope—Juliette could immediately tell the difference between the sisters. There was the matter of handwriting, of course. Rosalind's big loopy letters when she wrote in English or French and her wide, spread-out Chinese characters, as if each stroke were trying to run away from the others. Kathleen, on the other hand, always wrote like she was running out of space. She squished her letters and strokes until they overlapped, sometimes carving up the previous character with the brunt of the next. But beneath that, even if they had typed their letters out on a typewriter, Juliette could tell. Rosalind wrote on the state of affairs as anyone in this city would. She was bright and witty from years of education in classical literature. The sweetness of her words would drip onto the page as she bemoaned Juliette's absence and told her she would have been beside herself if she had seen Mr. Ping last week when his suit pants ripped down the middle. It wasn't that Kathleen wasn't as well read—Kathleen merely looked inward. She would never write a summary on the latest blood feud casualty and then offer a wise idiom on the cyclical nature of violence. She would lay out a step-by-step procedure on stopping further brutality so they could live in peace, then wonder why nobody in the Scarlet Gang seemed to be capable of doing so.

Juliette had always had an answer. She only never had the heart to tell Kathleen.

It was because they didn't want to.

"Madame deals with the riffraff day in, day out." Juliette set her chin in her hand. "Do you think she would be scared at the mere sight of a gun?"

Kathleen sighed irritably, smoothing down her hair. "Nevertheless, Juliette, it's not like—"

"You have been present at some of my father's business meetings, no?" Juliette interrupted. "I heard Māma say Jiùjiu brought you and Rosalind along for some time a few years ago, before you lost the stomach for it."

"It was only Rosalind who lost the stomach," Kathleen countered evenly, "but yes, our father did take us along for some negotiations."

"*Negotiations*," Juliette mocked, leaning back in the seat. Her voice came out in a sneer, but the derision wasn't directed at Kathleen. It was directed at the way the Scarlet Gang warped their own language, as if everybody did not already know the truth. They should begin calling it what it really was: extortion, blackmail.

Having arrived at their destination, the car slowed to an idle outside the mansion gates, its engine rumbling. The gates surrounding the house were new, replaced right after Juliette left. They were an utter nuisance for the men stationed out front whenever relatives arrived every five minutes hoping to enter, and now the two on duty hurried to pull the heavy metal spires open before Juliette could yell at them for being slow.

But that was the price for safety in the face of ever-present danger.

"You remember, don't you?" Juliette asked. "My father's tactics?" She had seen plenty during those short few months of her first return. Even before that, when Juliette was only a child, some of her earliest memories were of raising her arms to be picked up and smelling blood emanating off her father when he did so.

The Scarlet Gang did not tolerate weakness.

"Yes," Kathleen said.

"So if he can do it," Juliette continued, "why shouldn't I?"

Kathleen had nothing to say to that. She merely sighed a little sigh and flopped her hands to either side of herself in defeat.

The car came to a complete stop. A maid was already waiting to open the door, and though Juliette took the helping hand out, it was only a matter of courtesy; in her beaded dress, it was easy for her to scoot out of the car and step down from its high elevation. Kathleen, meanwhile, needed a few seconds to make a dignified exit, the confines of her qipao slowing her progress. By the time Kathleen's shoes crunched down on the driveway, Juliette was already heading toward the front door, angling her head toward the sunlight to warm her cold face.

It would all fall into place. She needn't worry. She had a name. First thing tomorrow, she would show up at this Zhang Gutai's place of work and confront him. One way or another, Juliette would stop this madness nonsense before her people suffered for it.

Then a shriek shot through the gardens. *"Ali, what's wrong with you?"*

Juliette whirled around, reacting fast to the panic echoing through the gardens. Her heart stuttered in horror.

It's too late.

The madness had come knocking on her doorstep.

"No, no, no," Juliette hissed, rushing toward the flower beds. There, Ali had been on her way back into the house, a laundry basket filled with clothing propped on her hip. Only now the basket was lying on the roses, bundles of folded clothing crushing them without mercy.

And Ali was tearing at her own throat.

"Get her onto the floor," Juliette yelled at the nearby gardener, the one who had gotten Juliette's attention in the first place with his shriek. "Kathleen, get help!"

Juliette took one of Ali's shoulders. The gardener took the other. Together they tried their hardest to force the maid down, but by the time Ali's head thudded against the soft soil of the rose beds, her fingers were already knuckle-deep into the muscle and tendon running through her neck. There was a horrible wet, tearing sound—a sensation of dampness as blood spurted outward—and then Juliette could see *bone*, could see clearly every ridge of ivory white spliced neatly through the pink-red of Ali's neck.

Ali's eyes turned glassy. Her hands slackened, the chunks of torn flesh sliding from her loosened grasp and dropping to the ground.

Juliette wanted to throw up. The blood pouring from Ali's throat ran and ran, seeping into the soil until the earth was stained dark, until the stain grew large enough to stop merely a few feet away from the former site of the old servants' house, where Nurse, too, had met her end.

This is why, Juliette thought numbly. *This is why we shall not love more than we need to. Death will come for everyone in the end—*

A terrified scream shot out from the main house.

Kathleen.

Juliette bolted to her feet. "Kathleen!" she roared. "Kathleen, where are you?"

"Juliette, *come!*"

Juliette slammed through the front door and sprinted through the living room, drawing concerned gasps from the few confused aunts who had risen from their gossiping on the couches. In a frenzy, she skidded into the kitchen to find Kathleen standing by the long counter, her body frozen in horror, hands pressed to her mouth and muffling her words in an effort not to scream.

A cook was writhing on the floor, blood already trickling down his forearms. Three feet away, under the doorway into the main hallway, another maid was in the process of collapsing, leaning against the jamb and striking herself to resist the madness.

"Step back—"

The maid collapsed. The first arc of blood from her throat flew wide, staining the intricate carvings of the doorway and painting the beige walls into an abstraction. Faintly, Juliette wondered if they would ever be able to get such a stain out, or if it would remain in this house forever. Even when painted over or scrubbed viciously from the jamb, its presence would remain, stinking up the room with the Scarlets' failure to protect their own.

The maid stilled. It seemed that was what finally jolted Kathleen into acting, because she surged forward then with a strangled gasp, her long hair swinging and shaking into her face in her haste.

This madness—it could be contagious.

"Stop!" Juliette shrieked.

Kathleen froze in her steps. The only sound that could be heard in the sudden silence was Juliette's heavy breathing.

She turned back, facing the two aunts who had cautiously crept into the kitchen. They covered their mouths in horror, but Juliette didn't give them time to be horrified.

"Send for some of the men out front to clean this up," she said. "Tell them to wear gloves."

Eleven

Juliette slammed the trunk of the car shut, clicking its latch so vigorously that the vehicle shuddered up and down on its tires.

"Ready," she called to the driver. "Go forth."

Through the rearview mirror, the driver gave a grim nod. The car started to pull away from the gravel driveway, rumbling in the direction of the front gate and toward the nearest hospital. The dead bodies in the trunk would be out of Juliette's hands then. She hoped the hospital appreciated how delicately the Scarlets had wrapped the corpses in thick bedsheets.

"Miss Cai."

Juliette turned, finding a messenger coming her way. "Yes?"

The messenger gestured back at the house. "Your parents have come downstairs. They ask what is occurring."

"Oh, *now* they come down," Juliette muttered under her breath. Not when there was screaming in the hallways. Not when Juliette was yelling obscenities so the gangsters would hurry up with the spare bedsheets and the maids would fetch water so the servants could attempt to scrub out the stains on the floorboards.

They were going to need to hire some heavy-duty cleaners.

"I'll go speak to my parents." Juliette sighed. She strolled past the messenger, shoulders heavy with anticipation. Her parents might have been taking a meeting upstairs, but dozens of relatives had witnessed the terrible deaths, and talk in this house spread fast.

But when Juliette came back into the living room, she had to do a double take, seeing what seemed to be the entirety of her family.

"Are we having a party I wasn't invited to?" Juliette jeered, halting to a stop at the threshold. There were still bloodstains in the kitchen, and her relatives were all gathered here en masse? Did they *want* to get infected and die?

Lord Cai stood, cutting off whichever relative had been speaking within the gathering.

"Juliette," he said, inclining his chin up the staircase. There was something in his hands. A few slips of creamy white paper. Expensive paper. "Come."

It was as clear a dismissal as any for the rest of the household. While everybody else dispersed, however, Tyler remained on the couch, his hands placed behind his head like he had all the time in the world. He cocked his head at Juliette's death glare, feigning obliviousness.

Juliette bit down on her tongue. She scuttled up the stairs after her father.

"What are we to do with the bloodstains?" she asked as they filtered into his office. Her mother was already there, seated on the other side of her father's desk and browsing through reports.

"We will have someone come to clean it," Lady Cai replied, looking up and flicking a phantom speck of dust off the sleeve of her qipao. "I am more concerned with *why* people were tearing their throats out in this house in the first place—"

"It's the madness," Juliette interrupted. "It's here, and it could be a viral contagion. We need to ask the other maids who were in contact with the victims to remain in their rooms for a few days."

Her father sat down in his own big chair and crossed his hands over his stomach. Her mother tilted her head quizzically.

"And how do you know it is a contagion?" Lord Cai asked. Though Juliette froze at the question, belatedly realizing she had relayed a detail from Roma, her father did not sound suspicious. He had only asked the question plainly, as he did in any everyday conversation. She told herself to calm down. If her father were suspicious, he was the type to make the fact simple and clear.

"Word on the street," Juliette replied. "It may only get worse from here on out."

Lady Cai pinched the bridge of her nose. She shook her head, waving off the thought. "Three dead in this household still does not stand up against the thousands being swayed by the political tide."

Juliette blinked. "But, *Māma*—"

"Don't you wish to know why everybody was gathered around in such fascination downstairs?" Lord Cai cut in. He pushed the paper in his hands onto the desk, angling them so that Juliette could get a good look. The conversation had moved on then; the madness was truly only an offshoot of politics in their minds.

Fine, Juliette thought. If she was the only one with the right priorities, then she could solve this whole damn thing on her own.

Juliette picked up the smaller slip of paper, her own name immediately catching her attention.

Miss Cai, I would love to see you there. —Paul

"What is this?" Juliette demanded.

"An invitation," Lady Cai explained, "to a masquerade party in the French Concession next week."

Juliette leaned in to read the bigger piece of paper, tutting under her breath. She didn't like the sound of this. Foreigners extending their hands in invitation could only mean demands and expectations.

"It is the French who are summoning us?" she asked.

"The function is a joint venture between the different foreign powers," her father replied softly. In a mocking tone, he added, "The French, British, Americans, and everyone else—they wish to come together and *celebrate the native powers of Shanghai*," reciting the text just as Juliette's eyes scanned over it.

Our hospitality is extended to all under the protection of Lord Cai, it read. This party was inviting every member of the Scarlet Gang.

Lady Cai scoffed. "If the foreigners wanted to celebrate us, they could begin by remembering this is our country, not theirs."

Juliette turned to look at her mother, curious. Distaste was fouling the lines in Lady Cai's face, deepening the grooves that she spent each morning covering with a layer of fine powder.

"However," Lord Cai continued, as if his wife hadn't made a scathing remark, "it is the French who wish to meet with us. There's another card lurking here somewhere."

After a few seconds of confused searching, Juliette lifted the bigger sheet of paper and found the third and final card, the same size as the one from Paul. This one was for her father, from the Consul-General of France in Shanghai. There were only two lines of writing. He was requesting a meeting at the party to discuss the situation in Shanghai, whatever that meant.

"Well," Juliette said, "does this mean trouble for us?"

"It may not be trouble." Lord Cai shrugged. "We will have to see."

Juliette narrowed her eyes. She didn't like how her parents had drifted into a pregnant silence, one that was waiting for something . . . something . . .

"I certainly hope you're not going to make *me* go to this masquerade," Juliette guessed contemptuously.

"I am not going to *make* you go like some tyrant," her father replied. "But I would strongly prefer it if you attended with me."

"Bàba," Juliette whined. "I did enough partying in New York to last nine lives. The French can say they want to discuss the state of affairs in Shanghai all they like, but we *know* they're useless."

"Juliette," her mother scolded.

"What?" Juliette retorted, righteous.

"No, no, she is right," Lord Cai said. "The French wish to meet only to discuss the Scarlet militia. They wish to hear how many people I have under my control and they wish to have my cooperation under the possibility of a Communist revolt. That is all true."

Her father leaned forward then, pinpointing his gaze on her, and suddenly Juliette regretted whining, because she felt like a child being told off for protesting an early bedtime.

"But we still need allies. We need power, we need customers, and we need their support. And I need you to be my little translator when they mutter among themselves in French, thinking I cannot understand them."

Juliette made a disgruntled noise at the back of her throat. "Very well," she said. She reached for the letter of invitation and shoved it in her pocket, wanting to examine it more in her own time. "I'll go, mais ce n'est pas de bon gré!"

She strode for the door, dismissing herself. She was so close—one hand was already on the handle and her body was in midstride—when her mother called out, "Wait."

Juliette halted.

"This . . . Paul," Lady Cai said. "Why is he calling after you?"

Lady Cai had said his name like it was some magic spell used for summoning. As if it held some grand weight to it rather than it be one syllable of lackluster annoyance.

"He is Walter Dexter's son," Juliette replied, apathetic. "They are still trying to hire us as middlemen for their drug trade."

Lady Cai mulled over that for a long moment. Then she said, "Is he handsome?"

"Ugh, please." Juliette pushed forward. "He is using me, Māma. It is that simple. Please excuse me now. I have work to—*what* are you doing?"

That latter part was directed at Tyler, who had been lurking close enough to the door that Juliette had hit his shoulder when it opened.

"Calm down," Tyler said. "I'm on my way to the washroom."

They both knew that was a big, fat lie—as wide as Tyler's monstrous smile and as long as his list of crimes.

Juliette closed her father's office door after herself with a solid *thud*. She stared at her cousin, waiting, and he only stared back. His cheek was still bright with its cut, having not yet fully scabbed over.

"Do you have something you'd like to say to me, Tyler?" Juliette asked.

"Only one," Tyler replied. His eyes flitted up, knowing her parents could still hear this conversation. "I'm very excited to attend this party. Le moment où tu n'es plus utile, je serai prêt à prendre ta place."

Juliette stiffened. Satisfied with the reaction he had incited, Tyler grinned again and merrily pivoted on his heel, strolling down the hallway with his hands shoved into his pockets and a low whistle sounding from his mouth.

When you stop being useful, I'll be here to replace you.

"Va te faire foutre," Juliette muttered. She took the stairs down two at a time, glared at the relatives who were still chatting on the couches, then made a beeline for the kitchen. There, she found Kathleen, who was still peering at the stains in the floor tiles. She was also chomping on an apple, though it was beyond Juliette how her cousin managed to have an appetite.

"Any luck?" Juliette asked.

"Oh, I gave up trying to clean out the stains ten minutes ago," Kathleen replied. "I'm just inspecting that one because it looks like a cat."

Juliette blinked.

Kathleen took another bite of her apple. "Too soon?"

"Way too soon," Juliette said. "Are you busy right now? I need your Communist ties."

"For the last time"—Kathleen threw her apple core into the trash can—"knowing who our spies are in the Party does not qualify me as a Communist. What am I finding?"

Juliette put her hands on her hips. "Zhang Gutai's home address."

Kathleen wrinkled her brow, trying to place the name. "You can't find his workplace? He edits that newspaper, doesn't he?"

"I can go poke around his workplace too," Juliette confirmed, "but I want alternatives."

"*Alternatives*" was a funny way of putting it. Juliette wanted his home address so she could break in and rummage around his belongings, should his answers in person prove lacking.

But she didn't have to clarify for Kathleen. Kathleen knew. She mocked a salute, her lips quirking. "On it."

"*Lice*?" Roma echoed in horror.

"Lice-*like*," Lourens emphasized, his correction accompanied by a sigh. He pointed to the strip of skin he had slit off the corpse, where the thick membranes were bulging with little pockets of dead insects. Benedikt was slightly green, and Marshall had his fingers pressed to his mouth.

"They jump from host to host through the hair, then burrow into the scalp," Lourens went on. He pushed down on an insect with his finger. Nearby, one of the scientists was blanching at the sight, unable to pull his curiosity away from the unconventional autopsy happening right atop the worktable. No matter—the White Flowers had seen stranger things.

"Good God," Marshall muttered. "We could have been infected."

Benedikt made an offended noise. "They're *dead* already," he replied, gesturing forward with his hand.

"And yet you made me pull one out," Marshall retorted. He shuddered, his full body vibrating with the motion. "So revolting—"

Roma tapped his fingers against the worktable. The lab was devoid of proper fresh air, and he had hardly slept the night before. His head was starting to pound with ferocity.

"Gentlemen," he prompted, trying to redirect Benedikt's and Marshall's attention back to Lourens. It did not work.

"The future well-being of the White Flowers thanks you."

"Oh, please, what will they know of my heroism?"

Roma exchanged a glance with Lourens and shook his head. There was no point trying to butt in when Benedikt and Marshall got like this. When they weren't scheming together, they were bickering together. It was almost always about the most nonsensical things that truly did not require an hour-long debate, yet regardless, Roma's two friends engaged in them, sometimes until their faces turned red. Roma wasn't sure if Benedikt and Marshall were fated to eventually kill each other or kiss each other.

"Anyhow," Lourens said, clearing his throat when there was the slightest lull in the argument, "with the resources we have here, we may be more advantaged than Shanghai's hospitals. I'd like to try to figure out how to engineer a cure, if that pleases you."

"*Yes*," Roma all but pleaded. "That would be great. Thank you, Lourens—"

"Don't rush to thank me yet." Lourens tutted. "I cannot find a cure for this odd infestation without the help of you youth."

Marshall quirked an eyebrow. Benedikt jammed his elbow into Marshall's ribs to keep him from making any sarcastic remark about his *youth*.

"Anything," Roma promised.

"I'll need to run experiments," Lourens said. He nodded to himself. "You must find me a live victim."

"A *live*—"

This time, it was Roma who jammed his elbow into Marshall's side.

"We're on it," Roma said quickly. "Thank you, Lourens. Truly."

When Lourens nodded his begrudging acceptance of such a sentiment, Roma pushed away from the worktable, gesturing for Benedikt and Marshall to follow suit, and the three of them took their leave. Roma was rather impressed that Marshall managed to stay silent until they pushed through the front doors. It was only when they were upon the sidewalk, under the thick clouds of the city, that Marshall finally erupted with: "How the *hell* do you propose we bring him a live victim?"

Roma sighed, shoving his hands deep in his pockets. He started back in the direction of the White Flower headquarters with his cousin trailing close on his tail. Marshall, meanwhile, as a bundle of unspent energy, bounced in front of them, walking backward.

"You're going to trip on a pebble," Benedikt warned.

"You're giving me a headache," Roma added.

"We don't know who's a victim of the madness until they succumb to it," Marshall went on, ignoring them both. "As soon as someone *is* succumbing, how would we keep them alive long enough to take them to the lab?"

Roma shut his eyes momentarily. When he opened them again, they felt like they weighed a thousand tons. "I don't *know*."

The throbbing in his head was only getting worse. Roma hardly contributed to conversation as they made their way home, and when the turn into the main building block appeared, he ducked through with a muttered goodbye, leaving Benedikt and Marshall to stare after him before they proceeded to their own living quarters. His friends would forgive him. Roma fell silent when he needed to think, when the city grew far too loud and he could hardly hear his own thoughts.

Roma eased the front door shut. All he needed was a moment of quiet and then he could have a grand ol' time trying to figure out a plan for Lourens—

"Roma."

Roma's head jerked up, his foot stalling on the first step of the staircase. At the landing of the second floor, his father was staring down at him.

"Yes?"

Without any prelude, Lord Montagov simply extended his arm, a piece of paper held between his fingers. Roma thought that his father would meet him halfway as he made his way up the stairs, but Lord Montagov remained where he was, forcing Roma to trek forward in a hurry so as not to keep his father waiting, almost panting by the time he was close enough to take the slip of paper.

It bore a name and an address, written in loopy scrawl.

"Find him," Lord Montagov sneered when Roma looked up for an explanation. "My sources say that the Communists may be the cause of this insipid madness."

Roma's fingers tightened on the slip of paper. "What?" he demanded. "The Communists have been seeking our help for years—"

"And given that we keep refusing them," his father cut in, "they are switching tactics. They make their revolution by squashing our power before we can counter their efforts. Stop them."

Could it be a motive as simple as politics? Kill the gangsters so there was no opposition. Infect the workers so they were angry and desperate enough to buy into any revolutionary screaming in their ear. Easy as a river breeze.

"How am I to stop a whole political faction?" Roma murmured, merely deliberating aloud. "How am I to—"

A hard knock came on his skull. Roma flinched, moving away from his father's knuckles to avoid a second blow. He should have known better than to muse within his father's earshot.

"I gave you an address, did I not?" Lord Montagov snapped. "Go. See how much truth there is in this claim."

With that, his father turned and disappeared back into his office, the door slamming. Roma was left behind on the stairs, holding the slip of paper, his head throbbing worse than before.

"Very well," he muttered bitterly.

Kathleen trailed along the waterfront, her steps slow against the hard granite. This far east, it was almost quiet, the usual screaming by the Bund replaced by clanging shipbuilding warehouses and lumber companies rumbling to finish their day's work. *Almost* quiet, but hardly peaceful. There was no place in Shanghai that would qualify as *peaceful.*

"Better hurry," she muttered to herself, checking the pocket watch in her sleeve. The sun would soon be setting, and it got cold by the Huangpu River.

Kathleen paced the rest of the way to the cotton mill, taking not the front entrance but a back window, right into the workers' break room. These laborers weren't offered many breaks, but as the end of their shifts crept nearer, more of them would come around to take a breather, and when Kathleen delicately climbed through the window, swinging her legs in, there was indeed a woman sitting there, eating rice out of a container.

The woman almost spat her rice out through her nose.

"Sorry, sorry, didn't mean to scare you!" Kathleen said quickly. "Would you be able to fetch Da Nao for me? Important Scarlet business. Boss won't mind."

"Scarlet business?" the woman echoed, putting her container down. She wore a red bracelet, so she was associated with the Scarlets, yet her voice sounded skeptical all the same. When the woman stood, she paused, taking a moment to squint at Kathleen.

Instinctively, Kathleen reached up to touch her hair, to make sure the wisps of her bangs lay just right above the arched brows she had delicately filled in. She was always careful not to touch her face too much—she spent far too long every morning doing her cosmetics until her face was soft and her chin was pointed to mess it up in the middle of the day.

A long moment passed. Finally, the woman nodded and said, "One second."

Kathleen heaved an exhale as soon as she was left alone. She hadn't realized how tense she had grown, how she had almost expected the woman to speak her mind, to ask what right Kathleen had to be here, digging her nose into Scarlet business. But at the end of the day, Kathleen was the one wearing the silk qipao and this woman was the one in a cotton uniform that likely hadn't been replaced in years. She wouldn't have dared.

The only one who did dare question her right to exist was her own father.

"Don't think about it," Kathleen muttered to herself. "Stop thinking about it."

She was already thinking about it. About the first argument they had when her father arrived in Paris, summoned because one of his three children had fallen ill.

It's influenza, the doctors had said. *She might not recover.*

Her father's temper was already at its breaking point, his French too elementary to understand the doctors. And when Kathleen tried to help, pulled him out into the hallway after the doctors left to make sure her father understood their options . . .

"I can't even listen to you right now," he sneered. He looked her up and down, eyeing her dress, the inspection dripping with distaste. "Not until you stop wearing such—"

"Don't," Kathleen cut in.

Her father reared back. Perhaps it had been the interruption that was more offensive. Perhaps it had been her tone, certain in her command without wavering.

"What have the tutors been teaching you?" he snapped. "You do *not* talk back to me—"

"Or what, Bàba?" she said evenly. "What will you do?"

For thousands of years, the worst crime in China was a lack of filial piety. Having children with no xiàoshùn was a fate worse than death. It meant being forgotten in the afterlife, a wandering ghost doomed to starve when no offerings came in from irreverent descendants.

But it was her father who had sent them out here, who had thinned the string that China tied around their wrists. He had sent them to the West, where they were taught different ideas, taught about a different afterlife that had nothing to do with burning paper money. The West had corrupted them—and whose fault was that?

Her father had nothing more to say. "Go," he snapped. "Go back into the room and join your sisters. I will speak to the doctors."

Kathleen did not protest. She had wondered in that moment, peering over her shoulder as her father stood there, if he ever cursed the universe for taking his wife in childbirth, if he regretted losing her in exchange for three strangers. For Kathleen, Rosalind, and Celia.

A girl who had been sickly all her life.

A girl who was in training to be Shanghai's dazzling star.

And a girl who just wanted to be left alone to live as she was.

Kathleen closed her fist tightly, her teeth gritted hard, forcing the memories back. Her father would have forced her into hiding if he'd had his way. He would have rather disowned her than let her back in Shanghai wearing a qipao, and Kathleen would have rather packed her bags and made her own way across Europe than go on being her father's prodigal son.

She supposed it was fortunate that Kathleen Lang—the real Kathleen—died of influenza two weeks after falling sick, her fourteen years of life coming to a close with no real friends, having been distant from her two sisters all her life. How were you supposed to mourn someone you never really knew? It was empty expressions under black veils and cold stares at the cremation vase. Even the thickest blood from the womb could run thin if given the empty space to bleed.

"I won't call you Celia," her father said at the port, lifting their suitcases. "That's not the name I gave you at birth." He cast her a glance askew. "But I will call you Kathleen. And save for Rosalind, you may tell no one. It's for your own safety. You must realize that."

She did. She had fought so hard all her life just to be called Celia, and now her father wanted to give her a different name and . . . she could accept it. The Lang triplets had been away from Shanghai for so long that not a soul had questioned Kathleen's changed face when they finally returned. Except Juliette—Juliette noticed everything, but their cousin had been quick to nod along, making the switch from Celia to Kathleen as quickly as she had made the switch to Celia.

Now Kathleen responded to this name as if it were her own, as if it were the only name she had ever known, and it was a comfort, no matter how strange.

"Hello."

Kathleen jumped at Da Nao's sudden appearance in the break room, her hand flying to her heart.

"Are you quite all right?" Da Nao asked.

"Perfectly," Kathleen breathed. She squared her shoulders, recovering back into business mode. "I need a favor. I'm after Zhang Gutai's personal address."

Though her cousin didn't know it, Juliette was actually familiar with Da Nao—whose name translated literally to Big Brain. He spent some hours working at this cotton mill and some as a fisherman along the Bund, retrieving fresh stock for the Scarlet Gang. He had been around during their childhood and had dropped by the Scarlet residence at least three times since Juliette's return. The Scarlet Gang liked their fish fresh. But they didn't need to know that their primary supplier was also their eyes and ears within the Party.

"Zhang Gutai," Da Nao echoed. "You want . . . the Secretary-General's personal address."

"Indeed."

Da Nao was pulling a face that said *What the hell do you need that for?* But he didn't ask and Kathleen didn't tell, so the fisherman tapped his chin in thought and said, "I can find it for you. But our next meeting is not until Saturday. It may have to wait until then."

Kathleen nodded. "That is fine. Thank you."

Da Nao left the break room without any fanfare. Mission achieved, Kathleen started to climb through the window again, only this time, as she slid onto the ledge, her hand came upon a flyer lying there, facedown and grimy with dirt and grease.

Kathleen flipped it over.

THE RULE OF THE GANGSTERS IS OVER. IT IS TIME TO UNIONIZE.

Her eyebrows shot straight up. She wondered if this was Da Nao's doing, but she couldn't imagine so. Yet at the bottom of the flyer, typed in a neat, faded line, it read *Distributed on behalf of the Communist Party of China*.

It would seem Da Nao was not the only employee here with Communist ties.

A sudden splashing noise by the wharf startled Kathleen out of her reverie, prompting her to hop off the ledge and back onto the ground outside the cotton mill. When Kathleen looked out into the water, she thought she caught a flash of something shiny darting through the waves.

"Strange," she muttered. She hurried home.

Twelve

They say Shanghai stands tall like an emperor's ugly daughter, its streets sprawling in a manner that only the limbs of a snarling princess could manage. It was not born this way. It used to be beautiful. They used to croon over it, examining the lines of its body and humming beneath their breath, nodding and deciding that it was well suited for children. Then this city mutilated itself with a wide, wide grin. It dragged a knife down its cheek and took the blade to its chest and now it worries not for finding suitors, but merely for running wild, drunk on the invulnerability of inherited power, well suited only for profit and feasting, dancing and whoring.

Now it may be ugly, but it is glorious.

Night always falls on this city with a quiet *clomp*. When the lights blink on—the buzzing of newly coveted electricity running through the wires that line the streets like black veins—it is easy to forget that the natural state of night is supposed to be darkness. Instead, night in Shanghai is vibrance and neon, gaslight flickering against the triangular flags fluttering in the breeze.

In this clamor, a dancer steps out from the most crowded burlesque club on her side of the city, shaking her hair free of its ribbons. She keeps in only one: a twirl of red, to mark her allegiance to the Scarlet Gang, to be left alone while she makes her way through Scarlet territory when walking back home, to signal to the gangsters who lurk in the alleyways by the Bund, picking their teeth clean with their sharp blades, that she is not to be hassled, that she is on their side.

The dancer shivers as she walks, dropping her long cigarette to the ground and putting it out with her shoe. Her hands freed now, she wraps them around her goose-bumped arms. She is ill at ease. There is no one following her; nor is there anybody before her. Nevertheless, somehow she is certain that someone is watching her.

It is not an utterly absurd concept. This city does not know itself; it will not feel the parasites that grow upon its skin until it is far too late. This city is a miscellany of parts smashed together and functioning in one collective stride, but place a gun to its head and it will only laugh in your face, misunderstanding the violence of such intent.

They have always said that Shanghai is an ugly daughter, but as the years grow on, it isn't enough anymore to characterize this city as merely one entity. This place rumbles on Western idealism and Eastern labor, hateful of its split and unable to function without it, multiple facets fighting and grappling in an ever-constant quarrel. Half Scarlet, half White Flower; half filthy rich, half dirt poor; half land, half water flowing in from the East China Sea. There is nothing more but water to the east of Shanghai. Perhaps that is why the Russians have come here, these flocks of exiles who fled the Bolshevik Revolution and even before that, when their home could no longer be a home. If you decided to run, you might as well keep running until you came to the edge of the world.

That is what this city is. The party at the end of the world.

Its flagship dancer has stopped now, letting the silence thrum in her ears as she strains to identify what it is that is prickling her nerves. The more she listens, the wider her hearing range stretches, picking up on the *drip-drip-drip* of a nearby pipe and the chatter of late-night workers.

The catch is this: It is not some*one* watching her. It is some*thing*.

And it comes to the surface. Something with a row of horns that grows from its curved back, glinting out of the water like ten ominous daggers. Something that raises its head and blinks opaque silver eyes at her.

The dancer flees. She panics, moving in such haste to get away from the horrifying sight that she stumbles right in front of a ship flying the wrong colors.

And the White Flower working to unload the ship catches sight of her.

"Excuse me!" he bellows down. "Are you lost?"

He has misinterpreted the dancer's idleness for confusion. He drops down from the ship's bow and starts walking toward her, only to halt abruptly upon spotting her red ribbon.

The White Flower's expression turns from friendly to thunderous in an instance. The dancer pulls her mouth into a tight, defeated grimace and throws her hands up, attempting to defuse the situation by shouting, "I'm sorry. I'm sorry. I wasn't watching the territory lines!" But he is already whipping out his pistol, aiming with one eye lazily shut.

"Bloody Scarlets," he mutters. "You think you can waltz wherever you want, don't you?"

The dancer, almost half-heartedly, scrambles for her own weapon: a small handgun strapped to her thigh.

"Wait," she calls steadily. "I'm not your enemy—there's something back there. It's coming—"

A splash sounds. A droplet of water lands in the soft flesh at the back of her knee, running a track down her leg. When the dancer looks down, she sees that the line of water is wholly black.

She lurches to her right, diving into an alleyway and pressing against a bend in the wall. Gunshots sound into the night as the White Flower interprets her fast pace to be an act of war, but by then she is already out of sight, shielding herself from the waterfront, her whole body shaking.

Then *something* erupts from the Huangpu River.

And screaming resounds into the night.

It is hard to say exactly what is occurring on the ports of Shanghai. While the dancer's mouth moves to silent prayers, hands clutched to her chest, knees folded until they press grooves into her forehead, the White Flower and all his other men still upon the ship stand within range of the chaos. They scrabble, and scream, and resist, but the infestation comes down on them, and there is no stopping it.

When the screaming stops, the dancer creeps out from the alleyway, hesitant in case there is calamity.

Instead, what she finds are insects.

Thousands of them—tiny, disgusting things crawling on the ground. They bump over one another and skitter about in random fashion, but en masse, they are all moving in one direction: toward the water.

For the first time, this city may finally fear the barrel pressed to its temple like a poisoned caress.

Because by the Huangpu River, the second wave of the madness unfolds, starting with the seven dead bodies lying motionless on the top deck of a Russian ship.

Thirteen

Juliette smoothed down the fabric of her qipao, pressing at the creases that were bunching up beneath her coat. She swallowed her discomfort in a hard gulp, as if it were nothing more than a bitter medicinal pill. It felt fraudulent, somehow, to put on a type of clothing that she hadn't worn in years. It felt like lying—to herself, to the image she had been building before she stepped foot back into this city.

But if she wanted to blend in within Zhang Gutai's daytime place of work, she had to look like any regular upper-class eighteen-year-old clacking around these streets with pearl earrings dangling in her loose, ungelled hair.

Juliette took a deep breath, tightened her grip on the sleeves of her coat, and marched into the building.

Zhang Gutai—as an important figure in a relatively new and fragile political party—was a secretive man. But he was also the chief editor of a newspaper called *Labor Daily*, and their address was public information. Though she hadn't expected to find much but a scant office complex when she wandered out here into the industrial edges of the Chinese part of the city, she was met with the absolute bustle of activity in the *Labor Daily*'s offices: people running around with bundles of paper and typewriters clutched in their arms as they yelled for the latest update on a batch that had proceeded forward into printing.

Her nose wrinkling, Juliette walked right past the front desk with her chin held high. These people were Communists, weren't they? They believed in equality, after all. She was sure they would also believe in letting Juliette take a look around by herself until she stumbled onto Zhang Gutai's office. She wouldn't need anybody to show her around.

Juliette smiled to herself.

The thick of the activity seemed to be coming in and out of a little set of stairs dropping into a basement level, so Juliette went there, snagging a clipboard from a table in an effort to look occupied. There was no natural light when she entered the basement level. She passed what may have been a back door, then turned left, entering the main space and scanning the scene before her. The floor and walls were constructed of cement. The only illumination came from the few light fixtures latched to the walls, which seemed terribly inconvenient for all these people down here at their desks, squinting in the dimness.

It reminded her of what cell blocks during the Great War might have looked like. Juliette supposed she wouldn't be at all surprised if it turned out this building really had been converted from an original use of holding prisoners.

She continued striding forward, deeper into the prisonlike office space, peering into each nook. Her heels were loud as she clicked through, but there was enough chaos down here that, for now, nobody thought much of her presence. Harried writers—both old and young—were busy scribbling, working fast on their typewriters, or taking phone calls. The wires that carried signals into this subterranean level were all tangled in a big mass at the back of the expansive space. As Juliette scanned the desks she passed, looking for anything of note, her attention snagged on one desk that appeared unoccupied.

Such an observation was peculiar enough in this little bubble of activity. She was even more intrigued when she craned her neck to read the writing atop the folders beside the telephone and saw, in Chinese, MEMO FOR ZHANG GUTAI.

Quickly she scrambled beneath the desk, clipboard shoved under her arm so she could search through the files. There was nothing noteworthy in the political reports, but when she dropped to a crouch and looked to the floor of the desk, she found *drawings*.

If everybody else is so busy, why is this *desk empty?* Juliette thought. And whose was it? Surely not Zhang Gutai, who most certainly had his own space. Shaking her head, she reached into the pile of drawings and pulled a few out, resolving not to look a gift horse in the mouth.

But when she looked upon the first drawing, she broke out in a cold sweat—all the way from the high collar at her neck to the edges of the qipao brushing her ankles.

One drawing was of wide, reptilianlike eyes. Another was of five claws gripping against a board of wood and scales somehow glistening despite the stray smears of ink along the page. Juliette's fingers froze, stunned as she took in the images—dozens of them, all depicting variations of the same thing.

"Guài wù," Juliette breathed. *Monster.*

Before she could overthink it, she snatched one of the drawings in the pile—the one that depicted a blur of a creature standing in its entirety—and folded it up, tucking the little square of paper into her coat pocket. It joined the masquerade invitation that she had placed there yesterday and forgotten to remove. With a cursory glance around to make sure she was still in the clear, Juliette stood and wiped the sweat off her palms. She marched for the little steps out of the basement level, her fists clutched tight.

Juliette paused suddenly, her foot hovering on the first step. To her left again was the back door.

And it was *shuddering.*

Suddenly all she could think of was the drawing in her pocket. She imagined a monster just on the other side of the door, breathing heavily, awaiting the prime moment to burst free and wreak havoc on innocents.

Juliette stepped toward the door hesitantly. Her hand came down to rest on the round knob. "Hello?" she called, her voice hoarse. "Is someone—"

"What are you doing there?"

Juliette jumped, snatching her hand away from the knob of the door. The frame had stopped shuddering. She swiveled around.

"Oh, me?"

The man who stood before her wore a fedora cap, his suit more Western looking than what everyone else down here was wearing. He had to be someone important, along the lines of Zhang Gutai's rank rather than a mere assistant who answered the phone.

"I'm here to see your chief editor for important business," Juliette continued. "I got a little lost."

"The exit is that way," the man said, pointing.

Juliette's smile grew cold.

"Official Scarlet business," she corrected. "My father—Lord Cai—sent me."

There was a moment of pause as the man digested her words, wariness setting in. Juliette had perfected the art of dishonest guiles; she hid her identity when necessary, then wielded it like a weapon when the time came. Only the man suddenly looked a little amused, too, much to Juliette's chagrin. Still, he nodded and gestured for her to follow him.

There was one more floor above the first floor, and the man spared no patience in hurrying Juliette along. He ascended the humble brown staircase three steps at a time while Juliette clacked up slowly, looking around. This staircase, with its thick handrails and long, polished panes, had the potential to be sweeping and decadent, if only the Communists were not so intent on giving the appearance of seeming grounded with the common people. Everything in this building could have been glorious. But glory was not the point anymore, was it?

Juliette leaned over the banister of the second floor with a sigh, peering at the frenzy of papers and typewriters below. When the man gestured at her impatiently from ahead, she grimaced and kept walking.

The man turned a corner and directed her into a spacious waiting area. There were two rows of chairs here, both pressed up against opposing walls and facing each other in front of a closed office door. Juliette finally understood his amusement. There was already someone sitting on one of the yellow chairs, legs stretched out in front of him.

Roma lurched upright.

"What are you doing here?" they demanded in unison.

The man in the fedora cap quietly removed himself. As soon as he was out of sight, Roma launched out of his seat and grabbed Juliette's arm. She was so offended he dared touch her that she couldn't react for a long second, not until Roma had already moved them to a corner of the waiting space, the wall cold against Juliette's back.

"Let go of me," she hissed, shaking her arm from his grip. Roma must have obtained the same information that she had. He wanted to know about Zhang Gutai's involvement in the madness.

Juliette bit back a curse. If the White Flowers got answers before she did, they would treat their findings like they treated the black market. They would do everything they could to secure a monopoly upon the information, pay off and kill sources until there was no way for the Scarlets to obtain what they knew. That way, only the White Flowers were safe, assuming there *was* a way to stop this madness. That way, the city only stacked up with the bodies of their enemies. Then people would begin to switch loyalties.

Then the White Flowers would be victorious. And the Scarlets would suffer.

"Look," Roma snapped. "You have to leave."

Juliette blinked rapidly, her head rearing back. "*I* have to leave?"

"Yes." Roma reached up, his expression dripping with derision, and flicked one of the earrings dangling from Juliette's ear. The pearl swung against her skin, brushing her jaw. Juliette barely stifled the whoosh of breath that threatened to escape, barely stifled the stream of fire she wanted to breathe from her throat.

"Play dress-up somewhere else," Roma went on. "I was here first."

"This is *Scarlet* territory."

"These people are Communists. You have no sway over them."

Juliette gritted her teeth, hard. Indeed, the Scarlet Gang had no control here. Her only consolation was that Roma didn't appear too happy himself, which meant the White Flowers had no sway over the Communists, either. For the time being, this neutrality was a good thing. The man in the fedora had shut his mouth immediately in learning Juliette's identity, precisely to avoid any unnecessary aggravation with the Scarlet Gang. But tiptoeing on thin ice wouldn't last forever. The Communists' very model of progress was overthrowing Shanghai as it was now—as it was for gangsters to thrive: sinful, profitable. Given the choice between killing all the capitalists and killing all the gangsters, they would choose both.

"Our relationship with the Communists is, as always, none of your business," Juliette said. "Now, if you would be so kind, get out of my face."

Roma narrowed his eyes. He took her command as a threat. Perhaps she had intended for it to be one.

"I'm not going anywhere."

God, the nerve. Juliette straightened to her full height. They weren't that far apart, she and Roma—he barely held half an inch over her when she was in heels. "I won't say it again," she hissed. "Get out of my face. *Now.*"

His lips thinned. Resentfully, and slowly, Roma submitted to the threat. He made a steady step back, glaring at her as he scrubbed a hand along his eyes. If Juliette didn't know better, she would have thought the gesture to be an act of self-consciousness. But no—it was exhaustion; the shadows under his eyes were almost smoky, like his bottom lashes were fringed with soot.

"Have you not been sleeping?" Juliette found herself asking suddenly. There was a direct correlation between her willingness to be civil and the distance between them. With him several strides away, she wanted to commit homicide a little less.

Roma's hand returned to his side. "I'll have you know," he answered, "that I am *well*, thank you very much."

"I wasn't asking after your well-being."

"Oh, give it a rest, Juliette."

Juliette folded her arms thoughtfully. Last night she had heard the news about the sudden spike in White Flower deaths, all lost to the madness. It was the biggest mass casualty yet. Which meant Roma wasn't going to leave just because she made a few barbed remarks—he was here now precisely because this strange madness had crept so close to home.

She tilted her chin at the closed door. "Is that his office?"

Roma didn't need to clarify who she meant. He nodded. "Zhang Gutai won't take visitors until the hour. Don't try anything."

Like what? Juliette thought nastily. It wasn't as if she could run Roma out without making a scene and offending the Communists, and she certainly refused to leave before she spoke to Zhang Gutai. To find answers, it was this or nothing.

Juliette marched to a chair and sat down. She tipped her head back and stared at the ceiling, resolute not to look anywhere else. Directing her mind elsewhere too, she reached into her coat pocket and fingered the drawing she had stashed away. It was uncertain whether these frightening sketches confirmed trouble with the Communists specifically, but it confirmed *something*. She would have to inspect it further, because she thought she recognized the background to be the

Bund. It was nothing more than a few harsh lines, but for somewhere as distinctive as the Bund, a few harsh lines were enough.

Meanwhile, Roma had settled back onto his seat along the other row of chairs, his fingers tapping to the *tick-tick-tick* of the clock on the wall. He kept his gaze pinned to Juliette, much to Juliette's annoyance. She could feel his inspection like it was a physical thing, as if he were inches away instead of across the room. Every sweep of his eyes felt like he was mechanically pulling her apart, piece by piece, until her insides were out in the open for inspection. Juliette could feel a flush creeping up from her chest, coloring her neck with discomfort, then spreading until her cheeks were blazing hot.

She was going to skin herself with her own damn knife. Her cells were betraying her on a molecular level. He was just *looking*, for heaven's sake. It did not qualify as an attack. Juliette was not going to rise to the bait. She would sit here until Zhang Gutai was ready to meet, and then—

"What?" Juliette snapped, unable to bear it any longer. She tore her gaze down, finally supplying her own ammunition against Roma's weaponized stare.

Roma made an inquisitive noise. He pursed his lips slowly, then tipped his chin. "What's got you so worked up?"

Juliette followed the direction of his gesture. She yanked her hand out from her pocket.

"Again, that would be none of your business."

"If it is to do with madne—"

"Why would you assume that?"

Roma's expression thundered. "Can I *finish* my sentence—"

The office door opened, cutting him off. A harried assistant came out and summoned Roma to go in before she quickly hurried away. With a huff, Roma shot Juliette a look that said *this isn't over*, before entering the office.

Juliette broiled in the wait, her toes tapping erratically against the hard floor panels and her fingers twisting around one another. For ten minutes she drove herself up the wall, envisioning Roma doing all in his power to convince Zhang Gutai to give *him* all the answers and disregard Juliette. Roma was a liar through and through—his tactics of persuasion knew no bounds.

When Roma came out, however, it was immediately clear in the slouch of his head that he hadn't gotten what he wanted.

"Don't look so smug," he whispered while Juliette passed him.

"That's just my face," she hissed back.

With her chin held high, Juliette walked into Zhang Gutai's office.

"Well, it must be my lucky day," Mr. Zhang declared when she entered, putting his fountain pen down. Despite his laudatory tone, he was frowning as he spoke. "First it was the heir of the White Flowers, now the Scarlet crown princess. What can I do for you, Miss Cai?"

Juliette flopped into one of the two large chairs placed opposite Mr. Zhang's heavy mahogany desk. In seconds she took in everything before her: the framed black-and-white photographs of his elderly parents, the hammer-and-sickle flag hanging from the side of the filing cabinet, the festive red calendar on the wall marked with daily meetings. Her eyes returning to the Communist before her, Juliette relaxed and made him see what she wanted him to see, letting out a small, careless laugh, vacuous as could be.

"You know how rumors work in this city, Mr. Zhang," she said. She held her nails out in front of her, squinting at a little chip marring her pinky. "They come to me, and I follow them. Do you know what graced my ear the other day?"

Zhang Gutai appeared mildly entertained. "Do tell."

"They say"—Juliette leaned in—"that *you* know why there is madness sweeping through Shanghai."

For a long moment Mr. Zhang said nothing. Then he blinked rapidly and replied, "Miss Cai, I haven't a clue why you would think that."

"No?" Juliette said lightly. "You didn't scheme up a madness to spread through the city? No plans at all to cause enough death until the gangsters are weak and the workers are frightened, until the factories have ripened into the ideal conditions for the Communists to swoop in and incite revolution?"

She digested his surprise, his astonishment at being confronted. Roma must not have asked him about the madness directly—he must have approached it in a more roundabout way, treading the waters to gather his conclusions instead of coming right out and saying it. That was to be expected. The direct approach was more of Juliette's arena.

"Miss Cai," Zhang Gutai said sternly. "That is *absurd*."

Juliette wasn't getting anywhere like this. She straightened in her chair and dropped her smile, her hands gripping the armrests. Now the easy flapper girl was gone. In her place sat the heiress of the most brutal gang in Shanghai.

"I will find the truth one way or another," Juliette said. "So speak now if you wish to be offered mercy. Else I will tear the answer from you limb by limb—"

"Miss Cai, I truly have no clue what you are speaking of," Mr. Zhang interrupted. "Please leave now. This is a place of work, and I won't have your ridiculous accusations taking up my time."

Juliette considered her options. Zhang Gutai's words were convincing, but he was uneasy. Unless he was a very, very good actor, he was no liar, but he kept glancing to the door, he kept tapping his hand against the flat of his desk. *Why?* What did he know that she didn't? Even if he did not scheme the madness, what was his involvement?

Juliette leaned back in her seat, relaxing her spine again into a false ease.

"And what if I have questions on the Communist Party?" she asked. "You are the Secretary-General, are you not?"

"You are welcome to attend our meetings if you wish to know about the Party," Mr. Zhang answered stiffly. "Otherwise, Miss Cai, please leave."

Juliette stood, taking her sweet time to stretch and work out the cricks in her neck. Then, bobbing a deep and exaggerated curtsy, she simpered, "Thank you for your gracious time," and left the office.

What now? she thought, closing the door behind her with a quiet click. She started to walk. *If he won't—*

"Oof!" Juliette staggered back, her head spinning as she rounded the corner and immediately collided hard with someone. The moment she looked up to see who the hell was in her path, she could only see red.

Roma caught her wrist before her hand could come down on him. He held her midmotion, their arms crossed like they were exchanging sword blows.

"Careful," Roma said quietly. His voice was too soft for the violence brewing under Juliette's skin. It was trickery. He was trying to divert her attention to his lips and breath and calm instead of whatever was going on here, with his harsh grip carving grooves into her wrist, and it was *working*. Juliette wanted to kill him for that alone.

Roma gave a mocking smile, like he knew what she was thinking. "Wouldn't want to make a scene in a Communist stronghold, would you?"

Juliette tried to tug her arm back, but Roma held firm. If he didn't let go in three seconds, she was drawing her gun. *One, two—*

Roma let go.

Juliette rubbed her wrist, smoothing a palm over her raging pulse and grumbling something inaudible under her breath. When Roma simply stood there, she demanded, "Why are you *still* here?"

Innocently, Roma pointed over to the chairs. "I left my hat behind."

"You weren't even wearing a hat before." But indeed, on the chair where he had originally been sitting, a hat was lying on its side. Roma, shrugging, merely went to pick it up. Juliette pivoted on her heel and left as fast as she could, hurrying from the building.

It wasn't until she was halfway down the road, pulling her coat tightly around her, that she stopped in her tracks, swearing.

"He better not have . . ." She plunged her hand into her pocket and came out with only one slip of paper. But when she unfolded it, she saw that the monster was still staring back at her, lines hazy with folding and refolding.

Juliette snorted. Roma had taken the masquerade invitation instead.

"Fool," she muttered.

When Juliette returned home, she found Kathleen already lounging on one of the couches in the living room. She went to join her cousin, complaining under her breath.

"What's wrong?" Kathleen asked absently, flipping the pages of her magazine.

"A lot of things," Juliette grumbled. "Did you find the address?"

Kathleen made a motion with her head that resembled a half nod. "Sort of. I'll have it in a few days."

"Good enough," Juliette muttered. "I've got the masquerade to worry about until then anyway."

A headache was starting in the space behind her ears. She was trying to plot her next move, but it was hard to decide where to look. There had to be a reason why Madame had heard what she heard. There had to be a reason why the Communists had said what they said. And if it was naught but a rumor, then Juliette could only put her suspicion to rest when she had exhausted every avenue to do with Zhang Gutai.

Juliette perked up slightly. Her hand reached into her pocket again, touching the drawing. She had yet to exhaust *everything*.

A whistle came from the front door then, interrupting Juliette's silent brooding. She looked up to find a Scarlet messenger hovering in the foyer space, gesturing at her with one hand and fixing the fit of his shoe with the other.

"Pass me that parcel beside you."

Juliette looked to her side. Indeed, a parcel was lying on the circular table beside the sofa she had chosen to collapse on, but what did this messenger think he was doing asking *her* to fetch him something that he could simply come get himself—

It clicked. *The qipao*. The Scarlet gangsters had become accustomed to shortcutting their association of her to glittery, beaded dresses and pomade in her finger-curled hair. As soon as she dressed in Chinese clothing instead, they saw right past her.

Juliette breathed in and found her lungs to be horribly tight. Could she never be both? Was she doomed to choose one country or the other? Be an American girl or nothing?

The messenger whistled again. "Hey—"

Juliette yanked out the knife sheathed at her thigh, right above where the slit of her qipao ended, and threw it. The blade embedded perfectly into the front door with a deep, sonorous *thud*. It drew a single drop of blood from the messenger's ear, where it had cut through.

"You don't whistle at me," Juliette said coldly. "I whistle at you. Understand?"

The messenger looked at her—really looked at her now. He reached up and touched his ear. The bleeding had already stopped. But his eyes were wide as he nodded.

Juliette took the parcel in her hands and stood. She walked right up to the messenger and passed it to him quaintly, as if she were delivering a lunch box to her friend.

"While you're at it," she said, "I need you to do something for me. Go to the Bund and interview the bankers who work along the main strip. Ask whether they've seen anything funny lurking about."

The messenger's mouth opened and closed. "All of them?"

"All. Of. Them."

"But—"

"Juliette, hold on," Kathleen called, rising from the couch too. "Let me."

Juliette raised an eyebrow. Kathleen waved a hand at the messenger in a *shoo*ing gesture, and the messenger took the opportunity to flee, closing the front door after him with the knife still embedded within it.

"You want to waste your time on *this*?" Juliette asked.

"It is not wasting my time if it is useful information you need." Kathleen reached into the coatrack by the door. "Why are you chasing after it?"

"I can send any one of the other messengers," Juliette continued, wrinkling her brow. Ordering her own cousin around didn't sit well with her. A specific task with specific goals was one matter, especially if Kathleen had contacts that benefited the mission. Sending her on a wild-goose chase was another matter entirely.

"Juliette—"

"I was mostly trying to frighten the messenger. It really is quite all right—"

Kathleen grabbed her cousin's wrist and squeezed, not hard enough to hurt, but hard enough for Juliette to know that this was serious.

"I'm not just doing this out of the kindness of my heart," she said firmly. "In some few years, this gang is either under your hands or someone else's. And knowing the other contenders . . ."

Kathleen paused. Their heads both went to the same people: Tyler first, then perhaps the other various cousins who might have a fighting chance only if Tyler mysteriously disappeared. They were all terrible and ruthless and hateful, but Juliette was too. The minuscule difference was that Juliette was also careful, intensely controlling with how much of that hate she let slip out to guide her hand.

"It could be under your hands too," Juliette said lightly. "We don't know what's going to happen in a few years."

Kathleen rolled her eyes. "I'm not a Cai, Juliette. That's not even in the realm of possibility."

There was little to argue back against that. Kathleen came from Lady Cai's side of the family. When Lord Cai was the face of the Scarlet Gang, it was unsurprising that only those sharing his name were seen to be legitimate. One only had to look at how easily his fellow cousins merged into the inner circle, while Mr. Lang, Lady Cai's brother, still had not won any favor in the two decades he had been around.

"It has to be you," Kathleen said. Her tone did not allow for dissent. "Everyone who may come for your crown is dangerous. And you are too, but"—she took a moment to think through her phrasing—"but at least you will never willingly bring danger inward just to soothe your pride. You're the only one I trust to hold this gang together as a steady steel structure, rather than a grappling hierarchy of whims. If you fail to be a good heir—if you *fall*—then this way of life falls. Let me do this for you."

Juliette's mouth opened, then closed. When all she could manage was a meek, "Okay," her cousin snorted.

The serious spell broke. Kathleen shrugged her coat on. "So, why do you need to know about the bankers at the Bund?"

Juliette was still mulling over her cousin's words. She had always thought of herself as the heir of the Scarlet Gang, but that wasn't it at all, was it? She was the heir to her father's version of the Scarlet Gang.

And was that so great? This Scarlet Gang was unraveling at its very seams. Perhaps a different one could have won the blood feud with the White Flowers generations ago. Perhaps a different one would have stopped the madness by now.

"Rumors of a monster," Juliette answered aloud, shaking herself out of her head. There were so many loose pieces floating around: a monster, a madness, the Communists—she had to focus on aligning them, not doubting herself. "I've reason to believe they might have witnessed something. My hopes aren't high, but a smidgen of it exists at least."

Kathleen nodded. "I'll report back with what I find." With that, her cousin waved goodbye and shut the door after her, the sound echoing back into the living room. The knife looked rather comical moving with the door like that. Juliette sighed and yanked it out, tucking the blade into her dress as she trudged up the stairs. Her parents were going to be horrified to find a gouge in the door. She smiled at the thought and remained rather amused, until she entered her room and spotted a lone figure on her bed.

Juliette almost jumped two feet into the air.

"Oh, heavens, you scared me," she gasped a moment later. The sisters were hardly ever in her room separately, so she hadn't immediately identified Rosalind, especially not while her cousin had her face inclined toward the beam of afternoon sun cutting through the window. "Are you and your sister both insistent on surprising me today?"

Rosalind looked a little miffed as she turned to Juliette. "You were with Kathleen just now? I've been waiting for you here for hours."

Juliette blinked. She wasn't sure what to say. "I'm sorry," she settled on, though her apology was confused and, as a result, disingenuous. "I didn't know."

Rosalind shook her head and muttered, "No matter."

This was one of the details that Juliette remembered from their childhood, before any of them had left for the Western world. Rosalind carried grudges like it was a contest. She was passionate and headstrong and had nerves of steel, but when you looked past her well-chosen, surface-level pretty words, she could also simmer on feelings long past their relevance.

"Don't grouch at me," Juliette tutted. She had to address it now or fear its flare-up long into the distant future. She knew her cousin, had borne witness to Rosalind's slow-building hatred toward the people who upset her—toward her maternal aunts who tried to take the place of her dead mother; toward her father, who valued the strengthening of his guānxì in the Scarlet Gang more than he valued caring for his children; even toward her fellow dancers at the burlesque club, who were jealous enough with Rosalind's growing star status that they tried to exclude her from their circles.

Sometimes Juliette wondered how Rosalind even managed to cope with so much absence in her life. And at that thought, she felt a little bad for not checking in with her cousin more often, though she hadn't been back in this city for all that long. Everyone always had more important things to be doing in the Cai family. Kathleen, at least, erred on the side of optimism. Rosalind did not. But constant care and outreach to your cousins was not a high priority when people were ripping at their own throats on the streets outside.

"What's wrong?" Juliette asked anyway. She could at least spare a minute if Rosalind had been waiting here for hours.

Rosalind didn't respond. For a moment Juliette almost feared that she hadn't absolved the burgeoning grudge. Then, all of a sudden, Rosalind dropped her face into her hands.

There was something haunting about that motion that struck Juliette to the core, something childlike and lost.

"Insects," Rosalind whispered, her words muffled into her palm. Now a coldness had settled into the room. Juliette felt all the little hairs at the back of her neck lift, standing so ramrod straight that her skin almost felt sensitive, sore to the touch.

"So many of them," Rosalind continued. Every crack of her cousin's voice sent a new shiver down Juliette's spine. "So many of them, all coming from the sea, all going back into the sea."

Slowly Juliette managed to lower herself into a kneel on her carpet. She craned her head to meet her cousin's drooped, terrified stare.

"What do you mean?" Juliette asked softly. "What insects?"

Rosalind shook her head. "I think I saw it. I saw it in the water."

It still didn't answer the question. "Saw what?" Juliette tried clarifying again. When Rosalind yet remained quiet, Juliette reached out and took her by the arms, demanding, "Rosalind, what did you see?"

Rosalind inhaled sharply. In that one motion, it was as if she sucked all the oxygen out of the room, sucked out all possibility that whatever she had witnessed could be something casually explained away. A second heartbeat was starting up along Juliette's skull, a pressure building from within to *listen, brace, prepare*. Somehow, she knew that what she was about to hear was going to change everything.

"Rosalind," Juliette prompted one final time.

"Silver eyes," Rosalind finally choked out with a shudder. Now that she had started speaking, it was coming out in a tumble. Her breathing grew increasingly shallow and Juliette's grip grew increasingly tight, fingers still clasped about Rosalind's arms. Her cousin barely seemed to notice. "It had silver eyes. And a curved spine. And sharp ridges. And scales and claws and—I—I don't know, Juliette. I don't know *what* it was. Guài wù, maybe. A monster."

A roar started to sound in Juliette's ears. With careful control, she pried her hands away from her cousin, then reached into her coat, retrieving the drawing she had stolen. She unfolded the worn sheet, smoothing out the lines of ink smeared upon it.

"Rosalind," Juliette said slowly. "Look at this drawing."

Rosalind reached for the thin piece of paper. Her fingers tightened upon it. Her eyes filled with tears.

"Is this what you saw?" Juliette whispered.

Ever so slowly, Rosalind nodded.

Fourteen

I f anyone asked Benedikt Montagov the one thing he wanted out of life, he had a very simple answer: to paint the perfect sphere.

Ask anyone else in the White Flowers and there would be an array of responses. Fortune, love, vengeance—all of these and more, Benedikt wanted too. But they faded into the background when he was painting, thinking of nothing save the movement in his wrist and the arc of his paintbrush, a task so careful, so tedious, so beautiful.

It was almost obsessive how badly he wanted to conjure the perfect sphere. It was one of those delusions that he had held since a child, a delusion that seemed to have formed fully fledged in his mind with no apparent origin, though if there was, perhaps it had been so early in his life he could simply no longer remember. It was all irrational anyway, a belief that if he achieved one impossible thing, then perhaps every other impossible element in his life would click together too, regardless of whether they truly correlated.

When Benedikt was five, he thought that if he could finish reciting the entire Bible from front to back, his father would survive his illness. His father died anyway, and then his mother too, six months later, from a stray bullet to the chest.

When Benedikt was eight, he convinced himself that he *needed* to run from his bedroom to the front door every morning within ten seconds, or else the day would be a bad one. This was back when he still lived within the central headquarters, in the bedroom next to Roma's on the fourth floor. Those days were always terrible and rough—but he didn't know how much of that was a result of his failures to run fast enough.

He was nineteen years old now and the habits hadn't faded; they had simply winnowed down and condensed themselves into the tightest possible ball, leaving behind one single wish, which rested atop a pyramid of other impossible desires.

"Dammit," Benedikt muttered. "Dammit, *dammit*." He ripped the sheet of paper from the canvas and bunched it up, throwing it hard against the wall of his studio. The futility bore down on him, thumping at his temples and invading his dry, tired eyes. Somewhere deep in the recesses of his logic, he knew what he wanted to do wasn't possible. What was a sphere? It was a three-dimensional circle, and circles didn't exist. A circle had points that were all equidistant from the center, and for them to be the same they would need to match to the most exact of precisions. How far would Benedikt go to find perfection? The brushstrokes? The particles? The atoms? If a true circle didn't exist in their very universe, how was he supposed to paint one?

Benedikt set down the paintbrush, scrubbing at his hair as he left his studio.

He paused down the hallway only when a voice floated from the adjacent room, bored and wry and low.

"The hell are you swearing about?"

Now he and Marshall shared the run-down building that sat one block away from the main Montagov dwelling, though Benedikt's name was the only one on the papers. In technicality, Marshall was living here as an illegal tenant, but Benedikt didn't mind. Marshall was an absolute loose cannon, but he was also an excellent cook and better than anyone at repairing a busted pipe. Perhaps it was all his practice putting together his own broken bones. Perhaps it was those early years of his life spent wandering on the streets and fending for himself before the White Flowers took him in. To this day, none of the Montagovs were aware of what exactly happened to Marshall's family. There was only one thing that Benedikt did know: they were all dead.

Marshall strolled out of his room, moth-eaten pajama pants slung low over his hips. When he lifted his arms to fold them across his chest, his bedraggled shirt rode up and showcased a crisscross of knife wounds that had scabbed over his lower torso.

Benedikt was staring. His pulse jumped once at the terrible realization, and jumped again at the thought of getting caught.

"You have more scars." His recovery was fast, barely stuttering even while his neck burned. This moment would probably come to him as he was trying to sleep, and then he would cringe so hard he would invert into himself, becoming an inside-out sheath of skin. Clearing his throat, Benedikt continued. "Where do they keep coming from?"

"This city is a dangerous place," Marshall answered without answering at all, his grin deepening.

He appeared to be teasing, buffing up his own bravado, but Benedikt started to frown. There were always five thousand different thoughts bubbling for attention in Benedikt's mind, and when one surged forward with a *particular* loudness, he paid attention to it. While Marshall wandered off down the hallway, disappearing into the kitchen to rummage about the cupboards, Benedikt remained there outside his studio, musing.

"Isn't that interesting though?"

"Are you still talking to me?"

Benedikt rolled his eyes, hurrying to join Marshall in the kitchen. Marshall was getting the pots and pans out, a stick of celery in his mouth. Benedikt didn't even want to ask why. He supposed Marshall was the type to chomp on raw celery for no good reason.

"Who else would I be talking to?" Benedikt replied, hoisting himself up onto the counter. "The city. It *is* becoming more dangerous, isn't it?"

Marshall took the celery out of his mouth and waved it in Benedikt's direction. When Benedikt only gave him a look, unwilling to open his mouth and take a bite, Marshall shrugged and threw the celery into the trash can.

"Ben, Ben, precious thing, I was only being facetious." Marshall lit a match for the gas. It flared to life between his fingers—a hot, burning miniature star. "This city has always been dangerous. It is the core of human flaw, the pulse of—"

"But of late," Benedikt cut in, leaning over the counter, his two hands propping him up against the hard granite, "haven't you noticed the crowds in the cabarets? The frequency of men who leap onstage to hassle the young dancers? The screaming on the streets when there aren't enough rickshaws for each patron to have his own? One would think that the numbers at the clubs would change, would grow lower and lower, what with the madness. But the nightlife establishments may be the only places that haven't slacked in paying rent to my uncle."

For once, Marshall needed a moment to respond, nothing held ready behind his tongue as soon as his moment came. He had the slightest smile on his lips, but it was pained, as if in sorrow.

"Ben," he said again. He paused. It might have been that he was struggling to find the words in Russian, starting and stopping a few times without coherence, so he lapsed into his mother tongue. "It's not that the city has gotten more dangerous. It's that it has changed."

"Changed?" Benedikt echoed, switching to Korean too. He hadn't taken all those lessons for nothing. He had a terrible accent, but at least he was fluent.

"The madness sweeps everywhere." Marshall retrieved a sprig of cilantro from the bag at his feet. He started chomping down on that too. "It moves like the plague: first all the reports were by the river, then they spread inward to the city, to the concessions, and now more and more mansions on the outskirts are sending victims to the morgue. Think about it. Those who wish to protect themselves will stay in, bar their doors, seal their windows. Those who do not care, those who are violent, those who delight in that which is terrible"—Marshall shrugged, waving his hands about as he chose the right words—"they *thrive*. They come outside. The city has not grown more violent. It is a matter of its people changing."

As if on cue, the sound of glass shattering swept through the apartment, startling Marshall enough to flinch while Benedikt simply turned around, frowning. They both listened, waiting to see if it was a threat. When they heard shouting about rent coming from the alley alongside the building, it was clear that they needn't worry.

Benedikt hopped off the kitchen counter. He rolled up his sleeves as he entered the hallway again, swerving into Marshall's bedroom to grab the nearest article of clothing he saw.

"Okay, let's go," he demanded when he came back into the kitchen.

"What do you mean?" Marshall exclaimed. "I'm making food!"

"I'll buy you food from a street stall." Benedikt threw the jacket over to him. "We've got a live victim to find today."

Marshall and Benedikt wandered about White Flower territory for hours with no luck. They knew that alleyways were common breeding grounds for madness, so they chose only to pick through those smaller paths of this city—twisting in and out of a labyrinth they were mightily familiar with. Before long, however, they realized it didn't matter how slow and careful they were, pausing in the mouths of the alleys when they heard the faintest rustling from within accompanied by an undeniably metallic smell. Twice now they had hurried in with a plan of attack, only to discover that the rustling was rodents, sniffing around a bloody corpse already long dead.

If it wasn't a corpse, then it was silence. It was alleyways that lay as static, undisturbed pictures, all of them reeking from overflowing trash bags and broken crate boxes because people were too frightened to venture far and dispose of their things properly. Benedikt was almost relieved when they finally stepped back onto a main street, reentering a world where wisps and snatches of conversation between vendors and shoppers drifted alongside him as he walked. *This* was the real part of the city. Those alleyways had become haunted versions of Shanghai: an underbelly transformed into a deadened husk.

"So that was a waste of time," Marshall remarked now. He checked his pocket watch. "Would you like to tell Roma of our colossal failure, or shall I?"

Benedikt pulled a face, blowing hot air into his stiff hands. It was not yet cold enough to require gloves, but the afternoon chill today was biting enough to sting.

"Where is Roma anyway?" he asked. "This was supposed to be his task too."

"He's heir of the White Flowers." Marshall tucked the watch away. "He can do whatever he likes."

"You know that's not true."

Marshall's eyebrows shot straight up, disappearing right into the dark mop of hair that fell over his forehead. Both of them were silent for a moment, staring at each other in a rare bout of confusion.

"I mean," Benedikt hurried to correct, "he has to answer to his father still."

"Oh," Marshall said shortly. He was wearing an unfamiliar, uneasy expression that made Benedikt uneasy in return. It gave Benedikt a sudden dip in his stomach, an urge to snatch the words he had just said out of the air, to shove them back into his mouth so Marshall could go back to his usual, relaxed disposition.

"Oh?" Benedikt echoed in question.

Marshall shook his head, laughing it off. The sound immediately relaxed Benedikt's stomach.

"For a second there I thought you meant he wasn't the heir."

Benedikt glanced up at the gray clouds. "No," he said, "that's not what I meant."

But privately they both knew. Benedikt Montagov and Marshall Seo were some of the only White Flowers who had publicly declared their allegiance to Roma. The rest were quiet, waiting to see if Roma would emerge victorious to his birthright, or if eventually he would be upstaged by whoever Lord Montagov decided to favor next.

"You want to go home now?"

Benedikt sighed and nodded. "We may as well."

On the next street over, as Benedikt and Marshall hurried south, Kathleen was moving north, dropping in and out of the banks along the Bund.

The Bund, she thought absently. What a strange way of translating it. In Chinese, it was wàitān, which should have lent itself to being called *the outer bank* in English. That was what it was: a strip of land that touched the part of the Huangpu River farthest downstream. By calling it the Bund instead, it became an embankment. It became a place to come and go, ships crowding in for a chance of the life inside the banks, for trading houses and foreign consulates buzzing with power.

It was here that wealth gathered most densely, amid the decadent, Beaux Arts–inspired, Western-funded buildings that only produced more wealth in a self-sustained cycle. Many of the structures were not yet finished, letting the sea breeze blow through its open beams of scaffolding. The clanging of builders working intensely rang frantic even at this late hour. They were not allowed to build *up* along the height-restricted Bund, so they could only build *well*.

Even half-constructed, everything here was beautiful. It was like every project was a competition to outshine the previous. Kathleen's favorite was the HSBC building—a huge, six-floor neoclassical thing housing the Hongkong and Shanghai Banking Corporation, glimmering on the outside as much as it did on the inside. It was hard to believe that such a colossal collection of marble and Monel managed to come together like this: in columns and lattices and a single roaring dome. It made the whole structure look like it belonged among ancient Grecian temples rather than the epicenter of Shanghai's financial golden age.

It was too bad that the *people* who worked in such welcoming buildings were about as welcoming as moldy rice.

Kathleen exited the HSBC building begrudgingly, emitting a long groan under her breath. Weary to her bones, she leaned against one of the exterior arches, taking a minute to consider her next steps.

I haven't a clue what you mean was the number one phrase that had been thrown at her today, and Kathleen hated failing at her tasks. As soon as these bankers realized Kathleen had not come to query about her credit account, but rather to ask whether they had seen any monsters on their way to work, they shut down immediately, rolling their eyes and asking her to please move along. Within these granite walls and thick, roaring vaults, she supposed the people who spent day after day here thought themselves safe from the madness, from rumors of the monster that brought it by.

Kathleen could tell. It was in the patient wave of their hands as they gestured for the next client, the leisurely manner of shrugging off Kathleen's question like it was simply beneath them. The rich and the foreign, they didn't truly believe it. To them, this *madness* sweeping the city was nothing except Chinese nonsense—only to affect the doomed poor, only to touch the believers caught in their tradition. They thought their glistening marble could keep out contagion because the contagion was nothing save the hysteria of savages.

When the madness comes through these columns, Kathleen thought to herself, *the people here won't know what hit them.*

And then, cruelly, she almost thought: *Good.*

"You, there! Xiǎo gūniáng!"

Kathleen swiveled around at the voice, her heart lifting in the hopes that a banker had come out to tell her that they recalled something. Only as she turned, her eyes landed on an elderly woman with a thick crop of white hair, shuffling nearer with both her hands clutching a large purse.

"Yes?" Kathleen asked.

The elderly woman stopped in front of her, eyes sweeping across the jade pendant pressed to her throat. Kathleen's arms prickled with goose bumps. She resisted the urge to touch her hair.

"I heard you asking"—the woman leaned in, her voice taking on a conspiratorial tone—"after a monster?"

Kathleen grimaced, shaking her goose bumps away with a small exhale. "I'm sorry," she replied. "I don't have any information, either—"

"Ah, but I do," the woman interrupted. "You won't get anywhere with these bankers. They hardly look up from their books and desks. But I was here three days ago. I saw it."

"You—" Kathleen looked over her shoulder, then leaned in, lowering her voice. "You saw it here? With your own eyes?"

The woman waved for Kathleen to follow her, and she did, looking both ways before they crossed the road. They walked up to the water, near the wharves that swept out into the river. When the elderly woman stopped, she set her bag down, then used both her arms to gesture.

"Right here," the woman said. "I was coming out of the bank with my son. Darling thing—but a complete bèndàn when it comes to his finances. Anyway, while he went to fetch a rickshaw, I stood by the bank to wait, and from the street there"—she moved her arms to gesture toward one of the roads that moved inward into the city—"this *thing* . . . came running out."

"A thing," Kathleen echoed. "You mean the monster?"

"Yes . . ." The woman trailed off. She had started this story with vigor, with the sort of energy that came with holding a rapt audience. Now it was fading, suddenly striking the woman with *what* she had truly seen. "The monster. Horrific, undying thing."

"But are you sure?" Kathleen urged. One part of her wanted to run home with this information immediately, tell Juliette so her cousin could gather the Scarlet forces and their pitchforks. Another part, the sensible part, knew this was not enough. They needed more. "Are you certain it was the monster, not a shadow or—"

"I am certain," the woman said firmly. "I am certain because a fisherman docking his boat tried to shoot at it as it lumbered along this very wharf." She pointed forward, to the wharf that extended out into the wide, wide river, currently rumbling with activity from the docked ships. "I am certain because the bullets merely bounced off its back, clinking to the ground as if it were not a *being* standing upright but a *god*. It was a monster. I am sure of it."

"What happened?" Kathleen whispered. A chill swept up her neck and down her arms. She did not think it was the sea breeze. It was something far ghastlier. "What happened next?"

The woman blinked. She seemed to come out of a slight daze, as if she had not quite noticed how intently she had gotten lost in her memory.

"Well, that's the thing," she replied, frowning. "My eyesight, you see. It's not the best. I watched the creature leap into the water and then . . ."

Kathleen leaned forward. "And then . . . ?"

The old woman shook her head. "I do not know. Everything got a little hazy. I thought I heard skittering. It looked like the darkness out there"—she extended her arm—"was moving. Like little things were being shot into the darkness." She shook her head again, more intensely this time. It did not look to do much, because the woman's voice had lost all of her initial energy. "My son had returned by then with the rickshaw. I told him to go look. I told him that I thought I saw a monster in the water. He ran along the wharf to go catch it."

Kathleen gasped. "And . . . did he?"

"No." The woman frowned, her gaze cast out toward the Huangpu River. "He said I was talking nonsense. Said he only saw a man, swimming away. He was convinced a fisherman had simply fallen off his boat."

A man. How could there have been a man in the water while the monster was there? How could he have survived?

Unless . . .

With a shuddering breath, the woman picked her bag up, then seemed to think twice, reaching out to grip Kathleen's hand instead.

"I recognize you from within the Scarlet Gang's ranks," she said quietly. "There's something stirring to life in the waters that surround this city. There's something stirring to life in so many places we cannot see." The elderly woman's fingers tightened until Kathleen could no longer feel her circulation within her palm.

"Please," the woman whispered. "Protect us."

Fifteen

ays later, Juliette could think of little else but the madness. She hardly reacted anymore when people called her name. She had ears only for the sound of screaming, and each time screams rang through the streets, she winced, wishing—*aching* to do something about it.

A monster, Juliette thought, her thoughts persistent in its cyclic loop as she leaned against the staircase in wait. *There's a monster spreading madness on the streets of Shanghai.*

"Ready to go?" Lord Cai called down to her, pausing at the top to straighten the collar of his coat.

Juliette forced herself back into the present. Sighing, she twirled the little clutch bag in her hands.

"Ready as ever."

Lord Cai descended the rest of the stairs, then stopped in front of his daughter, his expression set in a frown. Juliette looked down at herself, trying to determine what had drawn his disapproval. She was wearing her American dresses again, this one slightly fancier to fit the occasion, with bundles of tulle at her shoulders that fell into sleeves. Was the neckline too low-cut? Was this—for once—normal fatherly concern that wasn't about whether she could kill a man without flinching?

"Where's your mask?"

Close enough. I'll take it.

"Why bother?" Juliette sighed. "You're not wearing one."

Lord Cai scrubbed at his eyes. Juliette couldn't tell if it was his general tiredness in preparing to deal with the Frenchmen, or if he was exasperated with her childish behavior.

"Yes, because I am a fifty-year-old man," her father replied. "It would look ridiculous."

Juliette shrugged, then started for the front door. "You said it, not me."

The night was brisk when they stepped out into the driveway, and Juliette shivered slightly, rubbing her hands against her bare arms. No matter. It was too late to go back for a coat now. She climbed into the car with the chauffeur's help and slid down the seat to make room for her father. Most of their other family members who were attending the masquerade had already left. Juliette hadn't wanted to go anyway, so she had waited while Lord Cai took his time finishing up his work. He had only declared that it was time to get going when the sky turned pink and the burning orange sun started to brush the horizon.

Lord Cai got into the car. Once he settled himself into his seat, he rested his hands in his lap and glanced over at Juliette. His expression set into another frown. This time he was eyeing the necklace laced tightly across her throat.

"That's not a necklace, is it?"

"It is not, Bàba."

"That's garrote wire, isn't it?"

"Indeed it is, Bàba."

"How many other weapons have you concealed on yourself?"

"Five, Bàba."

Lord Cai pinched the bridge of his nose and muttered, "Wǒde māyā, have mercy on my soul."

Juliette smiled like she had been complimented.

Their car started forward and rumbled along smoothly, driving through the calmer, rural roads and into the city, honking every three seconds for the laborers and the men dragging rickshaws to get out of the way. Juliette usually made a habit not to look out the window, lest she make eye contact and a beggar approached. But for some inexplicable reason, she looked up tonight.

Right in time to see a woman bawling on the sidewalk, cradling a body in her lap.

The body was a bloody mess, hands stained red and throat so messy that its head was barely hanging on by the force of the neck bone. The crying woman cradled the head, pressed her cheek to its deathly white face.

The car started to move again. Juliette turned her gaze to the front, to the passing blur of the windshield in the front seat, and swallowed hard.

Why is this happening? she thought desperately. *Has this city committed such awful sins that we have come to deserve this?*

The answer was: yes. But it wasn't entirely their fault. The Chinese had built the pit, gathered the wood, and lit the match, but it was the foreigners who had come in and poured gasoline upon every surface, letting Shanghai rage into an untamable forest fire of debauchery.

"Here we are," the chauffeur said, braking.

Juliette, her jaw tight, got out of the car. In the French Concession, everything was a little bit shiny, even the grass beneath her feet. These gardens were usually gated, but they had been pulled wide open tonight specifically for this function. When Juliette walked through the gates, it was as if she had entered another world—one far from the dirty streets and tightly cramped alleyways that they had just driven through. Here it was greenery and climbing vines and slick intentions, little gazebos sitting patiently in quaint nooks and the darkness pulling in, pulling the shadows of the tall, wrought-iron gates that bordered this garden long into the grass, growing longer with every second of the violet sunset.

Despite the chill, Juliette was sweating a little as she browsed the crowds of people dispersed across these delicately kept gardens. Her first order of business was identifying where every relative had situated themselves. She found most of them easily, scattered about and socializing. Perhaps she *had* taken it a bit too far to bring so many weapons. Because of the knife strapped to the small of her back, her dress was too tight at her waist, and the white fabric at her knees was bunching up with every step. But Juliette couldn't help herself. By bringing weapons, she could fool herself into thinking she could act if disaster struck.

She tried not to acknowledge that there were some disasters she couldn't fight off with her knives. The foreigners here certainly did not care. As Juliette walked, she overheard more than one giggle about the rumors of madness, British men and Frenchwomen alike clinking their glasses in celebration regarding how intelligent it was to stay out of the local hysteria. They acted like it was a *choice*.

"Come, Juliette," Lord Cai prompted from ahead, straightening his sleeves.

Juliette followed obediently, but her eyes remained elsewhere. Under a delicate marble pavilion, a quartet was playing soft music, the sound floating toward a clearing where some foreign merchants and their wives were dancing. There was an even ratio of Scarlet gangsters and foreigners in attendance—merchants and officials alike—and a few were going so far as to be conversing in the fading twilight. She spotted Tyler within those groups, chatting with a Frenchwoman. When he saw her looking, he waved pleasantly. Juliette's mouth soured into a line.

Nearby, the strings of lights looped across the gazebo awnings flared to life with a sudden *whoosh*. The gardens became illuminated with gold, pushing out the darkness that would have otherwise crept in when the sun settled completely into the sea.

"Juliette," Lord Cai prompted again. Juliette had slowed her walk to a snail's crawl without noticing. Begrudgingly, she picked up her pace. She had noted that most of the attendants remained in groups with those to whom they were alike. British women who had moved here with their diplomat husbands laughed with one another, their laced gloves swirling their pastel parasols. French officers clapped one another on the back, howling over whatever unfunny joke one of their superiors just told. Yet dispersed in different sections of the garden, three loners stood unassociated despite their best efforts to look as if they were occupied in proper business.

Juliette stopped again. She cocked her head at one of them—the one who was intensely examining the plate in his hands.

"Bàba, doesn't that boy look Korean to you?"

Lord Cai didn't even follow the direction of her gaze. He put his hands around her shoulders and nudged her in the direction they were going. "Focus, Juliette."

It was a moot command. Juliette didn't require any focus when they approached the Consul-General of France because when the men spoke, she simply faded into the background. She was barely more than an ornament decorating the place. She tuned in and out of the main conversation, not even catching the Consul-General's name. Her focus was on the two men standing at attention behind him.

"Do you want to get a sandwich afterward?" the first man whispered to the second in French. "I hate this catering. They're trying too hard to appeal to that bland country across the ditch."

"You spoke my mind," the second responded quietly. "Would you look at them? A bunch of unrefined peasants."

Juliette had tensed, but with the remark about the ditch, it was clear that they were referring to the British, not the Scarlet Gang.

"They sip away on their tea and claim they invented it," the second man continued. "Think again, fool. The Chinese were brewing tea before you even had a king."

Juliette snorted suddenly—the irrelevant pettiness of the conversation completely taking her by surprise—then coughed to mask the sound. Lord Cai had nothing to worry about; bringing her here had been an unnecessary precaution. She turned her attention back to her father's conversation.

"They are wary, my lord," the Consul-General was saying. He spoke of his French businessmen, Juliette guessed. "The garde municipale keeps the French Concession safe for now, but if there is any trouble brewing, I need to know that I have the support of the Scarlet Gang."

If there was a revolt from the common Chinese people, from the unpaid workers who decided Communism was the prime solution, the French needed a way to maintain their hold on Shanghai. They thought they could obtain it with the weaponry and resources of the Scarlet Gang. They didn't quite realize that if there was a revolution, there would be no one left in Shanghai for them to do their business with.

But Lord Cai voiced none of that. He agreed easily, under the condition that the Scarlet Gang still had the jurisdiction to run their errands in the French Concession. The Consul-General of France exclaimed, in an attempt to mold his English with Americanisms, "Why, old friend, of course! That is not even in question," and when the two men shook hands, it seemed all was settled.

Juliette thought the whole thing theatrical and ridiculous. She thought it preposterous that her father had to ask permission to run business on land their ancestors had lived and died on from men who had simply docked their boat here and decided they would like to be in charge now.

The Consul-General of France, as if he could detect the hostility of Juliette's thoughts, at last turned his gaze to her.

"And how are you, Miss Juliette?"

Juliette smiled widely.

"You shouldn't get a say here." She was speaking before her father could stop her, her words dripping so sweetly that they sounded like admiration. "However flawed we are, however much we fight each other, this country is still not for people like you to dictate."

The Consul-General's bright expression faltered, but only slightly, unable to determine if Juliette was taking a dig or making an innocent remark. Her words were sharp but her eyes were friendly, her hands clasped together like she was making small talk.

"Have a good day," Lord Cai cut in before any of the French could formulate a response. He steered Juliette away firmly, marching her by her shoulders.

"Juliette," Lord Cai hissed the moment they were out of earshot. "I didn't think I had to teach you this, but you cannot say things like that to powerful people. It will be the death of you."

Juliette shook her shoulders out of her father's grasp.

"Surely not," she argued. "He is powerful, but he does not have the power to kill me."

"Very well," Lord Cai said firmly. "He may not kill you—"

"Then why can I not speak freely?"

Her father sighed. He breathed in, then breathed out, searching for his answer.

"Because," he said finally, "it hurts his feelings, Juliette."

Juliette folded her arms. "We stay quiet about the injustice of all this simply because *it hurts his feelings?*"

Lord Cai shook his head. He took his daughter by the elbow to lead her farther away, sparing a long look over his shoulder. When they were near one of the gazebos, he let go and clasped his hands before him.

"These days, Juliette," he said, low and warily, "the most dangerous people are the powerful white men who feel as if they have been slighted."

Juliette knew this. She knew this far more than people like her father and mother, who had only ever seen what the foreigners were capable of *after* they sailed their ships into Chinese waters. But Juliette—her parents had sent her off to America to be educated, after all. She had grown up with an eye pinned to the outside of every establishment before she walked in, searching for the segregation signs that demanded she keep out. She had learned to move out of the way whenever a white lady in heels was coming down the sidewalk with her pearls, learned to fake meekness and lower her gaze in the event that the white lady's husband would note the slight roll of Juliette's eyes and yell after her, demanding to know why she was in this country and what her problem was.

She didn't have to do a single thing in offense. It was the entitlement that drove these men forward. Entitlement that encouraged their wives to place a delicate handkerchief to their nose and sniff, wholeheartedly believing the tirade was deserved. They believed themselves the rulers of the world—on stolen land in America, on stolen land in Shanghai.

Everywhere they went—*entitlement*.

And Juliette was so *tired*.

"Everyone gets their feelings hurt," she said bitterly. "While he's here, he can experience it for once in his life. He doesn't deserve to have power. It's not his right."

"I know," Lord Cai said simply. "All of China knows. But this is the way the world works now. For as long as he has power, we need him. For as long as he has the most guns, he holds the power."

"It is not as if *we* do not have guns," Juliette grumbled anyway. "It is not as if we have not had an iron grip on Shanghai for the last century with *our* guns."

"Once it was enough," Lord Cai replied. "Now it is not."

The French needed *them*, but the Scarlet Gang did not *need* the French in the same way. What her father meant in actuality was that they needed French power—they needed to stay on their good side. If the Scarlet Gang were to declare war and take back the French

Concession as Chinese territory, they would be destroyed in hours. Loyalty and gang hierarchy was nothing against warships and torpedoes. The Opium Wars had proved that.

Juliette made a sound of disgust. Seeing her father's stern expression, she sighed and diverted the topic back to what was important. "Never mind. I heard nothing of interest from his men."

Lord Cai nodded. "That is fortunate. It means less trouble for us. Go enjoy yourself."

"Sure," Juliette said. By that she meant, *I'm getting food and then I'm leaving*. She had spotted Paul Dexter coming through the gates. He was searching through the crowd. "I'll be hiding—" Juliette coughed. "Pardon me, I'll be *hovering* by that tree."

Unfortunately, despite how quickly Juliette paced away, she still wasn't fast enough.

"Miss Cai, what a pleasant surprise."

Having reached the food table, Juliette set her clutch down and primly picked up an egg tart. She took a nibble, then turned around, facing the human equivalent of stale bread.

"How have you been?" Paul asked. He clasped his hands behind his back, stretching the blue fabric of his tailored suit. He wasn't wearing a mask, either. His green eyes blinked at her unfettered, reflecting the golden lights above them.

Juliette shrugged. "Fine."

"Excellent, excellent," Paul crowed. She didn't know why he was responding so enthusiastically to her uninspiring reply. "Let me say, it's most—"

"What do you want, Paul?" Juliette interrupted. "I already told you that we don't want your business."

Undeterred, Paul only ramped up his zeal and took Juliette by the elbow to lead her away from the food. At the back of her mind, she considered shooting him, but because this was a party with hundreds of rich foreigners mingling about, she decided that probably would not be the best course of action. She tensed her arm, but allowed Paul to lead her away.

"Just to talk," he said. "We've taken our business straight to the other merchants. Worry not. I have no more intentions to bother the Scarlet Gang."

Juliette smiled sweetly. Her teeth were gritted hard.

"And if that is the case, why are you bothering with me?"

Paul smiled sweetly back, though his expression appeared genuine.

"Perhaps I am after your affection, pretty girl."

Gross. She would bet her life savings that he only thought her pretty because she was digestible to Western standards. Her feminine beauty was a concept as fleeting as power. If she acquired a tan, put on some weight, and let a few decades pass, the street artists would not be rendering her face to sell their creams anymore. Chinese and Western standards alike were arbitrary, pitiful things. But Juliette still needed to keep herself in line, force herself to follow them if people were to look up to her. Without her looks, this city would turn on her. It would claim that she didn't deserve to be as competent as she was. The men, meanwhile, could be as tan, as fat, and as old as they wished. It would have no bearing on what people thought of them.

Juliette removed her arm from Paul's grip, pivoting on her heel to return to the food.

"No, thanks. My affection is not won with such humdrum energy."

It was as thorough a dismissal as any. Juliette thought she had been left alone when she picked up a drink. But Paul was persistent. His voice came over her shoulder again.

"How is your father?"

"He is well," Juliette replied, barely biting back the aggravation that wanted to climb into her words. Out of social courtesy, she asked him in a light voice, "And how is yours?"

Juliette was the queen of socialites. She had had nothing but practice. If she wanted to, she could have turned her slight, polite smile into a megawatt grin. But she did not think she could get any information out of Paul, and associating with him seemed pointless.

Perhaps Paul could tell. Perhaps he was smarter than Juliette gave him credit for. Perhaps he had indeed detected the restlessness of her tapping fingers and the ceaseless movement of her craning neck.

So he made himself useful.

"My father and I have started working for the Larkspur," Paul said. "Have you heard of him?"

The Larkspur. Juliette's tapping fingers halted midmovement. Lā-gespu. Larkspur. *That* was what the old man in Chenghuangmiao had been trying to say. Hearing one lunatic scream about a mysterious figure, claiming he had received a cure for the madness, was unworthy of notice. Hearing that same mysterious figure mentioned twice in a few days was strange. Her eyes focused properly on the British smooth talker before her, for once settling into a steady gaze.

"I've heard some things, here and there," Juliette replied vaguely. She tilted her head. "What do you do?"

"Run errands, mostly."

Now Paul was being deliberately vague, and he knew it. Juliette watched the lines of his small smirk, the curve of his eyebrows drawing together, and read him to an inch of his life. He wanted attention for his involvement with the Larkspur, but he was not allowed to give answers. He would hint at all he knew, but he would not give anything up just for gossip.

"Errands?" Juliette parroted. "I cannot imagine there is much to do."

"Oh, that's where you're wrong," Paul said, his chest puffing up. "The Larkspur has created a vaccine for the madness. He has merchants rushing for it in droves, and the organization of such a large affair requires workers the size of an army."

"Your salary must be fantastic." Juliette eyed the chain of a golden pocket watch draped through one of his buttonholes.

"The Larkspur sits upon stacks of money," Paul confirmed.

Is this Larkspur benefiting off the panic of the madness, then? Juliette wondered. *Or does he truly have a vaccine that is worth the money of these merchants?*

Juliette could have voiced her musings aloud, but Paul was looking too satisfied to give her a truthful answer. She only asked bluntly, "And does the Larkspur have a name?"

Paul shrugged. "If he does, I do not know it. If you would like, I could arrange for you to meet him."

At this Juliette straightened up, peering at him from underneath her blackened eyelashes, waiting for the catch.

"Though I must say," Paul continued, looking apologetic, "I am not yet very high in the ranks. You would have to stick around for some time while I work my way up. . . ."

Juliette barely refrained from rolling her eyes. Paul was still blabbering on, but she had stopped listening. He was only after a power trip. He couldn't make himself useful after all.

"Excusez-moi, mademoiselle."

Paul abruptly shut up as the voice spoke behind Juliette, giving her a blissful few seconds without his prattling. She silently thanked the French intruder, then took it back the moment she turned and faced the masked blond man standing before them.

Oh hell.

"Voulez-vous danser?"

Though Juliette could feel a vein in her forehead throbbing dangerously, pulsating with the rhythm of her anger, she took the opportunity to escape.

"Bien sûr," she said tightly. "À plus tard, Paul."

Juliette snagged Roma's sleeve and dragged him away, her fingers curled so tightly that her right hand turned numb. Did he think she wouldn't recognize him just because he was wearing a blond wig and a mask?

"Do you have a death wish?" Juliette hissed, switching to English as soon as Paul was out of earshot. Then, noting all the British ministers and merchants around her, she lowered her tongue into Russian instead. "I should kill you right now. Your audacity!"

"You wouldn't dare," Roma replied, his Russian fast and biting. "Would you risk allowing the Scarlet Gang to be seen as violent brutes in front of these foreigners just to get rid of me? The price is too high to pay."

"I—" Juliette clamped her lips shut, swallowing whatever else was poised on her tongue. They had paused in the fray of the dancing, amid a gathering of couples steadily increasing with the change in music. The pull of strings from the quartet was coming fast—the tune was livelier, the rhythm was teasing. Roma was right. Juliette wouldn't dare, but the foreigners had been the furthest thing from her mind. Juliette wouldn't dare because no matter how big her talk was, she still couldn't separate the hatred broiling in her stomach with the sudden lurch of adrenaline that came to life with his proximity. If her body refused to forget who Roma once was to her, how was she to make those same limbs rebel from their nature, make them destroy him?

"Penny for your thoughts?"

At Roma's switch back into English, Juliette's gaze jerked up. Their eyes locked. A tremor shuddered along the back of her hands. In the midst of so many swishing skirts, the stillness between them was starting to look suspicious. Really, Juliette wondered how Roma avoided looking suspicious anywhere he went. He moved too well. Had someone told her four years ago that he was a god in human form, she would have believed them.

"I doubt you have a penny on you," Juliette finally replied. Reluctantly, she took a step forward and raised her hand; Roma did the same. They didn't need to speak to make the complementing gesture. They had always known how to predict what the other was about to do.

"Indeed, but I have plenty of larger bills. Would you offer more thoughts for those?"

The music grew louder, spurring the couples all around them to move with a renewed vigor. Roma and Juliette were forced to circle each other, hands extended but not touching, hovering but not steady, needing to move to blend in but unwilling to make contact, unwilling to pretend to be more than what they were.

"What are you doing here, Roma?" Juliette asked tightly. She did not have the energy to play along with his trivial conversation. At such an intimate distance, she could hardly keep her breath even, could hardly hide the trembling that threatened to shake her extended hand. "I gather you are not risking your life just to have a little dance."

"No," he replied surely. "My father sent me." A pause. Only then did it seem like Roma was struggling to get his next words out. "He wishes to propose that the Scarlet Gang and White Flowers work together."

Juliette almost laughed in his face. She quavered at the rising numbers of the dead lost to the madness, yes, and she feared another outbreak within her own house—this time targeting those of her blood, those whom she knew well and held close to her heart. But it hadn't happened yet, and it wouldn't happen if Juliette could work fast enough—*alone*. No matter how much more efficient it was for the two gangs to work together, to join a divided city into one, she had no incentive at all to agree to Roma's proposal, and he appeared to think the same.

The words coming out of his mouth were one matter, but his expression was another. His heart was not in it, either. Even if working together could merge their territory, even if it could bring a momentary peace to the feud so they could discover *why* their gangsters were being picked off one by one, it wasn't enough. It wasn't enough to set down the hatred and the blood, to resolve the fury that Juliette had been nursing in her heart for four years.

Besides, why would Lord Montagov, of all people, propose an alliance? He was the most hateful of them all. Juliette could only come to one conclusion, the most likely: it was a test. If he sent Roma here and the Scarlet Gang agreed, then Lord Montagov knew the extent of their desperation. The White Flowers didn't truly want to work together. They only wanted to know how hard the Scarlet Gang had been hit, so they could use the information to strike even harder.

"Never," Juliette hissed. "Run home and tell your father he can *choke*."

Juliette whirled on her heel and broke away from their half dance, but then the music changed to suit a waltz, and Roma snagged her arm, pulling her back until her other hand landed on his shoulder and his came around her waist. Before she could do a thing about it, he had pulled her into the proper stance, chest to chest, and they were dancing.

It was like she was under compulsion. For a moment she allowed herself to believe they were fifteen again, spinning on the rooftop they liked to hide on, moving to the jazz club roaring beneath their feet. Memories were beastly little creatures, after all—they rose with the faintest whiff of nourishment.

She hated the knee-jerk way she leaned into him. She hated that her body followed his lead without resistance. They used to be unstoppable. When they were together, they never had an ounce of fear, not when they were hiding at the back of a noisy club playing cards, nor when they made it their mission to sneak into every private park in Shanghai, a bottle of whatever Juliette had stolen from the liquor cabinet tucked underneath Roma's arm, giggling like a pair of idiots.

It was all too familiar. The feeling of Roma's hands on her waist, his hand tucked in hers—those hands were of such grace, but she knew better than anyone that blood was soaked through and through the lines of his palms. Lines that read like scripture in appearance were in truth nothing but sin.

"This isn't proper," she intoned.

"You give me no choice," Roma replied. His voice was strained. "I need your cooperation."

The music rang sharp and then it moved fast, and as Roma twirled her outward, her skirts clinking alongside the tune, Juliette's resistance snapped to attention. When she came back, she wasn't content to let Roma lead. Despite their stance, the moves, the steps, the angle of their hands—despite everything about the waltz that determined she was the subservient partner, Juliette started to dictate where they were stepping.

"Why do you not dance with my father, then?" she asked, taking in a deep gulp of air as the next spin came. "He is the voice of this gang."

Roma was fighting back. His grip was tight on her hand, his fingers pressing into her waist like he was trying to press his fingerprints into her dress. If she had only heard his voice, she would not have known the pressure he was under. His voice was easy, casual.

"I fear your father would shoot me in the face."

"Oh, and you don't fear that I would do the same? It would appear my reputation *doesn't* precede me."

"Juliette," Roma said. "You have *power*."

The music came to an abrupt stop.

And they froze too, just as they were—eye to eye, heart to heart. As the people around them broke away in light laughter, switching partners before the music started again, Roma and Juliette simply stood there, heaving for breath, chests rising and falling, as if they had just engaged in close-contact combat instead of the waltz.

Step away, Juliette told herself.

The pain of it was almost physical. The years had worn on between them, had aged them into monsters with human faces, unrecognizable against old photos. Yet no matter how much she wanted to forget, it was like no time had passed at all. She looked at him and she could still remember the terrible dip in her stomach when the explosion happened, could still feel the tightness in her throat that signaled the onslaught of tears, worsening and worsening until she was breaking down against the exterior wall of her house, holding her scream back with nothing but the palm of her silk-gloved hand.

"You must consider it." Roma spoke quietly, like any loud noise could startle the bubble that had formed around them, could stomp down the strangeness between them, boiling and boiling to the surface. "I give my word that this is no ambush. This is a matter of preventing chaos from descending onto the streets."

Once, a long time ago, at the back of a library while a storm raged on outside, Juliette had asked Roma, "Do you ever imagine what life would be like if you had a different last name?"

"All the time. Don't you?"

Juliette had thought about it. "Only sometimes. Then I consider all that I would miss out on without it. What would I be if I weren't a Cai?"

Roma had lifted onto his elbow. "You could be a Montagov."

"Don't be ridiculous."

"Very well." Roma had leaned in, close enough that she could see the twinkle in his dark eyes, close enough to see her own blushing face in the reflection of his gaze. "Or we could erase both names and leave this entire Cai–Montagov nonsense behind."

Now she wanted to tear out the memories, launch them as a wad of spit right at Roma's face.

You give your word. But you have always been a liar.

She opened her mouth, the words to turn Roma away balanced right at the tip of her tongue. Then her gaze went to a rapidly approaching blur of movement coming toward him, and she blanched, her jaw wiring shut.

Roma became stock-still when he sensed the gun that Tyler had pointed to his head.

"Juliette," Tyler said. Where the loose sleeves of his dress shirt billowed with the light wind, his hands were perfectly still, not a single tremor to the steady grip on his weapon. "Step away."

Juliette considered the situation. Her eyes darted a quick inventory of the foreigners around them, taking in their scandalized gasps and their confused, wide eyes.

She needed to deescalate this *right now*.

"What is wrong with you?" Juliette scolded, feigning outrage as she stepped away.

Tyler frowned. "What—"

"Put away your gun and apologize to this kind Frenchman," she continued. She placed her hands on her hips, like she was Tyler's snappy aunt instead of a girl with a heartbeat that threatened to tear through her rib cage.

Tyler's expression morphed from furious to perplexed and back to furious again. He was buying it. It was working.

"Tyler," Lord Cai called from a distance away. "Gun away. Now."

"This is Roma Montagov," Tyler snapped. Gasps sounded from the British couple who stood behind him. "I know it. I could tell by his voice."

"Don't embarrass us by acting out like this," Juliette warned quietly.

Tyler responded by pressing the barrel of the gun deeper into Roma's neck. "I will not tolerate a Montagov parading around on our territory. The *disrespect*—"

Two figures stepped out of the shadows then, their guns already pointed on Tyler and snatching the words from his mouth. Benedikt Montagov and Marshall Seo had not even bothered wearing disguises. It was the Scarlet Gang's fault for not recognizing them. After all, Juliette had known they might be coming. She knew that Roma had snatched her invitation, that the White Flowers would have heard about this function even without it. And perhaps this was her own fault too. Perhaps some traitorous part of her had wanted Roma to show just so she could see him. That part of her—the one that had dreamed of a better world, that had loved without caution—was supposed to be *dead*.

Just like monsters were supposed to be mere tales. Just like this city, in all its glitter and technology and innovation, was supposed to be safe from madness.

"Stop," Juliette said, inaudible even to herself. This would end in a bloodbath. "Stop—"

A scream echoed into the night.

The confused rumblings began immediately, but then confusion turned to panic and panic turned to chaos. Tyler had no choice but to lower his gun when the British woman standing two feet away from him collapsed to the ground. He had no choice but to dart backward and give wide berth when the woman's hands launched at her delicate lily-white throat and tore it to pieces.

All around them.

One by one by one by one.

They dropped—Scarlets and merchants and foreigners alike. Those who had not been infected attempted to run. Some made it out the gates. Some succumbed as soon as they skidded onto the pavement outside the gardens, the madness kicking in with delay.

Juliette's lungs were tight again. Why was it spreading so damn *fast*?

"*No*," Juliette cried, rushing for a familiar figure on the ground. She got to Mr. Li right before he could place his hands on his throat, slammed her knee onto his wrist in the hopes that she could prevent him from acting.

The madness was too strong. Mr. Li yanked his arm out from underneath her and Juliette was sent toppling, her elbow skidding against the grass.

"Don't, don't!" she shouted, lunging forward and trying again. This time his hands made contact with his throat before she could reach him. This time, before she could try to wrap herself around her favorite uncle and force him to stop, someone was pulling her away, a rough grip pushing Juliette back onto the ground.

Juliette scrambled for the knife hidden in her back, her first instinct to brace for defense.

Then she heard, "Juliette, stop. I'm not attacking you."

Her hand froze, a cry caught in her throat. An arc of blood flew wide into the night, drops landing on her ankle, her wrists, dotting her skin like morbid, crimson jewelry. Mr. Li grew still. His face was frozen in his last expression—one of terror—so unlike the kindness that Juliette was used to.

"I could have saved him," she whispered.

"You couldn't," Roma snapped immediately. "You would have just infected yourself in the process."

Juliette let out a small, surprised breath. She scrunched her fists to hide their shaking. "What do you mean?"

"Insects, Juliette," Roma said. He swallowed hard as a nearby bout of screaming increased in volume. "That is how the madness is spreading—like lice through your hair."

For the shortest, uncensored second, Juliette's eyes widened, the web of facts in her head finally connecting, a thin line tracing from point to point. Then she laughed bitterly and brought her hand up to her head. She knocked upon her skull, and a hard, *crispy* sort of sound came from her hair, a sound that made it seem like she was knocking on cardboard instead. Her naturally straight hair needed at least three pounds of product to make her finger waves, or else the formation wouldn't harden in place. "I'd like to see them try."

Roma didn't say anything in response. He thinned his lips and looked out into the gardens. Those who were alive had chosen to huddle under a gazebo, somber and uncertain. Her father stood separated from the rest, his hands behind his back, merely watching.

There was nothing that anybody could do except stand there and watch the last of the victims die.

"One meeting."

Roma jerked his eyes to her, startling. "Pardon?"

"One meeting," Juliette repeated, as if his hearing had been the problem. She wiped the blood off her face. "That's all I can promise you."

Sixteen

J uliette took her time arming herself. There was something comforting about the act, something satisfying about the smooth, cold feeling of a gun pressed to her bare skin—one sticking out of her shoe, one at her thigh, one by her waist.

She was sure others would disagree. But if Juliette ran with the tide, she wouldn't be Juliette anymore.

After the incident in the French Concession gardens, it had been bedlam in the Cai mansion.

"Just listen to them," she had told her parents, her eyes burning because of the late hour. "There's no harm in listening—"

Disgruntled muttering had broken out immediately from the relatives gathered around on the couches—relatives who were inner-circle Scarlets and relatives who were absolutely clueless about what went on within the Scarlet Gang. Instead of going to sleep, they were all listening to a proposal that Juliette was directing only at her parents, and they all erupted with indignation, repulsed that Juliette would even entertain the notion of entering a meeting room with the White Flowers in peace. . . .

"Shut up!" Juliette screamed. "Shut up, shut up, *all of you!*"

Save for her parents, they all froze with their eyes wide, startled like raccoon dogs caught in the light. Juliette was heaving for breath, her face still marred with Mr. Li's blood. She looked a living nightmare.

Good, she thought. *Let them consider me callous. It is better than marking me weak.*

"Imagine," Juliette said when she could breathe evenly again. Her outburst had forced the living room quiet. "Imagine what the foreigners must think of us. Imagine what they discuss among themselves now as they watch their officers clean the dead. We merely confirm that we are savages, that this country is a place where madness spreads like disease, taking its people in droves."

"Perhaps that is good," Tyler called from the base of the staircase. He was seated casually, his elbows leaning back on a step while the rest of his body lounged on the hardwood floors. "Why not wait for this madness to run its course? Kill enough foreigners until they pack up their bags and run?"

"Because that's not how it works," Juliette hissed. "Do you know what will happen instead? They listen to the sweet nothings of their missionaries. They take it upon themselves to be our saviors. They roll tanks onto our streets and then they place their government in Shanghai, and before you know it . . ." Juliette stopped. She switched from Shanghainese to English, making her best attempt at a British accent. "Thank goodness we colonized the Chinese when we did. Who knows how they may have otherwise destroyed themselves."

Silence. Many of her relatives had not understood her when she switched to English. It did not matter. Those whom she needed to convince—her parents—understood her fine.

"The way I see it," Juliette continued, dropping into her natural American accent. "If our gangsters don't stop dying, then we lose control. The workers in the cotton mills and opium centers start grumbling, the whole city starts to stir with chaos, and then the foreigners take over, if the Communists don't get there first. At least the White Flowers are an even playing field. At least we are at an equilibrium, at least we *have* half the city as opposed to *none*."

"Speak plainly," Lady Cai said. She, too, slipped into accented

English. "You mean to say that putting aside the blood feud with the White Flowers is more acceptable than the risk of foreigners ruling us."

"Why can't they just speak běndì huà?" an aunt muttered bitterly in complaint, no longer able to track the conversation.

"Only for one meeting," Juliette replied quickly, ignoring the grumblings. "Only for long enough to join our resources and put a stop to the madness once and for all. Only so the white men keep their hands *off this damn country*."

And despite how strongly she had believed in her argument as she was delivering it, she'd still received the shock of her life when her parents had actually *agreed*. Now she looked into the mirror on her vanity, smoothed out her dress, and brushed a stray lock of hair back into her curls, pressing hard so it would mesh with the gel.

Her hands were shaking.

They shook on her way down the stairs, as her heels clacked along the driveway, as she slid into the back of the car, scooting to the end so Rosalind and Kathleen could jam themselves in after her. They kept shaking and shaking and shaking as she leaned her head against the window, staring out into the city streets as they drove. She watched the people with a new light, observing the vendors selling their wares and the barbers doing their jobs on the street sides, dropping their tuffs of thick black hair to the concrete.

The energy in Shanghai had disappeared. It was like some great big hand had reached down from the heavens and yanked the life out of every worker on the streets—took the volume away from the vendors, the vigor away from the rickshaw drivers, the lively chatter from the men who hung around shops for no reason other than to talk to passersby.

At least, until they saw the fancy car coming down the street. Then their scared eyes turned narrow. Then they did not dare openly rage, but they did stare, and such stares spoke monologues in itself.

The gangsters were the rulers of the city. If the city fell, the gangsters got the blame. And then all the gangsters would die—killed in political revolution, madness or no madness, foreigners or no foreigners.

Juliette leaned her head back against the seat, biting down on the inside of her cheeks so hard that the taste of metal flooded across her tongue. Unless she could stop it, this was going to come to a bitter, bitter end.

"Terrible, isn't it?" Rosalind whispered, leaning over to peer out the window.

"Not for long," Juliette said in reply, in promise. "Not if I can help it."

Her hands stopped shaking.

Alisa Montagova had memorized almost every street in Shanghai. In her head, instead of dendrites and synaptic nerves, she fancied there lived a map of her city, overlying her temporal lobes and amygdala pairs until all that she was made of was the places she had been.

When Alisa went missing from the places she was *supposed* to be, she was usually listening in on someone else's conversation. Either within her own household or the whole city, Alisa wasn't picky. Sometimes she would catch the most interesting snippets of the lives around her, bits and pieces that would come together in the most unexpected ways if she heard enough from different people.

Today was a disappointment.

Sighing, Alisa climbed out of the vent she had squirmed herself into, giving up on the argument between Mr. Lang and his elderly mother. There had been some rumors about instability within the Scarlet Gang, of Lord Cai being uprooted by his brother-in-law, but that proved to be a load of baloney. The only threat Mr. Lang posed was boring the ears off his own mother, whom he was visiting in her small city apartment, constantly complaining about the way she made her dumplings.

"Oh dear," Alisa said to herself. She peered down from the third-story rooftop she had found herself on, scratching her head. An hour ago, she had managed to sneak up here by climbing atop a street vendor's stall. It had cost her only one cent (to buy a vegetable bun) and then the old man had let her scramble onto the structure to get a leg onto the window ledge of the apartment block's second floor.

Since then the vendor had packed up and taken his conveniently tall cart with him.

Grimacing, Alisa searched for a ledge that could close the distance between the second floor and the hard ground, but she couldn't see anything of use on this side of the building. She would have to find another way down, and quickly too. The sun was hastening its descent, and Roma had threatened to take away all her shoes if she didn't attend the meeting tonight, which, to Alisa, was a threat that shook her to her easily cold toes.

"They will scrutinize us down to every last detail," Roma had said. "They're going to watch Papa's every move. They're going to notice Dimitri's prominence. *Don't* let them notice that you're missing too."

So Alisa pinched her nose and slid down the water pipe into the alleyway behind the building. There was so much trash dumped here that she even had trouble breathing through her mouth. It was as if the stench were being absorbed through her tongue.

Grumbling, Alisa waded through the trash, trying to estimate how late she was running. The sun was already too low, almost out of sight within the city, tucked behind the buildings in the distance. She was so preoccupied with her worrying that she almost didn't hear the wheezing until she passed right by.

Alisa froze.

"Hello?" she said, switching to the first Chinese dialect that her tongue landed on. "Is someone there?"

And in Russian, a weak voice replied: *"Here."*

Alisa scrambled back, hurrying through the trash bags in search of the person who had spoken. Her gaze landed on a blot of red. When she waded closer, the shape of a man appeared amid the trash by the wall.

He was lying in a pool of his own blood, his throat torn to shreds.

"Oh no."

It didn't take Alisa's usual genius to work out that this man was a victim of the madness tearing through Shanghai. She had heard her brother whispering about it, but he wouldn't tell her anything concrete, and he would never discuss it in the places she could listen in on. Perhaps he did that on purpose.

Alisa didn't recognize the victim before her, but he was a White Flower, and by the look of his clothes, he was supposed to be working a shift at the nearby ports. Alisa paused, unsteady. Her brother had warned her to stay far, far away from anyone who looked like they were even a little unbalanced.

But Alisa never listened. She dropped to her knees.

"Help!" she screamed. "Help!"

A sudden burst of activity erupted at the end of the alleyway, confused, annoyed muttering from other nearby White Flowers coming to see what the fuss was about. Alisa put her ear to the dying man's mouth, needing to hear if he was still breathing, if he was still alive.

She was just in time to catch his last, long sigh.

Gone.

Alisa rocked back, stunned.

The other White Flowers gathered around her, their annoyance transforming into sorrow as soon as they understood why Alisa had been screaming. Many took off their hats and held them to their chests. They were not surprised to see such a sight before them. They appeared resigned—another death to add to the hundreds that had already occurred before their eyes.

"Run along, little one," the White Flower closest to Alisa told her gently.

Alisa got to her feet slowly, letting the men deal with their own fallen. Somehow, in a daze, she navigated herself back onto the streets, looking up at the orange sky.

The meeting!

She started sprinting, cursing under her breath as she pulled up her mental map for the fastest route. Alisa was by the Huangpu River already, but the address she had memorized was much farther south, in the industrial sector of Nanshi, where the cotton mills rumbled and buildings turned from commercial to industrial.

The rival gangs were to meet there, far from the defined lines of their territories, far from the thoroughly established definitions of what was Scarlet and what was White Flower. In Nanshi, there were only factories. But amid those, there were either factory owners who were Scarlet funded or White Flower associated, or workers with grubby faces, living under gangster rule but ambivalent to the way the scales turned.

Some of those workers used to pledge their allegiance to one or the other, like the ones who were employed in the main city. Then the rural wages started to drop and the factory owners started getting richer. Then the Communists came in and started to whisper in their ears about revolution, and after all, you could only have a revolution if you cut off the heads of those in power.

Alisa flagged a rickshaw and clambered onto the seat. The man pulling it gave her a strange look, probably wondering if she was old enough to be running around on her own. Or maybe he thought her an escapee, one of those Russian dancers in the clubs fleeing her debts. Those girls were the cheapest stage props in all of Shanghai—too Western-looking to be Chinese and too Eastern-acting to be exotically foreign.

"Keep going until the buildings look like they're falling apart," Alisa told the rickshaw driver.

The rickshaw started moving.

By the time Alisa arrived, the sun was almost completely under the horizon, only a wedge floating above the jaundiced waves. She idled before the building that Roma had described, confused and shivering with the first hints of the nighttime cold. Her gaze swiveled from the closed door of the abandoned warehouse to ten paces left of it, where a Chinese girl was looking out into the river. This far south, the Huangpu was a different color. Almost foggier. Maybe it was because of the smoke that drifted through the air around them, some from the nearby flour mill, some from the adjacent oil mill. The French Water Works establishment was nearby too. No doubt that network was doing its part clogging up the place. Alisa stepped forward hesitantly, hoping to ask the girl for confirmation of their location. Her fur shrug was ruffling in the breeze, all of it some shade of orange under the sunset.

"It hasn't started yet. Don't worry."

Alisa blinked at the Russian words, taken aback for a short moment. Everything made more sense when the girl turned around and Alisa recognized her face.

"Juliette," Alisa said without thinking. She gulped then, wondering if she would get hit for using the heiress's name so casually.

But Juliette's focus was on the lighter in her hand. She was playing with it flippantly, turning the spark wheel and then quenching the flame as soon as it burst to life. "Alisa, yes?"

That came as a surprise. Everyone in Shanghai knew of Roma. They knew of his cold blood and his reputation as the careful, calculating heir of the White Flowers. But Alisa, who had little to do with anything, was a ghost.

"How did you know?"

Juliette finally looked up and raised an eyebrow, as if replying, *Why would I not?*

"You and Roma practically share a face," she said. "I hazarded a guess."

Alisa didn't know what to say to that; nor did she know what to say next in general. She was saved by a young White Flower opening the door to the warehouse and sticking his head out, spotting Alisa first and then glaring at Juliette. The animosity wasn't unexpected, even if they were supposed to be playing nice today. Merely organizing this meeting had put five of their men in the hospital after one of the messages being run into Scarlet territory had been delivered a little violently.

"You better come in, Miss Montagova," the boy said. "Your brother is asking after you."

Alisa nodded, but her curious gaze kept going back to Juliette.

"Aren't you coming in?"

Juliette smiled. There was some hidden amusement in that, the sort with a cause everyone would wonder about but no one would ever know.

"In a moment. You go ahead."

Alisa hurried inside.

The climate within the warehouse could be best described as frosty. Lord Cai and Lord Montagov were simply staring at each other from opposite sides of the room, both seated behind their respective tables on their halves of the warehouse.

There weren't many people here, and though the warehouse was small, the attendee numbers were meager enough for the space to feel roomy. Alisa counted less than twenty on each side, which was good. Gangsters had dispersed themselves into small clumps, pretending to be in conversation, but really, each side was watching the other closely, waiting for the slightest indication of an ambush. At the very least, it was unlikely any of these gangsters would act without instruction from Lord Cai or Lord Montagov. This meeting had forbidden upper-tier members of both the Scarlet Gang and the White Flowers from attending unless they were in the inner circle. Those with power were harder to control. Meanwhile, the errand runners and messengers in attendance did what they were told and conveniently acted as human shields in case things got messy.

She spotted Roma in the corner, standing stoic and far from

Benedikt and Marshall. When he caught sight of Alisa, he waved her over vigorously.

"About time."

Roma handed her the jacket he had been carrying in his hands. He brought it along because he knew Alisa always forgot her jackets and inevitably ended up shivering in the cold.

"Sorry," she said, shrugging on the jacket. "Has anything interesting happened yet?"

Alisa ran her eyes along the table on their side. Their father was seated icily. Beside him, Dimitri lounged back, one of his feet propped up against his other knee.

Roma shook his head.

"Why are you so late?"

Alisa swallowed hard. "I ran into someone interesting outside."

As if the mere mention of her was a summoning, Juliette came through the door then. Heads turned in her direction, but she simply looked ahead, her eyes speaking of no emotion.

Roma's mouth formed into a hard line.

"I shouldn't have to tell you this," he said quietly, "but stay well away from her. Juliette Cai is dangerous."

Alisa rolled her eyes. "Surely you don't believe those stories about her killing her American lovers with her bare hands—"

Roma cut her off with a sharp look. His scowl didn't last long, however, because his attention was wandering off, and whatever he had registered caused him to tense all over.

Alisa followed his gaze, confused. Juliette's expression was no longer one of cynical amusement. She nodded once at Roma. Noting Roma's equally serious expression, Alisa decided that she was definitely missing something here.

"Alisa."

She snapped her eyes back, facing her brother, who had already looked away.

"What?"

Roma frowned, then reached over and eased her hands away from her head. She hadn't even noticed that she was scratching intensely, pulling white-blond strands of hair out from their roots so that they were twisted around her fingertips like ropes of jewelry.

"Sorry," Alisa said, knotting her hands together behind her back. A hot prickling was spreading down her skin. It was possible that she was overheating with her jacket on, but a line of goose bumps along her collarbone said otherwise. "I'm so warm."

"What, do you want me to fan you?" Roma muttered. He pulled out a chair for Alisa, then took his own. "Sit still. Let's hope this doesn't go to shit."

Alisa nodded and sat back, trying not to scratch.

When Juliette walked into the room, it was the weight of her gun pressed against her thigh that focused her against the weight of the stares. She nodded at her parents to acknowledge that she had arrived, then moved her gaze across the rest of the room. In the first few seconds, she took in every face, matched them to a name, then ranked them in order of dangerousness.

There was Dimitri Voronin, who she had heard was aggressive and impossible to control, but today Lord Montagov valued diplomacy—or so he claimed—and so Dimitri would remain quiet. There was Marshall Seo, twirling what looked like a blade of grass between his fingers as if it were a real blade. Beside him, Benedikt Montagov sat with a neutral expression, looking like a pensive stone statue.

And there was, of course, Roma.

Juliette joined Rosalind and Kathleen at their seats, pulling a chair out and dropping in. With great reluctance, she concluded that none of the White Flowers seemed more volatile than Tyler, who was practically trembling in his seat in effort to keep silent.

"This is for you," Kathleen said, noting Juliette's arrival.

She slid over a square piece of paper. Juliette lifted a corner and read the brief scribblings of numbers and street names. Kathleen had done it. She had met with her contact again and retrieved Zhang Gutai's personal address.

"Did you find anything at the Bund?" Juliette asked, tucking the address away.

"The bankers were clueless," Kathleen replied. "Only one old woman had any information and she thought she saw a monster *in* the river."

Juliette chewed over the thought. She said, "Interesting."

Rosalind cleared her throat, leaning in. "What are we whispering about?"

"Oh." Juliette waved a hand. "Nothing important."

Rosalind narrowed her eyes. It looked as if she was going to say more, accuse Juliette of being dismissive. It would not have been undeserved—Juliette truly was trying to shut down unnecessary expansion on the subject, to keep quiet while they were in a warehouse full of White Flowers. But Rosalind took the hint. She changed the topic.

"Take a look at Tyler. He's two seconds away from throwing a tantrum."

Juliette turned around, her face pinched with distaste. His trembling had only intensified. "Maybe we should ask him to leave."

"No." Kathleen shook her head, then rose from her seat. "I'll talk to him. Asking him to leave would be making more trouble."

Before Juliette or Rosalind could protest, Kathleen was already off, pushing her chair back and walking toward Tyler, dropping into the seat beside him. Juliette and Rosalind couldn't hear what Kathleen was saying, but they could see that Tyler wasn't listening, even when Kathleen reached for his elbow and gave him a sharp shake.

"She's too kindhearted for her own good," Rosalind remarked.

"Let her be," Juliette replied. "Too many kind hearts turn cold every day."

A hush started to sweep through the warehouse. The meeting was starting. From the corner of her eye, Juliette caught sight of Roma's gaze once again. She wished Roma would stop looking at her. This whole thing felt strange for both obvious reasons and reasons she couldn't precisely decipher. In bringing the Scarlet Gang and White Flowers together, it felt like cooperation, but it also felt like defeat.

But they had no choice.

"Well, I hope everyone's having a nice evening."

Silence followed Lord Montagov's words immediately. He spoke in the Beijing dialect, the most common Chinese tongue that the merchants and foreign businessmen learned first, but it was accented. The older generation was not as fluent as their children.

"I will proceed right to the point," he said. "There is madness in this city, and it is killing Scarlets and White Flowers alike."

Lord Montagov seemed pleasant enough. If Juliette didn't know better, she would think him patient and unbothered.

"I'm sure that all will agree with me, then," he continued, "that this must stop. Man-made disease or natural occurrence, we need answers. We need to figure out why it is affecting our people so heavily, and then we need to put a stop to it."

Only silence followed.

"Really?" a sardonic voice said. It was not directed at Lord Montagov, but at the silent Scarlet Gang. Marshall Seo stood up. "While the whole city dies, you still refuse to speak?"

"It is simply in my belief," Lord Cai said coldly, "that when one announces a plan to put a stop to the madness, they should offer some of their own ideas first."

"Was it not your daughter who suggested this meeting?"

This came from Dimitri Voronin, who shrugged in a blasé, God-could-care sort of way.

"Our daughter," Lady Cai cut in, her tone thunderous, "sought to begin a dialogue. It was not a promise nor the guarantee of an exchange."

"Typical," Dimitri scoffed.

That remark didn't sit well with the Scarlet Gang. The errand runners who surrounded Lord Cai twitched in their seats, their hands inching closer and closer to the guns hidden at their hips. Lord Cai made an impatient gesture, telling everyone to calm down.

"This is the situation at present," Lord Cai said. He placed his hands upon the table, palms flat on the cold surface. "Under the current circumstances, we have leads and sources to work with should we wish to investigate this madness."

Lord Montagov opened his mouth, but Juliette's father was not done.

"That means," Lord Cai pressed on, "we do not *need* your help. Understand? We are here in *hopes* of furthering our knowledge and quickening our investigation. That is the position of the Scarlet Gang. Now, do the White Flowers wish to share their knowledge, their ideas, and indeed begin a cooperation, or did they attend this meeting simply to leech, as they have been doing for decades?"

While the back-and-forth occurred, eyes were shifting left and right; gazes met in all directions. Everybody was having an unspoken conversation, one person asking the ubiquitous question and another giving the most minuscule shake of the head.

It occurred to Juliette then that perhaps the White Flowers offered no further avenues of investigation because they had none to give. But to the White Flowers, admitting that they were clueless was just as bad as offering up all their trade secrets. It gave away power. They would rather have the Scarlet Gang think them hostile.

And some members of the Scarlet Gang bought it.

As Marshall Seo scoffed at the insult, muttering some inaudible retort beneath his breath, Tyler leaped to his feet, unable to hold himself back any longer. In two, three strides, he had crossed the divide.

Then Benedikt raised his gun, and Tyler froze in place.

The room collectively stopped breathing, uncertain what to do next, if now was a good time to react violently, if the simple act of raising a gun prompted retaliation. Juliette touched her own weapon, but she was more bothered with analyzing this turn of events, trying to connect them logically.

Marshall with the calloused hands was the one who had been threatened, but Benedikt with the paint-smudged fingers was the one reacting instead.

Juliette's hands moved away from the holster at her thigh. She understood. Benedikt had raised his gun to prevent Marshall from doing so first. Marshall would shoot, but Benedikt wouldn't.

"We thought this meeting was supposed to be peaceful," Benedikt said quietly, an attempt to unknot the tension before him. He didn't know who he was dealing with. Tyler wasn't one for reason; he lashed out and thought through how to weasel himself out of the consequences later.

"Oh, that's rich," Tyler sneered. "Whip out your gun and then claim you're talking of peace. *Peace.*"

In a flash, Tyler's own double-action revolver was in his hand and pointed at Benedikt. Juliette was on her feet in an instant, moving so fast that her chair fell over, only Tyler was faster and he was already pressing down on the trigger.

"I hate that word like I hate all you Montagovs."

He pulled the trigger. The sound of the shot echoed into the warehouse, provoked gasps from every direction.

But Benedikt only blinked, unharmed.

Juliette halted in her steps, breathing hard, her eyes wide as she turned around and searched for Kathleen.

Kathleen winked at Juliette upon making eye contact. She opened her palm to show her the six little bullets that rested there.

There had been no damage, but the damage was done. Chairs

were scraping back and gangsters were jumping to their feet; pistols were pointed and safeties were pulled; barrels were aimed—steady, even as the shouting began.

"If this is the way it is going to be," Lord Montagov announced above the noise and the accusations and the heated swearing, "then the Scarlet Gang and the White Flowers shall *never* cooperate—"

He didn't finish his declaration.

A choking noise was coming from the corner of the warehouse—a quiet gasping, over and over again. In confusion, the gangsters searched for the source, wary for any sense of a trick.

They didn't expect the noise to be coming from Alisa Montagova, who wheezed one last time before dropping to her knees, her fingers launching at her own throat.

Seventeen

Roma lunged for his sister, tearing her hands away from her throat in the flash of a second. Before she could shake him off with the frenzy of the madness, he already had her pinned to the ground, her hands twisted behind her back and her head pressed to the hard, concrete ground.

"Alisa, it's me. *It's me*," Roma gasped. Alisa tried to jerk forward. Roma hissed, craning his head back. "Stop that!"

He should have known better than to waste breath trying to talk her out of it. The madness was far from the whims of an unruly child. This was no longer only his sister—something had consumed her from the inside out.

"Help!" Roma called over his shoulder. "Get help!"

The White Flowers around him—each and every single one of them—hesitated. On the far side of the warehouse, the Scarlet Gang were ushering themselves out, leaving as fast as they could. This was not their problem to deal with, after all. When Juliette gave the appearance of lingering, her mother immediately pulled her away by the elbow and snapped something brief, as if speed was of the essence when outrunning a contagion.

At least they had a right to flee. What were the White Flowers doing flinching back?

"Don't just stand there!"

Benedikt finally snapped out of his daze and rushed over, rolling his sleeves up. He knelt and pinned one of Alisa's kicking legs to the floor. Face paling, Marshall was forced to join them too by mere principle, pinning down the other leg and snapping his fingers to prompt the messengers nearby.

"Roma," Benedikt said. "We have to take her to Lourens."

"Absolutely *not*." With his fervent exclamation, Roma almost lost his grip on Alisa's violent writhing. He quickly pinned her wrists down again. "We're not bringing Alisa in to be Lourens's experiment."

"How do you know that it won't do good?" Benedikt argued. His words were short and abrupt, a result of his exertion. "Those things are probably eating away at her brain as we speak. If we haven't tried removing them, how do we know we cannot?"

"Ben," Marshall chided. For once, on an occasion such as this, his strained voice was the quietest of the three. "We tried removing a *dead* thing from a *dead* man and we pulled out ten tons of brain matter. How can we risk it?"

"What *choice* is there?" Benedikt demanded.

Marshall let go of Alisa's leg, throwing the task between Roma and Benedikt to manage, then hurried to crouch near her head. "There is always a choice."

Marshall put his hands around Alisa's throat and squeezed. It took every working cell of Roma's rational mind not to attack his friend, not to push him away as Marshall counted beneath his breath. He knew exactly what Marshall was doing, knew that it was the necessary thing to do, but he burned with the need to protect.

Alisa stopped struggling. Marshall let go quickly, removing his hands like he had been scalded, then reaching back over again to check for her pulse.

He nodded. "She's okay. Only unconscious."

Heart thudding, Roma looped an arm around Alisa's neck, picking his little sister up like she weighed nothing—a paper doll of a girl. When Roma turned around, he saw that the warehouse was close to empty. Where the hell was his *father*?

"Let's go," Roma snapped, pushing the thought away for a later time. "We have to find the nearest hospital before she wakes up."

"Let me through!"

Roma slammed his fists on the door, shaking the frame so hard that the floor beneath his feet shuddered in fear. It didn't matter; the hinges stood strong, and on the other side, through the thin pane of glass, the doctor shook his head, telling Roma to turn around and go back to the waiting room, where the rest of the White Flowers had been told to remain.

"Let us take it from here," the doctor had said when they brought Alisa in. This hospital was smaller than some of the mansions on Bubbling Well Road, barely the size of a house that a British merchant might buy for his mistress. It was pitiful, but their best option. There was no telling how long Alisa could hold out, so they couldn't risk venturing out of Nanshi and into the city central. Even if this hospital was built to treat the frequent accidents of the nearby cotton mill workers. Even if Roma was convinced the weary-eyed doctors here did not look any more competent than the average street vendor.

"Keep her under," Roma had demanded as he handed Alisa over. "She needs oxygen, a feeding tube—"

"We must wake her up to know what is wrong," the doctor insisted. "We know what we are doing—"

"This is not a common sickness," Roma thundered. "This is *madness*."

The doctor had waved for his nurses, waved for them to push Roma out.

"Don't you dare," Roma warned. He was forced back a step, then two. "No—stop. Don't you dare lock me out—"

They had locked him out.

Now Roma slammed his fist on the door one last time, then pivoted on his feet, swearing viciously under his breath. He tugged on his hair, then tugged on his sleeves, pulling at everything in his immediate vicinity just to keep his hands moving, just to keep the sweats at bay and his anger concentrated in a tightly regulated radius. That was the problem with places like this—establishments far removed from the city central and run by people making pitiful wages. They did not fear the gangsters as much as they should.

"Roma!"

Roma squeezed his eyes shut. He let out a long, excruciating breath, then turned to face his father.

"What is the meaning of this?" Lord Montagov demanded. He had arrived with five men behind him, and now they all piled into this thin section of the hospital until the room felt airtight, until the off-white walls were almost slick with sweat. "How did this happen?"

Roma turned his gaze to the ceiling, counting backward from ten. He noted all the various cracks in the chipping paint, the way that decay seemed to lurk in every corner. This hospital seemed so industrial from the outside, so different from the Scarlet-funded facility in the French Concession that Juliette had taken him to, but they were each falling apart in their own way.

"What are you doing merely standing there?" Lord Montagov went on. He reached out to scuff Roma over the head.

That was the final thing to send Roma veering off the rails.

"What took *you* so damn long to get here?"

Lord Montagov narrowed his eyes. "Watch yourself—"

"Alisa was *dying*, and you merely stood by to watch how the Scarlet Gang would react? What's wrong with you?"

One of Lord Montagov's men shoved Roma back the moment

Roma leaned in too close. Perhaps it was something in his eyes, or something about the way fury set his words on fire. Whatever it was, it must have been threatening, because with a nod from Lord Montagov, the White Flower pulled a knife on Roma in threat for him to step back.

Roma remained where he was. "Go ahead," he said.

"You are making a fool of yourself," his father hissed. Lord Montagov thrived off the love of other people. He preened when surrounded and raged when stared at. Roma's dramatics were embarrassing him, and that gave Roma a perverse sort of pleasure.

"If I am a fool, then be rid of me." Roma splayed his arms. "Have Dimitri investigate this madness instead. Or better yet, why don't you yourself take it on?"

Lord Montagov made no move to answer him. If they were alone, his father would be yelling, hands slapping whatever flat surface was closest to make a loud noise—any loud noise, for as long as it could make Roma flinch, his father would be satisfied.

It wasn't obedience that Lord Montagov sought. It was the reassurance of his power.

At this moment Roma was reckless enough to take that away.

"I suppose you are too busy. I suppose Dimitri has more important tasks to uphold, more important people to sweet-talk. Or perhaps"—Roma's voice grew quiet, speaking like he was reciting a poem—"it is because neither you nor Dimitri is brave enough to get close to the madness. You fear for yourself more than you fear for our people."

"You—"

A terrifying scream rang from within the locked doors, and Roma pivoted immediately, uncaring if his sudden movements earned him a knife in his back. He was already reaching into his coat pocket and drawing his gun, shooting once, twice, three times until the glass panel of the door crumbled entirely, opening a space for him to insert his arm through and turn the lock on the other side.

"Alisa," he bellowed, slamming open the doors. *"Alisa!"*

He skidded into the emergency room, a hand slamming up to cover his eyes from the harsh lights fixed to the droopy ceilings. Nobody objected to his presence. They were far too busy grabbing ahold of Alisa's writhing body, keeping her still for just long enough to press a syringe into her neck. She fell slack in seconds, the bloodstained strands of her lanky blond hair falling over her eyes.

"What did you do to her?" Roma demanded, rushing forward. He brushed her hair back, swallowing the lump in his throat. Her eyelids—so pale and translucent under this lighting that her blue-purple veins stood out starkly—fluttered briefly, then remained closed.

The doctor, the same one who had locked him out and assured him of his sister's safety cleared his throat. Roma looked to him, barely holding back his anger.

"We have injected her to keep her comatose." The doctor thinned his lips, then scrubbed his forehead vigorously, as if he was thinking through a fog in his mind. "I—we—" He cleared his throat, then tried again. "We do not know what is wrong with her. She must remain asleep until there is a cure."

Eighteen

Roma descended the stairs. Though his physical body had carried him here, had moved him through the motions of waving his thanks at the bartender, through lifting the curtain at the back of the bar, his head remained miles away, still hovering outside the hospital room and watching Alisa in her induced coma—her arms and legs strapped down to the bed for her own safety.

"I am undefeated!"

At the roar that traveled up the spiraling staircase, Roma's mind returned to him, and his anger slammed back into full force. Blood boiling, he jumped the last five steps, landing upon the floorboards with a heavy, wooden *thump*.

Roma ventured deeper into this shallow underground, navigating the room underneath the bar. The construction of this place had sucked up almost all of his father's funds a few years back—the floors were uneven from overuse and the lights on the low ceiling flickered on and off at random. It smelled of sweat and piss and there were so many voices shouting over one another that this could have been a gathering for delinquents, but there was no doubting the exorbitant design of this place. One look was enough—at the fighting pit in the center of the room, at the flashes of silver built into the ropes that secured the ring—

to know that this underground arena was one of Lord Montagov's most prized investments. It was no wonder, given the betting charges down here had earned him back his losses within weeks.

"Don't you two have better things to do than hang out amid all this?"

Roma dropped into a seat at a spectator's table, inspecting the ceramic cups in front of Benedikt and Marshall.

"That's what I've been saying," Benedikt replied.

"This is the last time. I promise," Marshall said. "Afterward—*no, get him by the legs!*"

Marshall's attention had been drawn away momentarily by the fight. The crowd around the barrier cheered as the loser went down and the victor pumped his fists into the air.

"Terrible form," Marshall muttered, turning his gaze back.

Disgruntled, Roma lifted the cup in front of Benedikt and took a cautionary sniff. His cousin snatched it from his hands.

"Don't drink that," Benedikt warned.

"Vodka?" Roma asked in response, at last identifying the smell that had been wafting under his nose. "In a teacup? Really?"

"Not my idea."

Marshall leaned in with a sly grin. "Yes, don't blame your sweet cousin. It was mine."

Their table suddenly shuddered with the impact of another man going down in the ring, the crowd roaring with cheers. A woman was marking the scores with a piece of chalk. In flocks before every fight, spectators ran to her with cash, calling out bets on who would win.

Roma wasn't entirely surprised to see Dimitri Voronin stepping into the ring next. He seemed like the type to spend all his free time down here, mingling with the filth that coated the floors and feeling right at home. Roma, meanwhile, made it his goal to avoid this place. He would come down only if the matter couldn't wait, as was the case now.

"I just spoke with my father at home," Roma said. He angled his head so he didn't have to watch Dimitri pump his fists and bare his teeth to the crowd. "He has stopped caring about the madness. He thinks it is something that can be waited out. He thinks that Alisa will simply wake up and snap out of it when she has grown tired of trying to tear out her throat."

That was a half truth. Lord Montagov no longer wished to investigate the madness, but it was not apathy. It was because Roma had hit a nerve and struck him right where it hurt most. This inaction was punishment. For calling his own father a coward, Lord Montagov would show him just how cowardly he could be, and let Alisa wilt away.

"He is an idiot." Marshall paused. "No offense."

"None taken," Roma muttered. It was as if his father did not realize that they could not run a gang without gangsters. Lord Montagov had too much confidence in himself—most of it undeserved. If the worst-case scenario arrived, he probably thought he could face off with death and demand their assets back.

"I have to do something." Roma held his head in his hands. "But short of siphoning all of our funds to the lab so Lourens has more resources to work on a cure—"

"Hold on," Marshall said. "Why wait for Lourens to make a cure from square one when there is word on the street about someone already having made a vaccine? We can steal the vaccine, run our research—"

"There is no way to know if the vaccine is real," Benedikt cut in. "If you are speaking about the Larkspur, he sounds like an utter charlatan."

Roma nodded in agreement. He had heard the rumors too, but it was nonsense—merely a way to profit off the panic sweeping through the city. If trained doctors could barely understand the mechanisms of this madness, how could one foreign man have dreamed up the cure?

"We must still find that live victim Lourens requires," Roma decided. "But . . ."

The sound of bones being crushed rang out from the ring, and the woman shouted for another contestant to take on the "godly Dimitri Voronin." Roma cringed, wishing he could block out all the noise.

From the table beside them, a man rose and ran up excitedly.

"But," Roma tried to continue over the uproar, watching the man go with a grimace, "we cannot sit idle and wait for a cure that Lourens may or may not find. And truly, I am at a loss as to what else—"

A roar came from the crowds then, this one not of murderous joy but of outrage and disappointment. Roma whipped around, cursing when he saw why the fight had been interrupted.

Dimitri had pulled a gun on his next competitor.

Benedikt and Marshall rose, but Roma quickly held out a hand, telling them to sit down. Dimitri's competitor, on closer appraisal, was not Russian. Roma had missed it before in his cursory glance when the man was running up, but the sweep of pomade in his hair gave him away as American.

"Let's calm down now, old boy." The American laughed nervously. His accent confirmed Roma's assessment. "I thought this was a fight, not a showdown in the Wild West."

Dimitri pulled a face, failing to comprehend what the American was saying. "Scarlet merchants who sneak in here face the consequences."

His competitor's eyes widened. "I—I'm not with the Scarlet Gang."

"You trade with the Scarlet Gang. I have seen your face on their side of the streets."

"But I am not affiliated," the man protested.

"In this city, you are one or the other."

Roma got out of his chair. He cast his two friends a sharp look, warning them not to follow, then turned, his face locked in its harsh expression. The American continued stammering away in the ring. Dimitri strode closer with his gun. By the time Roma had pushed his way through the crowd and climbed over the ropes, Dimitri was directly in front of the American, his nostrils flared wide in his anger.

What is he so worked up about? Roma genuinely wondered. Slights like these could be easily ignored. It wasn't as if this man was a true Scarlet. If he was stupid enough to come into a White Flower fight club, his ship had probably landed in Shanghai only days ago.

Roma jumped into the ring, his steps smooth until he was sliding right between the American and Dimitri's barrel. "That's enough."

"Move, Roma," Dimitri thundered. He pushed his gun forward in threat, until the cool metal pressed an indent into Roma's forehead. "Run off—this does not concern you."

"Or what?" Roma replied coolly. "You'll shoot me?"

Up here, under these lights, surrounded by a crowd of White Flowers, Roma was safer than he could ever be. There was a gun to his head, but he was unafraid. Dimitri had one choice here, and with an ear perked to the dissatisfied screaming coming from the spectators, he seemed to be realizing that Roma had him trapped. To Dimitri, perhaps Roma was the annoying kid in the household that Lord Montagov did not trust. To the people around them, Roma was heir of the White Flowers—a killer of Scarlets and neck-deep in every drop of blood he had spilled in the name of vengeance. Like it or not, Roma was still a Montagov, and Montagovs had power. If Roma said this American wasn't a Scarlet, he wasn't a Scarlet.

Roma waved for the American to leave.

But as soon as the American stepped out of the ring, hurrying for the exit, Dimitri aimed and shot him anyway.

"No!" Roma roared.

The crowd became a mixed cacophony of cheering and horrified booing, split between those who had secretly been waiting for Dimitri to draw the blood they craved and those who were eyeing the situation warily now, wondering what role Roma played here if he could not get Dimitri to listen to him.

Roma had been simmering all day. He could not get the doctors to heed his demands. He could not convince his own father to see reason. He was the heir of the White Flowers—heir to an underground empire made of killers and gangsters and toughened merchants who had fled a country ravaged by war. If he could not hold on to their respect, could not rule over them and feed on their fear, then what the *hell* did he have?

Dimitri made one move against him, and suddenly Roma was surrounded by the jeering of the people he was supposed to command, looked at as if he were a *child* and not their heir. If it had been Dimitri at the hospital, perhaps the doctors would have listened. If Dimitri had told Lord Montagov that the madness was threatening the city more furiously than they had ever anticipated, Lord Montagov would have listened.

Roma's control was slipping through his fingers like fine grains of sand. When he closed his fist, there were almost no grains left for him to hold on to. His hands were almost empty.

If he lost the respect of these White Flowers around him, he lost his status. If he was no longer Roma Montagov, heir of the White Flowers, then he could not protect those he actually cared to keep safe.

He had already failed Alisa.

He didn't want to keep failing.

"We will not tolerate the Scarlet Gang!" Dimitri was pumping his fists up and down, his handgun raising and lowering callously, riling up the spectators. "We will kill them *all*!"

A long time ago, Roma had told Juliette that her anger was like a cold diamond. It was something she could swallow smoothly, something to be placed upon other people, gliding along their skin in glitter and glamour before they realized far too late that the diamond had sliced them into pieces. He had admired her for it. Mostly because his own anger was the precise opposite—an uncontrollable wave of fire that knew no subtlety.

And it had arrived.

In two quick motions, Roma lunged for Dimitri and disarmed him, throwing the gun into the crowd.

"You didn't give the American a fair fight," Roma said. He gestured for Dimitri to approach. "So I'll let you make it up."

The crowd screamed their approval. Dimitri stood still for a second, trying to decipher Roma's motivation. Then, with a glance outward into the cheering, he cricked his neck and charged.

Roma refused to let this descend into the monstrous, bestial grappling that these places were known for. As soon as he slammed his arm up for his first block, he remained quick, light on his feet, each one of his punches thrown with intent. The ring was rocking with the intensity of the spectators, the entire club raging so loudly that its sounds were ringing with a faint echo.

To the observers, everything was a rapid blur.

To Roma, it was all instinct. He had spent years pretend sparring with Benedikt, and it was finally counting for something. Roma switched from offense to defense within heartbeats; his right arm came up to block a punch and his left arm tore forward at the same time, landing a hit so solidly upon Dimitri's jaw that the other boy stumbled back, a mania playing in his eyes.

It did not matter how furious Dimitri was. Roma was not tiring. It almost felt supernatural, this exhilaration rushing through the lines of his limbs, this pulsating, absolute need to *win* against the favorite, to have the people remember who was the actual Montagov and who was the fraud, who was the one deserving of dignity as the heir.

Then Dimitri got a hit on Roma's cheek, and something *stung*, far more than he expected.

Roma hissed, stumbling back three steps to gather his bearings. Dimitri swung his arms, rolling out his shoulders, and under the lights, a flash of something glinted between his index and middle fingers.

He has a blade between his fingers, Roma realized dimly. Then, as if it was new information: *Cheater.*

"Ready to give up?" Dimitri bellowed. He thumped his chest. Roma could not look away from the glinting flashes of the blade. He couldn't stop the fight now without losing face. But if he continued, all it would take was one swipe of Dimitri's fist across Roma's neck to kill him.

The panic set in. Roma started to get sloppy. Dimitri kicked out and Roma took the hit. A fist flashed in his periphery, and in his haste to get away, Roma dodged too hard, overjudging his balance and stumbling. Dimitri struck again. A flash of the blade: a slit opened on Roma's jaw.

The crowd jeered. They could sense Roma's energy depleting. They could sense that he seemed to have given up before the fight had even finished.

Are you a Montagov, or are you a coward?

Roma tore his gaze back up, steeling his throbbing jaw. What was he fighting so damn fair for? What kind of deluded world was he living in where the White Flowers wanted someone who ruled by honor, instead of sweat and blood and violence?

Roma reached out and grabbed a fistful of Dimitri's shoulder-length black hair. Dimitri hadn't been expecting it. Nor had he expected Roma to slam a knee right into his nose, to take his arm and twist backward until Roma had a grip on his neck and a foot stomping down on the back of his knees.

Dimitri fell flat to the ground of the ring. The crowd rushed for the ropes, shaking and shaking and shaking the ring.

Roma had him now. With his hands positioned where they were, he could snap Dimitri's neck if he wanted. He could do anything and play it off as a mere accident—a slip of the moment.

"Roma Montagov, our victor!" the woman with the chalkboard announced.

Roma leaned down to Dimitri, close enough so Dimitri could not mishear his words over the roar of the crowd.

"Don't you forget who I am."

With that, he stood, wiping his forearm across his bleeding mouth roughly. He ducked under the ropes and landed solidly amid the crowd. This place was a boiling pot of volatile activity and emotions. Roma couldn't get away fast enough.

"You," he snapped. A man with a white handkerchief in his pocket jerked to attention. "Get someone to take the American's corpse out of here."

The man ran off to fulfill his task. Roma found his way back to his friends, dropping into his seat with the weight of a thousand years.

"What a hero," Marshall crooned.

"Shut up," Roma said. He breathed in deeply. Again. Then again. In his head he saw the American crumple to the ground. Alisa's unmoving body. The complete lack of emotion on his father's face.

"Are you quite all right?" Benedikt asked in concern.

"Yes, I'm fine." Roma looked up with a glare. "Can we go back to what we were discussing before? With Alisa in the state she is in"—flashes of her face were burned into his mind, vivid and stark and already wasting away—"I need answers. If this madness sprouted from somebody's bad intention, I must hunt them down."

"Didn't your father send you after the Communists?"

Roma nodded. "But it's a dead end. We have only struck dead ends wherever we go."

"We could plead with the Scarlet Gang for their information," Marshall suggested. "This time with more guns—"

Benedikt pressed a hand over the Marshall's mouth, shutting him up before he could expand further on a nonsensical plan.

"Roma, I truly cannot fathom what else there is to do," Benedikt admitted. "I think the meeting made it clear that the White Flowers know nothing. We are at a loss unless we wish to spread our resources thin and put an ear in every corner of Shanghai."

"How many spies do we still have in the Scarlet Gang?" Roma

asked. "Perhaps they can figure out what it is. The Scarlet Gang practically admitted to having information, but they won't tell us—"

"I doubt asking the spies would be effective," Benedikt interrupted. His hand was still over Marshall's mouth. Marshall appeared to have started licking Benedikt's palm in an effort to be released. Benedikt acted as if he hadn't noticed. "If the Scarlet Gang really do know something, it would be discussed within the inner circle. Letting rumors slip to the regular gangsters is a surefire route toward causing panic."

Marshall finally writhed free of Benedikt's hand.

"By God, you're both dull in the head," he said. "Who in the Scarlet Gang keeps appearing everywhere you go, who appears to also have a personal stake in finding the necessary answers?" He leveled his gaze with Roma's. "You've got to ask Juliette for help."

Suddenly, Roma held up his finger, asking Benedikt and Marshall to be patient as he thought it over.

When he finally seemed to have ruminated on it for some time, he said, "Pass me that bucket over there."

Benedikt blinked. "What?"

"Bucket."

Marshall stood and retrieved the bucket. As soon as he brought it under Roma's nose, the brutal heir of the White Flowers stuck his head within it and retched as a result of all the violence at his hand.

A minute later Roma resurfaced, the contents of his stomach emptied.

"Okay," he said bitterly. "I'll ask Juliette alone for her help."

Nineteen

I'm worried. Can you blame me?"

Lady Cai pulled the brush through Juliette's hair, frowning each time she hit a tangle. Juliette was certainly old enough to manage this herself, but her mother insisted. When Juliette was a little girl with hair that grew down to her waist, her mother used to come into her room every night and brush it until all the knots were gone, or until Lady Cai was at least satisfied by the state of her daughter's head, which occasionally included the thoughts within it too. Now that Juliette was back for good, her mother had reinstated the practice. Juliette's parents were busy people. This was her mother's way of still having some role in her life.

"No matter what it is in this city, there are too many people invested," Lady Cai continued. "Too many people with personal stakes. Too many people with too much to lose." Her frown deepened as she spoke, both in accordance with the words coming out from her mouth and in frustration with her task. Juliette's hair was bobbed now—there was not much left to brush—but it was still a struggle to work through all the remnants of product that Juliette heaped on every day to maintain her curls.

"Māma, you will have more to worry about if"—Juliette winced as the brush went through a clump of gel that hadn't washed out—"the madness spreads to every corner of this city. Our dwindling numbers

213

are more a cause for concern than the toes I step on while sticking my nose into Communist business."

Dwindling numbers in the Scarlet Gang. Dwindling numbers in the White Flowers. Their blood feud was nothing compared to both gangs dying out, yet Juliette seemed to be the only person who believed this madness potent enough to sweep the rug out from under everyone. Her parents were too proud. They had grown too used to situations they could control, adversaries they could defeat. They did not see this situation as Juliette did. They did not see Alisa Montagova trying to tear out her own throat every time they closed their eyes, as Juliette did now.

The girl was so young. How had she gotten caught up in this?

"Well." Lady Cai sniffed. "It is inevitable that you shall step on some toes. It is simply that I would prefer to send men with you while you're doing so."

Juliette bristled. At the very least, her parents were taking the madness seriously now. They still did not think it required their personal interference—or rather they did not see how they could possibly be of any help when it came to a disease that had people tearing at their own throats—but they cared enough to officially put Juliette to the task, excusing her from her other duties. No more chasing rent. Juliette was on a one-woman mission for the truth.

"Please do not assign me an entourage," Juliette said, shuddering. "I could outfight them in my sleep."

Lady Cai glared at her through the mirror.

"What?" Juliette exclaimed.

"It is not about the fight," her mother replied firmly. "It is about image. It is your people having your back."

Oh God. Juliette could immediately sense the incoming lecture. It was an innate ability of hers, like how some people sensed incoming storms by the ache in their bones.

"Don't forget, your father has been overthrown once or twice during his time."

Juliette closed her eyes, sighing internally before forcing them open again. Four years had passed and her mother still delighted in recounting this story as if it taught the greatest life lesson known to mankind.

"When that despicable Montagov avenged his father's death by killing your grandfather," her mother said, "your father should have been the one to lead next."

Lady Cai pulled the brush through another knot. Juliette winced.

"But he was even younger than you are now, so the businessmen removed him and decided one of their own would have the final say. They dismissed him as nothing but a boy and said that if he wanted to lead with no reason save his bloodline, then he should join the monarchy instead of a gang. But then, in—"

"—1892," Juliette interrupted, taking over the story with theatrics, "with the people on the streets of Shanghai directionless and running amok, with both the Scarlet Gang and the White Flowers taken over by irrelevant associates while the rightful young heirs were shoved to the background, they at last revolted—"

Juliette snapped her mouth shut upon seeing the deathly glower her mother was giving her through the mirror. She grumbled an apology, folding her arms. She admired her father's ability to climb back to the top, just as she could detachedly acknowledge that Lord Montagov—who had also been uprooted when *his* father died—was intelligent enough to do the same. Except in this period of time, while both gangs were led by men who cared naught for bonds and allegiance, only efficiency and money, the blood feud had been at its *quietest*.

"Your father," Lady Cai said sharply, tugging on a strand of hair, "reclaimed his rightful title when he was older because he had people who believed in him. He appealed to the common majority—those who you see protecting him now, those who you see willing to give up their lives for him. It is all a matter of pride, Juliette." Lady Cai ducked her head, pressing her face against her daughter's until they were both staring ahead into the mirror. "He wanted the Scarlet Gang to be a force of nature. He wanted membership to be a badge that declared power. The commoners in the gang could think of nothing else more desirable, and behind him, they toppled the businessmen who had no choice but to accept their subservience."

Juliette raised an eyebrow. "In summary," she said, "it is a game of numbers."

"You could say that." Her mother clicked her tongue. "So don't start believing that skill is all it takes to stay at the top. Loyalty plays its dirty hand too, and it is a fickle, ever-changing thing."

With that Lady Cai set down her brush, squeezed Juliette's shoulder, and said good night. Brisk, quick, and abrupt—that was her mother. She strode out of Juliette's bedroom and shut the door behind her, leaving Juliette to mull on those parting words.

The rest of the world didn't see it, but while Lord Cai was the face of the Scarlet Gang, Lady Cai did just as much work behind the scenes, running her eyes through every piece of paper that passed into the house. It was Lady Cai who had convinced her husband that a daughter would be far more capable of leading the Scarlet Gang next, rather than a male relative. So Juliette had been given the crown, and Lord Cai expected the gang to bend at the knee when Juliette became the head one day—out of expectation, out of blood loyalty.

Juliette leaned toward the mirror, touching her fingers to the lines of her face.

Was it loyalty that created power? Or was loyalty only a symptom, offered when the circumstances were favorable and taken away when the tides turned? It helped that Lord Cai and Lord Montagov were men. Juliette wasn't naive. Their every messenger, every errand runner, every lower-tiered but fiercely loyal gangster was male. Most of the Scarlet Gang feared and revered Juliette now, but she was not in control yet. How would they react when Juliette tried to exert true power over them? Would she have to shed all that she was—ditch the glittery dresses and wear suits to be listened to?

Juliette finally pushed away from her vanity table, rubbing at her eyes tiredly. The day had worn on for far too long, yet her body felt restless instead of weary. When she collapsed onto the blankets atop her bed, her nightgown was sticky against her skin. She could hear her heartbeat thudding, and with the longer she lay there in the dark, the thudding only became more intense, until the sound was playing through her eardrums.

Wait—

Juliette bolted upright. Someone was *knocking* rhythmically on the glass doors of her second-floor balcony.

"No," Juliette said aloud dully.

The knocking came again, slow, purposeful.

"No," she repeated.

More knocking.

"Ah!"

Juliette clambered to her feet and stormed toward the sound, opening the curtains with more force than necessary. As the fabric settled, she found a familiar figure seated casually on the railing of her balcony, his legs swinging and his body backlit by the glow of the crescent moon. She swallowed hard.

"Really?" Juliette demanded through the glass door. "You climbed my house? You couldn't have simply thrown a few pebbles?"

Roma looked down into the gardens below. "You don't have any pebbles."

Juliette rubbed her eyes again, forcefully this time. Maybe if she rubbed hard enough, she would realize this was all a fever dream and she'd wake up peacefully alone in her room.

She removed her hand from her eyes. Roma was still there.

They really needed to upgrade their security.

"Roma Montagov, this is unacceptable," Juliette declared tightly. This was all too reminiscent, too wistful, too *much*. "Leave before you get shot."

Even with his face shrouded in the shadows, Roma managed to convey a frown that reached Juliette with maximum effect. He looked around, seeing no one in the gardens below him.

"Who will shoot me?"

"*I'm* going to shoot you," Juliette snapped.

"No, you're not. Open the door, dorogaya."

Juliette jerked back, horrified not by the command, but by his term of endearment. With delay, Roma seemed to realize too what had slipped out, his eyes widening a fraction, but he didn't fumble or take it back. He merely stared at her in wait, like he hadn't just pulled out a relic from their past, one that they had smashed to pieces.

"The door stays closed," Juliette said coldly. "What do you want?"

Roma hopped off the railing, his shoes landing on the balcony tiles with a soft sound. When he came up close against the glass, Juliette noted a deep scratch marring his jaw, and she wondered if he'd stumbled here right after a fight. It was almost enough to have her reach for her gun and really send him running, but then, quietly, Roma whispered, "I want to save my sister."

Something inside of Juliette came loose. Her hard eyes softened the smallest of fractions.

"How is Alisa?" she asked.

"They've tied her up at the hospital like some asylum patient," Roma replied. His eyes were focused on his hands. He kept flipping them over—palm, back, palm, back—searching for something that wasn't there. "She tried to go for her throat again when she regained consciousness, so they're injecting her with something to keep her asleep. They're keeping her asleep until there's some way to cure this madness."

Roma looked up. There was a madness, a desperation, in his own eyes.

"I need your help, Juliette. All the trails from my end have gone cold. There's nothing else I can chase, nowhere I can go, no one I can call. You, however—I know you know *something*."

Juliette didn't immediately respond. She stood there unmoving, wrestling with the pit in her stomach and realizing she was uncertain if this feeling was still hatred . . . or *fear*. Fear that if the madness went on, she too would find herself in Roma's position, watching someone she loved die. Fear that by mere consideration of Roma in such a sympathetic manner, she had crossed the line.

The problem with hatred was that when the initial emotion weakened, the responses still remained. The clenched fists and hot veins, the blurred vision and quickened pulse. And in such remains, Juliette was not in control of what they might develop into.

Like yearning.

"You ask me for help," Juliette said quietly, "and yet—how much blood is on your hands, Roma? In the time I was gone, how many of my people asked you for help, for mercy, right before you shot them?"

Roma's eyes were wholly black under the moonlight. "I have nothing to say to that," he answered. "The blood feud was the blood feud. This is something utterly new in itself. If we don't help each other, we may both die out."

"I am the one with information," Juliette warned, her skin pricking uncomfortably. "Try to refrain from making sweeping generalizations about us both."

"You have information, but I have the other half of the city," Roma countered. "If you act alone, that's half of Shanghai you cannot work with. If I act alone, I cannot enter any Scarlet territory. Think, Juliette—when the madness is hitting us both, there is no telling in which territory the answers will be found."

A chill swept through her room, bitter and cold and correct. Juliette tried to ignore it. She forced a laugh, the sound hard.

"As you're proving right now, I don't think a lack of permission is stopping you from prancing into my territory."

"Juliette." Roma pressed his hands against the glass. His pleading stare was utterly, utterly unguarded. "*Please*, she's my *sister*."

God—

Juliette had to look away. She couldn't bear it. The heaviness twisting her heart was undeserved. Any vulnerability that Roma Montagov showed was an act, a carefully constructed facade he would bide his time with until the chance came to strike. She *knew* this.

But perhaps Juliette would never learn. Perhaps her memories of Roma would pull her toward ruin, unless she reached into her own chest and ripped out all remains of softness.

"For Alisa," Juliette managed roughly, finally turning her gaze back, "and for all the little girls in this city falling victim to a game they never asked to play, I will help you. But do your part, Roma. I help you and you help me find the solution to this madness as quickly as possible."

Roma exhaled, breathing relief and gratitude onto the glass. She watched him carefully, watched the tension drain from his shoulders and the terror in his eyes meld into hope. She wondered how much of it was true and how much of it was for her benefit, so she would think she was making the right decision.

"Deal."

This could ruin her. It could ruin everything. But what mattered now was not Juliette, nor her feelings—it was finding a solution. If the possibility of saving her people meant risking her reputation with them, then it was a sacrifice she had to make.

Who else would make it? Who else but Juliette?

"Okay," Juliette conceded quietly. She supposed there was no going back. "I have Zhang Gutai's home address. My next move was breaking in and rummaging around, but"—she shrugged, the gesture so forcefully casual on her part that she almost believed it—"we can go there together to begin, if you wish."

"Yes," Roma said. If he nodded any harder, his head might roll right off. *"Yes."*

"Tomorrow, then," Juliette decided. Suddenly the memories of their past together—the ones she had spent four years trying so hard to *forget*—came barreling into her mind with full force. She had no choice but to invoke them, ignoring the clenching tightness in her lungs. "Meet me at the statue."

The statue—a small stone rendering of a crying woman—was a forgotten artifact hidden in an unnamed park in the International Settlement. Four years ago, Roma and Juliette had stumbled upon it by chance and spent an afternoon trying to work out its intentions and origins. Juliette had insisted it was Niobe, the woman in Greek mythology who had cried so much after her children were slain that the gods turned her to stone. Roma had maintained it was La Llorona, the Weeping Woman in Latin American folklore who cried for the child she had killed. They had never decided on an answer.

If Roma was surprised or taken aback by her reference to the statue, he didn't show it. He only asked, "When?"

"Sunrise."

It was only at that which Roma appeared mildly concerned. "Sunrise? That's ambitious."

"The earlier the better," Juliette insisted. She winced. "It reduces our chances of being seen together. This goes without saying, but no one can know we're collaborating. We would—"

"—both be dead if they knew," Roma finished. "I know. Until sunrise, then."

Juliette watched him swing his legs back over the railing of the balcony, hanging along the elaborate metal designs like another piece of the sculpting. Under the low-hanging light of the moon, Roma was a black-and-white study of sorrow.

Roma paused. "Good night, Juliette."

Then he was gone, his lithe shadow working quickly down the exterior wall and darting through the gardens. One jump and he was over the gate, off the Scarlet Gang's grounds and on his way back to his own world.

Juliette drew her curtains tightly, adjusting the fabric until not a sliver of silver was shining through. Only then did she allow herself to emit a long exhale, pushing the moonlight out of her room and its changing faces out of her heart.

Twenty

A t sunrise, it was early enough that the ports were quiet, the waves rocking against the floating boardwalk. It was early enough that the smell of the wind was still sweet, untainted by the smog of morning factories, absent of the aromas that rose from the fried food and sloppy soups cooked in the stalls pushed upon the streets.

Unfortunately, it still wasn't early enough to avoid a Nationalist rally.

Juliette halted in her step, freezing on the pavement underneath a swaying green tree. "Tā mā de," she cursed under her breath. "What are—"

"Kuomintang," Roma answered before Juliette could finish the question.

Juliette shot him a dirty look when he stopped beside her. Did he think her incapable of spotting the little suns on their hats? It wasn't exactly an obscure logo. The Kuomintang party—and their Nationalists—was growing incredibly popular.

"I *know*," Juliette said, rolling her eyes. "I was going to ask what they're doing. This is my city. I don't need you educating me."

Roma cast her a glance askew. "Is it though?"

He hadn't even put any venom behind his tone, and yet those

few words sent a dagger hurtling right through Juliette's heart. *Is it though*? How many times had she asked herself that question in Manhattan? How many times had she climbed up to her building's rooftop and gazed out on New York's skyline, refusing to let herself love it, because loving one meant losing another, and losing Shanghai meant losing everything?

"Now, what is that supposed to mean?" she asked tightly.

Roma looked almost amused by the question. He made a vague gesturing motion toward her, indicating her dress, her shoes. "Come on, Juliette. I've been here a lot longer than you have. You're an American girl at heart."

And the implication of the words left unspoken were clear: *Do us all a favor and go back.*

"Ah yes," she muttered. The sharpness in her chest only twisted deeper. "Me and my American democracy, how am I managing in such a climate?"

Before Roma could rebut anything further, Juliette started walking again, veering off their intended route. Instead of passing the rally gathered about the wide road, she hurried into a nearby alleyway, barely pausing for Roma to follow after her. He registered the change quickly. Soon the two of them were picking their way through trash bags and overturned food carts, scrunching their noses at stray animals and grimacing at the frequent puddles of blood. While they walked through the city's back roads, they were content to lapse into silence, content to pretend the other was not present.

Then Roma whirled around, spinning so fast to face the scene behind them that Juliette immediately assumed they were under attack.

"What?" she snapped, pivoting back too. She grabbed her pistol, then pointed wildly, waiting for something to jump out. "What is it?"

Except Roma remained weaponless. He merely searched the street behind them, his brow scrunched.

"I thought I heard something," he said. They waited. A bird dived into a garbage can. An exterior pipe gushed dirty water on the streets.

"I don't see anything," Juliette said quietly, putting her weapon away.

Roma frowned. He waited another second, but the scene was still. "My mistake. I apologize." He straightened his sleeve cuffs. "Let us continue."

Hesitantly, Juliette turned and started to walk again. They were not far now from the address that Kathleen had given her. This was a familiar part of the city.

The goose bumps, however, remained on her arms.

He's only being paranoid, Juliette tried to reassure herself. The fear of being spotted together was already keeping both of them on their toes. Juliette had her coat collar pulled high to shield her face. Roma wore his hat low over his forehead, which was a good decision when he presently looked so unkempt that any onlooker on the street might run in the other direction upon sighting him. In the bright daylight, the cuts on his face were stark against his pale skin. Judging by the shadows beneath his eyes, Juliette would not be surprised if he had not slept last night, likely tossing and turning in worry over Alisa.

Juliette shook her head. She needed to clear her mind of her assumptions. For all she knew, he could also have been out killing Scarlets.

"It's one of these buildings," Juliette said when they came upon the correct street. The houses here were dilapidated and crowded, the spaces between each building barely wide enough for a child to squeeze through. This area wasn't far from the French Concession, yet a tangible line could be drawn as a border between the two districts, and it was clear which half this street fell on. A long rectangular structure lay half-crumbled under Juliette's feet. Perhaps a grandiose village gate had stood here once, etched with golden characters to welcome its incomers, but it was gone now, torn apart for cityscapes and depravity.

"Are you sure this is the right place?" Roma asked. "Surely a newspaper job pays more than enough to move elsewhere."

"Of all people, Roma Montagov," Juliette said, "you should understand the importance of image." *One and the same, with the people, among the people.* The Communists never stopped preaching such ideals. If the common worker had to suffer, then Zhang Gutai must too—else what other basis did he have for their respect?

Juliette started toward the building her address indicated. Then— two paces away from the main entrance—she abruptly paused. She pointed. "Look."

Roma stifled his sharp breath. *Insects.* A collection of their deadened husks, lying out in the open by the entrance of this apartment block. If this didn't scream *guilty*, Juliette didn't know what did.

Pulse thudding, she pushed at the apartment building's entry door. The rusty lock came free, and the door swung open.

Juliette gestured for Roma to move faster. They worked their way up the stairs, grimacing at the cramped conditions. The stairs staggered up the building along one wall, then trickled straight into a parallel hallway with four doors not so far removed from one another. North, then south, north, then south—they trekked up the stairs, passed the doors on the floor, then moved up the next set of stairs, continuing the process in a dizzying sort of pattern. Roma was more used to this; Juliette was not. She hadn't lived within the city limits for years, nor felt the shift of the floorboards sigh under her feet as the entire structure seemed to heave.

"Which apartment is it?" Roma asked. He sniffed as they passed a windowsill on the third floor's landing, eyeing the flowerpots pushed right to the edge, one little nudge away from shattering on the pavement below.

Juliette only stuck her index finger up at the sky. They kept climbing—up, up, up to the very top, reaching a floor with a sole door waiting right where the stairs ended.

They paused. They exchanged a look.

"He's not home," Juliette assured Roma before he could ask. She bent down on one knee, producing her thin, needlelike dagger from the folds of her dress. "I scanned the calendar in his office. Meetings with important people all day today."

Only as soon as Juliette inserted the dagger into the lock, her tongue poking out from her mouth in concentration, she heard the very distinct, undeniable echo of footsteps shuffling inside the apartment and toward the front door.

"Juliette!" Roma hissed, rushing forward.

Juliette bolted up, stashing the knife into her sleeve. She held her arm out to stop Roma in his tracks, gathering herself just in time before the door flung open and an old man blinked at them with filmy, squinting eyes. He was surely pushing sixty, frazzled and weary-looking, as if he hadn't gotten enough sleep since he came out from the womb.

"Hello," the man said, confused.

Juliette thought fast. They could salvage this. This wasn't beyond saving.

"Good morning. We're from the university," she exclaimed, dropping into another dialect—Wenzhounese—so promptly that Roma jolted back the smallest inch, unable to conceal his astonishment at her quick switch. "Are you well on this fine morning?"

The man leaned his ear forward, grimacing. In Shanghainese, he replied, "Speak běndì huà, would you, girl? I don't understand."

Wenzhou was a city only days of travel to the south of Shanghai, but its local dialect was so incomprehensible to outsiders that Juliette would never have learned it had Nurse not taught her. Nurse used to say that the closest sound resembling Wenzhounese was not a neighboring tongue like Shanghainese, but the chirping of songbirds. In a city not only bustling with foreigners but also native Chinese from every corner of the country, most civilians shared a language, but they did not share the same way of speaking it. Two Chinese merchants could carry on an entire conversation with each one speaking his own dialect. They didn't need to meet in the middle. They only needed to understand.

Juliette, however, hadn't expected the old man to understand her at all; she had only one goal. Before he could squint closely at her face and recognize her for the heir of the Scarlet Gang, she had to make him think she was a careless immigrant girl from elsewhere.

"My apologies." Juliette switched to Shanghainese, task accomplished. "As I was saying, we're from Shanghai University and terribly excited to see you today. We're hoping to found the first student union club and need some advice. Is Mr. Zhang home to speak?"

The old man straightened, brushing his hands over his knitted cardigan. Juliette expected him to turn them away, to tell them to come back some other time, so they could skitter out of sight and mark this off as a temporary failure. As long as they didn't raise suspicion, they could come back. As long as this man didn't pay too much attention to their faces and thought them regular university students who weren't worth remembering.

She didn't expect the man to clear his throat imperiously and say, "I am Mr. Zhang."

Roma and Juliette exchanged a perplexed glance.

"Er . . . no, you're not."

The man's posture sagged. He blew out a breath and abandoned his assuming air. "Fine. I am Qi Ren, Mr. Zhang's personal assistant. You may come in."

Juliette blinked—first in confusion over this man's peculiarity, then in surprise, that he was inviting them in instead of turning them away. As she stood there, she felt a nudge from Roma, asking why she wasn't moving when Mr. Qi turned on his heel and shuffled away on his hard slippers.

This wasn't her original plan, but Juliette was nothing if not adaptable.

"Come on," she muttered to Roma. They hurried in after Mr. Qi.

"How shall I address you?" Mr. Qi called over his shoulder.

Juliette didn't miss a beat. "Zhu Liye. And this is Mr. Montague.

Lovely couches you have." She sat down before he could invite her to.

Mr. Qi, frowning, moved aside a variety of folders on the nearby table, turning them over so his two-character name and *Labor Daily*'s watermark were facedown. "Will this take some time?"

"If that works for you," Juliette replied brightly.

Mr. Qi sighed. "I will go make some tea."

As soon as Mr. Qi had moved far enough into the adjoining kitchen, busy with his task of boiling water, Roma turned to Juliette and hissed, "*Montague? Really?*"

"Shut up," Juliette hissed back. "I couldn't think of anything else and I didn't want to pause suspiciously."

"You're fluent in Russian and *that's* the best you could come up with?" Roma asked, flabbergasted. "What is a *Montague*? It sounds Italian."

"There are Italian Communists!"

"Not in Shanghai!"

Juliette was prevented from responding when Mr. Qi stuck his head back in and asked what sort of tea they wanted. Once he returned deeper into the kitchen, satisfied with their polite answers that anything would do, Juliette ducked her head and said, "Okay, we can still do what we came here to do. You must distract him."

"Say again?" Roma demanded. "You're going to leave *me* here to entertain?"

"Is that a problem?"

"Yes, it's a problem." Roma leaned back in the couch, his hands placed in his lap. "How do I know you're going to share whatever information you find if it doesn't benefit you?"

He was perfectly valid to suspect her, but that didn't mean Juliette liked the insinuation she would sabotage this operation.

"Stop arguing with me," she replied. "Our usual job description is intimidation and gunfire. If we can even pull this off, we should count ourselves lucky."

"Frankly, that's—"

"Do you wish to save Alisa, or not?"

Roma fell quiet. He clenched his fists, and Juliette couldn't tell if it was in reaction over her reminder about Alisa, or if it was to resist reaching out and strangling her. Mr. Qi returned right on cue, with a teapot and three round teacups balanced in his frail arms. Wasting no time, Juliette shot to her feet and asked for the washroom. Mr. Qi absently pointed down the hallway while he placed the cups onto the table, and Juliette flounced off, leaving Roma to glare daggers after her as he started making up a story on the spot about the founding of Shanghai University's Communist union club, which neither of them were actually sure existed. It was his problem now. Juliette had bigger fish to fry.

With her ears perked to ensure Roma was still rambling on about socialist solidarity, Juliette paused at the end of the dilapidated hallway. There were four doors: one wide open into the washroom, two propped ajar and leading into bedrooms, and the fourth shut tight, unyielding when Juliette jiggled the knob lightly. If Zhang Gutai had anything to hide, it would be behind this door.

Juliette braced, then smacked the flat of her palm so hard upon the knob that the simple lock clicked out of commission. Freezing for a brief second, Juliette waited to see if Mr. Qi would come running. When there was no interruption in Roma's spiel, she turned the knob and slipped through the door.

Juliette looked around.

There was a red flag with a yellow hammer-and-sickle stretched across one of the walls. Beneath it, a large desk was overflowing with folders and textbooks, but Juliette didn't waste time scanning it when she approached. She dropped to her knees and pulled at the bottom drawer along the side of the desk. Immediately, the first thing she saw was her own face, and though the paper was flimsy and thin, the press of ink crooked, the rendering of her features completely awry and mis-

calculated, it was undoubtedly still *her* under a heading proclaiming
RESIST THE SCARLET GANG.

"Interesting," Juliette muttered, "but not what I'm looking for."

She pushed the posters aside and dug deeper. All she found were
papers upon papers of propaganda that had no relevance to her,
smeared ink written with inciting terror in mind.

In the second drawer, however, she discovered envelopes, all
embellished with the scrawls of thick ink nibs that spoke of power
and wealth. Juliette thumbed through them quickly, throwing aside
invitations from Kuomintang politicians and thinly veiled threats
from bankers and businessmen, throwing aside anything that looked
vaguely like it could waste her time. Her attention was snagged only
when she came upon a little white square, an envelope far smaller than
the others. Unlike the rest, it did not have a return address.

Instead, it had one little purple flower in the corner, pressed in by
a custom-made rubber stamp.

"A larkspur," Juliette whispered, recognizing the image of the
flower. She scrambled to retrieve the paper inside the envelope. It was
merely a small slip of script, typewritten and snipped to fit.

> It was a pleasure to meet and discuss business.
> Let me know if you change your mind.
> —Larkspur

For a long moment Juliette could only stare at the note, her pulse
pounding. What did it mean? What were all these *pieces*, part of a
bigger puzzle, floating separate to each other but so clearly made to
be joined?

Juliette shoved the envelope back in and slammed the drawer shut.
She smoothed down her dress and, before any more time could pass
to incite suspicion over her absence, she strode out of the office, closing the door behind her with a soft click.

She took two very deep breaths. Her heartbeat leveled down to its usual rate.

"—and really, our goals extend much further beyond revolution," Roma was saying when she casually wandered back into the sitting room. "There's planning to be done, opponents to eliminate."

"All of which require resources much bigger than ourselves, of course," Juliette interjected, settling back onto the couch. She smiled wide enough that her canines slid over her bottom lip. "Now, where were we?"

"Zhu Liye."

Juliette jerked to attention, eyes narrowing as she looked upon Roma. She had to squint because the sun was glaring brightly behind his head, flaring rays that illuminated him into overt clarity while they walked down the pavement.

"Are you still on about the names?"

"No, I—" Roma made a sound that could have been a chuckle, if not for the hostility. "I just understood. You translated Juliette into Chinese. Ju-li-ette. Zhu Liye."

Roma had clearly been musing over that specific conundrum since the moment they left Zhang Gutai's apartment. After quickly telling him what she found in the office, Juliette had been content to walk without conversation as they picked their way back down to the streets. Roma had seemed compliant to the example Juliette set, until now.

"Nice detective work," Juliette intoned. She hopped down from the sidewalk to avoid a puddle, her heels clicking onto the road. Roma followed closely.

"I actually—" Roma tilted his head to the side. It was almost birdlike in the way he did it—quick and curious and void of ulterior motive. "I don't know your Chinese name."

Juliette's eyes narrowed. "Does it matter?"

"I'm only being civil."

"Don't be."

Another lull. This time Roma didn't hurry to fill it. This time he only waited. He knew that Juliette detested silence. She detested it so viciously that when it followed her around with the air of a ghoul, when it skipped between her and whomever she was walking with, whether it be enemy or friend, Juliette would scrape away at herself just to find a weapon to counter it.

He stayed silent. And Juliette caved.

"Cai Junli," she said monotonously. "Change up the pronunciation a little and Junli turned into *Juliette*."

Her name was no secret; it was merely forgotten. She was just Juliette, the heiress who came from the West—with the American girl's dress and the American girl's name. If the people of Shanghai dug deep into the recesses of their memory, they would find Juliette's Chinese name lurking somewhere between the age of their grandfather and the residential address of their third-favorite aunt. But it would never rise to their lips upon instinct. What was instead spoken was what Juliette had slowed down and distorted earlier into a full name: *Zhūliyè*.

"You never told me," Roma said. He was staring ahead. "Back then."

"There were a lot of things I didn't tell you," Juliette replied. Just as dully, she too added, "Back then."

Four years ago, the city was not the same. Many men still kept their hair long, in what was called a queue, one braid trailing down their back with the front of their scalp shaved. The women wore their garments loose, their pants straight.

So everywhere Juliette went, she went in her bright dresses. She sneered at the ugly clothes other girls wore, and when her mother dared attempt to have her adhere to the usual fashion, she tore the bland shirts from her closet and ripped them into shreds, letting the strips flush in swirls down the newly renovated plumbing. She trashed every qipao and tossed aside every silk scarf Lady Cai tried to compromise with. To avoid being recognized when she colluded with Roma, she threw coats over her gaudy costumes, of course, but she was always treading the line of recklessness. Juliette had almost preferred the thought of being caught a traitor over putting on the same clothes as everyone else. She would have rather been an outcast than admit the blood in her veins was a product of the East.

Juliette liked to think she had come down a bit from her high horse since then. The second time she returned to New York, she had seen the darkness behind the glamour of the West. It was no longer so great to be a child constructed with Western parts.

"I picked it myself."

Roma visibly startled at her words. He hadn't expected her to say anything more.

"Your name?" he clarified.

Juliette nodded. She did not look at him, did not even blink. She said, "The kids in New York made fun of me. They asked what I was called and then they laughed when I told them, repeating those foreign syllables back at me over and over again as if speaking it in song made it funny."

She had been five years old. The wound of the mockery was healed now, covered by tough skin and rough calluses, but it still stung on bad days, as all old injuries did.

"My name was too Chinese for the West," Juliette continued, a wry smile on her lips. She didn't know why her face had morphed itself into amusement. She was anything but amused. "You know how it is—or maybe you don't. A temporary thing for a temporary place, but now the temporary thing is burrowed in so deep it cannot be removed."

As soon as *those* words came out, Juliette felt a pang of nausea hit her throat—an immediate visceral realization that she had said too much. Ditzy flapper Juliette, who was meant to help her survive the West, had dug her claws in so deep that the real Juliette didn't know where the facade stopped and where her true self began—if there was even anything left of her true self, or if there was anything in there to begin with. All her cousins—Rosalind, Kathleen, Tyler—they had English names to accommodate to the flood of Westerners controlling Shanghai, but their Chinese names still existed as part of their identity; their relatives still addressed them as such on the occasion. Juliette was only ever Juliette.

The air was sticky. They had been walking for long enough to enter the French Concession, strolling alongside a row of identical houses with glaringly bright walls and generous patches of greenery. Juliette pulled at her collar, grimacing when Roma opened and closed his mouth.

"Juliette—"

Was the line between enemy and friend horizontal or vertical? Was it a great plain to lumber across or was it a high, high wall—either to be scaled or kicked down in one big blow?

"We're done here, right?" Juliette asked. "Do what you will with this information. I'm sure the link between Zhang Gutai and the Larkspur will give you plenty to work with."

Juliette veered left, picking a shortcut through a yard that would take her to the next street. The grass here grew up to her ankles. When she dropped her shoe down, the ground seemed to swallow her, dipping and softening simply by her step. It felt like a welcome—a *hurry*, a *come through*.

Until Roma clamped a hand on her shoulder, forcibly stopping her.

"You have *got*"—Juliette spun around, slapping his hand off her—"to stop doing that."

"We're not finished," Roma said.

"Yes, we are."

The shadows of the nearby house were heavy. Roma and Juliette stood right where the shadows ended, right at the strict divide between light and gloom.

Roma looked her up and down.

"You still think it's a scheme within the Communists, don't you?" he asked suddenly. His voice dropped an octave, as if realizing that they needed to minimize the volume of their argument while standing on a street like this. In the early-morning light, it was hard to remember what danger tasted like. But one wrong move—one wrong person looking out their window at the right time—and they would both be in deep trouble.

"Roma," Juliette said coldly, "we're done collaborating—"

"No, we're *not*," Roma insisted. "Because this isn't something you can investigate on your own. I can see what you're planning just by looking at you. You think you can simply insert yourself into the Communist circles with your Scarlet resources—"

Juliette took a step closer. She didn't know if it was the bright glare of sunlight reflecting off a nearby window, or if she was angry enough to be seeing white flaring into her vision.

"You," she seethed, "don't know *anything*."

"I know enough to see a *pattern* here with the Larkspur." Roma clicked his fingers in her face. "Snap out of it, Juliette! You're only ignoring this clue because you wish to walk away from our collaboration and begin investigating other Communists! It won't do anything! You're on the wrong path and *you know it*."

His words had a physical force to them—multiple stinging hits that struck her skin. Juliette could hardly breathe, never mind find the energy to speak, to continue the staged whispers of their screaming match. She hated him *so much*. She hated that he was right. She hated that he was inciting this reaction in her. And most of all, she hated that she *had* to hate him, because if she didn't, the hatred would turn right back on herself and there would be nothing to hate except her own weak will.

"You can't do that," Juliette said. She sounded more sad now than angry. She hated *this*. "You don't get to do that."

If she leaned in, she could count the individual specks of pollen that had landed on the bridge of Roma's nose. The atmosphere here was too heady and strange and pastoral. The longer they remained— lined up with the pearly white walls, standing in the swaying grasses— the more Juliette felt ready to slough off a whole layer of skin. Why could she never remake herself—why was she always bound to end up here?

Roma blinked. He eased up on his temper too, his whisper turning into a soft one. "Do what?"

See me.

Juliette turned away. She wrapped her arms around her waist. "What are you suggesting?" she asked in lieu of a reply. "Why have you latched on to the Larkspur so intently?"

"Think about it," Roma said. He matched her steady, low tone. "Zhang Gutai is the rumored maker of the madness. The Larkspur is the rumored healer of the madness. How can there *not* be a link? How can there *not* have been something that passed between them at their meeting?"

Juliette shook her head. "Link or no link, if we want to fix this at the root, we go to the *maker*, not the *healer*—"

"I'm not saying the Larkspur has all the answers," Roma hurried to correct. "I'm saying the Larkspur can lead us toward getting more out of Zhang Gutai. I'm saying it's another way to the truth if Zhang Gutai won't talk."

He has some sense to his logic, Juliette thought. *He's not . . .* wrong.

Yet Juliette remained difficult. Her mother once told her that she had almost been born the wrong way around—feetfirst—because Juliette always refused the easy way out.

"Why do you insist on convincing me?" she asked. "Why not go about confronting the Larkspur alone, bid me good riddance?"

Roma looked down. His fingers twitched in her direction; he might have been trying to resist reaching out for her, but Juliette booted that out of her thoughts as soon as it came in. Softness and longing were sentiments of the past. If Roma were ever again to run a tender finger down her spine, it would be to count her vertebrae and gauge where he could stab his knife in.

"Listen, Juliette," he breathed. "We have two halves of one city. If I act alone, I am locked out of Scarlet territory. I won't risk losing out on a cure for my sister as soon as possible just because of our blood feud. The feud has taken enough. I won't let it take Alisa."

His eyes shifted back to her, and in that gaze lay both sadness and rage, pooling outward until it surrounded the space between them. Juliette was right in the heart of that conflict too, horrified to have to counter this madness with the boy who had torn her to pieces, yet aching for this city, for what had come down upon it.

Roma extended his hand. Hesitant.

"Until the madness stops, that's all I ask. Between the two of us, we put the knives and guns and threats down for as long as it takes to stop our city from falling. Are you willing?"

She shouldn't have been. But he had worded it just right. To Roma, saving Alisa was everything. Regardless of monsters or charlatan magical cures, all he wanted was for her to wake up again. To Juliette, it was the city that came first, and the city she put first. She needed her people to stop dying. It was fortunate that these two such goals came together.

Juliette extended her hand, tucked it into Roma's to shake. There was a jolt between them, a terrible, hot spark as they both seemed to realize that, for the first time in four years, this was skin-to-skin contact without malice. Juliette felt like she had swallowed a burning-hot coal.

"Until the madness stops," she whispered.

They pumped twice, then Roma turned their hands, so his was

at the bottom and Juliette's was at the top. If they couldn't have anything, then they could at least have this—a second, a whimsy, a fantasy—before Juliette came to her senses and jerked her hand away, returning it to her side with her fist clenching.

"Tomorrow, then," Roma decided. His voice was rough. "We hunt the Larkspur."

Twenty-One

Her expression forcefully neutral, Kathleen slipped into the early-morning Communist meeting, putting one foot in front of the other and walking right past the people guarding the door.

This was something she was very good at: seeing without being seen. Kathleen could strike a balance between confidence and timidity like it was a natural reflex. She had learned to pick up the bits and pieces that others built themselves upon, pulling their attributes and molding them into an amalgamation of her own. She had adopted the way Juliette tilted her chin up when she talked, demanding respect even at her worst. She had learned to imitate the way Rosalind sank her shoulders down when their father engaged in his endless rants, becoming small by intent so he would remember that she was demure and stop, even if there was an imperceptible smirk playing on her lips.

Sometimes it was hard for Kathleen to remember that she was still her own person, not just shards of a mirror, reflecting back a thousand different personalities most fitting for the situation.

"Excuse me," Kathleen said absently, extending her hand to push past two Communists chatting intently. They gave way without much notice, allowing Kathleen to keep moving through the crowded space. She didn't know what she was heading toward. She only knew she had to keep moving until this meeting started, or else she would look out of place.

The meeting was being held in a large hall space, the ceiling hollow and tall, curving up to meet the steepness of the roofing. In another country, perhaps this might have been a church, with its stained-glass windows and thick wooden beams. Here it was merely used for weddings involving foreigners and events that the rich put on.

Ironic that the Communists were renting it out now.

"Get in, get out," Kathleen muttered to herself, echoing Juliette's words from earlier that morning. When Juliette came to her and Rosalind for help, she had been bustling with frantic energy, half an arm already jammed into her coat.

"There has to be a reason, right?" Juliette had asked. "The Communists wouldn't be muttering about one genius in the Party dreaming it all up if they didn't have some sort of proof. If Zhang Gutai is innocent, then the proof should say so too, and point us in another direction. So we need to go to the proof."

Rosalind was already needed elsewhere, at the club, for an important meeting that Lord Cai would be taking with foreigners who required impressing, who needed to see Shanghai at its most extravagant, glittering glory. By the pinched look on Rosalind's face, she likely had not been eager to be sent off to the Communists anyway. Kathleen, on the other hand, didn't quite mind. Try as she might to despise this climate, there was something too to be enjoyed while neck-deep in the chaos and activity and broiling, growing tensions. It made her feel like she was a part of something, even if she was just the little flea latched on to a sprinting cheetah racing for prey. If she understood politics, then she understood society. And if she understood society, then she would be well equipped to survive it, to manipulate the playing field around her until she could have a chance of living her life in peace.

As much as she loved her sister, Kathleen didn't want to survive the way Rosalind was surviving, among the lights and jazz music. She did not wish to get into a costume and powder her face until she was as pale as a sheet of paper like Rosalind did every day, with a sneer on her lips. Juliette didn't know how lucky she was to have been born into her natural skin, into her white cheeks and porcelain-smooth wrists. There was so much luck to be had in the genetic lottery; one different code and it was a whole lifetime of forced adaptation.

All Kathleen could do to survive was forge her own path. There was no alternative.

"I am a first-year university student," Kathleen muttered under her breath, rehearsing her answer should anybody ask who she was, "working as a reporter for the campus paper. I am hoping to learn more about the exciting opportunities for workers in Shanghai. I was raised in poverty. My mother is dead. My father is dead to me—*oof*."

Kathleen froze. The person she had run into made a small bow of apology.

"Please forgive me. I wasn't watching where I was going." Marshall Seo's smile was bright and forceful, even while Kathleen stared and stared. Did he not recognize her? Why was he here?

Probably for the same reason you are.

"Nothing to forgive," Kathleen replied quickly, inclining her head. She turned to go, but Marshall sidestepped faster than she could blink, placing himself right into her path. She narrowly prevented herself from slamming her nose right into his chest.

"In such a hurry?" Marshall asked. "The meeting won't start for another few minutes."

He definitely recognized her.

"I wish to find a seat," Kathleen replied. Her heart started to thud in her chest. "The acoustics in this room are deceiving. Better to be as close to the stage as possible."

It didn't matter that neither of them was wearing gang colors, attending a meeting run by a group that rejected them both. They were on opposite sides—a clash was a clash.

"Oh, but stay a while, darling!" Marshall insisted. "Look, over there—" Marshall put his hand on her elbow. Kathleen's hand immediately snapped to her waist, her fingers curling around the handgun sitting underneath her jacket.

The air stilled. "Don't do that." Marshall whispered it almost sadly. "You know better."

A clash was a clash—so why wasn't he chasing her out? This was White Flower territory. It would be poor decision-making on her part to shoot at him, but *he* could shoot at *her*—he could kill her and the Scarlets could do nothing about it.

Slowly, Kathleen eased her fingers away from the gun. "You don't even know what I was about to do."

Marshall grinned. The expression came on in a flash—serious one second, then overjoyed the next. "Don't I?"

She didn't know how to respond to that. She didn't know how to respond to this conversation at all—how to respond to a sort of flirtation that seemed to be more a personality trait rather than something performed with a goal in mind.

How to respond to the simple little fact that he was not pointing his gun at her.

A trick. The White Flowers knew how to play the long game.

Marshall remained standing there. His gaze moved about her forehead and her nose and the pendant at her throat, and though Kathleen instinctively wanted to flinch away from scrutiny, she copied the slouch of his relaxed shoulders instead, almost challenging him to say something more.

He didn't. Marshall smiled, like he was simply having fun with their staring contest.

"Well, this has been a nice chat." Kathleen took a step back. "But I want to find my seat now. Goodbye."

She hurried away with a huff, dropping into the first free chair she found near the front. She hadn't even wanted to sit down. She was trying to speak with the Communists. Why was she so bad at staying on task?

Kathleen looked around. To her left, an old woman was snoring away. To her right, two young university students—real ones, unlike her, if their notepads were any indication—were intently focused on discussing their plans for after this meeting.

Kathleen craned her neck, then craned some more, her fingers tapping the back of the chair frantically. A ticking clock appeared in her mind's eye each time she blinked, as if her time here were a measurable thing that would soon run out.

Kathleen's gaze snagged on a group of three balding men two rows behind. When she strained her ears and focused, she noted that they were speaking in Shanghainese, gibbering on about the state of the Northern Expedition, fingers stabbing down on knees, and tongues moving fast enough to spray spittle in all directions. The way they gestured made her think they weren't just casual attendees. Party members.

Perfect.

Kathleen made her way over, dragging her chair until she could plop down right next to them.

"Do you have a second?" she cut in, pulling their conversation to a halt. "I'm from the university." Kathleen produced a recording device from her pocket and held it out in front of her. The thing was actually broken, dug out from—strangely enough—a pile of unused bullets from the armory in the Cai mansion.

"We always have time for our students," one of the men replied. He puffed his chest out, readying himself.

I'm recording your voice, not taking your picture, Kathleen thought.

"I'd like to publish a piece on the Party's Secretary-General," she said aloud. "Zhang Gutai?" Her eyes flicked to the stage. There were people gathering on the platform now, but they were speaking among themselves, shuffling around their notes. She had a few minutes before the place went quiet. She couldn't ease these men into her questions. She needed to extract the information she wanted as quickly as possible, prime them into what she wanted.

"What about him?"

Kathleen cleared her throat. "The revolution needs a leader. Do you think his capable nature will be an asset?"

Silence. For a moment she was afraid that she had started far too strong, stepped her bare foot into a nest of vipers and scared them back into their holes.

Then the men started to guffaw.

"His capable nature?" one parroted with a wheeze. "Don't make me laugh."

Kathleen blinked. She had hoped her leading questions would prompt them into thinking she knew more than she actually did. It seemed a fair guess that Zhang Gutai would be capable, did it not? There were very few other personality traits fitting for a mastermind who had schemed up an epidemic. Instead, her stab in the dark had landed in the other direction.

"You do not think Mr. Zhang to be capable?" she asked, perplexity soaking into her voice.

"Why would you think him to be?" one of the three men shot back, returning the genuine bemusement.

Up on the stage, a speaker tapped the microphone. Sharp feedback rang through the whole building space, bouncing through the little nooks in the ceiling alcoves.

"It is a fair assumption."

"Is it?"

Kathleen felt a tic begin in her jaw. She could not keep playing a game. She was untrained in the art of speaking untruths.

"Rumor has it that he has created the madness sweeping through Shanghai."

The three men stiffened. Meanwhile, the first speaker onstage started to welcome the attendees, thanking them for coming and prompting those at the back to come closer to the front.

"What sort of piece are you writing anyway?" The whisper floated over to Kathleen from the man seated farthest from her. He spoke in a way that moved only half his mouth, the words pushed out through the gaps of his teeth and the slit of his lips.

Kathleen's hands were heavy with the recording device. Carefully, she scrunched it into her fist, then put it away, determining it had served her purpose.

"A study of power," she replied, "and the madness that comes with it. A study of the powerful, and those who are scared of him." Allowing no mistake over the meaning of her words, Kathleen whispered, "The uncovering of the madness."

Applause rang through the hall. From somewhere afar, Kathleen thought she heard a brief whine of sirens merging with the noise, but when the applause stopped, all she could hear was the next speaker—a real Bolshevik who had come all the way from Moscow—hailing the benefits of unionizing.

"Make no mistake." The man nearest to her met her eyes briefly before he leveled his gaze on the stage again. Had he not beheld this information, Kathleen would never had thought him a Communist. What was it that made this man different from the others on the street? At what point did mere political self-interest cross into fanaticism, enough to die for a cause? "If you wish to uncover Zhang Gutai's role in this madness, it is not his power that elevates him."

"Then what does?" Kathleen asked.

None of the men jumped to answer her. Perhaps the Bolshevik's speech onstage was far too captivating. Perhaps they were simply scared.

"You claim to be heralds of equality." Kathleen tapped her foot on a discarded flyer lying upon the ground. The big, bold text was bleeding ink, soaked with droplets of someone's spilled tea. "Live up to your claim. Allow me to expose Zhang Gutai for the false scoundrel he is. No one needs to know that the information came from you. I don't even know your names. You are anonymous soldiers for justice."

A beat passed. These men were itching to tell her. She could see it in the glint of their eyes, the frenzy of the high that came when one thought they were doing good in the world. The Bolshevik onstage took a bow. The hall erupted in a wave of applause.

Kathleen waited.

"You want to write a study on his power?" The man closest to her leaned in. "Understand this: Zhang Gutai is not powerful. *He has a monster doing his bidding.*"

A cold draft wafted into the room. With the applause dying, the audience grew quiet once more.

"What?"

"We saw it," the second one said firmly. "We saw it leave his apartment. He sends it out like a leashed demon to kill those who upset him."

"The whole Party knows," the third man added, "but no one speaks against dishonor while the tide rushes forward in our preferred direction. Who would dare?"

Under the technicolor shadows of the stained windows, the whole audience seemed to shift forward, awaiting the next speaker while the stage remained empty. Kathleen might have been the only one turned in another direction.

These men think sightings *of the monster cause madness,* she realized. They thought the monster to be an assassin on Zhang Gutai's instruction, killing those who looked upon it. But then how did the insects play into the equation? Why had Juliette been muttering on about lice-like creatures spreading madness instead?

"That sounds like power to me," Kathleen remarked.

"Power is something achievable by few." A shrug. "Anyone can be

247

the master to a monster should their heart be wicked enough."

The room suddenly roared with havoc, jostling chairs and screeching sounds echoing into the sonorous space. Suddenly Kathleen remembered hearing the faraway sirens and brushing them off, but indeed, they *had* been sirens, bringing with them enforcement that did not enforce law at all, only the way that things were. This was White Flower territory. They paid the garde municipale here a mighty amount to keep the gangsters in power, which included storming the meetings of Communists, storming every attempt this party made in their progress toward igniting revolution and eradicating gangster rule.

"Halt immediately and put your hands up," one of the officers boomed.

The activity only erupted further as people streamed out the doors and dove under tables. Dimly, Kathleen considered doing the same, but an officer was already marching right for her, his expression set on harassment.

"Venez avec moi," the officer demanded. "Ne bougez pas."

Kathleen made a contemplative noise. "Non, monsieur, j'ai un rendezvous avec quelqu'un."

The officer jumped in surprise. He hadn't expected the Parisian accent. He himself did not have the features of the white French commonly seen in the Concession. Like so many other officers in the garde municipale, he was only a product of French rule, shipped up for his labor from Annam or any one of the various countries south of China that had not managed to keep the foreigners out of its government.

"Maintenant, s'il vous plaît," the officer snapped, his hackles visibly rising with Kathleen's insolence. All around them, Communists were being pushed to the ground and rounded up. Those who had not run off fast enough would be processed and placed on a list, names to watch should the Party grow any bigger and need culling.

"Ah, leave her be."

Kathleen whipped around, her frown heavy. Marshall was waving the officer off, waving a hand adorned with a ring that quite clearly belonged within the collection of Montagov heirlooms. The ring glinted in the light and the officer's irate expression dulled. He cleared his throat and left to hassle the next nearest victim.

"Why did you do that?" Kathleen asked. "Why do you offer your help when it has not been requested?"

Marshall shrugged. From out of nowhere, he seemed to have conjured a glistening red apple. "They step on us enough. I wish to aid." He took a bite out of his apple.

Kathleen tugged at her jacket. If she pulled any harder, the fabric would permanently have a wrinkle to it.

"What is that supposed to mean?" she asked coldly. "The garde municipale is on your side. They will never step on *you*."

"Of course they do." Marshall smiled, but this time it did not reach his eyes. "They all do. They cannot wait to polish their shoes and stomp down with finality. People like us are dying every day."

Kathleen did not move.

Marshall took no notice of her discomfort. He went on, gesturing around with his apple.

"Just as those Communists you were speaking to would find the first opportunity to drag down their Secretary-General."

Kathleen made a noise of offense. "Were you eavesdropping on my conversation?"

"And if I was?"

The arrests seemed to be slowing now. There was a straight path from here to the door and then Kathleen would have freedom, escaping with her newly acquired information bundled to her chest.

Too bad the White Flowers had the exact same information now.

"Mind your business," Kathleen snapped.

Before Marshall Seo could steal anything more, she marched away.

Twenty-Two

Morning turned to noon with an exhausted flop, beams of gray daylight streaming through the dirty windows of the burlesque club. Juliette waved at the cigarette smoke that wafted below her nose, grimacing and holding back her cough.

"Is the radiator broken?" Juliette yelled, her voice carrying loudly. "Turn the heat up! And get me more gin!"

She was already wearing a long coat lined with fur thicker than her father's account books, but each time the doors slammed open, a cold breeze swirled in and further chilled the brisk day.

"You finished the whole bottle already?" one of the waitresses remarked. She had a cloth in her hand, scrubbing at a nearby table, her nose scrunched in the direction of the glass in front of Juliette.

Juliette picked up the empty bottle, examined the delicate detailing, then set it down again upon a flyer. She had found the thin piece of paper on the streets before she came in. The corner was rumpled now from how much she had been fiddling with it.

GET VACCINATED, the flyer read in large lettering. At the very bottom, there were two printed lines offering an address in the International Settlement.

"Tone down the judgment before I fire you," Juliette replied, the threat delivered without much conviction. She clicked her fingers at a passing kitchen hand. "Come on! Another bottle!"

The kitchen hand hurried to accommodate. The crowd in the burlesque club during the day was sparse, and for the gangsters who came during these hours, there was nothing to do except dawdle around and watch Rosalind's watered-down daytime routine. At night, all the stops were pulled out and Rosalind kicked and *cha-cha*-ed her way into extravagance. The lights would glow to their fullest capacity and the hum from the floor would be enough to power the chandeliers, which twinkled gold against the hazy red ceiling. But while the sun was up outside and the bodies scattered amid the round tables were few, it was as if the place were hibernating. Rosalind usually worked two hours during the day and she clearly hated them, if her inability to pay attention was any indication. From the stage, she had raised an eyebrow at Juliette, wordlessly asking why Juliette was throwing a fit from the audience and, in the process, missed the first few notes of her next song.

"Drinking at one in the afternoon?" Rosalind remarked when she came up to Juliette an hour later, finally finished with her set. Having changed out of her flashy stage dress, she slumped onto the chair opposite Juliette in her dark-green qipao, blending into the deep green of the seat. Only her black eyes stood out in the bland lighting. Everything else became strange and gray.

"Well, I'm *trying*."

Juliette poured deftly, then offered the half-full cup to Rosalind.

Rosalind took a sip. She grimaced so severely that her usual pointed chin morphed into three.

"This is *awful*." She coughed, wiping at her mouth. She looked around then, eyeing the empty tables. "Are you meeting someone here again?"

A merchant, Rosalind was suggesting, or perhaps a foreign diplomat, a businessman—people in power who Juliette was supposed to be rubbing shoulders with. But since Walter Dexter, who had been more of a pest than anything, her father hadn't given her anyone else to meet with. She had one task only: find out why the people of Shanghai were dying.

"Every time I knock on my father's door to ask if there are any important people he would like me to sweet-talk, he waves me off like—" Juliette performed an exaggerated imitation of her father's harried expression, flicking her wrist quickly through the air like a limp fish.

Rosalind bit back a laugh. "You don't have anywhere better to be, then?"

"I'm merely spending some time in your talent," Juliette replied. "I'm so *bored* of these ordinary people who don't know the difference between a dropkick and a flat kick. . . ."

Rosalind pulled a face. "*I* don't even know what the difference is. I'm almost certain you just made those terms up."

Juliette shrugged, then threw the rest of her drink down. The answer she had given was the truth. She only needed to be seen at the burlesque club for long enough that it would not be suspicious when dusk came and she slipped out to meet Roma.

Juliette shuddered. *Slipping out to meet Roma.* It was too reminiscent. A wound so long removed, yet still fresh and open and sore.

"Are you okay?"

Rosalind jolted. "Why wouldn't I be?"

The cosmetic application was good, but Juliette spent a long time every morning fiddling around with her pots and jars too. Without looking very closely at all, she could tell where Rosalind had heaped on the creams and powder, could track the exact line where her real skin ended and a false layer began to cover up the shadows and dark circles.

"I worry that you're not getting enough sleep," Juliette replied.

A loud crash came from their left. The waitress who had been cleaning the table had knocked over a candleholder.

Rosalind shook her head—it could have been a motion both in disapproval over the waitress and in response to Juliette. "I've been sleeping, just not well. I keep having dreams about those insects." She shuddered, then leaned forward. "Juliette, I feel helpless merely sitting around while the city falls apart. There must be something I can do—"

"Relax," Juliette said gently. "It is not your job to take on."

Rosalind placed both her hands flat on the table. Her jaw tightened. "I wish to help."

"Help me by getting some sleep." Juliette tried for a smile. "Help us by dancing with all your beautiful brilliance, just so we can forget—even for a few minutes—that people are looting stores and settings fires in the streets."

Just so they could forget that madness was striking every little corner of this city, that this was not a force police officers or gangsters or colonialist powers could fight back against.

Rosalind did not respond for a long moment. Then, to Juliette's shock, she asked, "Is that all I am good for?"

Juliette jerked back. "Pardon?"

"One would think that I don't even need to be a Scarlet anymore," Rosalind said bitterly. Her voice was almost unrecognizable, forged by a shard of broken glass. "All I am is a dancer."

"*Rosalind.*" Juliette leaned forward too, then, her eyes narrowing. Where was this coming from? "You are a dancer, yes—but one in the Scarlet inner circle, privy to meetings and correspondences even your own father cannot stick his nose into. How can you doubt whether or not you are a Scarlet?"

But Rosalind's eyes were haunted. The bitterness had given way to anguish, and the anguish ate away at her temper until she was only gazing forward in defeat. That monster sighting—it had affected her more than she had let on. It had sent her on long nights and spirals, and now she was questioning everything that her life was stacked atop of, which was dangerous for someone like Rosalind, whose mind was already an eternal, sepulchral place.

"It is only that it feels unfair sometimes," Rosalind said quietly, "that you are allowed to *be* in this family and you shall have your place in the Scarlet Gang, but I am a dancer or I am nothing."

Juliette blinked. There was nothing she could say to that. Nothing except:

"I'm . . . sorry." Juliette reached out, placed a hand on her cousin's. "Do you want me to talk to my father—"

Rosalind shook her head quickly. She laughed, the sound brittle.

"Please, never mind me," Rosalind said. "I'm just . . . I don't know. I don't know what's wrong with me. I need more sleep." She stood then, squeezing Juliette's hand once before letting go. "I have to get home now to rest if I want to be ready for my shift tonight. Are you coming?"

She wasn't, but she also didn't want to let Rosalind go while it seemed like there was still a conflict here—a conflict between them—that had been left unresolved. It was unnerving. The hairs at the back of Juliette's neck were standing up as if she and her cousin had just had a fight, but she could not pinpoint where the friction lay. Perhaps it was her imagination. Rosalind's eyes had cleared now, injecting more spirit into her spine. Perhaps it had only been a brief moment of internal calamity.

"You go on," Juliette finally replied. "I have some more time to waste."

Nodding, Rosalind smiled once more. She walked out the door and another cold draft blew in, this one shaking Juliette so viciously that she curled her entire neck into her coat, becoming a girl swallowed in fur. Now there was not even a show to keep her entertained. She had no choice but to people-watch her Scarlets.

"How long have you been wiping at that table for?" Juliette called.

The waitress looked over, sighing. "Xiǎojiě, the stains are persistent."

Juliette shot to her feet and clacked over on her heels. She extended her hand for the cleaning cloth.

The waitress blinked. "Miss Cai, it's not proper for you to get your hands dirty—"

"*Pass* it."

She passed it. Juliette scrunched it up in her fist. In three quick, violent motions—her hand coming down on the table so hard that it made a sound—the surface was smooth and clear and shiny.

Juliette gave the cloth back. "Use your elbows. It's not that hard."

"I had a thought."

Benedikt looked up from his sketch pad, squinting in his attempt to focus on Marshall's face. It was an overcast day, yet there was still a blinding brightness glaring through the thick clouds and streaming into their living room. The result was a terribly depressing sky without the comfort of proper, heavy rain.

"My ears are on the top of my head."

Marshall flopped down on the long couch too, carelessly shoving Benedikt's legs aside. He pretended not to hear Benedikt's sound of protest, not moving even when he almost sat right on his friend's bare foot.

"Don't you think it is a little peculiar that Lord Montagov has been sending us on so many Scarlet missions lately? How is he getting this information?"

"It is not peculiar." Benedikt's focus returned to the movement of pencil against rough paper. "We have spies in the Scarlet Gang. We have always had spies in the Scarlet Gang. They certainly have spies among our ranks too."

"We have spies, certainly, but not to this extent," Marshall replied. He always looked so somber when he was trying to concentrate. Benedikt found it a little funny, if he was honest. It didn't suit Marshall—it was like a jester wearing a three-piece.

"What? You think we have managed to infiltrate their inner circle?" Benedikt shook his head. "We would know if that were the case. Can you stop wriggling around so much?"

Marshall did not stop wriggling. It seemed that he was trying to adjust his seat to get comfortable, but the couch cushions were going to detach and fly right off if he kept at it. Finally, he settled in and propped his chin on his fist.

"The information has just been so accurate lately," Marshall said, a hint of awe entering his voice. "He had the time of the masquerade before Roma did. This morning he sent me after Kathleen Lang and had her exact location. How is your uncle doing this?"

Benedikt looked up from his drawing, then looked down again, his pencil moving in a quick arc. A line of a jaw merged with the curve of a throat. A smudge in the shading became a dimple.

"Lord Montagov sent you after Kathleen Lang?" he asked.

Marshall leaned back. "Well, he's not going to send you or Roma into a Communist meeting. You speak the language, but your face does not blend in as mine does."

Benedikt rolled his eyes. "Yes, I understood that. But why are we following Kathleen Lang now?"

Marshall shrugged. "I don't know. I suppose we want the information she acquires." He squinted at the weather outside the window. A beat of silence passed, nothing but the rapid sound of shading from Benedikt's nub of a pencil.

"Should we resume our pursuit for a live victim today?" Marshall asked.

Benedikt supposed they should. They were running out of time. Alisa was counting on them, and if they had more avenues to exhaust in order to find a cure, wasn't it on them to at least try?

Sighing, Benedikt tossed his sketchbook onto the table. "I suppose we must."

"You may always resume drawing after we fail and call it a night,"

Marshall promised. He craned his neck and peered at the sketchbook. "But my nose is not that big."

At sunset, Juliette slipped out of the burlesque club with her head down, her chin tucked into her collar. It was both an effort to avoid being seen and to brace against the frigid breeze—a gale that stung her skin with every point of contact. She didn't know what it was about today that brought the early winter in with such a bite.

"Buns, hot buns for two cents! Get them now, get them hot—"

"Miss, miss, we're selling fish for cheap—"

"Fortune-telling! Palm-reading! Xiǎojiě, you look like you need—"

Juliette swerved left and right through the open markets, staring at her shoes. She pulled the hood of her coat up until most of her hair was buried in the fur, most of her face swallowed by the fuzz. It wasn't that it was dangerous to be recognized—she had ten thousand excuses up her sleeve as to where she was going, but she wasn't in the mood to spin lies. This city was her old friend. She didn't need to look up to find her way around. This way and that way and this way and that, soon she was moving along Avenue Edward VII, finally lifting her head and bracing her cheeks against the cold to search for Roma.

The activity along this street all headed in one direction—toward Great World. It wasn't quite fair to call the place an "*arcade*" like Juliette was fond of doing. Rather, it was an indoor entertainment complex with everything under the earth. Distorted mirrors and tightrope walkers and ice cream parlors came together in a cacophony of activity that worked to suck away a day of your life and all the money in your wallet. The central attraction was the Chinese opera, but Juliette had never liked it much. Her favorite was the magicians, though she hadn't been inside the arcade for years, and by now all the magicians she had once been familiar with had probably moved on or been replaced.

Sighing, Juliette scanned the five blockbuster Chinese characters sitting directly atop Great World. They burned against the glow of the fading sun, backlit with the barest hint of fiery orange.

White . . . golden . . . dragon . . . cigarettes, she translated, the task more confusing than it had to be. She had forgotten for the shortest second to read right to left instead of left to right, which she had gotten used to in the last few years.

"Focus," she muttered to herself.

Juliette's wandering attention dropped to follow the stream of faces coming in and out of the doors to Great World. She searched carefully—scanning the masses in the rapidly falling night as they followed loud advertisements into every vice readily available—until her gaze came to the front of a dress shop. Leaning upon a signpost, Roma stood with his hands buried deep in his pockets, shadows under his eyes.

Juliette strolled over, her shoes silent against the gravel for once. She prepared to chide him for standing so far from the building and making it hard to find him. Only when she came near, something about his expression cut her off before she had even started.

"What's wrong—"

"Don't look back," Roma began, "but you were followed."

"I was not."

Her denial came fast and unwavering, though it was more an act of rebellion on her part than true certainty. As she spoke, her first instinct was to swivel around and prove Roma wrong, but logic instructed her to refrain. She held herself still, all the tendons in her neck pulled taut. She had indeed been deep in thought while making her way over, concentrating on keeping her face hidden from those in her view rather than watching for the lurkers in her peripheral. Could she have picked up a tail?

"A white man stopped right when you did," Roma said. "He pulled a newspaper from his pocket and started reading it in the middle of the street. I don't know what your thoughts are, but that is highly suspicious to me."

Juliette started rummaging through her pocket, cursing under her breath.

"He might not be a threat," she insisted. "Perhaps he is one of yours—doing surveillance on your activities."

"He is not Russian," Roma countered immediately. "His clothing and hairstyle say British, and we have none of those within our ranks."

Juliette finally found what she was looking for and pulled out her facial powder. She opened the box and angled the mirror folded within, scanning the darkening streets behind her without turning around.

"Found him," Juliette reported. "Yellow handkerchief in the front pocket?"

"That's the one," Roma replied.

She didn't know how Roma had distinguished the tail as British. He looked like any other foreigner on the street.

Juliette peered closer at her mirror. She changed the angle slightly, slightly . . .

"Roma," she said, her voice rising. "He's got a gun."

"Every foreigner in this city has a gun—"

"He's pointing it at us," Juliette cut in. "He just drew it from behind his newspaper."

Tense silence fell between the two as they desperately thought through their options. Around them, Shanghai continued moving, alive and vibrant and unbothered. But Roma and Juliette couldn't merge back into this crowd without being followed to wherever they were going next. There was no cover to hide behind and disappear from, nowhere to draw their own weapons before the Brit could see and shoot first.

"Untie your coat and embrace me," Roma said.

Juliette choked on her sudden laugh. She waited for the pin to drop, but Roma was being serious.

"You're kidding," she said.

"No, I'm not," Roma countered evenly. "Do it, so I can shoot him."

Their British tail was more than a hundred paces away. There were dozens of civilians walking back and forth in the space between. How did Roma expect to shoot him amid all those conditions, while *embracing* Juliette?

Juliette gave the ribbon around her waist a tug, loosening her coat and lifting her arm in the same movement. In her other hand, she snapped her mirror closed, cutting off all her sights on the tail.

"I hope you know what you're doing," she whispered. Her lungs were tight. Her pulse was a raging war drum.

She wrapped her arms around Roma's neck.

Juliette heard his breath catch. A quick inhale, hardly perceptible had she not been so near. Perhaps he had not considered the fact that asking Juliette to act his cover would mean coming close to her. He certainly hadn't expected her chin to automatically find its place in the crook where his shoulder met his neck, just as it always used to.

They had both grown tall and grown thorns. Yet Juliette had slotted back so easily—far too easily for her own liking.

"Lean closer," Roma instructed. She felt his arm moving, retrieving his pistol behind the cover of her coat as it billowed on either side of them in the breeze.

Juliette remembered when Roma swore to her that he would never pick up a gun. He had never grown comfortable with automatic weaponry like she had. In those few months she had spent in Shanghai at fifteen, Roma hadn't been living the same life as she had. While he operated in his comfortable claim as the heir of the White Flowers, Juliette was fighting to be seen, hanging on to her father's every word in fear that missing a single instruction would place her into obscurity.

We do not have the luxury of mercy, Juliette. Look at this city. Look at the starvation that squirms under the layer of glamour.

Her father's favorite teaching tactic had been to take her to the attic of the house, so they could peer through the highest window together and squint at the city center on the horizon.

Empires can fall in mere hours. This one is no different. Here in Shanghai, whoever shoots first has the best chance of surviving.

Juliette had learned her lesson. It seemed that Roma had picked up the same sentiment in the years she had been gone.

"Don't miss," Juliette whispered.

"I never do."

A *bang* sounded from the space between them. Juliette immediately whirled around to catch the British tail collapsing where he stood, a bright-red spot blooming on his chest. There was a smoking hole in Juliette's coat, but she barely noticed. Her mind was on the screams resounding around her as they sought the source of the sound, on the flurry of movement that had started atop the cobblestones.

Gunshot sounds were common in Shanghai, but never in a place so occupied, never in a place that the foreigners liked to brag about to their friends back home. Gunshot sounds belonged to gangsters and conflicts across territory lines, in the hours when the devil prowled the streets and there was moonlight beaming down from the sky. Now was supposed to be reserved for the warmth of the sunset. Now was supposed to be a time of pretending Shanghai wasn't split in two.

Yet in the chaos, there were three other places of absolute stillness.

Juliette hadn't been followed by one man. She had been followed by four.

So they needed to run *now*.

"The arcade," Juliette commanded. She turned to Roma, frowning over his slowness. "Come *on*. This is the first time I've actually had to run from a crime I've committed."

Roma blinked. His eyes were pulled wide, disbelieving. He didn't seem to be entirely present as they dove into the crowd, pushing against the abundance of hands and elbows that were surging in all directions in an attempt to find safety.

"A crime *you* committed?" Roma echoed softly. Juliette had to strain to hear him. "*I* shot that gun."

Juliette scoffed, turning. "Do you really need credit for—" Her sentence died against her lips. She had thought Roma was correcting her, claiming ownership over the crime, but then she saw the expression on his face. It had been an accusation.

He hadn't wanted to shoot.

Juliette turned away quickly, shaking her head as though she had seen something she wasn't supposed to. Here she was, thinking that he had finally adapted to the gun, and in the very next second he was surprising her with his playacting. How much of his exterior was a mere image? Juliette hadn't considered before this moment that while Roma was being swept into the rumors on *her* cruelty, thinking her transformed into someone else, perhaps Juliette had been falling into the exact same trap, buying into the tales of ice and coldness that had originated from within the White Flowers themselves.

Juliette frowned, ducking to surge through a small gap between two open parasols. When she emerged on the other side, her eyes wandered over to Roma again—to his clenched jaw and his calculating stare.

She never seemed to know what was real and what was not when it came to Roma Montagov. She thought she knew him, and then she did not. She thought she had adjusted after he betrayed her, marked him off as wicked and bloodthirsty, but it seemed he still was not.

Maybe there was no truth. Maybe nothing was as easy as one truth.

"Quickly," Juliette said to him, shaking her head to clear her mind.

They managed to enter Great World, pausing at the entranceway to check for their pursuers. Juliette glanced over her shoulder and found two of the three men she had spotted before, each pushing their way through the crowd, their eyes glued on her. They moved strategically, always behind a civilian, always ducked low to the ground. Roma was tugging at her shoulder to keep her moving, but she was searching for the third man, her hand going to her ankle.

"Where is he?" she asked.

Roma searched the crowd, and after a fraction of a second, pointed to the very side, where the man was running, perhaps looking for an alternate entrance into Great World so that he could corner them inside.

Juliette pulled her pistol from her sock. The man was seconds from disappearing from view.

Even if Roma was not the brutal heir this city thought him to be, that did not mean Juliette's reputation was any less true.

The running man crumpled as Juliette's bullet embedded into his neck. Before her pistol had stopped smoking, Juliette had already pivoted on her heel and was shoving deeper into the building.

Inside Great World, most of the attendees hadn't heard the gunshots, or had simply thought them part of the arcade's sound and atmosphere. Juliette wove through the crowd, her reflection darting by in the corner of her eye as she tried to navigate past the exhibit of distorting mirrors.

"How are we going to lose the other two?" Roma called.

"Follow me," Juliette said.

They pushed through the thickest part of the crowd and burst outdoors, into the hollow center of Great World. An opera show was in full swing here, but Juliette was busy searching for another inner entrance back into the building of Great World, frantically eyeing the external staircases that zigzagged from floor to floor. Juliette surged forward again and plowed through a family of five, then ran into a woman carrying a birdcage, wincing when the cage clattered to the floor and the bird gave a squawk of death.

"Juliette," Roma chided from behind. "Watch it."

"Hurry up," Juliette snapped in response.

His carefulness was slowing him down. Juliette caught a flash of one pursuer coming through the mirror exhibit. The other collided with an exasperated love-letter scribe making for the exit.

"Where are we going?" Roma huffed.

Juliette pointed to the wide white stairs that loomed into view. "Up," she said. "Quick, quick—no, Roma, *duck!*"

The moment they pulled up onto the stairs, elevating atop the crowd, the pursuers had clear shots at them. Bullets ricocheted through the open space, urging Juliette to take the steps three at a time.

"Juliette, I don't like this!" Roma shouted. His footfalls were heavier than hers, taking four at a time to stay at her speed.

"This isn't my idea of fun, either," Juliette shouted in response, stumbling onto the second-floor landing and bursting back inside the central, circular building. "Keep up!"

This floor was occupied by people, not attractions: pimps and actors and barbers all offering their services to those who were searching.

"This way," Juliette said, panting. She dashed past the startled row of earwax extractors and barged through two swinging doors. Roma followed suit.

"In here, in here."

Juliette grabbed Roma's sleeve, yanking him furiously into the racks of lace-hemmed robes.

"Are we . . . ? Are we hiding?" Roma whispered.

"Only temporarily," Juliette replied. "Squat."

They squatted into the clothes, holding their breath. A second later the doors burst open and both remaining pursuers entered, heaving loudly into the quiet of the dressing room.

"Check that side," one demanded of the other. British accent. "I'll check over here. They couldn't have gone far."

Juliette watched the two men part, following their progress with their feet, waiting until the two pairs of shoes were a good distance separated.

"That one is yours," Juliette whispered, pointing to the set of shoes coming closer and closer. "Kill him."

Roma grabbed her wrist, the motion whip quick. "No," he hissed quietly. "It's two against two. They can be spared without harm."

A metallic *clang!* rang through the room. One of the men had tipped over a clothing rack.

Juliette pulled her wrist away harshly, then nodded just so they weren't wasting more time arguing. She scuttled forward. While the man she had assigned to Roma had stopped near him, likely scanning his surroundings, the other kept pacing, and to keep up with him, Juliette had no choice but to spring up from her squat and move fast, breaking into a run through the racks with her back hunched.

She didn't know what gave it away. Perhaps her shoe had squeaked or perhaps her hand had brushed up against a hanger that clinked against metal, but suddenly the man stopped and whirled around, his gun firing into the racks, his bullet skimming past Juliette's ear.

Another shot fired nearby. Juliette didn't know if that had been the other man or Roma. She didn't know what was happening except she was darting out from the racks and aiming at the man, needing to pinpoint her shot within the millisecond before he took aim again.

Her barrel smoked. Her bullet embedded into the man's right shoulder, and his weapon dropped to the floor.

"Roma," Juliette called, her eyes and aim still pinned on the Brit. "Did you get him?"

"Knocked him out cold," Roma replied. He strolled closer, coming to a stop right behind Juliette while she pointed the gun forward.

"Who sent you?" she asked their last pursuer.

"I don't know," the Brit said quickly. His eyes swiveled from the door to her gun's barrel and back to the door again. He was twenty paces away from the exit.

"What do you mean you don't know?" Roma demanded.

"Other merchants spread the word that there was money from the

Larkspur for whoever killed Juliette Cai or Roma Montagov," the man stammered. "We tried our hand at it. Please—come on, just let me go. It seemed too good to pass up, you know? We thought we would have enough trouble finding you separately, but then you showed up together. It's not like we actually would have succeeded. . . ."

The man trailed off. By the widening of his eyes, it seemed that he was realizing what he held in his inventory. He knew. He knew that Roma Montagov and Juliette Cai were working together. He had seen their embrace. That gave him information to take to the Larkspur; that gave him power.

The man lunged for the door. Roma yelled out in warning—it was incomprehensible whether he was directing his shout at the Brit or at Juliette—and darted after the Brit furiously, one hand outstretched in a bid to grasp his collar and haul him back into the room like a stray dog.

By then Juliette had already pulled the trigger. The man dropped to the floor, slipping out of Roma's grasp with a heavy finality.

Roma stared down at the dead man. For the briefest moment Juliette caught shock marred in his wide eyes, before he blinked once and shuttered it away.

"You didn't have to kill him."

Juliette stepped forward. There was a splotch of blood on Roma's pale cheek, running an arch so that his cheekbone was stark in the dim bulb's light.

"He would have killed us."

"You know"—Roma dragged his eyes up from the body—"that he got pulled into this. He didn't choose it like we did."

Once upon a time, Roma and Juliette had come up with a list of rules that, if followed, would have made the city something tolerable. It wouldn't make Shanghai kind, only salvageable, because that was the best they could do. Gangsters should only kill other gangsters. The only fair targets were those who chose the life they led, which,

Juliette later realized, included the common workers—the maids, the chauffeurs, *Nurse*.

Fight dirty but fight bravely. Do not fight those who cannot understand what it means to fight.

Nurse had known exactly what working for the Scarlet Gang entailed. *This* man had pulled at a hint of glitter in the ground expecting a nugget of gold and disturbed a hornet's nest instead. They would leave him here, in a puddle of his own blood, and soon someone would come in and find him. The poor worker to make the discovery would call the police and the municipal forces would arrive with a weary sigh, looking upon the man with no more emotion than someone observing a dead wheat field—displeased with the general loss upon the world but overall void of any personal attachment.

By all their old rules, these men chasing after them should have been spared. But Juliette had lost those old rules the second she lost the old Roma. When conflict erupted, she thought about herself, her own safety—not that of the man waving a gun in her face.

But an agreement was still an agreement.

"Fine," Juliette said shortly.

"Fine?" Roma echoed.

Without quite looking at him, Juliette pulled a silk handkerchief from her coat and passed it forward. "Fine," she said again, as if he hadn't heard her the first time. "You said to spare them, and though I agreed, I still went against it. That is my wrongdoing. While we keep working together, we listen to each other."

Roma brought the handkerchief to his face slowly. He dabbed an inch away from where the splatter actually was, wiping at nothing except the brutal line of his jaw. Juliette thought he would be content with her poor attempt at an apology, would at least nod in satisfaction. Instead, his eyes only grew more distant.

"We used to be pretty good at that."

A pit formed in Juliette's stomach. "What?"

"Working together. Listening." He had stopped wiping at his face. His hand merely hovered in the air, its task undetermined. "We used to be a team, Juliette."

Juliette strode forward and yanked the silk from Roma's hands. She was almost insulted that he was so aggressively bad at wiping up a simple blood splatter; in one furious swipe, she had stained the white of her silk with a deep red and his face was beautiful once more.

"None of it," Juliette hissed, "was *real*."

There was something awful about the shrinking distance between them—like the coiling of a spring, winding tighter and tighter. Any sudden movements were bound to end in disaster.

"Of course," Roma said. His tone was dull. His eyes were electric, like he, too, was only remembering just now. "Forgive me for that particular oversight."

A tense moment passed in stillness: the slow release of the spring back into its usual position. Juliette looked away first, moved her foot so it wouldn't touch the puddle of blood growing upon the rotting wood floors. This was a city shrouded in blood. It was foolish to try changing it.

"It would appear that while we search for the Larkspur, the Larkspur looms closer to us," she remarked, gesturing to the dead man.

"It means we're onto something," Roma said surely. "We're closer to saving Alisa."

Juliette nodded. Somehow, it seemed that the Larkspur knew they were coming. But if he thought a few merchants were enough to scare them off, he would be sorely disappointed.

"We must arrive at his location before the night grows late."

She produced the flyer heralding the vaccination, folding it so that the address at the bottom was on display. Absently, she used her other hand to wipe at a damp feeling on her neck, wondering if she had, in fact, also acquired blood splatter on herself without noticing.

Roma nodded. "Let's go."

Twenty-Three

O nce it must have been silent here. Perhaps there had been the occasional horse tearing by on its hooves, passing pasture after pasture until the grooves it forged into the dirt created a trail. In a few quick years, trails forged from centuries of heavy footfalls had been paved over. Pebbles that had thought themselves immortal were crushed into nothing; trees older than whole countries were felled and destroyed.

And in their place, greed grew. It grew into train tracks, linking village to village until there were no boundaries. It grew into wires, and pipes, and apartment complexes stacked atop one another with little planning.

Juliette thought the International Settlement might have gotten the worst of it. The invaders couldn't erase the people already living within the area they decided to call their own, but they could erase everything else.

Where did the lanterns go? Juliette wondered, stopping at the streetside and craning her head up. *What is Shanghai without its lanterns?*

"We're here," Roma said, cutting into her reverie. "This is the address on the flyers."

He pointed to the building behind the one Juliette was staring at. For a second, as Juliette looked upon it, she thought her eyes were playing tricks on her. Tonight was a dark night, but there was enough low, oil-fueled light streaming through its windows to illuminate rows upon rows of people outside: a line starting from the front door that was so long it curled thrice around the building.

She charged ahead.

"Juliette!" Roma hissed. "Juliette, wait—"

It doesn't matter, Roma, she wanted to tell him. She knew what he was thinking, or at least some variation of it: They had to be careful. They had to avoid being spotted together. They had the Larkspur's assassins on their heels, so they had to watch who they were upsetting. *It doesn't matter,* she wanted to scream. If their people didn't stop dying, if they couldn't save what they were trying to protect, nothing in this world mattered anymore.

Juliette shoved her way to the front of the line. When an elderly man near the door tried to push her back, she spat the nastiest curse she could summon in Shanghainese, and he shrank like his life had been sucked from his veins.

Juliette sensed Roma's presence behind her when she came to a stop in front of the towering man who guarded the door. Roma settled a cautious hand on her elbow in warning. This man was twice as wide as her. A head-to-toe glance under the oil lamp's light told her he was possibly hired help, from a country farther south than China, from places where hunger was fuel and desperation was the engine.

The prodding at her elbow increased. Juliette moved her arm away, shooting a cautionary glance back at Roma, commanding him to stop.

Roma had never been so worried for their safety.

He had been in plenty of shoot-outs with the Scarlet Gang in the years Juliette had been away. Despite his hatred of the White Flower fight club, he had been in more street brawls than he would care to admit and grabbed his fair share of scars because his first reaction to a blade was always to block instead of move. It was inevitable; even if he hated the violence, the violence found him, and he was either to cooperate or be cut down.

But he had always had backup. He had several sets of eyes working his every angle.

This right now was just him and Juliette against a shadowy third threat that was neither Scarlet Gang nor White Flower. This was just the two of them against a force that wanted them both dead, that wanted the present powers in Shanghai crushed until there was only anarchy.

"Let us through," Juliette demanded.

"Employees of the Larkspur only," the guard said, his words a deep, deep rumble. "Otherwise you've got to wait your turn."

Roma peered over his shoulder, his breath coming as quick as his rapid motions. They were mostly flocked by the interlocked lines, but a few men and women weren't standing quite right. They weren't *in* the line; they were hovering just outside it—keeping the peace without giving themselves away as personnel.

"Juliette," Roma warned. He switched to Russian to avoid being understood by eavesdroppers. "There are at least five others in this crowd who have been hired with the Larkspur's dirty money. They have weapons. They *will* react if you pose yourself as a threat."

"They have weapons?" Juliette echoed. Her Russian always had a twang to it; it wasn't quite an accent—her tutor had been too good for that. It was an idiosyncrasy, a way she spoke her vowels that made them uniquely Juliette. "So do I."

Juliette swung her fist. In an arc that started at her stomach and pulled outward, she backhanded the guard so hard that he dropped like a stone, falling out of the way to allow Juliette to kick open the door and pull Roma through before he had even caught up with the chain of events.

She used her gun, he realized belatedly. Juliette hadn't suddenly obtained the strength of a wrestler—she simply had her pistol clutched backward in her fist and had used the butt of it against the guard's temple. The guard hadn't even seen her retrieve it. Her sleight of hand had remained completely off the radar while his focus remained on her face—on the set of her jaw and her cold smile.

Juliette embraced danger with open arms. It seemed that Roma couldn't do so even when his whole world was at risk, even while Alisa was strapped down by her arms and legs. He almost feared what it would take to push him to the brink, and he hoped it would never happen, because he himself didn't want to see it if that time came.

"Bolt it," Juliette said.

Roma returned to reality. He eyed the thin steel door and slammed it shut, turning the lock. He warily eyed Juliette too, then the four walls they had found themselves within. They were at the base of a stairwell, one that ascended so steeply that Roma couldn't identify what awaited at the end.

"We have five minutes at most before they break through this flimsy thing," Roma estimated. The banging against the door from the outside was already starting.

"Five minutes should be plenty," Juliette said. She jabbed a thumb in the direction of the door. "My worry is we'll have even less because of this noise."

She took the stairs up two at a time, the pistol in her hand disappearing out of sight. Despite having his eyes pinned on her the entire time, Roma wasn't sure where it had gone. Her coat had one shallow pocket. Her dress inside was only a long slip of fabric with a multitude of beads. *How is she concealing all her weapons?*

At the second to last step, the smell of incense wafted under Roma's nose. He supposed he wasn't entirely surprised when he arrived at the landing and took in the scene. It reminded him of the storybooks Lady Montagova had read to him when he was young, about Arabian nights and djinn in the deserts. Colorful silk curtains fluttered with the breeze that Roma and Juliette's commotion was stirring up, revealing the crumbling windowsills underneath, edging dangerously close to the candles burning on the ground. Plush, woven rugs were splayed on both the floors and walls, humming with warmth and giving off a unique *old* sort of odor. There wasn't a single chair to be seen, only a maelstrom of pillows and cushions, each "seat" occupied by the many under the Larkspur's thumb.

In the center of it all, a low table was situated between a woman with a needle and a man with his arm out. They both sat on pillows too.

"Mon Dieu," the man at the table cried out. Juliette's pistol had returned. It was pointed at the woman with the needle.

"Are you the Larkspur?" she asked in English.

Roma scanned the twenty odd other occupants in the room. He couldn't quite decipher who was under the employment of the Larkspur and who was here for the vaccine. Half had sat up straighter, signaling their involvement in the scheme, but it didn't look like they were about to interfere. Their elbows trembled; their necks sank into their shoulders. These were all people like Paul Dexter, who had called on the White Flowers once or twice too now. They thought themselves powerful and prized, but ultimately, they were gutless. They would hardly even dare speak about seeing Roma and Juliette working together, in case they could not produce proof.

The woman did not respond immediately. She withdrew the needle and cleaned the tip, opening a small case beside her. On one side, a row of five red vials glistened under the firelight. On the other side, a row of four blue ones sat waiting.

With the longer the woman drew out her answer, the more likely it seemed that she *had* to be the Larkspur and the masculine pronouns everybody was using were simply an assumption.

Until the woman looked up suddenly—her kohl-dark eyes and thick eyelashes glaring at the muzzle of Juliette's pistol—and said, "No, I am not."

She had an uncommon accent, leaning into French but not quite. The Frenchman sitting opposite her was completely frozen. Perhaps he thought if he didn't move, he wouldn't be registered in Juliette's sight.

"What is in those injections?" Juliette asked.

Her other hand, the one that wasn't clutching a pistol, was jerking around by her side as she spoke. Roma didn't understand what she was doing for a long moment, until it clicked that she was *pointing* at the vials. She wanted him to grab one.

"Now, if I told you," the woman said, "we would go out of business."

While Roma inched closer and closer to the vials, there was nothing Juliette wanted to do more than to pull the trigger. A long time ago, one of her tutors had said that being terribly hot-headed was her fatal flaw. She couldn't remember which tutor it was now—Chinese literature? French? Etiquette? Whatever subject it was, it didn't matter; she had lashed out in indignation because of the comment and directly proved her tutor correct.

She would breathe deeply now. *Smile,* she told herself. Before meeting every stranger in New York, she went through the same routine: smile, shoulders back, eyes heavy. She was light and bubbly and the epitome of the flapper girl, working ten times as hard to maintain the perception she wanted just because of the skin she wore.

"Answer this, then," Juliette said. Her grin forced its way out, as if she found this impossibly entertaining, as if the pistol in her hand weren't level with the woman's eyes. "What does the Larkspur know of the madness? Why would he have the cure when no one else does?"

Roma had bent into a crouch while Juliette handled the talking. He clapped a hand over the Frenchman's neck in an attempt to intimidate him, giving him instructions in French to get up and get out of his sight. While Roma spoke, he was leaning closer, pretending to get a kick out of looming over the man. The reality was that he was leaning so he could take up as much of the table as possible, until his arm hovered right above the case of injection vials, and with a flick of his finger, he had slid a blue vial down his sleeve.

Meanwhile, oblivious to what was going on right under her nose, the woman shrugged, infuriatingly calm. Her aloofness spilled gasoline upon the tension already brewing thick in the room, one spark away from explosion.

"You will have to ask the Larkspur yourself," the woman replied, "but I am afraid nobody knows where—or who—he is."

Juliette almost pulled the trigger then and there. She didn't *want* the woman dead; nor did she enjoy killing people for fun. But if they got in her way, they needed to be moved. It wasn't a kill she wanted, but action. Her people were dropping like flies to some madness she couldn't control, her city was shaking in fear at the thought of some monster she couldn't confront, and she was so sick of doing *nothing*.

Anything would be better than standing motionless. When Juliette wanted to blow up in frustration, the only solution was blowing something else up.

Roma straightened up from his crouch and touched her elbow.

"I have it," he muttered softly in Russian, and Juliette—with her teeth gritted so hard that she sent sour pains spiriting up and down her jaw—lowered her gun.

Juliette cleared her throat. "Very well. Keep your secrets. Do you have a window we could jump from?"

"Is it time to go home yet?"

Benedikt rolled his eyes. They were strolling the streets, ears perked for chaos but otherwise on low alert. It wasn't as if they hadn't expected this. Their searches had been futile every time. Those who fell to the madness were either resisting until the very last second or already dead.

"This was a waste of time," Marshall whined. "A waste, Ben! A waaaaaa—"

Benedikt pressed his hand into Marshall's face. This motion was so familiar that he did not need to look; he simply extended his hand outward as they walked side by side and smashed his fingers into whatever flesh he could find.

Marshall only put up with it for three short seconds. After that he was prodding at Benedikt wildly, cackling as Benedikt yelled for him to stop, his words unintelligible in his effort not to laugh while his ribs ached.

He would have been content to laugh, to fill the night with good spirits even if the night would give nothing back. Only then he heard it.

A strange, strange sound.

"Mars," Benedikt gasped. "Wait, I'm serious."

"Oh, you're serious, are you—"

"I'm serious. *Listen!*"

Marshall stopped suddenly, realizing that Benedikt wasn't kidding. His hand slowly loosened from his deathly grip on the other boy's wrist. He turned his ear to the wind, listening.

Choking—that was the sound.

"Excellent," Marshall said, rolling up his sleeves. "Finally. *Finally.*" He charged forward, shoulders folded like he was barging into battle with a shield in one hand and a spear in the other. That was Marshall. Even when he had nothing with him, he could carry the guise of something.

Benedikt ran after his friend, moving on his toes in his attempt to see over Marshall's shoulder, trying to locate the victim. It was a silhouette that Benedikt saw first—a primordial thing hunched over in two, looking more like an animal than a person.

They were dead center in White Flower territory, in the easternmost section of the eastern half of the city. Benedikt had expected one of their own to be dying. But it wasn't a White Flower coughing in the alleyway. As the figure lifted their head in apprehension over Benedikt's and Marshall's nearing voices, swinging back a long rope of black hair that reflected silver in the moonlight, Benedikt caught sight of uniformed shoulders: the clothing of the Nationalist army.

"Grab her," Benedikt commanded.

The woman took a step back. She had either understood Benedikt's Russian or she had heard something in his desperate tone.

She didn't get very far. Her foot staggered one step in reverse and then she was pressed against the brick wall, backing into nothing. If she had had more control over herself, she would have pivoted on her heel and run out the other end of the alleyway. But she was lost— delirious to the insects working against her nerves as they instructed for her to tear at her throat.

"Are you joking?" Marshall hissed. "She's a Nationalist. They'll come after us—"

Benedikt surged forward, his hand going for his gun. "They won't know."

Usually it was Marshall making the erratic decisions. Marshall was only ever sensible when he was trying to keep Benedikt away from trouble.

"Ben!"

It was too late. As hard as he could, Benedikt slammed the butt of his revolver against the Nationalist's head, arching his shoulders forward to keep his own skull far away. Once she dropped to the ground, her neck lolling back on the concrete and her hands splayed outward with blood coating the first inch of her fingers, Benedikt hauled her up with a grunt, carrying her around the waist like a rag doll.

There was blood dripping down her forehead. More rings of blood stained the space around her neck, but at least there wasn't any leak around a major vein. She would stay alive until they could get her to the lab.

This is a person, a voice in the deepest corners of Benedikt's mind was hissing. *You cannot abduct a person off the streets for experimentation.*

She was going to die anyway.

Do you get to decide when?

More people would die otherwise.

You have killed too many people to claim you care about human life.

"Help me," Benedikt said to Marshall, struggling with the woman's deadweight.

Marshall grimaced. "Yeah, yeah," he muttered, inching over. A flash of a blade in his hand; then the woman's long braid detached, landing with a dispassionate thump on the floor.

"Helps prevent contamination to us," Marshall explained. He grabbed her legs, taking on some of the burden. "Now, let's move. Lourens is probably closing up."

Twenty-Four

Juliette was clenching her fist.

Open, closed, open, closed. Her hands were absolutely *itching* for something to do.

Mostly, they were begging to get ahold of the vial that Roma had tucked in his sleeve. Juliette hadn't asked for it—she wouldn't overstep her bounds that far and have him think she mistrusted him that much. But it was a true test of strength to keep her hands to herself and not attempt a snatching.

"It's just around this corner," Roma assured, either oblivious to her internal turmoil or misinterpreting it. "We're nearly there."

He spoke to her like she was a startled rabbit about to bolt. Juliette was antsy, but just because she was on White Flower territory didn't mean she was about to let herself be attacked, and the more Roma tried to be kind to her, the more her nose wrinkled.

"You are more nervous than I am right now," Juliette commented.

"I am not," Roma shot back. "I am simply a cautious person."

"I don't recall you looking over your shoulder every second when you came into the Scarlet burlesque club."

In fact, she recalled him looking rather confident, which had annoyed her immensely.

Roma gave her a sidelong glance, narrowing his tired eyes. He needed a moment to find his answer, and when he did, he simply muttered, "Times have changed."

They had indeed. Starting from the mere fact that Roma and Juliette were walking side by side and yet Juliette's arms were casually swinging, positioned far from her weapons.

When they turned the corner, Juliette immediately spotted the research facility Roma had described. Among the row of buildings, it was the only one more silver-toned than brown, bearing metal platings that shone under the moonlight, where others, constructed of plaster or wood, only glowed dully. She took her time admiring the sight, but Roma ran up to the door quickly, long accustomed to the appearance of such detailing.

"Did you fund this?" Juliette asked.

She eyed the fancy lock that Roma was twirling around. His eyes were focused on the rapidly spinning numbers that appeared above the panel, moving the dial into the hundreds before dropping back to 51, 50, 49 . . . Though the inside of the glass-paned doors was dark, she could make out a long hallway and one sole door that gleamed with light.

"*I* did not," Roma replied.

A heavy sigh from Juliette. "Did *the White Flowers* fund this place, you wet blanket?"

The lock clicked. Roma pulled the door open and signaled for Juliette to go ahead. "Indeed."

Juliette nodded. There was some surprise, some acknowledgment, and just the smallest hint of approval in that small jerk of her head. The Scarlet Gang would never fund something like this. She assumed the White Flowers probably tested their products here, making sure that the drugs they traded were what the merchants said they were, but with technology like this, there were infinite possibilities in research and innovation.

The Chinese were still very much people of the past. They emphasized classical texts and poetry over science, and it showed—in the dingy, cramped basements that the Scarlet drug testers were placed in, in the thousands of poems Juliette had been given to memorize before she was taught the basics of natural selection.

She looked up at the neatly spaced electric lights, all currently extinguished into darkness. Even while swathed in shadow, she could pick out the unblemished lines in the ceiling, the bulbs that were undoubtedly polished by cleaners every weekend on the clock.

"Lourens, let me in."

The hallway suddenly lit up, but not from the bulbs. The one door that had been brimming with light had opened.

"Zdravstvuyte, zdravstvuyte," Lourens bellowed, sticking his head out with his greeting. He faltered upon seeing Juliette. "Ei—nǐ hǎo?"

His confusion was almost endearing.

"You don't have to switch, sir," she said in Russian, walking toward the lab. Internally, Juliette quickly ran through the possibilities of his accent. "But we can speak Dutch if you'd like."

"Oh, that's not necessary," Lourens said. The wrinkles near his eyes crinkled deeply in amusement. He had never looked so charmed. "Poor Roma here would feel terribly left out."

Roma pulled a face. "Excuse *me*, I—" He stopped. He turned to the doorway, appearing to be listening hard. "Is somebody coming?"

Indeed, in that moment, two figures burst through the doorway, carrying between them a prone form—an unconscious woman in a Nationalist uniform. Benedikt Montagov blinked in bewilderment, taken aback to see Juliette standing mere meters away from his cousin. Marshall Seo only snorted, waving his hand for them to move aside so they could enter the lab. It was after hours now. The worktables had been cleared and emptied, wiped down and polished to ready a nice, spacious surface that the Nationalist could be set down upon. As soon as she was placed upon the table, her body stilled, but her hair rustled about, sections of her scalp *twitching*.

Juliette pressed her hand to her mouth. Her eyes tracked the dots of blood marring the Nationalist's neck, little crescent moons that seemed to be the result of sharp nails. This woman was infected with the madness. But she was not yet dead.

"Sorry to barge in," Marshall Seo said. He sounded a little too proud of himself to be truly apologetic. "Are we interrupting anything?"

Roma placed his vial down on another worktable. The blue of its liquid glistened under the glaring white light.

"Only the answer to whether the Larkspur really made a true vaccine, but it can wait," he said. "Lourens, you wanted to run tests on a live victim of the madness, yes?"

"Certainly, but—" Lourens gestured to Juliette. "There's a lady in the room."

"The lady is interested in seeing you run your tests, please," Juliette said. With the exception of her brief surprise upon her first sighting of the Nationalist, it would have been impossible to find any sort of shock from Juliette. She spoke as if this were an everyday occurrence.

Lourens blew out a breath. He wiped his brow, his movements slow even while the world around him sped up at the appearance of this dying Nationalist. "Very well, then. Let us see if we can find a cure."

He began.

Juliette watched in fascination as the scientist hauled out a box and retrieved its contents, filling the lab with equipment and machinery more fitting for a hospital than a drug-testing facility. Lourens took blood samples and tissue samples and—with his lips thinned—he even took hair follicles from the Nationalist on the table, putting them under a microscope and jotting notes at record speed. Juliette folded her arms and tapped her foot, ignoring the whispering between the three White Flowers on the other side of the room. Her ears would begin to burn if she listened in. She didn't know what other topic could possibly engross them so much, would prompt Roma to gesture wildly with his hands as he hissed in low tones to his two friends.

"This is unfortunate."

Lourens's remark rapidly reeled back in the attention of the three in the corner.

"What did you find?" Roma asked, breaking away from his friends.

"That is the very problem," Lourens replied. "Nothing. Even with advanced equipment, I see nothing that the doctors across Shanghai don't already see. There is nothing about this woman's vitals that would suggest infection of any kind."

Juliette frowned, then leaned on the table behind her, remaining silent.

Marshall demanded, "Then is there no way to cure the madness?"

"Impossible," Roma countered immediately. For his sanity, he had to believe that a cure existed. He could not even allow himself to entertain the notion of a doomed investigation, of Alisa never waking again.

"Perhaps it is not that there is no cure," Benedikt added, speaking more evenly. His words were all enunciated to the cleanest degree, like he had practiced the sentence in his head before he spoke it aloud. "You said that this madness was somebody's creation, after all. If there is a cure, it is not for us to see. If there is a cure, only whoever engineered the madness has the instruction."

Lourens pulled off his gloves. The machines around him were humming at different pitches, filling the lab with an almost musical air.

"Too many factors," Lourens said. "Too many secrets, too much information we do not have. It would be absurd to try attempting it—"

"You haven't tried everything yet," Juliette said.

Every pair of eyes in the room—those who were conscious, anyway—turned to look at her. Juliette lifted her chin.

"You took her blood, looked at her skin—it's all too human, too bodily." Juliette walked toward the unconscious Nationalist, peered down at this entity of flesh, a vessel for life that had been altered. "This madness is not natural. Why try to engineer a cure the natural way? Slice her head open. Pull the insects out."

"Juliette," Roma chided. "That's—"

Lourens was already picking up a scalpel, shrugging unceremoniously.

"Wait," Benedikt said. "Last time—"

The tip of the blade sank into the Nationalist's scalp. Lourens pulled gently on only a small section of her hair to make a parting and clear space to extract an insect. . . .

The Nationalist spasmed viciously. The entire table rocked, and Juliette didn't know if it had shifted seriously enough to make a terrible creaking noise or if it was actually her ragged gasp that echoed through the room. One second the woman on the table could have rivaled the dead. The next she was writhing, her hand clutched to her chest and her legs rigidly straight. Her eyes remained closed. The only way they could tell when she died was when her hand fell from her chest and swung down from the table, waving back and forth like a heavy pendulum.

Her hair, once again, stirred. This time, it was not just the insects settling—they were leaving, some streaming down her neck in little lines of black, hurrying down her body in a mass evacuation with such order that they resembled a dark fluid.

Others flew wide, springing out with no warning whatsoever to latch on to whatever was nearest.

For two insects, the nearest host was Lourens's beard.

The landing happened in slow motion to Juliette's eyes, but Roma was already moving. By the time she had registered the horror of what it meant to see two little black specks disappearing into the tufts of white, Roma already had a knife in his hand. By the time she even thought to call out a warning, Roma took the knife and sheared through Lourens's beard as close as he dared to get to skin, flinging the white hairs to the ground.

They waited.

The machines had gone to sleep. Now the labs were filled only with heavy breathing.

They waited.

Two insects surged out from the clump of hair on the ground. Roma stomped down hard, crushing them without mercy. A hundred more insects had been released into the night when they shot through the crack underneath the lab door before anyone could stop them, but at least killing two out of the thousands was better than killing none.

Lourens touched his bare chin. His wrinkled eyes were pulled uncharacteristically wide.

"Well," Lourens said. "Thank you, Roma. Let's move on to the vaccine you brought me, then, shall we?"

Twenty-Five

S o," Roma said, "may I warn you not to report back your findings about this facility?"

They were waiting now on the first floor, seated upon the metal chairs scattered along the far wall. At some point they needed to get rid of the corpse that lay in front of them, but for now it remained—its scrunched, anxious face frozen in death while Lourens poured the vaccine into little test tubes, squeezing various chemicals into some and placing others into the rumbling machines he had on the second floor, humming under his breath while he worked above them.

"As if your feeble warning would work," Juliette replied. "You should know that by now."

Roma slumped in his seat, his head lolling against the backrest. "Should I have blindfolded you?"

Juliette scoffed. She tapped her shoes rapidly, twisting the heel left and right like windshield wipers while her eyes did the same, darting from sight to sight. "Even if I wanted to play spy," she said, "this information would be useless." She eyed a particularly sharp silver thing coming down overhead like an icicle. It descended from a machine, hanging where the ceiling of the first floor meshed into the railing of the second floor.

"Useless?" Roma echoed in disbelief. His sharp tone drew the attention of his two friends, who had otherwise been staring off into space, seated on chairs along the perpendicular wall.

"Deemed unnecessary," Juliette corrected. She wasn't quite sure why she was carrying on this conversation. It wasn't as if she owed him an explanation, and yet all the same, it didn't seem like it would hurt to explain. "The Scarlet Gang remains in the age of traditional herbs. Perhaps one or two metal machines. We are nowhere near"—she waved her hands around—"this."

Her parents would not care about these findings if she ran back with them. If she could even get their attention for a short minute, they would rather ask why she had been in a White Flower facility and hadn't thought to burn it down.

Roma folded his arms. "Interesting."

Juliette narrowed her eyes. "Now are you going to report *that* information back?"

"Why would I?" Roma had a sly sort of smile playing on his lips, one that he wasn't letting slip out completely. "We already knew that."

Juliette stamped her foot down in a fit of feigned anger, but Roma was too quick. He moved his toes away, and all Juliette achieved was a shock rocketing up her ankle.

Her ankle throbbed; a genuine snort of amusement slipped out. It was an acknowledgment that she had been bested on this small matter, that she had fallen back on her old petty tricks and forgotten that Roma knew those well.

"Can't do that—" Roma said.

"—else you have to step on me in return," Juliette finished.

At once their smiles faded. At once they were remembering the times when Juliette had giggled at Roma's superstition, the times when he would have her hold still after she had stomped on his foot and gently—ever so gently—stepped on her toes too.

"We will be fated to have an argument if I do not return the gesture," Roma had chided the first time upon Juliette's confusion. "Hey—stop laughing!"

He had laughed too. He had laughed because the idea of an argument driving them apart had seemed so absurd when they were fighting the forces of their families to be together.

Look where they were now. Separated by a mile of bloodshed.

Juliette turned away. They lapsed back into silence, allowing the humming of the machines to roar and ebb as it pleased. Occasionally, Juliette heard a rare hoot from outside, and she would angle her head whichever way the noise came from, trying to figure out if it was an owl or a dog or the monster on the streets of Shanghai.

Finally, Juliette couldn't stand her boredom. She stood and started to wander about the lab, picking things up at random and setting them down after inspecting them: the beakers lined along the floor, the little metallic spoons gathered in the corners, the neatly organized files at the end of the worktables. . . .

A hand snatched the files away from under her nose.

"Those aren't for your prying eyes, lovely," Marshall said.

Juliette frowned. "I wasn't prying," she countered, "and if I were, you would not have been able to tell."

"Is that so?" Marshall set the files down, then shuffled them away from her. She resented the action. She was putting her own neck on the line to work with Roma. In what world would she take the risk to be a double-crosser?

"Marshall, sit back down," Roma called from across the room. Benedikt Montagov did not even bother looking up from the sketch pad he had retrieved from his bag. Lourens, on the other hand, cast a worried glance down from the second floor. If the direction of his gaze was any indication, he was not afraid of a brawl starting, but rather that any rough nonsense would damage the glass beakers around the labs.

"Why don't I show you some of my inventions?" Lourens tried, his voice a loud bellow. "They may be the most innovative materials that Shanghai has yet to see."

Neither Juliette nor Marshall paid him any heed. Juliette took a step in. Marshall matched her.

"Are you insinuating something?" Juliette asked.

"Not just insinuating." Marshall grabbed her wrist. He pulled it out toward him, then reached for the hem of her sleeve, where he yanked out the blade she had hidden. "I'm accusing. Why did you bring weapons, Miss Cai?"

Juliette made a noise of disbelief. She caught Marshall's other wrist with the hand she had free and twisted. "It would be stranger if I *didn't* bring weapons, you—*ow!*"

He hit her.

To be fair, it had certainly been on instinct—a jerk of his elbow in reaction to the pressure she was applying to his arm—but Juliette staggered back, her chin smarting from the blow of bone against bone.

From his seat, Roma bolted up and shouted, "Mars!" but Juliette was already pushing Marshall back, her throbbing jaw giving way to anger and her anger intensifying the pulsating pain making its way to her lip. This was the way of the blood feud: a small infraction and then a return without thinking, furious jabs and fast hits moving before the mind could register—no reason, only impulse.

Marshall grabbed ahold of Juliette's arm again, this time twisting it hard until her whole limb was folded against her back. The fight could have ended there, but Marshall still had her knife in his hand, and Juliette's first instinct was to fear. Temporary peace or not, she had no reason to trust him. She had every reason to kick a foot against the nearby worktable and propel herself upward, until she was using the tight grip Marshall had on her arm to roll over his shoulder, spinning over him and landing with a solid *thump* on her two feet. The maneuver applied enough pressure on Marshall's arm that he was sent hurtling to the floor, his skull thumping to the linoleum with a grunt as he lost his balance from her brutal yank.

Quickly, Juliette swooped for the knife he had dropped. In that moment, she didn't know if she even intended to kill him. All she knew was that she did not think when she fought; she only knew enemy from friend. She only knew to keep moving, to bring the knife up in the same motion that she had retrieved it, raise it high until it caught the light, only moments away from an arc that would end with it buried in Marshall Seo's chest.

Until Marshall started *laughing*. That sound alone—it tore her out from her haze. It stopped Juliette in her tracks, the knife loosening in her grip, the tension in her arms collapsing.

By the time Roma and Benedikt hurried near enough to stop the fight, Juliette was already extending a hand toward Marshall, pulling him back onto his feet.

"Whew. How long did it take you to practice that move?" Marshall asked, dusting his shoulders off. He propped his shoe on the corner of the table as Juliette had and tested his weight. "You were truly defying gravity for a second."

"You're too tall to pull it off, so don't try," Juliette replied.

Roma and Benedikt blinked. They had no words. Their faces said it all.

Marshall lifted his head up, addressing Lourens. "Can we still see your inventions?"

Lourens's mouth opened and closed. The animosity in the room had now given way entirely to curiosity, and it seemed the scientist didn't know what to do with it. Wordlessly, he could only leave his machines to rumble and trek down the stairs. He waved them to the shelves near the back of the first floor, eyeing Juliette and Marshall, who followed him eagerly while Roma and Benedikt trailed with more hesitation, watching the two like they were afraid this peace was merely part of a longer fight.

"These little knickknacks were not made with White Flower funds and are unrelated to your gangster nonsense, so don't you go babbling to your father, Roma," Lourens started. He picked up a jar of blue salts and popped it open. "Take a sniff."

Juliette leaned in. "It smells good."

Lourens grinned to himself. The motion looked a little funny with the new bald patch at the center of his chin. "It induces seizures in birds. I usually sprinkle it in the grassy area at the back of the building."

He moved on to a gray powder, bringing it down for Marshall to see. Marshall passed it to Benedikt, who passed it to Roma, who passed it back. Between the latter two, they hadn't collectively looked at the jar for more than a second.

"This creates a sudden, quick explosion of air when mixed with water," Lourens explained when it came back into his hands. "I usually throw it into the Huangpu River when I am having a stroll and the birds are trying to waddle along with me. It scares them off rather well."

"I'm starting to pick up a pattern," Juliette said.

Lourens pulled a face, his elderly features sagging low. "Birds," he muttered. "Miniature little devils."

Juliette tried not to laugh, scanning through more of the labels on the shelf. Her Dutch was mostly conversational, so it was difficult to comprehend what each jar was tagged as. When her inspection snagged on a small jar at the back, she wasn't sure what had been the cause of her interest—that DOODSKUS was printed along the side or that it was the most opaque, white liquid she had ever seen. It reminded her of the whites of her eyes: impenetrable, solid.

"What's that one?" Juliette asked, pointing.

"Oh, that one is new." Lourens practically rose onto his tiptoes in excitement as he stretched to retrieve it. With the jar nestled in his palm, the scientist handled it with special care, slowly easing off the lid. Juliette caught a whiff of what smelled like a garden of roses.

It was sweet and fragrant and reminded her of bygone days running around in the backyard with dirt in her hands.

"It is able to stop an organism's heart," Lourens explained reverently. "I have not perfected it quite yet, but ingestion of this substance should create a state that appears like death for three hours. When it wears off . . ." He clicked his fingers. The sound lagged, a result of his stiff, aging joints. "The organism awakes, like it was never dead."

At that moment, a loud *ding!* echoed through the lab, and Lourens exclaimed that the machine was done, returning the jar to its original spot and hurrying up the stairs back to his worktable. Roma and Benedikt were quick to follow on his heels, exclaiming their hypotheses over what he would find. Juliette, meanwhile, reached a hand onto the shelf. Before Lourens could peer over and see, her palm swallowed the jar of impenetrable white material and she shook it into her sleeve. She had been fast enough to evade Lourens's eyes, but not fast enough to evade Marshall's. Juliette looked right at him and dared him to say something.

Marshall only quirked his lip and turned, hurrying after the others. It seemed fitting that he would feel slighted when she was peeping through their lab reports but this would amuse him.

"Let us see," Lourens was saying when Juliette finally joined them. He lifted the lid to a machine and extracted a strip of thin paper with black lines running from length to length. Making a sound under his breath that Juliette couldn't quite interpret, Lourens then pushed past her to another machine, checking the dark screen on this one and looking at the strip of paper again. When that was done, his final stop was the books on his desk.

"Well," Lourens finally said after he had browsed through his books and kept everyone simmering in complete silence for five minutes. He stopped his finger at the bottom of a yellowed page, tapping twice on a list of formulae that he had printed out by hand, as if that meant anything. "With our limited starting point, I cannot conclude whether this is a true vaccine like they say. I have nothing to compare it against." Lourens squinted at the paper again. "But it is indeed a mixture of some use. The primary substance is an opiate, one that I believe has been introduced to the streets here as something called *lernicrom*."

Juliette stopped cold. She felt a tremor shake down her spine, a revelation dropped straight from the heavens and onto her shoulders.

"Tā mā de," she cursed softly. "I know that drug."

"Well, we have both started dealing it, albeit sparsely," Roma said, recognizing the name too.

"No, that's not it," Juliette said tiredly. "*Lernicrom.* It's the drug that Walter Dexter was trying to sell to the Scarlet Gang in bulk." She closed her eyes, then opened them again. "He's the Larkspur's supplier."

Twenty-Six

The next night, Juliette was buried deep inside her head. All those times when she had brushed Walter Dexter off, she could have been gathering information instead. Now it would appear suspicious if she tried sidling back into his good graces. Perhaps this was why people were warned not to burn their bridges, even if it was a bridge leading to a no-good merchant.

Juliette stabbed her chopsticks down angrily. Suspicious or not, she needed to get back in contact with Walter Dexter without arousing distrust. And in brainstorming how to do so, no matter which path she went down, all roads seemed to lead back to his son, Paul Dexter.

She wanted to strangle herself at the thought.

Perhaps I do not have to hunt him down, Juliette thought weakly. *Perhaps I am only chasing ghosts. Who is to say he will even know anything?*

But she had to try. Everything in this whole bizarre affair was circumstantial. Just because Walter Dexter was supplying the Larkspur didn't mean he knew anything more about the Larkspur's identity and location than they did. Just because the Larkspur was making a vaccine didn't mean he could lead them to a cure for this wretched madness.

Equally, it also meant that the Larkspur *could* know, and so might Walter Dexter.

Dang it.

"Where are you tonight?"

At Rosalind's sharp summons, Juliette looked up from her food, stopping herself just a moment before her chopsticks mindlessly closed on air.

"Right here," she said, frowning when Rosalind pulled a face that said she didn't believe her.

"Really?" Rosalind gestured across the table with her chin. "Why'd you ignore Mr. Ping when he asked for your opinion on the worker strikes, then?"

Juliette's attention shot to Mr. Ping, a member of her father's inner circle who used to like asking about her studies whenever he saw her. If she recalled correctly, a favorite topic of his was astrology; he always had something to suggest about the alignment of the Western zodiacs, and Juliette—even at fifteen—always had a quip to fire back about fate working through science and statistics instead. Right now he was pouting on the other side of the circular table, looking especially wounded. Juliette winced.

"It's been a long day."

"Indeed," Kathleen muttered in agreement from Rosalind's other side, massaging the bridge of her nose.

The racket of their private room was loud enough to compete with the rest of the restaurant outside. Lord Cai was in the seat beside her, but these dinners were not opportunities for father-daughter discussions. Her father was always too occupied with other conversation to utter a single word to her, and her mother was taking charge of the second table in the room, leading the conversation there. This wasn't the setting for personal conversations. This was prime time for members of the Scarlet Gang's inner circle to jostle and brag and drink to the edge of death against one another to win favors.

Tyler was usually one of the loudest people at these tables. Today, however, he was off chasing rent money instead, as he had been for the past few days. While Juliette was put in charge of the madness, Tyler was running her heiress roles in her place, and he reveled in them. Juliette stiffened each time she heard him yelling through the house, gathering his entourage so they could set out—and it was happening often. It seemed like every minute had a new dodger, a new account going into the red. Tyler would wave his gun and threaten store owners and house tenants until they coughed up the necessary amount, until the Scarlets had made back what they were owed. It was hypocritical for Juliette to be looking down on Tyler for simply doing what was technically her job, she knew, but performing such a job in this climate made her uneasy. People were not refusing to pay now because they wished to rebel; they were simply not making enough income because all their customers were dying.

Juliette sighed, twiddling her chopsticks. The food spun before them on the glass turntable, presenting roasted ducks and rice cakes and fried noodles without pause. Meanwhile, Juliette was mechanically picking up servings from the center and bringing them to her plate, putting food in her mouth without really tasting it. It was a shame, really. One glance at the decadent greens of the vegetables, at the gleam of the scaled fish, at the glistening oils dripping off the meat was enough to water the mouths of anyone.

Except Juliette had zoned out yet again. Realizing that she was raising the ashtray to her mouth instead of her ceramic teacup, she shook herself back to reality and caught the very last syllable coming out of Rosalind's mouth—not nearly enough to determine any of what her cousin had said, but just enough to know that it had been a question and something needing a worthwhile answer out of Juliette instead of a smile and a generic, inquisitive noise.

"I'm sorry, what?" Juliette said. "You were talking, weren't you? I'm sorry, I'm terrible—"

And she was about to be even more terrible because she would never know what Rosalind had asked. At that moment, her father was clearing his throat, and the two tables in the private room fell silent immediately. Lord Cai rose, his hands clasped behind his rigid back.

"I hope everyone is well," her father said. "There is something I must address tonight."

Some gut feeling in Juliette tightened. She braced.

"Undeniable proof has come to my attention today that there is a spy in the Scarlet Gang."

Utter quiet sank into the room—not an absence of sound, but a presence in itself, like an invisible, heavy blanket had been settled over all their shoulders. Even the servers stopped—one boy who had been pouring tea froze midmovement.

Juliette only blinked. She exchanged a glance with Rosalind. It was almost common knowledge that there were spies in the Scarlet Gang. How could there not be? The Scarlets certainly had people among the common ranks of the White Flowers. It wasn't too much of a stretch to consider the White Flowers had invaded their messengers, especially given how often their people got the jump on the Scarlet Gang.

Lord Cai continued.

"There is a spy in the Scarlet Gang who has been invited into this room."

For a short, horrific second, Juliette felt a pang of fear that her father was referring to *her*. Could he have found out about her association with the White Flowers—with Roma Montagov—and taken it the wrong way?

Impossible, she thought, clenching her fists beneath the table. She hadn't given away any information. Surely something had to have happened to damage their business to elicit a declaration like this from her father.

She was right.

"Today three important potential clients pulled out of their planned partnerships with us." Juliette's father was holding himself with the air of exhaustion, as if he was sick and tired of battling nervous clientele, but Juliette saw through the guise. Her eyes skipped over him and traced the tense lines of her mother's stiff shoulders across the room. They were furious. They had been betrayed.

"They knew of our pricing before it had even been proposed," Lord Cai continued. "They went to the White Flowers instead."

Doubtlessly after the White Flowers had approached them with lower prices. And how could a spy know of such protected information unless they were in the inner circle? This wasn't the work of a messenger who had vague ideas regarding drop-off locations. This was the very core of Scarlet business, and it had sprung a leak.

"I know all your backgrounds," Lord Cai went on. "I know you are all born and bred of Shanghai. Your blood runs thousands of years back to ancestors who link us together. If there is a traitor here, you have not been turned by true loyalty or anything of that caliber, but rather by the promise of money, or glory, or false love, or merely by the thrill of playing spy. But I assure you . . ." He settled back into his seat and reached for the teapot. He refilled his ceramic cup, his hand completely steady as the leaves overflowed to the very, very brim, spilling onto the red tablecloth and staining it until the darkness looked like a bloom of blood. If he poured any longer, Juliette feared the hot tea would spill down the tablecloth and burn her legs. "When I uncover who you are, the consequences by my hand will be far greater than what the White Flowers may do upon the notification that you will no longer act the traitor."

To Juliette's relief, Lord Cai finally set the pot down just before the overspill reached the edge of the table. Her father was smiling, but his eyes, despite the aged crinkle of crow's feet, stayed as blank as an executioner's. In this moment, Lord Cai didn't choose verbal words to deliver his message. He let his expression speak for him.

There was no doubt which parent Juliette had received her monstrous smile from.

"Please," Lord Cai said, when nobody moved after the close of his threat. "Let us continue eating."

Slowly the powerful men and the wives who whispered into their ears picked up their chopsticks again. Juliette couldn't quite sit still anymore. She leaned toward her father and whispered that she had to run to the washroom. When Lord Cai nodded, Juliette rose, making for the door.

Outside the Scarlet Gang's private room, Juliette leaned against the cold wall, taking a second to catch her breath. She saw the other patrons of the restaurant to her left, where the volume was at a roar—a collective effort of different small tables each fighting to be heard over the others. To her right, there were separate doorways leading to the kitchen and the washrooms. With a sigh, Juliette marched into the washroom.

"Calm yourself," she told herself, leaning her head against the large metal sink. She drooped her neck, breathing deeply.

What would her father say if he knew that she was working with Roma Montagov? Would he see it the way she did, that giving up this one point of pride could help all their people if they managed to stop the madness? Or would he get stuck on the very core of Juliette's betrayal: that she had had unlimited chances to shoot Roma in revenge for all the blood his hands had spilled, and hadn't?

Juliette pulled her chin up, facing the distorted bronze mirror before her. All she saw was a stranger.

Perhaps she was in over her head. Perhaps the correct course of action was to break off any alliance with Roma Montagov and go to her own people instead, to figure out a way to corner Walter Dexter with brute manpower and make him talk—

A scream pierced her ear. Juliette startled, registered it as coming from the main restaurant.

She barged out of the washroom. In seconds, she had hurried to the source of the scream, panting for breath as she searched for victims. She found only one man collapsed on the ground. Her eyes landed on him in the same second that his hands launched around his neck.

But nobody went forward to help him. Even as he tore into his throat, littering chunks of skin outward along a small radius and eventually stilling into death, the people of the restaurant continued on. Only one elderly lady at the back waved down a waiter to clean the scene. Some others had hardly flinched, acting as if they had not noticed, as if not acknowledging death would offend it enough to have it go away.

Civilians were ripping out their own throats and the people of this city had become so desensitized that they were content to continue their dinner like it was a regular Tuesday. Juliette supposed it was. If this continued, it would be the norm until the whole city collapsed. It was only a matter of time until every small establishment in Shanghai emptied out, either because their customers had succumbed to the madness or because others wished not to attend places where infection was likely. A matter of time until Scarlet-assisted businesses ate through their savings and could no longer make rent even despite Tyler's threats, until large restaurants of this size crumbled too. There were red roses sprouting forward on every second door along Scarlet territory. Warnings upon warnings, but what good were warnings in the face of madness?

"Hey," Juliette snapped when the waiter crouched near the dead man. "Don't touch him." Her tone scared the waiter enough to send him scrambling back. "Put a tablecloth over the body and call a doctor."

Nothing was a guarantee. She needed Roma's help to fix this city. But she also needed to stop sitting around and making excuses.

She needed to weasel her way beside Paul Dexter.

At this hour it was hard to find the line in the horizon where the waters ended and land began, where the Huangpu River bled into the bank on the other side. When Benedikt was sitting by the water's edge, looking out into the night, it was easy to forget the swirling concoction of red and gold and smoke and laughter that existed in the city behind him. It was easy to believe that this was all there was: an unshaped land, blotted with the faintest dots of glitter from the other bank.

"I thought I would find you here."

Benedikt turned at the voice, letting his leg swing over the board-walk. The light that framed Marshall stung at Benedikt's unadjusted eyes when he looked upon him.

"It is not like I go anywhere else."

Marshall shoved his hands into his pockets. He was dressed nicely in a Western suit tonight, which was rare but not unusual, not if Lord Montagov had just sent him somewhere on an errand.

"Do you know how long the Huangpu River is? You're picky, Ben. I don't think I've ever found you in the same spot twice."

Beneath them, the river seemed to rock in response. It knew that it was being gossiped about.

"Did something happen?" Benedikt asked.

"Were you expecting something to happen?" Marshall replied, coming to sit beside him.

"Something is *always* happening."

Marshall pursed his lips. He thought for a second. "No, nothing happened," he finally said. "When I left him, Roma was drafting a reply to a message from Juliette. He's been at it for three hours. I think he's going to pull a muscle."

Roma did nothing half-heartedly. Whenever he visited Alisa's bed-side, he would stay for almost half the day, his other tasks be damned. The only reason Lord Montagov allowed such inactivity from him was because he knew Roma would enact his other tasks with his full attention eventually, as soon as he left the hospital.

"Better to pull a muscle than to pull out his own throat," Benedikt muttered. He stopped. "I don't trust her."

"Juliette?"

Benedikt nodded.

"Of course you don't," Marshall said. "You shouldn't. It doesn't mean she's not useful. It doesn't mean you have to dislike her." He gestured toward the alleyway. "Can we go home now?"

Benedikt sighed, but he was already getting up, dusting off his hands. "You could have gone home on your own, Mars."

"Where's the fun in that?"

Benedikt would never understand how often Marshall needed to be surrounded by people. Marshall was allergic to lonesomeness—he had once genuinely developed a rash because he sat down in his room and forbade himself from leaving until he balanced an account book. Benedikt was the opposite. People made him sticky. People made him think about his words twice as hard and sweat when he didn't pick them right.

"I don't suppose you're in the mood to stop by a casino first?" Marshall asked when they started to walk, grinning. "I heard there's—"

Midspeech, Marshall suddenly halted in his steps, throwing an arm out to snag Benedikt back. Benedikt needed a few seconds to see why they had stopped. He needed a few more to truly *comprehend* what he was seeing.

A shadow—stretching on the pavement in front of them. They were still midway inside this alleyway, too deep inside to look past the tall buildings on either side and determine what was making the looming shadow. The streetlamp was not far; the outline shining down was stark and well defined, leaving no mistake for the sight of horns, for limbs that moved with a pained stagger, for a size that was incomprehensible for anything natural.

Chudovishche. Monster. The same one that all of Shanghai had been seeing, lurking in the city's corners.

"Good God," Benedikt muttered.

The shadow was moving toward them, toward their very alleyway.

"Hide!"

"Hide?" Marshall hissed in echo. "You want me to magically shrink myself?"

Indeed, the alleyway was too thin to offer a viable hiding spot. But there was a wide blue tarp lying atop the discarded wooden boxes. With no time to give instruction, Benedikt grabbed the tarp and pushed Marshall down roughly, shushing him when Marshall winced, and folded himself down too, until they were curled up alongside the boxes and hidden under the thin sheet.

Something heavy passed through the alley. It sounded effortful, like feet that did not quite come down right, like nostrils that were too thin to pass breath, so only a wheeze could come out.

Then a rough splash of water rang into the night. Droplets came down onto the river surface as if it had started raining only in one section of the sky.

"What was that?" Marshall hissed. "Did it jump into the water?"

Benedikt grabbed a corner of the tarp, slowly inching his head out into the open. Marshall gripped his shoulder and tried to do the same, until both of them were peering out from their hiding place, squinting into the dark, trying to get a look at the river beating on at the other end of the alleyway.

A shape was floating in the water. Under the moonlight, it was hard to catch much except the glint of what could have been the spine, rows of protrusions that were distorting and changing and . . .

Benedikt swore, pushing Marshall down. "Hide, hide, *hide*!"

A burst of movement erupted from the water—*from* the monster. Miniature dots—spitting into the air, barely visible until they landed on the boardwalk, barely visible until they skittered forward under the moonlight, looking like a moving carpet spreading into the alleyway.

Marshall yanked the tarp up and Benedikt slammed his foot down on the edge of it, pressing the tarp hard into the ground lest the insects crawl through. There was the sound of skittering. The sound of a thousand little legs brushing up against rough gravel, dispersing into the city.

Silence. A long minute passed. The silence only continued.

"I think they're gone," Benedikt whispered. "Mars?"

Marshall made a choking noise.

"Marshall!"

Benedikt moved fast enough to disrupt the air around him. He placed his hands on both sides of Marshall's face, squeezing hard to demand Marshall's attention and sanity, squeezing hard in case he needed to stop him from clawing himself to death.

But instead of falling to madness, Marshall snorted. A beat later an amused laugh escaped. "Ben, I'm only kidding."

Benedikt stared at Marshall.

"Mudak," he hissed angrily. When he took his hands back, he had to resist the urge to hit Marshall. "What's wrong with you? Why would you joke about such a matter?"

Marshall appeared confused now, like he didn't understand the fury being thrown in his direction. "They hadn't crawled upon us," he said slowly. "Why would you take me seriously?"

"Why wouldn't I?" Benedikt snapped. "You don't joke about that, Marshall. I will not lose you!"

Marshall blinked. He tilted his head curiously, in the same way he usually did when he was trying to predict Benedikt's next move during a sparring match. In a true match, Benedikt had always been better at predicting Marshall's lazy feigns, tracking Marshall's guess-work and acting the opposite.

But here, while they sat nose to nose, he would never have expected Marshall to reach out and touch his cheek—the brush of a finger feather-soft, as though to test whether Benedikt was really there.

Benedikt jerked away. He tore the tarp off them, getting to his feet in a whirlwind of motion.

"I need to tell Roma what we just saw," he snapped. "I'll see you at home."

He hurried off before Marshall could follow.

Roma finally sent his letter of reply five hours after he started writing it. Once he had proofread it a tenth time, he wasn't entirely sure anymore whether he had spelled his own name correctly.

"Should I have included my patronymic?" he muttered to himself now, flipping to the next page of his book without taking in any of the words. "Is that strange?"

The whole thing was too strange. Four years ago, he had sent Juliette so many love letters that when he sat down to write *this* letter—to agree that they should gather as much information as possible from their separate sources on Walter Dexter, before meeting in Great World tomorrow—his immediate reaction upon scribing "Dear Juliette" was to make a comparison of her hair to a raven.

Roma sighed, then put the book down on his chest, closing his eyes. He was already lying on his bed. He figured he may as well take a nap until it was time for him to go sticking his nose into the White Flower factories. Someone there had to have information on Walter Dexter's ongoings.

But the moment he started dozing, there was a heavy thudding on his bedroom door.

Roma groaned. "What is it?"

His door opened. Benedikt came barreling in. "Do you have a moment?"

"You're interrupting my quality time with Eugene Onegin, but that's quite all right." Roma removed his book from his chest and set it down on his blanket. "He's unnecessarily pretentious anyway."

"The monster. The insects. They're one and the same."

Roma bolted up. He demanded, "Say again?"

Benedikt took a seat at his cousin's desk, his anxiety releasing through the rapid tapping of his fingers. Roma, on the other hand, had scrambled up and started to pace the entirety of his bedroom. There was too much tension building up between his bones.

"The insects come *from* the monster," Benedikt said in a rush. "We saw it. We saw it leap in the water and then . . ." He mimed an explosion outward. "The nonsense all makes *sense* now. Those who say that sightings of the monster create the madness are correct, just not in the way they think. The monster makes the insects. The insects make the madness."

Roma was suddenly very short of breath. Not in panic, but in understanding. As if he had been presented with a gift box of information, disassembled in little pieces, and if he didn't put it together quickly enough, the gift would be taken away.

"This is colossal," Roma said, forcing himself to go slowly. "If we trust Lourens when he says these insects operate identically to one another, if we assume they are all being controlled by one entity, and that one entity is in fact the monster . . ." Roma stopped pacing. He almost dropped to his knees. The monster was real. *Real.* And it wasn't that he hadn't believed the sightings prior to this moment, but he'd accepted them the way he accepted the foreigners in the concessions—as something of an inconvenience but not his biggest threat. The sightings were outside his field of concern, secondary to the madness. But now . . .

"If we kill the monster, we kill each and every one of these peculiar insects in Shanghai. If we kill the monster, we stop the madness."

Then the insects embedded in Alisa would die. Then she would no longer be under the clutches of the madness. Then she could wake up again. It was as good as a cure.

Benedikt thinned his lips. "You say that as if it will be easy. You didn't see it."

Roma paused in his pacing. "Well—what did you see?"

A loaded quiet set into the room. Benedikt seemed to consider his answer. He tapped his knuckles against the desk a few times, then did it again for good measure. Finally, he gave his head a minuscule shake.

"You've heard the stories," Benedikt replied tightly. "They're not so far off from the truth. I wouldn't worry about its appearance yet. Before we can even consider killing it, how do we find it again?"

Roma resumed his pacing. "Marshall said the Communists saw it coming from Zhang Gutai's apartment."

If Roma had been paying close enough attention, he would have seen his cousin's expression suddenly crumple—not in a grimace or a sneer but rather a flash of pain. It was fortunate that all Montagovs knew how to switch to a blank stare in the blink of an eye. By the time Roma glanced over, Benedikt had resumed a neutral expression, waiting for his cousin to continue.

"I need you and Marshall to stake out Zhang Gutai's apartment," Roma decided. The plan was coming together while he talked, each piece slotting in mere moments after the one before had clicked. "Watch for any appearance of chudovishche. Confirm for me that Zhang Gutai is guilty. If you see the monster appear with your own two eyes, then we know he is controlling it to spread madness across Shanghai. Then we know how to find the monster to kill it: by finding Zhang Gutai."

This time Benedikt did grimace plainly. "You wish for me simply to *watch*? That sounds . . . tedious."

"I would worry for your safety if it were exciting work. The more boring, the better off you are."

Benedikt shook his head. "You bored us enough searching for a live victim of the madness, and look where that got us," he said. "Why can't you and Juliette do it? You're already on the investigation. I have my own life to tend to too, you know."

Roma narrowed his eyes. Benedikt crossed his arms. *Is there something about this assignment that is too much of an ask?* Roma wondered.

What is his resistance to it? It is merely another chance to goof off with Marshall, which he does on a daily basis anyway.

"I won't waste our collaboration with Juliette on stalking Zhang Gutai," Roma answered, sounding offended at the notion.

"I thought this monster was our concern, not the Larkspur."

"I *know* that," Roma shot back. He was bristling, unable to hold the sharpness from his tone. Alisa's life was a stake—he did not have the energy to debate such petty matters. "But we cannot be certain Zhang Gutai is truly linked to the monster *until we see something*. Until then we need an alternate plan for answers on the monster and its madness. Until then we need to get to the bottom of this Larkspur figure so we can gather why he knows what he knows and use it to get back to the monster."

But Benedikt was still insistent on digging his foot in. "You cannot stalk Zhang Gutai *after* you find the Larkspur? Obviously he is linked with him in some fashion if you found correspondences between them."

"Benedikt," Roma said firmly. "It was only one correspondence from the Larkspur's end." He shook his head. His cousin was side-tracking him. "Look—you and Marshall have to do it because we don't know how long it could take for the monster to make an appearance."

"Can't you just tell a lower-ranked gangster to keep an eye on him?"

"Benedikt."

"And truly, you only need one person on this task—"

"Are you," Roma interrupted, his tone suddenly cold, "a White Flower or not?"

That shut him up. Benedikt clamped his lips together, then said, "Of course."

"So stop arguing against my command." Roma placed his hands behind his back. "Is that all?"

Benedikt stood. He made a mock bow, his mouth twisted sourly.

"Yes, Cousin," he said. "I'll leave you to your heir duties now. Make sure not to overly exert yourself." A gust of wind followed his fast escape. The slam of the door echoed loudly enough to shake the house.

Heir duties. What a jokester. Benedikt knew full and well that Roma could either be the heir or be a ghost. Benedikt might have been one of the only people who actually understood that Roma did not fight so hard to remain heir because he enjoyed the power but because it was the only place he could control his personal safety. If the heavens opened and offered Roma a little villa in the outskirts of the country, where he could move himself and his loved ones out to live a life in obscurity, he would choose it immediately.

Benedikt's dig rolled right off Roma's shoulders. His cousin could complain all he liked and take his anger out on Roma, but he was too logical to dismiss the task outright. He would do it and complain like hell about it, then shut up when it mattered. Besides, Benedikt could not grumble for long. Whatever had knotted his intestines in such a state was bound to loosen soon, and then he would forget why he threw such a fit.

Roma sighed and flopped back onto his bed.

He had always known that sitting at the top came with its prickles and thorns.

But in this city, void of any alternative path, at least this was better than not being heir at all.

Later that night, a knock came down on Kathleen's door, startling her from her reading. She was snuggled into her blankets already, half considering feigning sleep so she would not need to get up, put her pendant on, and answer the door, when the door simply opened on its own.

"Thank you for waiting on my response," she droned, eyeing Rosalind as she came in.

"You weren't going to open it," her sister replied knowingly.

Kathleen grimaced, closing the magazine she was reading. She supposed this season's latest shoe designs could wait. "I might have been asleep."

Rosalind looked up. She pointed at the small chandelier, then at the three golden lamps scattered around the room. "You sleep with the lights on?"

"Pft. Maybe."

With a roll of her eyes, Rosalind sat down at the foot of the bed. She seemed to gaze at nothing for a long while, before drawing her legs up to her chest and resting her face delicately on the flat surface of her knees.

Kathleen frowned. "Ça va?"

"Ça va." Rosalind sighed. "Lord Cai scared me tonight."

"Me too." It was a mighty big claim to insist a spy had made its way into the Scarlet inner circle. The circle was only so big. "We have enough trouble with people *dying*. This is going to divide even further."

Rosalind made a noise—it could have been one of agreement; it could have been nothing but a need to clear her throat. Another few seconds passed by. Then she asked:

"You don't think it's Juliette, do you?"

Kathleen's eyes widened. "No!" she exclaimed. "Why would you even think that?"

Rosalind thinned her lips. "I'm just thinking out loud. You've heard the same rumors as I have."

"Juliette would never."

The air was getting a little thick. Kathleen hadn't expected this, hadn't expected a wary silence to follow when she wanted agreement instead.

"You can't be too trusting all the time."

"I'm not *too* trusting," Kathleen snapped, prickled now.

"Oh, really?" Rosalind shot back. The volume of their voices was growing. "What is this quick need for defense, then? I was just throwing the possibility out there and you're acting like I'm biting your head off—"

"Talk is dangerous," Kathleen cut in. "You know this. You know what a few thoughtless words can do—"

"Who *cares* what talk can do! She's Juliette!"

Kathleen jerked against her nest of blankets, shocked. Her ears were ringing, like her sister's outburst had been an explosion rather than an exclamation. Though they were both close to Juliette, Rosalind's relationship to their cousin was different from hers. Rosalind and Juliette were too similar. They both coveted the leading role, the right to have the ultimate decision. When they clashed, only one could be right.

But . . . this wasn't a clash. This was just . . .

"God, I'm sorry," Rosalind said suddenly, her voice softening. "I don't—I'm sorry. I love Juliette. You know I do. I'm just . . . I'm scared, okay? And we don't have the same safety she does. Lord Cai is going to stop at nothing to find out who's acting the traitor, and you know he'll suspect outsiders like us first."

Kathleen stiffened. "We are hardly outsiders."

"But we are not Cais, at the end of the day."

Much as Kathleen hated it, her sister was right. It mattered little that they were more closely related to the beating core of the Cais than the other second, third, fourth cousins. So long as their last name was different, there would always be that doubt in the family over whether Rosalind and Kathleen truly belonged here. They came from Lady Cai's side—the side that had been brought into this house rather than the side that had been raised in it for generations.

"I guess we need to be careful, then," Kathleen mumbled. "Make sure we have no reason to be accused."

People like Tyler would not have to worry. Even if they were all just as related, he bore the Cai name. Anything he did, anything he achieved was something wonderful reflecting back on the family, on the generations of ancestors who had built them from the ground up. Anything Kathleen and Rosalind were a part of reflected back to the Langs instead, and Kathleen knew absolutely nothing about that side of her family history, short of the grandmother she visited once a year.

"Yeah," Rosalind whispered. She sighed, scrubbing her forehead. "Okay, I should go. I'm sorry for yelling." She hopped off the bed. "Get some sleep. Bonne nuit."

"Good night," Kathleen echoed. The door had already closed. When she lay back down and picked up her magazine again, she could no longer return her attention to the shoes.

You've heard the same rumors as I have.

"Wait," Kathleen whispered aloud. "*What* rumors?"

Twenty-Seven

Juliette was a hairsbreadth away from snapping.

The air was crisp that afternoon, a product of clear skies and the sea breeze. As she strolled along the pavement under the delicate shade of the waving green trees, she was surrounded by the sounds of rushing fountain water and chirping birdsong—the sounds of the International Settlement when it was still a little dazed from its previous wild night, only awakening with the golden sunbeams caressing its edges.

It should have been peaceful, calm. Too bad she was strolling with Paul Dexter, who hadn't yet given her any substantive information to work with, despite the hours they had spent together already.

"I have a surprise for you," Paul was saying now, giddy with his enthusiasm. "I was so delighted to receive your letter, Miss Cai. I'm thoroughly enjoying our time in each other's company."

That makes one of us.

It was almost as if he knew what game she was playing at. Every time she mentioned his father's job, he diverted it to talk about how hardworking Walter Dexter was. Every time she mentioned *his* work with the Larkspur, Paul steered into Shanghai's climate and how terribly difficult it was to find reputable work. Briefly, she wondered if Paul had perhaps heard about Juliette rushing into one of the vaccination houses and now suspected her of trying to take down the Larkspur, but it seemed improbable that the information would pass to someone as irrelevant as Paul Dexter. She also wondered if he had received the same instruction from the Larkspur as those other merchants—on killing Juliette for a price—but she couldn't imagine how he was planning to play his hand if that were the case. It was more likely that he was sitting on everything he had, simply so he could keep her around for longer.

"A surprise?" Juliette echoed absently. "You shouldn't have."

He had to know that she was digging around for *something*. That fact alone gave him the upper hand—gave him the right to tug Juliette around as he pleased. But there was no chance he knew specifically what she was looking for, and Juliette held *that* close to her chest. There was no chance he realized she knew about his father's role as the Larkspur's supplier and that she was after every little thread of information the Dexters had on the Larkspur's identity.

Somebody who was supplying the Larkspur with the very drug he needed for his vaccines had to have an address to work with. It was absurd to think otherwise. How else would Walter Dexter make deliveries? By leaving drugs in a designated hole within a brick wall?

"Oh, but I did." Paul spun suddenly. Rather than walking at her side, he was now two paces ahead of her, strolling backward with his hand outstretched so he could look at her. Juliette forced herself to take his hand. "You will love it. It's at my house."

Juliette perked up. It was most improper for Paul Dexter to be showing her something at his house, but it was a brilliant opportunity to maximize her snooping. Let him dare try something unsavory. He would find himself most incapacitated.

"How exciting," Juliette said.

Paul must have sensed her lift in mood, because he beamed at her. In fact, he did not stop beaming as they continued walking; nor did he stop jabbering, going on and on about his thoughts on the city, the nightlife, the casinos—

"Have you heard about the strikes?"

Juliette's heel came down hard on a crack in the sidewalk. Paul reached out fast, grabbing her elbow so she did not fall, but Juliette did not think to thank him as she glanced up to his kindly expression. She only blinked, a small, disbelieving laugh escaping.

"What do *you* know about the strikes?" she asked.

"Plenty, Miss Cai," Paul replied confidently. "There are two types of Communists now: those who are dying because they are too poor to deserve the Larkspur's cure and those who are angry enough from this fact that they wish to rise up."

Too poor *to* deserve . . . *What kind of tomfoolery*—

"Those strikes are happening in the Scarlet-funded factories," Juliette said. Her voice came out too tightly, and she coughed, trying to lighten her tone so Paul would not think her acting aggressive. "It will be fine. We have it under control."

"Certainly," Paul agreed, but he sounded like he was merely humoring her, which was an insult in itself. "Ah, here we are."

As Paul stopped outside a tall gate, pressing a button to alert somebody within the house to manage the lock, Juliette squinted through the bars. The house was tucked inward enough that she saw nothing save hills and hills of green grass lawns.

"Is your father not home?" Juliette asked.

"No. He is in a meeting," Paul replied. "The rent will not pay itself, after all."

The gate slid open, resounding with a firm *click*. Paul offered his arm.

"Indeed," Juliette muttered. The rent *wasn't* paying itself. So how much could a merchant be making to afford this, and how could he have made so much so fast? Other houses along this road were occupied by bankers and lieutenants and well-to-do diplomats. Walter Dexter had marched into Shanghai desperate enough to beg the Scarlet Gang for an audience. He had slunk into the burlesque club with

315

a suit that bore a small rip at the sleeve. He certainly had not started out in this house. He certainly had not swept into this city already brimming with money.

And yet the evidence before her said otherwise.

They passed the statues installed on the lawns, depictions of goddesses and sprites piled over one another, faces forlorn and marble skin glistening. The front door, which Paul pulled open for her, was etched with gold, bold against its other entranceways and against the swooping exterior staircases that framed the house.

"It's beautiful," Juliette said quietly.

She meant it.

Juliette came through the foyer and entered a circular living room, her shoes echoing loudly on the hard flooring and drawing the attention of the servants who were folding linens. Upon sighting Paul, they gathered their things and hurried out, exchanging knowing glances. None of the servants bothered closing the quaint doors at the side of the living room—doors that were framed by pots of flowers and gave way to an expansive backyard. They were pulled wide open, letting a strong breeze trail in with confidence, billowing at the gossamer white curtains in a way that reminded Juliette of dancing showgirls.

Paul hurried to the doors and pulled them closed. The curtains settled still, fluttering to a sad stop. He remained there for a second longer than necessary, staring out into his yard, his eyes gleaming with the bright light outside. Juliette came to stand beside him, breathing in deeply. Standing here, if she tried hard enough, she could almost forget what the streets of Shanghai looked like. She could be anywhere else. Rural England or the American South, perhaps. The air smelled sweet enough. The sights were pleasant enough.

"Magnificent, isn't it?" Paul asked softly. *"A September sun, losing some of its heat if not its brilliance . . ."*

"We are far from the Colorado range, Mr. Dexter," Juliette replied, catching his quote.

Paul jumped, unable to hide his surprise. Then he grinned and said, "Brilliant. Absolutely brilliant. For a Chinese woman, your English is extraordinary. There is not a trace of an accent to be found."

Juliette placed her hand on the doors. When she pressed down, she felt the cold of the delicate glass seep into her bones.

"I have an American accent," she replied dully.

Paul waved her off. "You know what I mean."

Do I? she wanted to say. *Would I be less if I sounded like my mother, my father, and all those in this city who were forced to learn more than one language, unlike you?*

She said nothing. Paul took the opportunity to touch her elbow and lead her into the rest of the house, speaking excitedly about his surprise. They wound through the long halls, passing surrealistic paintings that hung from the pearl-white walls. Juliette craned her neck every which way, trying to inspect the rooms she could glimpse into, but they were walking too speedily for her to get a good look.

It turned out that Juliette needn't have worried about searching for Walter Dexter's locus of business. Paul led her right into it. They came into a large office space—likely the biggest room in the entire house— with smooth wooden flooring and high bookshelves lining the walls. Here the air felt different: murkier, more humid, a result of the sealed windows and thick curtains. Juliette's eyes went to the giant desk first, taking in the menagerie of files and stacks upon stacks of papers.

"Hobson," Paul called. "Hobson!"

A butler appeared behind them: Chinese, dressed in a Western getup. There was no way his name was truly Hobson. Juliette would not have been surprised if Paul had merely assigned him this name because he did not wish to pronounce his Chinese one.

"Sir?"

Paul gestured into the room, to the spacious area in front of the desk where there was an oval gray rug and, atop it, four easels with four large canvases, covered by a coarse cloth.

"Would you do the honors?"

Hobson bowed. He strode into the room, his spine straight and his white-gloved hands held in front of him. When he pulled off the cloth, the fabric blended with his gloves.

Juliette looked at the four canvases.

"Oh . . . my . . ."

"Do you like them?"

Each canvas was a painting of her: two as a study of her facial features and the other two involving scenery, placing her in a garden or what might have been the world's loneliest tea party. Juliette didn't know what was more horrifying, that Paul thought this was a gift she would be pleased to receive, or that he actually spent his hard-earned dirty money from the Larkspur on this. She didn't even know what to say, perhaps except: "My nose isn't that high."

Paul jerked back, ever so slightly. "What?"

"My nose"—Juliette pulled her elbow from his grasp and turned to face the paneled windows, so he could see her side profile—"is rather flat. I am beautiful from the front, I know, but my side profile is rather lackluster. You've given me too much credit."

Hobson started to fold up the cloth sheet. The sound was too loud in the abrupt quiet that had settled into the room. Paul's lips were slowly turning down, faltering—finally, finally, for the first time all day, picking up on Juliette's attitude. This was not ideal. She was supposed to be winning his trust, not trashing it, no matter how creepy he was. She quickly turned to face Paul again, beaming.

"But I'm so incredibly flattered. How very kind of you. How could I thank you for such a gift?"

Paul grasped her offer of recovery. He inclined his head, pleased once more, and said, "Oh, it is my pleasure. Hobson, pack up the paintings and send someone to take them to Miss Cai's house, would you?"

Juliette was looking forward to tossing the canvases in the attic and never looking at them again. Or maybe she should burn the horrific things instead. If Rosalind saw them, she would never let Juliette live it down.

"Shall we continue our walk, then?"

Juliette startled. If they left Walter's office now, could she find the time to come back without being spotted? The house was full of servants, and she doubted anyone would hesitate to tell on her if they caught her lurking about.

Hobson cleared his throat, meaning to inch past Juliette with one of the canvases in his arms. Absently, still contemplating her options, Juliette took a step away and cleared a path, her back pressing to the cool wooden column behind her. It was mightily warm in this part of the Dexters' house. Unnaturally warm.

As Hobson exited, inspiration struck.

"All this excitement," Juliette said suddenly, placing a hand to her forehead. "I—" She feigned a swoon. Paul rushed forward to catch her. He was quick enough to stop her from hitting the ground, but by then she had settled herself solidly into a crumpled position, her knees curled up beneath her.

"Miss Cai, are you—"

"It is merely the heat. It rushes right to my head," Juliette assured him breathlessly, waving off his concern. "Do you have tiger balm? Of course not—you British have no clue about our medicines. I'm sure one of your house servants must know what I'm talking about. Can you fetch me some?"

"Of course, of course," Paul stammered quickly. Harried, he let go of her gently and hurried off.

Juliette immediately scrabbled up.

"I'm really making a habit out of snooping around other people's desks," she muttered to herself. With the countdown ticking, she shuffled through the files, her eyes scanning for any mention of the Larkspur. She found dozens of calling cards, dozens of letters containing contact information, but there was no invoice with the Larkspur—not even anything to do with *lernicrom*. He was certainly still trying to sell the drug, so where was the evidence?

There was no time to mull further. Footsteps were coming back down the hallway.

Cursing under her breath, Juliette tidied the ordered stacks of files, then returned to the spot where she had collapsed, leaning onto her elbows. She didn't look up when Paul appeared before her, pretending to be too dizzy to lift her head higher than a few inches from the ground.

"Apologies for my delay," Paul puffed. "I accosted Hobson and demanded this elusive tiger balm of him, but he was unreceptive to my hurry. He said he had already placed some in my briefcase last week when I complained of my headache. I had to hunt down my briefcase."

Two *clicks* rang through the room. Juliette peered through her darkened lashes and saw Paul shuffling around the mess in his briefcase. As he stuck his hand into one of the pockets on the lid, muttering when his fingers got stuck in the tight space, Juliette caught sight of business logs lying in the case, delivery invoices marked with such tiny font that it was a miracle her eyes caught ATTN: LARKSPUR.

Juliette barely held back her gasp. Paul perhaps interpreted the sound she emitted as one of gratitude, because he twisted open the jar and gingerly touched the balm, slathering enough on his finger to bring it to her temple.

At least he knew enough about this balm to know where it was supposed to be applied. His fingers were awfully cold.

"Thank you," Juliette said. She forced her eyes to wander, so that Paul wouldn't note where her attention had snagged. "I feel much better. I don't suppose I could have a drink of water? I'll feel much better once hydrated."

Paul nodded eagerly and rushed off once again, this time leaving behind his open briefcase.

Juliette snatched the business logs.

Invoice #10092A
September 23rd, 1926
ATTN: Larkspur
10 boxes—lernicrom

The signature below certifies responsibility on behalf of signee that he will assure the remaining passage of the product to the intended recipient.

Deliverer: Archibald Welch

"Archibald Welch," Juliette muttered in echo. She had never before heard the name. But the invoice in her hands made it as clear as day that this man had personal contact with the Larkspur, running between Walter Dexter as the middleman. Quickly, she flipped through each sheet in the pile, finding them all to be different dates with various amounts of boxes, but identically signed. It wasn't the same as directly finding the Larkspur's address, but it was one step closer.

Juliette placed the logs back neatly. Paul returned, a glass of water in hand.

"How are you feeling?" he asked. He gave her the glass and watched her take a sip. "Does your head feel clearer?"

Smiling, Juliette set the glass down. "Oh," she said demurely. "Everything is clearing up now."

"You're home late."

Juliette tossed her jacket onto her bed, then tossed herself on too, rocking the entire frame with her weight. Kathleen was almost thrown out of the comfortable position she had made herself at the foot of the bed. She shot her cousin an evil glance as the bed stilled, but no glare from Kathleen ever looked sincere.

"I'm heading out *again* in half an hour." Juliette groaned, throwing her arm over her eyes. Merely a second later, she quickly removed her arm, rubbing the stray cosmetics from her skin and wincing, knowing that she had smeared the product on her lashes. "Where's Rosalind?"

Kathleen rested her chin in her hand.

"She was needed at the club again."

Juliette frowned. "More foreigners?"

"The French are getting antsy with this madness," Kathleen replied, "and if they cannot do anything about it, they will pretend they are being useful by asking for continuous meetings to discuss their next course of action."

"There *is* no next course of action," Juliette said dryly. "At least not from them. Unless they wish to mobilize their armies against one monster lurking in the shadows of Shanghai."

Kathleen sighed in response. She flipped to the next page of her fashion magazine.

"By the way, your father came around earlier looking for you."

"Oh?" Juliette said. "Did Bàba want something?"

"Said he was merely doing a head count." Kathleen grimaced. "He's on edge about the White Flower spy. It seems he's contemplating evicting some distant relatives from the house."

"Good," Juliette muttered.

Kathleen rolled her eyes, then extended her hand. Juliette threaded her fingers through her cousin's, immediately less burdened, the tension in her body softening.

"Are you still following the Communists?" Kathleen asked.

"No, we—" Juliette paused, her pulse jumping. Quickly, she corrected, "*I'm* waiting on more confirmation before I make any accusations."

Kathleen nodded. "Fair." She flipped another page in her magazine with her other hand. When she had flipped three and Juliette had not said anything more, opting to stare at her ceiling instead, Kathleen wrinkled her nose.

"What's wrong with you?"

"Trying to mentally organize my time," Juliette replied wryly. She pulled her hand away and rolled over, squinting at the little clock ticking on her vanity. "I need a favor."

Kathleen closed her magazine. "Go on."

"I need all the information there is on a man named Archibald Welch. I need to know how to find him."

"And is there a reason?" Kathleen asked. Though she questioned, she was already getting off the bed, grabbing her nearby coat and shrugging it on.

"He may have the Larkspur's true identity."

Kathleen pulled at her coat collar, then tugged out the hair that had gotten caught inside. "I'll send a messenger over with whatever I find. Do you need it before your meeting?"

"That would be optimal, yes."

Kathleen mocked a salute. She moved fast, her objective square in her head, but just as she came to the doorway, Juliette called, "Wait."

Kathleen paused.

A beat passed. Juliette sat up straighter, drawing her knees to her chest. "Thank you," she said, her voice suddenly shaky. "For sticking by me. Even when you disapprove." *Even when my hands are dripping with blood.*

Kathleen almost seemed amused. Slowly, she came back into the room and settled into a delicate crouch before her cousin.

"I get the feeling you think I'm a little judgmental of all you do."

Juliette shrugged. Earnestly, she asked, "Aren't you?"

"Juliette, come on." Kathleen got out of her crouch, opting to sit beside her cousin instead. "Do you remember Rosalind's friend? The annoying one?"

Juliette wasn't sure where this was going, but she searched her memory anyway, sifting through the few friends she remembered Rosalind to have had.

She came up blank.

"Was this before we all left for the West or the first time I came back?"

"The first time you came back. Rosalind was working at the burlesque club already."

By the look of Juliette's constipated expression, Kathleen figured she wasn't remembering.

"Her name was some gemstone," Kathleen kept trying. "I can't remember exactly what, but . . . Ruby? Sapphire? Emerald?"

It clicked suddenly. A suppressed laugh escaped from Juliette, and then Kathleen—even as she tried to clamp her lips together— was laughing too, though the memory was hardly something to be humored over.

"Amethyst," Juliette said. "It was Amethyst."

Amethyst had been at least five years older than all of them, and Rosalind had worshipped the ground she walked on. She was the long-legged star of the stage, the one training Rosalind to become the next dazzling meteor.

Amethyst also drove Kathleen up the wall. She was always telling her to buy those whitening creams, to get a new qipao fitted, edging closer and closer toward the most offensive insinuations—

Until the day Kathleen finally snapped.

"Juliette!" she remembered her cousin yelling from the back of the burlesque club. "Juliette!"

"*What* is going on?" Juliette had muttered, leaving her table and moving toward the sound of Kathleen's call. Eventually, she found herself slipping into Rosalind's dressing room, and though Rosalind was nowhere to be found, Kathleen was pacing the length of it, guarding a slumped figure sprawled on the floor.

"I think she's dead," Kathleen cried. "She tried to *grab* me, so I pushed her and she hit her head and—"

Juliette waved a hand for her cousin to stop speaking. She knelt on the ground and put a hand on Amethyst's neck. There was a small smattering of blood coming from the girl's temple, but her pulse was thudding just fine.

"What is she even doing in here?" Juliette asked. "Did she follow you?"

Kathleen nodded. "I got so angry. I was only defending myself! I didn't mean to—"

"Oh, hush, she's fine," Juliette said, standing. "I'm more concerned about how loudly you yelled for me to come—"

Rosalind's dressing room door flew open then. Two other dancers barged in, with Rosalind in tow. Immediately, the dancers rushed for Amethyst on the floor, crying out in concern.

"What happened?" Rosalind asked, horrified. The two dancers immediately looked to Kathleen. Kathleen looked to Juliette. And in that moment, as Juliette and Kathleen exchanged a glance, an understanding had clicked into place. One of them was always safe. The other was not.

"Maybe Amethyst should mind her own business," Juliette said. "Next time I'll hit harder."

One of the dancers blinked. "Excuse me?"

"Do I need to repeat myself?" Juliette said. "Get her out of my sight. In fact, get her out of this club. I don't want to see her face ever again."

Rosalind's jaw had dropped. "Juliette—"

It didn't matter how much Rosalind tried to make a case for Amethyst. With a wave of Juliette's hand, Amethyst was escorted out in seconds, still unconscious.

"To this day," Juliette said now, "Rosalind still thinks I attacked Amethyst for no reason. We never did find the heart to tell her that her friend was awful, even after she sent word that she wasn't coming back to dance."

"I don't think anybody is brave enough to come back to their place of employment after the Scarlet heiress drives them out."

"Oh, *psh*. I've threatened plenty of people in this city. You don't see everyone running home crying."

Kathleen rolled her eyes, but it felt kindly. She reached out, placed a hand on Juliette's arm.

"Listen to me, biǎomèi," she said quietly. "You and Rosalind are my only family. The only family that matters. So *please*, stop thanking me every second like a damn Westerner just for helping you. I will never judge you. I could never. I'll always be on your side, no matter what." Kathleen checked the time again, then stood, smiling. "Understand?"

Juliette could only nod.

"I'll get a note to you as soon as possible."

With that, Kathleen got up and made her exit, hurrying to her destination before the sun could fully set. The room fell quiet, hosting only the sound of the clock's ticking hands and Juliette's soft, grateful exhale.

"Thank you," Juliette whispered anyway, to the empty room.

Twenty-Eight

Roma had chosen a seat at the back of the performance room, at a long table that saw visitors to Great World coming and going every few seconds. They would gulp down their drink, slam it down, then be swept back into the audience of the show going on at the front. They were fast, and ferocious, and definitely bursting with a dozen different drugs in their system.

In contrast, Roma must have appeared downright leaden while he sipped from his glass and waited. His hat was pulled low over his face, preventing those around him from looking too closely. If they recognized him, they would start whispering about sighting Roma Montagov watching the singsong girls who high-kicked on the stage with dresses slit to their armpits, and heaven knew how his father would react to that. He had warned Roma against Great World since Roma was a child, warned that places like these—places that teemed with life, pieces of entertainment slotted together with Chinese ingenuity—would corrupt the mind faster than opium. Here, visitors squandered their wages and traded food for forgetting. As much as Great World was looked down upon, it was still a marker of success. Those who worked in the factories out in Nanshi were not making enough in a day's wages for a mere admission ticket.

Roma sighed, setting his drink down. With his face shielded, the only person who would be able to find him among the drunken masses and screaming visitors knew exactly how to look.

"Hey, stranger."

Juliette slid into the diagonal seat, brushing a stray lock of hair out of her face, melding it back into her curls. She did not mind being identified here, in Great World. She only needed to mind being seen with the heir of the White Flowers.

Roma kept his gaze on the stage. They were setting up the tightrope now. He wondered how many bones had been broken in this building.

"Have a drink," he said, pushing his mostly full cup in her direction.

"Is it poisoned?"

At that, Roma jerked his eyes to her, horrified. *"No."*

"Missed opportunity, Montagov." Juliette brought it to her reddened lips. She took a sip. "Stop looking at me."

Roma looked away. "Did you find anything?" he asked.

"Yet to be determined, but"—she checked a pocket watch; Roma wasn't sure where she had pulled it out from, seeing as her dress did not give the appearance of pockets—"I may have something in a few minutes more. You go first."

Roma was too exhausted to argue. If the gangsters in this city were constantly as tired as he was, the blood feud would come to a complete halt within the hour.

"They're one and the same," Roma said. "The monster. The madness. If we find the monster, we stop the madness."

He told her all that had been seen. All that had been deduced.

"That is as good as confirmation," Juliette exclaimed. Noting the volume her voice had taken, she looked around, then said in a hiss, "We must act—"

"It has only been seen leaving his apartment," Roma said. "No one has seen Zhang Gutai himself ordering it around."

"If the monster was seen where Zhang Gutai lives, he *must* be controlling it." Juliette would not allow for argument against this. She stabbed a finger down on the table. "Roma, think about it. Think about everything else. This madness keeps growing in waves, and in each wave, it's always a large group who die *first* before the insects disperse out into the city. The gangsters by the ports. The White Flowers on the ship. The Frenchmen taking dinner. The businessmen outside the Bund."

Roma couldn't deny this. He said, "It seems it's always gangsters or merchants who are the initial targets."

"And who else would want these specific groups dead?" Juliette went on. "Who else would take down the capitalists like this? If Zhang Gutai is responsible, if he has the answers to *stopping* this all, then why would we waste time on other avenues—"

"But it's useless if he won't talk—"

"We *make* him talk," Juliette exclaimed. "We hold a damn knife to his throat. We torture him for answers. We have not exhausted every avenue with him yet—"

"He's a *Communist*." It was becoming increasingly hard not to turn to Juliette while they argued back and forth. There was something instinctual about turning toward her, like the way all living things shift their attention when there is a loud sound. "He has been trained to keep secrets and take them to the grave. Do you think he is afraid of death?"

What was a threat if you didn't mean to carry through? If they wanted him to give them the monster, give them a way to stop the havoc he was causing with the madness, then killing Zhang Gutai did nothing save destroy any chance of the city's salvation. How could they convincingly threaten to kill him if they did not truly wish to?

"If he is the only one who can lead us to the monster," Roma went on, "I won't risk us endangering such information. He may prefer to kill himself than to talk. I won't risk Alisa's life on such a bet."

Juliette thinned her lips. She was unhappy, he could tell. She would have continued protesting too, had a Scarlet not approached her at that moment, whispering in her ear.

Roma stiffened, looking away and pulling his hat lower. It was impossible to hear what the Scarlet was saying over the noise in the expansive room, over the hoots from the audience, over the clinking of glasses and the popping of mini fireworks exploding on the stage. From the corner of his eye, he watched the Scarlet hand over a large beige-colored file and a smaller note. With a nod from Juliette, the Scarlet left, leaving her to scan the note. Satisfied, she reached into the file, shaking out the papers within. If Roma was reading the text along the side correctly, it said: SHANGHAI MUNICIPAL POLICE—ARREST FILE—ARCHIBALD WELCH.

"We still have alternate options," Roma said, when it seemed safe to continue their conversation. "The Larkspur may tell us exactly what we wish to know, may offer the cure we seek. If he does not, only then should we resort to torturing Zhang Gutai on how to stop his monster. Agreed?"

Juliette sighed. "Fine. It is my turn to divulge my findings, then." She slid the file across the table. It moved fast, sliding smoothly across the flat surface toward Roma until he slammed his hand down on it.

"Archibald Welch," Roma read aloud, confirming what he thought he had sighted. A mugshot stared up at him: a black-and-white clipping of a man who was staring ahead blankly and had a vicious scar marring a line from his brow to the corner of his lip. "Who is that?"

Juliette stood from her seat and gestured for them to take their leave. "The only deliveryman who has the Larkspur's address. And if his history of arrests is any indication, he frequents the most dangerous place in Shanghai every Thursday."

Roma quirked a brow. "Today is Thursday."

"Precisely."

Despite his efforts, Benedikt ended up sitting on a rooftop across from Zhang Gutai's apartment, entering the third hour of their stakeout.

It was growing cold. He had accidentally stepped in a puddle on his way up too, so he was doing his job while hovering in a strange half crouch, wanting to rest but not wanting to spread the damp stain on his pants any further.

Marshall had laughed himself out with how ridiculous Benedikt looked. Benedikt thought he would never stop. But at least laughter was preferable to silence. At least Marshall's mirth upon Benedikt's misfortune was a signal that they should forget the strangeness that had bloomed between them in the alleyway.

"Hey," Marshall warned suddenly, pulling Benedikt out of his daze. "Someone's coming in."

Straightening from his ridiculous crouch, Benedikt hurried close to the roof's edge. There he joined Marshall, eyes narrowed.

"It's another foreigner," Benedikt remarked, leaning back with a sigh. From the location they had chosen, they had a perfect view into the sliding doors that separated Zhang Gutai's living room from his mini balcony. The balcony itself was barely big enough to fit two pots of flowers, but the glass doors were wide enough to allow Benedikt and Marshall a full view of foreigners coming and going on the hour. It was a mystery. Zhang Gutai wasn't even home. Yet foreigners continued arriving at his front door, ushered into the living room by a man who bordered middle-aged onto elderly—Qi Ren, his assistant, if Roma's debrief was correct—to sip tea for a few minutes and leave soon after. The buildings in this district were built closely enough that when the wind didn't howl too heavily, Benedikt could strain his ear and pick up bits and pieces of the conversation ongoing inside the living room.

Qi Ren's English was not great. Every two words, he would lapse into Chinese, then start muttering about how much his back hurt. The foreigners—some American, some British—would try to discuss politics or Shanghai's state of affairs, but since none of them managed to get anywhere, it was no surprise they would leave so soon.

Why would Zhang Gutai assign his assistant to take these meetings?

They all sounded like they wanted something from the Communist Party. Qi Ren sounded like he hardly cared what they were talking about. He wasn't taking notes or anything of the like to pass on to Zhang Gutai.

By now the foreigner who had walked in was already standing, preparing to leave when Qi Ren started to doze, midsentence. With a roll of his eyes, the white man strolled out the door, disappearing into the rest of the building to make his way down the winding staircases.

"Did you catch that?" Marshall asked.

Benedikt turned to him. He didn't speak for a moment. Then: "Catch what?"

"Honestly, Ben, you're here looking so pensive and I'm paying more attention than you are," Marshall pretended to chide. Jutting his chin in the direction of the building, he said, "He introduced himself as a designated official of the French Concession. Scarlet-assigned. This is White Flower territory. Do we rough him up?"

It wasn't a serious question; they didn't have time to be stirring trouble in the streets. But it did give Benedikt an idea to figure out exactly what they had been witnessing all afternoon.

"Stay here," he told Marshall.

"Wait. Are you really going to rough him up?" Marshall called after him, eyes wide. "Ben!"

"Just stay here!" he replied over his shoulder.

Benedikt moved fast, afraid that he would lose the English-speaking Frenchman. Fortunately, when he rounded the corner to come to the front of Zhang Gutai's apartment complex, the Frenchman was just coming out, busying himself with the buttons on his vest.

Benedikt grabbed the man and hauled him into the nearby alley-way.

"Ey!"

"Be quiet," Benedikt snapped. "What is your business on White Flower land?"

"Why, I'll be . . . ," the man hissed. "Get your hands off me."

Briefly, Benedikt wondered if the people coming and going from the apartment had anything to do with the monster business. What if they were all keepers of the creature, giving reports disguised in code to Qi Ren? But he took one look at this Frenchman and brushed it off. Men this brusque could not pull together such an intricate scheme.

Benedikt retrieved a knife from the waistband of his pants and pointed it. "I asked a question."

"My business with Zhang Gutai is none of yours," the man replied sharply. He wasn't as scared as he ought to be. Something was changing in this city.

"You stand on White Flower territory. Zhang Gutai cannot save you here."

The Frenchman laughed coarsely. It was like he hadn't even noticed the blade aimed to his chest. To him, his neatly pressed suit was as good as a suit of armor.

"We could invade this entire city if we wished," he spat. "We could have this country sign another treaty, hand over all this land. We only refrain because—"

"Hey!" A policeman blew his whistle from the other end of the alleyway. "What's happening over there?"

Benedikt withdrew his knife. He jerked his chin at the Frenchman. "Shoo."

The Frenchman harrumphed and marched off. Satisfied that there would be no altercation needing intervention, the policeman walked off too. Benedikt was left in the alleyway, bristling in his quiet anger. This would never have happened a few months ago. The settlement officials, the merchants, the foreigners alike—they only grew mighty now because the gangs were weakening. Because the madness was taking their people in droves, collapsing their chains and drilling holes in their structure.

They were vultures, all of them—the British and the French and every other newcomer. Circling above the city and awaiting the carnage so they could gorge themselves until they were full. The Russians had arrived in this country and merged inward, wishing to learn the way of things and do better. These foreigners had sailed in and grinned at the crime. They looked upon the slowly fracturing pieces before them and knew they only needed to wait for the madness to take its victims, wait for the political factions to split this city just enough until it was time to swoop in. They did not even have to make their own kill. . . . They only had to wait.

Benedikt shook his head and hurried out of the alleyway.

"Learn anything interesting?" Marshall asked when Benedikt returned.

Benedikt shook his head. He dusted off his damp pants and dropped to a crouch. "See anything interesting?"

"Well," Marshall remarked, "no monster sightings. But in my dreadful boredom with your absence, I did notice . . ." He pointed forward, letting Benedikt see for himself.

"What am I looking at?"

Marshall tutted, then reached out to physically turn Benedikt's head, changing the direction of his gaze. "There, by the lower-left corner of the balcony."

Benedikt hissed inward.

"You see it?"

"Yes."

There, by the lower-left corner of the balcony: a series of angry claw marks, trailing down the little ledge.

Twenty-Nine

O f all venues," Roma exclaimed, craning his neck to squint at the broken neon sign propped against the roof, "*this* had to be the place our man likes to frequent?"

The sun had set half an hour ago, turning the earlier red-hazed sky into vivid black ink. A light mist was coming down too, though Juliette wasn't sure when that had started. She simply realized upon staring into the hazy blue iteration of M NTUA that there were little flecks of water coming from the sky, and when she touched her face, her fingers came back slick with moisture.

"Honestly?" Juliette said. "I expected more debauchery."

"I expected more gunfire," Roma replied.

Mantua was slotted perfectly between Scarlet Gang and White Flower territory, a brothel and bar establishment bursting with the thrill of its own taboo. This was one of the most dangerous places in Shanghai, but in a strange, roundabout way, it was also the safest place for Roma and Juliette to be seen together. At any point, unruly men could get up and kill each other, women could whip out their pistols and shoot, bartenders could smash their glasses and decide to start a war. It was this adrenaline rush, the anticipation, the waiting that the people of Mantua were after. Who would believe the whispers coming from a place like *this*?

"By my knowledge, there have been at least five disputes here in the past week," Roma reported, matter-of-fact. They were still standing outside. Neither had made any move to go in. "The municipal police attempt to raid it almost every second week. Why would a Brit come here so often?"

"Why does *anybody* come here?" Juliette asked in reply. "He likes the excitement."

It took the same amount of effort as it would if she were wading through tar, but Juliette pulled at the creaky old door and stepped into Mantua, letting her eyes adjust to the dark and dreary interior. Though it was hard to see, certain areas were lit with streams of neon, wires flashing brightly enough to burn her retinas. Looking around, Juliette could almost have convinced herself that she had stepped into a speakeasy in New York, if not for the murkier glow.

Roma closed the door tightly after himself, then waved a hand before his nose, trying to disperse the thick cloud of smoke that wafted his way. "Do you see him?"

Juliette scanned her eyes through the dark shadows and bright spots of neon, squinting past the three American men on the dance floor attempting to teach a prostitute how to do the Charleston. The bar was flocked with customers, an ever-changing crowd of already drunk patrons carelessly tossing different currencies onto the alcohol-sodden floor. As soon as one was drawn away from the bar and up a small staircase nearby, entwined with a stranger and no doubt on their way to further sin, another took their place.

Archibald Welch was seated at the very left of the bar, with a clear bubble of space between him and everybody else. Where others simply hovered around their plump, red velvet seats, Archibald was seated firmly: a hulking mass of a man with ginger hair and a neck thicker than his face. The scar tissue that ran across his face glowed under the bar's blue light. The picture in his arrest file did not do his size justice.

"Huh," Roma said upon spotting their target. "I don't suppose we can try to intimidate him."

Juliette shrugged. "We may as well try."

The two surged forward, pushing through the crowds of Mantua and coming to a stop on either side of Archibald, settling themselves onto the velvet stools to the left and right of him. Archibald barely stirred. He didn't acknowledge their presence, though it was quite clear that Roma and Juliette were here for him.

Juliette turned to him and smiled.

"Archibald Welch, I believe?" she said sweetly. "Do you go by Archie?"

Archibald threw his drink down. "No."

"Really?" Juliette kept trying. "Archiboo, then?"

Roma rolled his eyes.

"All right, that's enough," he cut in. "We know about your business with the Larkspur, Mr. Welch, and I'm sure you know who we are. So, unless you want both the Scarlet Gang and the White Flowers coming down on your ass, I suggest you start talking. *Now.*"

Roma had decided to go rough in contrast to Juliette's niceties, but it seemed neither tactic was working. Archibald didn't give any indication that he had processed or even heard Roma's threat. He just kept drinking his drinks.

"Come on, it's not even information about *you* that we need," Juliette said, allowing a whine to slide into her voice. "We only want to know how to find the Larkspur."

Archibald remained quiet. The jazz music raged on in the background and the prostitutes mingled about, searching for their next clients. One came near, a fan clutched in her delicate fist, but she pivoted on her heel almost immediately, sensing the tension in that little nook of the bar.

Juliette's fingers worked at a bead on her dress. She was prepared to prompt the man again, when, to her shock, he set down his glass and said, "I'll tell you."

His voice was gravel against rubber. It was the collision of a ship against the coastal rocks that would take it down with all its men.

Roma blinked. "Really?"

Juliette had a suspicion Roma hadn't meant for that reaction to slip out. Upon Roma's response, Archibald's face split into a smile. His eyes became swallowed by his heavy lids, consumed into dark whorls.

It was the scariest sight Juliette had ever seen.

"Sure," Archibald said. He signaled to the bartender, who abandoned her present order to cater to him immediately. He was holding three fingers up. "But let's make this fun. One question answered for every shot you take."

Roma and Juliette exchanged a perplexed glance. How did that benefit Archibald Welch in any way? Was he that desperate for drinking buddies?

"Sounds fair," Roma grumbled. He eyed the liquid that had been set down before him with more disgust than his usual neutral expression.

Archibald raised his shot glass with a grin. "Gānbēi."

"Cheers," Juliette muttered, clinking her glass with his and Roma's.

The liquid went down fast, fire hitting the back of her throat. She cringed more at the taste than the heat, at the terribly cheap brand that her tongue immediately revolted against.

"God, what is this hellfire?" Juliette coughed, clinking the empty glass down. Roma did the same, careful to keep his expression steady.

"Tequila," Archibald said. He gestured for the bartender. "Next question?"

"*Hey*," Juliette protested. "That didn't count."

"I *said* one shot for each question, Miss Cai. No exceptions."

Three more shots landed before the three of them. This one tasted even worse. Juliette could have been drinking the gasoline that fueled the Scarlet cars.

"We'll start simple," Roma said once those glasses clinked down, jumping in before Juliette could squander another question. "Who is the Larkspur?"

Archibald shrugged, feigning apology. "I do not know his name; nor have I seen his face."

It felt like a lie. At the same time, Juliette could not imagine that this man had any reason to protect the Larkspur. He did not have to engage in this conversation at all if he wished to tell nothing.

Juliette resisted the urge to crush the shot glass in her fingers. "But you have interacted with him? He is a real person with a real place of operation?"

Archibald made a noise of consideration. "I believe there are two questions lurking in that."

Six glasses this time. Juliette took her two smoothly, having prepared herself this round. Roma had to hold back a cough.

"Of course he is real," Archibald replied. "Who sent you my way—Walter Dexter?"

Just to be petty, she should have made *him* drink for the answer to his question, but it likely would have done nothing substantial. It seemed like the alcohol was hardly affecting Archibald.

"Sort of."

Archibald nodded, satisfied enough. "I make direct deliveries to the Larkspur. Does that count as interaction by your terms?" He tipped his glass upside down, shook out the last few drops. "I pick them up from Dexter's warehouse and take everything to the top floor of the Long Fa Teahouse in Chenghuangmiao. That is where the Larkspur makes his vaccine."

Juliette let out her breath in a quick exhale. That was it, then. They had their address. They could speak to the Larkspur directly.

And if this didn't work out, then she didn't know what the hell they would do to save their city.

"Is that all tonight?" Archibald asked. Something about his voice was teasing. He did not expect this to be enough. He was looking at Juliette like he could read her mind, could see the cogs turning rapidly beneath her skull.

"That's all," Roma said, already rolling up his sleeves, preparing to leave.

But Juliette shook her head.

"No." This time *she* waved for the bartender. Roma's eyes bugged. He started to mouth something at her in horror, but she ignored him. "I have more questions."

"*Juliette*," Roma hissed.

The shots appeared. Archibald chuckled—a big and heavy hoot that came right from his stomach and smelled of fumes—slapping his hand down on the table in amusement. "Drink up, Mr. Montagov."

Roma glared at the glass, and drank.

"His vaccine," Juliette started, when the heat in her throat eased, "is it real? You must know if you make the delivery. You must have seen more than the average merchant."

This gave Archibald pause. He gargled his drink in his mouth, thinking for a long moment. Perhaps he was deliberating whether to keep silent on this question. But a promise was a promise; Juliette and Roma had already paid for their knowledge.

"The vaccine is both legitimate and not," Archibald answered carefully. "The Larkspur makes one strain in his lab, using the opiate I deliver. The other strain is simply colored saline."

Roma blinked. "What?"

If the madness was not stopped, at some point, it would spread to every corner of Shanghai. With two strains of the vaccine, one that was true and one that was not, the Larkspur controlled who was immune and who was not.

The weight of this revelation smacked Juliette dead center in the chest.

"The Larkspur is essentially picking and choosing who lives and who dies," she accused, incensed.

Archibald shrugged, neither confirming nor denying what she had said.

"But how?" she demanded. "How does he have a true vaccine to begin with?"

Archibald waved for the bartender. Juliette tossed down her next drink before he could prompt her, slamming the glass down furiously. Roma was the slowest this time, grimacing severely as he wiped his mouth.

"You're overstepping the extent of my knowledge, little girl," Archibald replied. "But I can tell you this: The first delivery I made, I watched the Larkspur work from a little leather book. He referred back to it continuously, as if he was unfamiliar with the supplies I dumped at his feet." The cheeky glint in Archibald's eye seemed to fade. "You wish to know about his true vaccine? The Larkspur was working from a little book made of tough leather found *only* in Britain. Do you understand?"

Roma and Juliette exchanged a glance.

"That he is British?" Juliette asked.

"He prefers his notebooks made traditionally?" Roma added.

Archibald looked at them like they were both missing brain cells. "Tell me, if a merchant from Britain set sail for Shanghai when news of madness broke out, would he be here by now?"

Juliette frowned. "Depends how fast the ship is going—"

"Even the fastest ship would not explain the short time between the outbreak of the madness and rumors of the Larkspur's vaccine," Archibald interrupted. "And yet his book came from Britain. Which means he had the formula to a vaccine before the madness had even broken out here."

Without warning, Archibald suddenly lurched in his seat. For a frightening moment, in her frantic train of thought, Juliette assumed he had been shot, but the movement was only so he could lean forward and wave down the bartender again.

"I believe that answer warrants a few more shots. It was a good one, wasn't it?"

Juliette's head was spinning. She was uncertain if it was over the information or the alcohol.

"The book," she said to Roma. "I shall get the book—"

"Oh, don't bother," Archibald cut in. "I never saw it again. I did, however, see charring marks on the floorboards. He burned it. Once he had the methods memorized, do you really think he would risk people like you stealing it?"

It was a good question. Juliette thinned her lips, but Archibald only grinned at such an expression and pushed closer the two shots in front of her. Juliette took one without much hesitation. It was the final hurrah, after all. They had gotten what they had come for.

"Juliette Cai," Archibald said, extending his second glass, "you have been a fantastic drinking partner. Mr. Montagov needs some more work."

"Rude," Roma muttered.

Carefully, making sure her hand wasn't shaking, Juliette picked up her second glass too and raised it. Roma followed suit, and then the last shot of poison was going down, working its havoc. Wasting no time, Archibald stood as soon as he finished, clapping a heavy hand over Juliette's left shoulder and another over Roma's right shoulder in a gesture of camaraderie.

"It's been a pleasure, kids. But the clock strikes past eleven o'clock, and my sources have told me it's time to go."

He hurried away, merged into the pulsing crowd and fading with the neon. An absolute agent of chaos. Juliette hardly knew the man and she respected him on principle.

She squeezed her eyes shut, shaking her head and forcing her focus to clear. She was fine. She could manage this.

"Roma?" she prompted.

Roma tilted sideways and pitched onto the floor.

"Roma!"

Juliette scrambled off her chair and knelt beside him, woozy enough to see in doubles but not enough to lose balance. She gave his face a light smack.

"Just leave me here," he said with a groan.

"How are you this bad?" Juliette asked in disbelief. "I thought you were Russian."

"I am Russian, not an alcoholic," Roma muttered. He squeezed his eyes shut, then opened them wide, blinking at the ceiling with a stunned expression. "Why am I on the floor?"

"We're leaving," Juliette commanded. She hauled at his shoulder, trying to get him back onto his feet. With a grunt, Roma complied. Or attempted to—on his first try, he only managed to sit up. Juliette gave him another tug, and then he was standing again, albeit with some swaying.

"We're leaving?" Roma repeated.

Suddenly, sirens were filling the room, a piercing wail cutting over the roar of jazz music. There was screaming and then there was a stampede of people running in all directions in such a whir that Juliette could no longer comprehend where the exit was. Outside, a voice on the loudspeaker was demanding that all patrons of Mantua come out with their hands up. Inside, people were pulling the safeties off their guns.

"We're not leaving anymore," she corrected. "Unless we want to get shot by the municipal police. Up, it is. Come on."

She grabbed his sleeve and dragged him toward the little staircase she had noticed earlier in the corner of the establishment. While all of Mantua's patrons rushed and pushed and stepped over one another to get to the exit, the brightly dressed girls booked it to the stairs instead, slipping up and out of sight.

"Careful, careful," Juliette warned when Roma stumbled on the first step.

They were both breathing heavily by the time they came to the top of the stairs, trying to stand still while the world spun. On the second floor, the hallway was so narrow that Juliette couldn't extend both her arms. The carpet was incredibly plush, half her heel sinking deep into the threads. The neon glow that pervaded the walls downstairs was absent here. This level was lit with the occasional dim bulb along the ceiling, illuminating just enough to see where they were going and to cast long, dancing shadows on the peeling wallpaper.

Juliette opened the first door she came upon. Two distinct yelps of surprise sounded as light seeped into the tiny room. Juliette squinted and saw a man with his pants down.

"Get out," she demanded.

"This is *my* room," the woman on the bed protested.

Below their feet, there was a heavy thud, then gunfire.

"Oh, I'm sorry, let me rephrase," Juliette said. It was getting very hard now to stay serious. For the most absurd reason, she had laughter bubbling up into her throat. "Get. Out!"

The man recognized her first. He was probably a Scarlet, judging by the speed at which he pulled his pants back on and hightailed it out of there, nodding to Juliette on his way out. The woman was a slower case, begrudgingly stepping off a bed that took up half the room. There was one window above the bed, but it was too small to push a cat out, never mind a person.

"Move faster," Juliette snapped. She could hear footsteps thundering up the stairs.

The woman brushed by and exited, throwing a glare back. Juliette tugged Roma into the vacated room and slammed the door shut.

"I don't think she liked you very much," Roma said.

"I don't care to be likable," Juliette replied. "Get under the blankets."

Roma visibly cringed. Screams reverberated into the second floor. "Must I? Do you know what people get up to under those—"

"Do it!" Juliette hissed. She reached into her dress and pawed through her money pouch, digging out an acceptable amount. It was rather difficult given that she couldn't really read the numbers anymore.

"Fine, fine," Roma said. Just as he stumbled onto the bed and drew the blanket over himself, an earth-shattering banging sounded upon the door.

Juliette was ready.

She opened the door a sliver, not enough for the officer to barge in but enough so he could get a good look at her face, at her American dress. That was usually all it took to put the dots together, and she waited—she waited for that millisecond when the realization set in.

It set in.

"This room is empty," she instructed him, as if she were putting the officer under hypnosis. He was Chinese, not British, which was fortunate for Juliette, because it meant he was more likely to fear the Scarlet Gang. Juliette passed the cash in her hands, and the officer inclined his head, tipping at her the coat of arms of the International Settlement on his dark-blue peaked cap.

"Understood," he said. He took the cash and then he was on his way, marking the room off as examined and leaving Juliette to shut the door and lean against it with her heart thudding.

"Is it safe now?" Roma asked from within the blankets, his words muffled.

Sighing, Juliette marched over and whipped the blankets off him. Roma blinked in surprise, eyes wider than saucepans, his hair flopped in all directions.

Juliette started laughing.

The giggle bubbled up from the warmth in her stomach, spreading all over her chest as she plopped down on the bed with her arms wrapped around her middle. She didn't know what was so funny. Nor did Roma when he sat up.

"This is . . . your . . . fault," Juliette managed to hiccup.

"My fault?" Roma echoed in disbelief.

"Yes," Juliette managed. "If you could handle your alcohol, we would have left when Archibald Welch did."

"Please," Roma said. "If I hadn't fallen over, you would have."

"Lies."

"Yeah?" Roma challenged. He gave her shoulder a hard shove. Juliette's entire, unstable body teetered backward onto the bed, her head spinning wildly.

"You—"

She came at him with her two hands, though she didn't quite know what her intent was. Perhaps she was to throttle him, or pluck out his eyes, or go for the gun he had in his pocket, but Roma was faster even in his inebriated state. He caught her by the wrists and pushed, until she was on her back again and Roma was hovering over her, smug.

"You were saying?" Roma asked. He didn't move away once he had proved his point. He remained—his hands holding her wrists down over her head, his body hovering over hers, his eyes strange and dark and on fire.

Something had changed in Roma's expression. Juliette inhaled sharply, a small, quick breath. It might have gone unnoticed, if Roma hadn't been so close. He noticed.

He always noticed.

"Why do you flinch?" Roma asked. His voice dropped to a conspiring, merciless whisper. "Do you fear me?"

A hot fury swept into Juliette's stilled veins. Such an insolent question reawakened all of her dulled senses, sweeping back the numbness of the alcohol.

"I have *never* feared you."

Juliette reversed their bodies in one deft push. Bitter and resentful and aggrieved, she hooked her legs around his and twisted her hips until Roma was the one flat on his back and she loomed over him, kneeling on the sheets. Though she attempted to pin his shoulders down as he had done to her, it was a half-hearted, head-spinning attempt. Roma merely looked upon the ire in her manner and responded in kind.

He sat up fast, shaking her grip loose. But he did not act further. They remained as they were—too close, too entwined. She was straddling his lap; he was hovering merely inches away.

One of his hands landed on her ankle. Her hand came down on his neck.

"Perhaps," Roma said, his words barely audible, "you do not fear me. But"—his hand was moving higher and higher, brushing her calf, her knee, her thigh. Juliette's palm sank lower, until it was gripping the space underneath the smooth collar of his white shirt—"you have always feared weakness."

Juliette snapped her gaze up. Their eyes met, murky and drunk and alert and challenging all at once, the loosest they had ever been and sharper than ever, somehow—somehow.

"And is this weakness?" she asked.

She didn't know who was breathing harder—her or Roma. They hovered a gasp away, daring the other to make the first move, daring the other to give in to what neither wanted to admit they wanted, what neither wanted to admit was something that was happening, what neither wanted to admit was a mere replay of history.

They both gave in at once.

Roma's kiss was just as she remembered. It filled her with so much adrenaline and exuberance that she could burst. It made her feel too ethereal for her own body, as if she could tear out of her own skin.

The alcohol had tasted terrible in its glass, but its remnants were wholly sweet on Roma's tongue. His teeth grazed her lower lip, and Juliette arched against him, her hands running across his shoulders, down the hard muscles along his sides, up his shirt, and against the burning warmth of his bare skin.

Her blood was roaring in her ears. She felt his lips move from her mouth to her jaw to her collarbone, burning everywhere he touched.

Juliette couldn't think, couldn't speak—her head was spinning and her world was spinning and she wanted nothing else in this moment than to continue spinning, spinning, spinning. She wanted to veer off course. She wanted to be out of control forever.

Four years ago, they had been innocent and young and good. Their love had been sweet, something to protect, simpler than life itself. Now they were monstrous; now they were pressed against each other and giving off the same heady perfume of the brothel they hid inside, drunk off more than just cheap tequila. Hunger and desire fueled their every move. Juliette tore at the buttons down Roma's front and she was pushing his shirt off, gripping at the scars and the old wounds that ran down his back.

"Call a truce," Juliette murmured against his lips. They needed to stop. She couldn't stop. "You are torturing me."

"We are not at war," Roma replied softly. "Why call a truce?"

Juliette shook her head. She closed her eyes, let the sensation of his lips brushing against her jaw roll through her. "Aren't we?"

We are.

The realization hit Juliette like a bucket of ice, sinking into her bones with a sort of cold found six feet underground. She burrowed her face into the crook of Roma's neck, forcing herself not to break, not to cry. Roma sensed the change before Juliette had even realized it herself, his arms coming around to hold her.

"What are you doing, Roma Montagov?" Juliette whispered, her voice only a rasp. "What are you doing to me?"

Wasn't playing with her heart once enough? Hadn't he already torn her in two and left her to the wolves once before?

Roma did not say anything. Juliette could read nothing from him, not even when she lifted her head and looked at him with wide, blinking eyes.

Juliette lurched away suddenly, scrambling to stand. Only then did Roma react. Only then did he reach out and grab her wrist, whispering, "Juliette."

"What?" she hissed back. "What, Roma? Do you wish to explain what this is between us, when you made it achingly clear four years ago where your heart stands? Shall I hold you at gunpoint until you have no choice but to admit you are once again *playing* me—"

"I am not."

Juliette reached into her dress, tore out the gun she had hidden in its folds. With the hand she had free, she pulled the safety and pressed the barrel to the underside of his jaw—to the soft part where her mouth had been merely minutes before—and all Roma did was lift his chin so the gun would sink in further, until the muzzle was only another press of a kiss against his skin.

"I cannot fathom it," she breathed. "You destroy me and then you kiss me. You give me reason to hate you and then you give me reason to love you. Is this a lie or the truth? Is this a ploy or your heart reaching for me?"

His pulse was beating hard enough that Juliette could sense it, could feel it thundering away even as she stood over him with her hand so close to his neck. An arc of moonlight had shifted in through the small window, and now it ran along Roma's body: his bare shoulders and his bare arms, braced to either side of him but making no move to stop Juliette from threatening his life.

She could pull the trigger. She could save herself the agony of hope.

"It is never as simple as one truth," Roma replied hoarsely. "Nothing ever is."

"That is not an answer."

"It is all I can give you." Roma reached up, closed his fingers around the barrel slowly. "And it is all that you could bear to hear. You speak to me as if I am still the same person you left behind, who betrayed you four years ago, but I am not. And *you* are not the same Juliette I loved, either."

Juliette was the one holding the gun, but suddenly she felt like *she* had been shot. Mantua was silent now, the raid finished and the municipal police packed up. Below, all that moved was the reflected glow of the building's neon sign, rippling in the shallow rain puddles.

"Why?" she rasped. The question she should have asked four years ago. The question that had been bearing on her all those years, a weight chained to her heart. "Why did you launch that attack on my people?"

Roma's eyes fluttered shut. It was like he was waiting for the bullet to come.

"Because," he whispered, "I had no choice."

Juliette withdrew her gun. Before Roma could say anything more, she ran out.

Thirty

Juliette buried her hands deep in the rich soil. She pressed and melded, closing her fingers around the bits of mulch that lined her gardens.

She had been working on the flower beds at the front of her house since dawn, easing her pounding headache with sunshine and the sounds of nature. If the frown on her face was any indication, however, it wasn't working. When she had gardened as a child, cleaning the soil beds with fistfuls of dead petals clutched in her fists, it had meant that she was in a bad mood and that she was trying to work off her aggression without shooting her pistol. It was practically Scarlet urban legend: speak to Juliette when she had a plant in her hand and risk the consequences.

Nobody had tended to these gardens since Ali bled to death in them.

Juliette breathed out deeply. She unwrapped a small purple hyacinth, settling it neatly into the hole she had dug. Before the bulbous flower could misalign and tip over, Juliette pushed the soil back into the hole.

She wished she could fill herself up like this. She wished she could press mounds of rich soil into the gaps of her heart, occupying the space until flowers could take root and grow roses. Maybe then she wouldn't be hearing Roma's voice in her head over and over again, taking up every inch of her thoughts.

Juliette's knees were covered in little, scarred-over scratches. She had fallen a quarter of a mile away from Mantua, and stayed there with her palms grazing the gravel, her dress soaking up mud and rainwater. It had stung badly during the rest of her trek home, but the pain now was good. The coolness of the earth underneath her, the morning sun cutting a golden line down her face, the crisp sharpness of the little rocks and twigs digging into her skin—it reminded her that she wasn't untethering from space itself and floating up into the clouds.

It is all I can give you.

None of this made any sense. If Roma Montagov had not hated her all these years, then why pretend he did? If he *had* hated her all these years, then why say such things now—why pretend, with such agony in his words, that his betrayal had hurt him just as much as it had hurt her?

I had no choice.

Juliette gave a sudden scream, smashing her fist into the soil. Two maids working nearby jumped and skittered away, but Juliette paid them no heed. For crying out loud, she had already *done* this four years ago. She had long ago drawn up two columns in her head: Roma's actions and Roma's words, utterly unable to pit them up against each other, unable to comprehend *why*—why—he would betray her when he said he loved her. Now she could not fathom him yet again, could not align the way he reached for her with the hate that he claimed to possess, could not understand the sadness in his eyes when he spoke of her being a new, cold Juliette he could not bear to see.

It is never as simple as one truth. Nothing ever is.

Juliette grabbed the shovel beside her, the anger in her veins raging to a crescendo. Planting flowers was child's play. She staggered to her feet and raised the shovel instead, smashing the lip of the metal hard into the plots she had just spent hours making beautiful. Again and again, her shovel sank into the flower beds until the flowers were all shredded to pieces, sharp petals littering the black soil. Someone called her name from afar and that mere summoning incensed her even more, to the point where she turned around and made a new target out of the first thing her eyes landed on: a thin tree that was twice as tall as she.

Juliette stormed toward the trunk. She raised the shovel, and thwacked, and thwacked, and thwacked—

"Juliette!"

The shovel snagged midmotion. When Juliette whirled around, she found Rosalind's delicate hand and her manicured nails gripping the shovel hard, holding it back from another gouge upon the tree.

"What is wrong with you?" Rosalind hissed. "Why have you become *unhinged*?"

"Leave me be," Juliette replied sharply. She tugged the shovel from her cousin's hands and hurried inside the house, leaving a track of soil and the gardening materials in the foyer, hardly caring about the mess she made as she trekked up to her bedroom. There she found her most drab oversize coat and tugged it on, hiding her dress and hiding her face, covering every element that gave away her stature. Almost out of habit, she pulled the hood on too to cover her hair, but that was unnecessary; she hadn't styled her signature finger waves. Loose black locks of hair brushed her neck instead. Juliette touched a strand that sat above her ear and gave it a tug, as if to check if it was real.

She marched out of her house, walking with her eyes in front of her, checking her surroundings only once. Was she still being followed? She hardly cared. Not when her heart was pounding a war cry in her ears. Not when she could not stop clenching her fists, a desperate effort to distract her trembling fingers.

Juliette had always prided herself on her priorities. She knew how to sight what was important, like explorers knew how to sight the north star. Her city, her gang, her family. Her family, her gang, her city.

But could an explorer still find the north star if the whole world turned upside down?

One ragged boot in front of the other, Juliette walked. At some point, she was passing through the Bund, weaving through the motor vehicles that pulled in and out of their parking spaces hazardously and merged onto the neatly pressed roads like a zip.

Dimly, Juliette wondered what it would be like to cease walking forward and err sideways instead, right down the wharves into the river. She could just keep going and drop straight into the water, becoming nothing more than another box of lost stock, another stray mark in the catalogs, another statistic of lost revenue.

Juliette moved on from the Bund, out of the International Settlement, and onto White Flower territory at last.

She pulled her hood higher. The action wasn't warranted—it was far easier for her to blend into the streets here where the Montagovs reigned than it was for Roma to sidle into her territory. Without Scarlet colors twined around her wrist or clipped into her hair, without any of her usual identifiers, as far as any of the patrolling White Flowers knew, she was just another Chinese girl who happened to live nearby.

"*Oi!*"

Juliette winced, angling her head down before the person she had accidentally shouldered could get a good look at her face.

"Sorry!" she called back. Just before she hurried around the corner, she thought she caught a glimpse of blond atop a pair of eyes staring curiously after her.

"The strangest thing happened," Benedikt announced.

He dropped into the open seat, unwinding the scarf around his neck and setting it down on their small corner table. Marshall nodded in a gesture for Benedikt to go on, but Roma acted as if he hadn't even heard his cousin. He was staring blankly at the other side of the restaurant, and—much to Benedikt's concern—was looking like he hadn't slept for days. Ever since Alisa became infected with the madness, the exhaustion on Roma's face had been wearing deeper and deeper, but something about his expression now was . . . different. It seemed that not only had his body reached its breaking point, but his mind had too, teetering past the point of bouncing back and now merely sitting idle, in wait for something to shift it back into cognition.

Benedikt wondered if Roma had even gone home last night, given his cousin was wearing the same wrinkled white shirt as the previous day. He wondered if he should ask what was wrong, or if it was better to pretend that all was well and treat his cousin no differently.

Afraid of the answers to the former, he chose the latter.

"I think I just saw Juliette Cai."

Roma's knee jerked up, colliding with the bottom of the table so roughly that the plate in front of Marshall almost slid off.

"Hey, watch it," Marshall chided. He put his hands protectively around his slice of honey cake. "Just because your food hasn't come yet doesn't mean you should ruin someone else's."

Roma ignored Marshall.

"What do you mean?" he demanded at Benedikt. "Are you certain it was her?"

"Calm down," Benedikt replied. "She was minding her own business—"

Roma was already leaping out of his chair. By the time Benedikt had even registered what was happening in that sudden flurry of motion, Roma was long gone, the doors of the restaurant swinging and swinging.

"What . . . was that?" Benedikt asked, stunned.

Marshall shrugged. He shoved a big spoonful of cake into his mouth. "You want cake?"

Meanwhile, Juliette had wandered deep into White Flower territory using only the basis of her memory, backtracking and doubling up on routes that she thought she remembered. Eventually, the streets started to bear some resemblance to the images she had in her head. Eventually, she found one very familiar alleyway and ducked in, lowering her head to pass through the collection of low-hanging laundry lines, wrinkling her nose against the damp smell in the air.

"Disgusting," Juliette muttered, wiping away the drops of dirty laundry water that landed upon the back of her neck. Just as she paused, intending to fling away the water, she caught sight of a tall and imposing figure entering the other end of the alleyway.

All the muscles along her shoulders froze stiff. Quickly, Juliette forced herself to scrunch her hand small, to continue strolling forward at an unsuspicious pace. Backing away now and running from the alleyway would immediately mark her as guilty, as a trespasser on enemy ground.

Fortunately, Dimitri Voronin didn't seem to recognize her as he passed. He was busy muttering to himself, straightening the fabric of his sleeve cuffs.

He disappeared from the alley. Juliette emerged out the other side too, breathing a sigh of relief. She scanned the apartment complexes laid out before her, matching her memory to the changed sights. She had been here before, but so much time had passed that the colors of the walls were different and the tiles had faded. . . .

"Are you out of your mind?"

Juliette gasped, barely registering Roma's voice before he had looped an arm around her waist to drag her aside, hauling her into the alleyway by the apartment building. When Juliette struggled back onto her own feet, she barely stopped herself from stomping on Roma's toes.

"I can *walk*, thank you," she hissed.

"You seemed to be taking your sweet time lingering in full view of every single window in my house!" Roma hissed back. "They will *kill* you, Juliette. Do you consider us a joke?"

"What do you think?" Juliette shot back. "All my dead relatives would say otherwise!"

They both fell silent.

"What are you doing here?" Roma asked quietly. His gaze was focused on a point just above her shoulder, refusing to make direct eye contact. But Juliette was looking right at him. She couldn't stop looking. She looked at him and she wanted to burst with all that she wanted to say, all that she wanted to hear, all that she wanted to be rid of. Everything—everything—was tight: her lungs, her skin, her teeth. She was too big for her body, bound to erupt into pieces and become a segment of the natural world growing in the cement cracks.

"I'm here," Juliette managed, "because I am sick to death of running away and remaining in ignorance. I want the truth."

"I told you—"

"You cannot *do* this." Juliette had started yelling. She had not intended to yell, but she was—four years of silence escaping all at once. "Don't I deserve to know? Don't I deserve at least a modicum of what the hell was going through your brain when you decided to tell your father exactly how to set an ambush on my—"

Juliette stopped midsentence, her eyebrows lifting so high they disappeared into her bangs. There was a blade held to her heart. *Roma* was holding a blade to her heart, his arm straight and long.

A beat passed. Juliette waited to see what he would do.

But Roma only shook his head. He suddenly *felt* so much like his old self again. Like the boy who had kissed her for the first time on the rooftop of a jazz club. Like the boy who didn't believe in violence, who swore he would rule his half of the city one day with fairness and justice.

"You're not even afraid," Roma breathed, his voice hitching, "and do you know why? Because you *know* I cannot push this knife in—you have always known, and even if you doubted my mercy upon returning, you discovered what the truth was pretty soon, didn't you?"

The tip of the blade was ice-cold even through her dress, almost soothing against the hot flush emanating from her body.

"If you know that I will not be afraid," Juliette asked, "then why hold your blade out?"

"Because *this*—" Roma closed his eyes. Tears. Tears were falling down his face. "This is why my betrayal was so terrible. Because you believed me incapable of hurting you, and yet I did."

He pulled away then, removing the tip of the blade from her heart and letting the cold air rush to fill the space. Without warning, Roma turned and threw his knife; it sank to the hilt, the whole blade embedded into the opposite wall. Juliette watched it all numbly, like she was some specter floating high above. She supposed she had expected this. Roma was right. She could not be afraid even when her life was in his hands. After all, she had been the one to walk her life into White Flower territory, to place it upon waiting palms.

"Then why?" Juliette asked. Her words came out a rasp. "Why did you do it?"

"It was a compromise." Roma scrubbed at his face harshly. His eyes slid to the mouth of the alleyway, checking for threats, checking that they were uninterrupted, unwatched. "My father wanted me to kill you outright, and I refused."

Juliette remembered the white flower lying on the path of her house, the note written from Lord Montagov. It had been dripping with mockery.

"Why not?"

A hard laugh. Roma shook his head. "Must you ask? I loved you."

Juliette bit down on her tongue. There was that word again. Love. *Loved.* He spoke as though all that had happened between them was real up until push came to shove, and Juliette could not comprehend this, could hardly accept this when she had spent so long convincing herself that their whole past was a lie, nothing save a spectacular act on Roma's part to fulfill his ultimate deed.

She *had* to convince herself. How could she bear to think that he had *loved* her and yet destroyed her anyway? How could she bear to face the truth that she had loved him too, so deeply that remnants yet remained, and if it hadn't been some grand master plan to sink his claws into her mind . . . then the pull in her fingertips now could be attributed to nothing save the weakness of her own heart.

The taste of metal flooded her mouth. With a wince of pain, Juliette eased her jaw loose, but she remained quiet still, the broken skin under her tongue throbbing.

"You can believe what you want to believe," Roma went on, noting the look on her face. "But you wanted the truth, so here it is. My father found out, Juliette. Some spy reported to him that we were lovers, and to rid the Montagov name of the insult, he gave me a knife"—Roma pointed to the knife in the wall—"to sink into your heart."

She remembered how deeply Roma had feared his own father, had feared the feats that the White Flowers were capable of. She remembered how Roma used to ponder day in and day out the ways he would change things when the White Flowers came under his hand. And she remembered her own fondness for such ambition, that spark of hope flaring in her chest every time Roma said that the future was theirs, that the city would be theirs one day, united as one, as long as they had each other.

Juliette stared at the knife in the wall. She whispered, "But you didn't."

"I didn't," Roma echoed. "I told him I'd rather take my own life, and he threatened exactly that. My father has been waiting for me to screw up since I was born, and it finally happened. He said he could launch a hit on you—"

"He couldn't have," Juliette interrupted. "He doesn't have the power—"

"You don't know that!" Roma's voice cracked, splitting apart into fragments. He turned away again; he spoke while facing the mouth of the alleyway. "And I didn't know that, either. My father . . . It may not seem like it because he does not act on it often, but he has eyes everywhere. He has always had eyes everywhere. If he made up his mind to kill you as he promised, if he wanted to set the scene to look as if we had both killed each other in the middle of Shanghai and kick off the blood feud to new heights, then he could do it. I had no doubt."

"We could have fought him." Juliette did not know why she bothered offering solutions to a situation long passed. It was instinct at this point, a way of protecting herself from the possibility that Roma had—perhaps—made the correct decision. "Lord Montagov is still human. He could have taken a bullet to the head."

Roma choked out another laugh, utterly, utterly devoid of humor. "I was *fifteen*, Juliette. I couldn't even defend myself against Dimitri's aggressive shoulder slaps. You think I could put a bullet through my father's head?"

I *could have done it*, Juliette wanted to say. But she didn't know if it was wishful thinking, if she would truly have been capable enough before anger turned her skin from fire to hardened rock. Back then she had believed just as Roma did, believed that this divided city could be sewn back together. She believed it when they sat under the velvet night and looked out at the haze of lights in the distance, when Roma said he would defy everything, everything, even the stars, to change their fate in this city.

"Astra inclinant," he would whisper into the wind, so heartachingly sincere even when quoting in Latin, "sed non obligant."

The stars incline us, they do not bind us.

Juliette breathed in shallowly. She felt something inside her unravel.

"What happened?" she managed. "What happened to change his mind?"

Roma started rolling up his sleeves. He was looking for something to do with his hands, something to occupy his restless energy because he could not stand there as Juliette did—a soldier turned to stone.

"My father wanted you dead because he felt insulted. He wanted me dead because I dared rebel." A long pause. "So I went to him and gave him a better plan. One that would cause more loss to the Scarlets. One that would put me back on his side." And Roma finally glanced at Juliette again, finally looked her eye to eye. "It would hurt you more than death, but at least you would be alive."

"You—" Juliette raised her hand, but she didn't know what she was trying to do. She ended up pointing a finger at Roma instead, like this was nothing but a small scolding. "You—"

You didn't have the right to make that choice.

But she couldn't even articulate herself.

Roma reached out, smoothed a palm over her hand so she was making a fist instead. His hands were steady. Juliette's were shaking. Repenting.

"I can't be sorry if you're looking for an apology," Roma whispered. "And . . . I suppose I am sorry that I am not more sorry. But given the choice between your life and your Scarlets . . ." Roma let go of her hand. "I chose you. Are you satisfied?"

Juliette squeezed her eyes shut. She didn't care anymore that that was dangerous, that she was breaking apart in the middle of White Flower territory. She pressed her fist to her forehead, feeling the sharpness of her rings dig into her skin, and breathed, "Indeed, I never shall be satisfied."

He chose me. She had believed him callous, believed him to have performed the greatest possible betrayal when she had offered him love.

Instead, the truth was that he had gone against everything he stood for. He had stained his own hands with the lives of dozens of innocents, placed razor blades in his own heart just to keep Juliette alive and safe, far from the threats of his father. He hadn't used the information he gleaned from his time with her as a tool of power. He had used it as a tool of weakness.

Juliette almost laughed out loud—in deliriousness, in sheer disbelief. This was what this city did to lovers. It tossed blame around like a slick coat of blood, mixing and merging with everything else until it had left its stain. This was why he hadn't wanted to tell her. He'd known that she would reach this conclusion—this realization that, in a roundabout way, Nurse's blood was now on her hands too. If Roma had not truly loved her, *her* life would have been the one the blood feud took instead—a simple, clean exchange.

She opened her eyes and looked to the skies. Gray, dreary skies of the first day of October. Down here, in the shadows of the cold alleyway, she could remain a lurker in the dark, could reach out and brush away the teardrop hovering at Roma's jaw and know that nobody could act a witness. She resisted. Somewhere above, past those low clouds and brisk winds, the north star was spinning, spinning atop the world with no regard for anything else.

Her city, her gang, her family. Her family, her gang, her city.

"Very well."

Roma blinked. "I beg your pardon?"

Juliette returned her hands to her sides, smoothing down her dress. She tried for a smile, but she was sure that she merely looked to be in pain.

"Very well," she repeated. "We hardly have time to be wasting on our personal dramas, do we? Mystery solved."

She walked over to the knife and pulled it out from the alleyway. It was beautiful. The handle was etched with a lily, the blade shiny, sharp, golden.

This city was on their shoulders. They could not collapse now, no matter how badly Juliette wanted to lie down in the grass and become still for the next millennia. And no matter how much it pained her, she glanced over her shoulder and looked to Roma, looked upon him right as he settled his mask back on, as he turned from mournful to cold once more.

You chose me four years ago. Would you choose me still? Would you choose this version of me—these sharp edges and hands far bloodier than yours?

Her city, her gang, her family. The better thing to do now would be to walk away, walk away from anything that would distract her from what was important. But she couldn't. She . . . hoped. And hope was dangerous. Hope was the most vicious evil of them all, the thing that had managed to thrive in Pandora's box among misery, and disease, and sadness—and what could endure alongside others with such teeth if it didn't have ghastly claws of its own?

"We still have a monster to catch," Juliette said firmly, even knowing, knowing better. "Chenghuangmiao is White Flower territory. Let's go."

She feared Roma would say no. That he would walk away even if she couldn't. There were so many people bustling about Chenghuangmiao on the daily—Chinese or otherwise—that it would be impossible to keep the Scarlet Gang out. She did not need Roma's help to find the Larkspur at this stage. They did not have to keep cooperating. He knew this.

Roma's eyes were blank. His posture was easy, spine straight.

"Let's go," he said.

Thirty-One

Tyler Cai was the first to receive news of rumblings within the city. He prided himself on keeping an ear on the grapevine, face turned outward for whispers that flowed downwind of any burning source, eyes pinned on those who needed them. Average civilians were fickle little creatures. They could not be trusted to go about their lives sensibly. They needed overseeing, a gentle, kind hand to prod them around and move the strings that held their fates as necessity dictated, else the strings became entangled and people choked to death on their own bumbling foolishness.

"Mr. Cai." The news came from a messenger named Andong, whom Tyler had taken especially under his wing, trained with the express directive of coming to him first, before anybody else. "It's really bad."

Tyler straightened up at his desk, setting down his calligraphy pen. "What happened?"

"A strike at a factory in Nanshi," Andong said, breathless. He had run in, barely avoiding a collision with the doorjamb in his hurry. "Casualties. There are casualties this time."

"Casualties?" Tyler echoed, his whole brow furrowing. "They are merely workers making up a fuss—how did they manage casualties? Did the madness strike at the same time?"

"No, it's the Communists," came the harried reply. "There were people from the worker's union planted inside the factory, instructing the workers and smuggling in weapons. The foreman is dead. Found with a meat cleaver in his head."

Tyler frowned deeply. He cast his memory back to the rallies on the streets, to the political parties that the Scarlet Gang had been trying to keep under control. Perhaps they had aligned themselves wrongly with the Nationalists. Perhaps it was the Communists they should have been watching more closely.

"With what do they take issue?" Tyler sneered. "How dare they revolt against those who give them safety!"

"They do not view it as such," Andong replied. "The workers who are not dying from the madness are dying from starvation. They're lining up en masse for that stupid vaccine, and instead of blaming this blasted Larkspur for overcharging, they worship him for the safety of his magical vials and blame the Scarlet factories for not paying enough to let them have both the vaccine and food."

Tyler shook his head. He hissed, "Ridiculous."

"Yet the Communists are thriving in this climate."

They were. They were taking full advantage of the chaos to turn the people of Shanghai against their rulers, to tear down the reign the gangsters had built. But it was not a big deal. The Scarlet Gang still held the crown. If they couldn't get the Communists in line eventually, they would simply destroy them.

"It is not an isolated incident," Andong warned when Tyler remained silent. "It may be an uprising. The Communists are planning something today. The factories all through Nanshi are starting to mutter unhappily. There will be more murders before the day is done."

Off with their heads and down with the rich. The workers were hungry enough that they would cut down the gangsters and use the sound of screaming to insulate the spaces between their ribs.

"Send warnings to our Scarlet affiliations," Tyler instructed. "Immediately."

The messenger nodded. He seemed to start back in the direction he came, but paused before he could move, stilling. "There's . . . another thing."

"More?" Tyler said. He threw his hands behind his head, rocking back on his chair.

"*I* did not see this with my own eyes, but"—Andong stepped farther into the room, then lowered his head. Instinctively his voice grew quiet, as if matters of death and revolution could be discussed at a normal speaking tone but petty gossip required reverence—"Cansun said he witnessed Miss Juliette in White Flower territory. He said he saw her . . ." Andong trailed off.

"Spit it out," Tyler snapped.

"He saw her with Roma Montagov."

Tyler lowered his hands slowly. "Oh?"

"It was a mere glimpse," Andong continued. "But he thought it suspicious. He thought you may like to know."

"Indeed, I do like to know." Tyler stood. "Thank you, Andong. If you would excuse me now, I must find my dear cousin."

Roma and Juliette had reached a peculiar sort of peace. It felt almost as if they were no longer enemies, and yet they were colder with each other than they had been before Mantua—far more stiff, more reserved. Juliette snuck a glance at Roma while they pushed their way through Chenghuangmiao, eyeing the way his hands were curled, the way he kept his elbows close to his core.

She hadn't realized that they had gotten comfortable around each other until they were uncomfortable again.

"I'm not remembering wrong, am I?" she asked aloud, aching to break the tension. "The Long Fa Teahouse *is* what Archibald Welch said?"

Juliette paused to inspect the shops they were passing, and in those few seconds, three shoppers rammed into her, one after the other. She wrinkled her nose, almost hissing out an exclamation before she stopped herself. Being invisible was better than being recognized, she supposed. It didn't mean she enjoyed it, even if blending in with the bustling crowd in her drab coat and drabber hairstyle was doing her a huge favor.

"I cannot imagine why you would ask me for confirmation," Roma replied. "I was on the floor."

"Nothing wrong with scrubbing the floor once in a while. It shows your humility."

Roma did not laugh. She hadn't expected him to. Silently she gestured for them to proceed before the shoppers here could bowl them over and recognize their faces.

"Come on, floor-scrubber."

Juliette set off, her stride purposeful. They passed the cream sellers and the puppet shows, then walked by the whole row of xiǎolóngbāo stores without once pausing to inhale the steam that smelled like delicious meats. They wound their way around the yelling performers and ducked beneath the archway leading into the central hustle and bustle of Chenghuangmiao, and there, Roma stopped suddenly, squinting ahead.

"Juliette," Roma said. "It's that one."

She nodded, gesturing for them to hurry that way. The Long Fa Teahouse sat near the ponds and to the left of the zigzag Jiuqu Bridge, a five-floor construction with an extravagant roof curving at its gold-lined edges. The building had probably been standing since China was first ruled by emperors in the Forbidden City.

Roma and Juliette stepped through the open doors of the teahouse, lifting their feet over the raised section framing the doorway. They paused.

"Up?" Roma asked, peering around the ground level, empty save for one stool tucked in the corner.

"Top floor," Juliette reminded.

They climbed the stairs. Floor after floor, they passed customers and servers, activity spilling over the edges as orders were shouted and bills were thrown forward. But when Juliette stomped her way up the last staircase, arriving at the top floor with Roma close on her heels, they found only one tall wooden door blocking them from anything on the other side.

"Is this it?"

"It must be," Roma replied. Hesitantly, he reached out with the back of his hand and knocked.

"Come in."

A British accent. Low, rumbly, like they had a bit of a cold or a nasal infection.

Roma and Juliette exchanged a glance. Roma shrugged and mouthed, *May as well.*

Juliette cracked open the door. Her brow immediately furrowed with what she found: a tiny space—no more than ten paces across. In the center of the room, a desk was laid out, though half of it was covered by an enormous white curtain that stretched to the ceiling. By the light filtering through the window, Juliette could make out a silhouette behind the curtain, his feet placed upon his desk and his arms tucked behind his head.

"Welcome to my office, Miss Cai and Mr. Montagov," the Larkspur said. He spoke like he had gravel lodged in his throat. Juliette wondered if it was his true voice, or if it was feigned. And if it was feigned . . . why? "I can't say I was expecting you, and I usually take meetings by appointment only, but come in, come in."

Juliette slowly strode toward the desk. On closer examination, as she peered at the wall behind the Larkspur, she realized that it was *not* a wall—it was merely a temporary divider. This "room" was as large as all the floors below. Behind the divider, the rest was surely the lab Archibald Welch had mentioned.

The Larkspur thinks he's being so sneaky, Juliette thought, eyeing the line where the divider met the ceiling. *He should learn to do a better paint job.*

"Come, sit," the Larkspur bellowed. Through the curtain, the outline of his arm showed him gesturing at the seats before him. However, his arm's silhouette would split the moment it came close to the curtain.

Juliette narrowed her eyes. She searched for a second source of refracted light behind the curtain that would create such an effect and found her answer upon the wall, where a mirror half faced the ceiling instead of the onlooker. It offered the illusion of decoration, but all it took was a glance up to where the mirror pointed and the discovery of another mirror to reveal the truth.

They couldn't see the Larkspur, but he could certainly see them.

"We won't take up much of your time," Roma assured. He sat down first. Juliette followed his lead, though she only perched on the edge of her seat, ready for a quick getaway.

"It's about your vaccine," Juliette said tightly. She did not have time to play around. "How are you making it?"

The Larkspur chuckled. "Miss Cai, you realize how detrimental it is to my business if I tell you. It would be like me asking you to give up your client lists."

Juliette slammed her hand onto his desk. "This is about people's *lives.*"

"Is it?" the Larkspur shot back. "What are you going to do with the formula of my vaccine? Make a preventative cure? I'm trying to run a business based on demand, not a research facility."

Roma grabbed Juliette's elbow. He was telling her to ease back, not to upset the Larkspur before they had gotten what they came for. But his touch startled her, and when she jumped in shock, her already fraught nerves rose from tense to catastrophic.

"What is your business with Zhang Gutai?" Roma asked. "Surely you must have heard the rumors about his role as the maker of the madness. You must realize how suspicious it is that you seem to be the healer."

The Larkspur only laughed.

"Please," Roma said through clenched teeth. "We're not accusing you of anything. We are merely putting together names, finding a way to *fix* this mess—"

"You've made it so far into your little investigation and you still can't put it together?"

Juliette was seconds away from lunging over the curtain and beating the Larkspur until his cryptic answers had some damn clarity.

"What do you mean?"

"What do you think, Miss Cai?"

Juliette shot out from her chair so quickly that the chair flew backward and turned over. "All right. That's it."

She reached over, and in one quick, deft movement, tore at the curtain, her strength ripping the fabric from the rings that held them onto the ceiling.

The Larkspur leaped up, but Juliette didn't catch a face. She couldn't. He was wearing a mask—one of those cheap Chinese opera masks that every vendor in the open markets sold to curious children, decorated with wide, bulging eyes and red and white swirls to emphasize the nose and mouth. It hid every part of his features, but Juliette was quite sure that the Larkspur was looking rather pleased with himself right now.

He was also pointing a gun at her.

"You are not the first person to do that, Miss Cai," the Larkspur said, almost sympathetically, "and I killed the last one who tried."

Juliette's weapon was tucked inside her dress. By the time she reached for it, she would have given the Larkspur plentiful time to shoot.

Still, she put on her bravado.

"Who do you think can shoot faster?" Juliette sneered.

"I think by the time you reach for your pistol, there will already be a hole in your head."

Juliette looked over at Roma. His jaw was gritted so hard that she feared he would soon have cracks in his molars.

"It is merely one question," Roma said quietly. He asked again: "What is your business with Zhang Gutai?"

The Larkspur considered them. He cocked his head and made a noise, then gestured with his free hand, meaning for Roma and Juliette to come nearer. They did not move. Instead, the Larkspur sidled closer to the table and leaned in, as if he was to release a great, big secret.

"You wish to know my business with Zhang Gutai?" he whispered gutturally. "Zhang Gutai is turning *himself* into a monster. I am making the vaccine using information *he* is giving me."

"Why?" Juliette demanded as they hurried down the stairs. "Why would he tell us this? Why would Zhang Gutai give him the formula to a vaccine?"

The world was moving too fast. Juliette's pulse was thudding at breakneck speed. Her breath was coming too rapidly, even when they reached the ground level and stopped to find their bearings, stopped to gather their thoughts, realizing they now had every puzzle piece they needed to stop the damned madness tearing Shanghai apart.

Didn't they?

"It doesn't make any sense," Juliette spat. "He must know we aim to kill the monster. He must know that we will hunt Zhang Gutai now with this knowledge. Why would he give this up? Without the monster, there is no madness. With no madness, he goes out of business."

"I don't know, Juliette," Roma replied. "I can't think of any viable answer either. But—"

"Down with the gangsters!"

The shout drew Roma's attention and Juliette's horror immediately, startling the two badly enough that they grabbed each other. It had come from the Jiuqu Bridge, from a raving old man who kept yelling until a Scarlet gangster nearby threatened to beat him up. The sight, however, was not met with indifference, as per usual. Instead, at the intrusion of the tough-talking Scarlet, the civilians started to mutter among themselves, throwing rumors and speculations to the wind. Juliette caught snippets of whispers: of striking workers and factory revolts.

She dropped Roma's hand quickly, taking a step away. Roma did not move.

"Why would he say such a thing?" Juliette muttered, her eyes still on the scene. Why did that old man feel emboldened enough to wish death on the gangsters?

"If the reports I read this morning were any indication, it's trouble from the Communists," Roma replied. "Armed strikes in Nanshi."

"Nanshi," Juliette echoed, knowing the area was familiar for a particular reason. "That's—"

Roma nodded. "Where Alisa is, stuck in a hospital right by the factories," he finished. "We may be running out of time. The workers will storm the building should an uprising occur."

If the workers rebelled from their tasks, instructed to cause chaos, they would seek to harm every gangster, every capitalist, every high-ranking foreman and factory owner in sight, child or not, conscious or not—including little Alisa Montagova.

"We kill him," Juliette decided. "Today."

Kill the monster, stop the madness. Wake Alisa and save her from the chaos building up around her.

"He will still be in his office," Roma said. "How do we want to do this?"

Juliette checked her pocket watch. She bit her lip, thinking hard. There was no time for her to consult her parents. She doubted they would approve anyway. They would want to think things through, draw up plans. She could not ask for official Scarlet backup. She would do this by her own terms. "Gather your closest reinforcements, your weapons. We meet by the *Labor Daily* offices in an hour's time."

Roma nodded. His gaze searched her face, sweeping from her forehead to her eyes to her mouth, as if he was waiting for her to say something else. When she did not, puzzled over what he was waiting for, Roma did not explain himself. He merely nodded again and said, "See you then."

Tyler pulled back from where he had been lurking, pressing up against the exterior wall of the Long Fa Teahouse. He moved himself out of view just soon enough to avoid being spotted by Roma Montagov, who hurried into the crowds of Chenghuangmiao and disappeared.

Taking one last drag of his cigarette, Tyler pinched the lit end to stub it out, then dropped it to the ground, uncaring of the new burns on his fingers.

Tyler had seen them. He could not hear their conversation, but he had seen them—working together, reaching out for each other.

"Tā mā de, Juliette," he muttered. *"Traitor."*

Thirty-Two

M essage for you, Miss Lang."

Kathleen rolled over, moving from one end of Juliette's neatly made bed to the other. She was the maids' worst nightmare. There were plenty of chairs for her to occupy in this house, but whenever Juliette left her room, Kathleen came wandering in to take ownership of her bed.

To be fair, it was an absurdly comfortable bed.

"For me?" Kathleen asked, waving the messenger in. This was unusual. There weren't many callers for her.

"It says both Lang Selin and Lang Shalin at the front, but I cannot find Miss Rosalind," the messenger responded, sounding out the syllables of their names awkwardly. When he showed her the front of the note, she realized that her Chinese name—Lang Selin—had been written out in its romanized equivalent instead of its Chinese characters.

It had to be Juliette. No one else would be so cryptic.

Kathleen quirked a brow, extending her hand for the note. "Thank you."

The messenger left. Kathleen unfolded the slip of paper.

I need your help. The Secretary-General of the
Communist Party is the monster. Meet me by his work
building. Bring guns. Bring silencers. Tell no one.

"Oh, *merde*."

Juliette was trying to kill the Secretary-General of the Communist Party.

Kathleen threw the note down and bolted off the bed, hurrying for the armory next door. They kept their weapons in this small room, with the grandfather clocks and the rotting settees, in a row of cabinets that would have otherwise appeared inconsequential to a casual observer. She moved fast, tearing open the drawers and loading up two pistols, spinning the silencers on tightly. She checked the ammunition, clicked each loose component tightly, then shoved both weapons in her pockets.

Kathleen stopped. Her ears perked suddenly, hearing sound from the other side of the wall, from Juliette's room.

Footsteps. Who was walking about?

Prickled, Kathleen rose quietly, keeping her footsteps light as she padded out of the armory and back toward Juliette's bedroom. With her breath held, she poked her head through the doorway and sighted a familiar figure. She relaxed. It was only Rosalind, holding the note.

"What the *hell* is this?" Rosalind demanded.

Kathleen immediately tensed again. "I . . . thought the words were rather self-explanatory."

"You can't be serious." Rosalind's eyes dropped down to Kathleen's pockets. She traced the shapes of the weapons, gaze sharpening—hollowing. "You're not actually going to go, are you?"

Kathleen blinked. "Why would I not?"

A moment passed. That moment would be something to mark

forever: the first time Kathleen looked at Rosalind—really looked—and realized she had no clue what could possibly be going through her sister's head. And when Rosalind exploded outward, Kathleen felt the impact like a piece of debris sticking right through her gut.

"This is *absurd*!" Rosalind shouted suddenly. "We do not have the right to go killing Secretary-Generals as we please! Juliette cannot pull you into this as she pleases!"

"Rosalind, stop," Kathleen pleaded, hurrying to close the door. "She is not pulling me into anything."

"Then what is this note? A mere suggestion?"

"This is *important*. This is a matter of stopping the madness."

Rosalind's lips thinned. Her volume dropped, until it was not loud but cold, not angry but accusatory. "Here I was, thinking you were the pacifist of the family."

Pacifist. Kathleen almost laughed aloud. Of all the words to describe her, pacifist could not be farther from the truth. All because she did not care for bloodshed, and suddenly she was an almighty saint. She would pull a switch to instantly end all life in this city if it meant she herself could have some peace and quiet.

"That is your mistake," Kathleen said evenly. "That is everyone's mistake."

Rosalind folded her arms. If she clutched the note in her fist any harder, she would put a hole right through the words. "I suppose Juliette is the only person exempt from being a fool in your eyes."

Kathleen's jaw almost dropped.

"Do you *hear* yourself right now?" she asked. Perhaps she had stepped into a machine that took them back to being petulant toddlers.

But Rosalind did not care to consider herself. The bitterness had risen to the surface and now it could not cease in overflowing.

"Look at how casually Juliette has approached this whole madness," she hissed. "Look at how she treats it like it is merely another task to impress her parents with—"

"Stop it." Kathleen's hands closed around the hem of her shirt, scrunching her fingers into the thick fabric. "You haven't been around for most of it."

"I *saw* the monster!"

"This isn't Juliette's *fault*. It's not her fault that she has to treat it like her job because it *is*—"

"You don't get it," Rosalind hissed, rushing forward. She stopped right in front of Kathleen and clutched at her shoulders. "Juliette will never face the consequences to anything she does. We will. We feel every goddamn part of this city when it breaks—"

"*Rosalind,*" Kathleen pleaded, "you're really, really stressed right now." She untangled her hands from her shirt and held them out in front of her. It was both an action to keep Rosalind at a distance and to placate her sister like she would placate a feral animal. "I get it, I do, but we're all on the same side."

"Her family name is Cai!" Rosalind exclaimed. "How can we be on the same side when they will never fall? They are invulnerable. We are *not!*"

Kathleen could not keep listening to this. Time was running out. The weapons in her pocket grew heavier with each passing second. She removed Rosalind's tight grip from her shoulders, unspeaking, and turned to leave.

Until Rosalind said, "Celia, please."

Kathleen froze. She whirled around.

"Don't," she hissed. "There are ears everywhere in this house. Don't put me in danger just to make a point."

Rosalind looked away. She let out a long breath, seemed to gather herself, and whispered, "I'm only looking out for you."

Now is not the time to look out for me! Kathleen wanted to snap. What part of this was so hard to understand? She shook her head. She swallowed her words, forced herself to soften her tone.

"It's a simple matter, Rosalind. Will you help, or will you not?"

When Rosalind met her eyes again, Kathleen only found apathy in her sister's expression.

"I will not."

"Very well," Kathleen said. "But please do not stop me."

This city was teeming with monsters in every corner. She would be damned before she let her own sister stop her from putting down at least one.

Kathleen walked out of the room.

Thirty-Three

Juliette stood around the corner of the *Labor Daily* office building, her body tucked in the shadows of the exterior walls and protruding pipes. She had chosen a small swath of grass where the building curved inward a little, near the rusty back door that looked like it hadn't been cleaned in weeks. A climbing plant was growing in this nook, flying across the walls and dangling right above Juliette's head. From a distance, she may have looked like a statue, staring straight ahead with dead-dull eyes. She couldn't blink too much. If she did, she might collapse then and there, become a twin to the Niobe made of marble that stood in the International Settlement, and then she would never get up again.

"Juliette—oh *God*."

Juliette was also standing here because she had found a corpse. A victim of the madness: an older woman with her throat in shreds. She remained here because she did not know what to do, whether it was best to leave the victim be or do something—or if killing Zhang Gutai today would be enough as that *something* bearing on her shoulders.

Juliette turned, exhaling a breath at the sight of her cousin. Kathleen covered her mouth in horror, ducking under the trail of vines.

"Before you ask," Juliette said, "I found her like this. Did you bring a silencer?"

"Right here," Kathleen said. She passed Juliette one of the pistols in her pocket, her gaze still locked on the dead woman slumped against the wall.

"Where's Rosalind?" Juliette asked. She rose to the tips of her toes to look over Kathleen's shoulder, as if Rosalind had merely been walking a little slowly.

"She could not come," Kathleen replied. She dragged her gaze away from the dead victim. "The burlesque club needs her. It was too suspicious to leave."

Juliette nodded. She would have preferred to have another trusted pair of eyes and hands here, but there was nothing to do about it.

"Now can you tell me what's going on?" Kathleen demanded.

"Exactly as my note said," Juliette replied. "The madness stops today."

"But—" Kathleen scratched the inside of her elbow, drawing angry lines over her skin. "Juliette, surely you don't mean for just the two of us to storm what is essentially a Communist stronghold. This may be a workplace, but I've no doubt some are carrying weapons."

Juliette grimaced. "About that . . ." She spotted three figures approaching along the pavement. She raised her hand, catching Roma's attention. "Don't panic. I'll explain everything later."

Kathleen whirled around. As always, when somebody said not to panic, the first thing one did was panic. She physically darted back a few steps when Marshall Seo grinned at her and waved. Benedikt Montagov reached over and yanked the other boy's hand down.

The White Flowers ducked under the vines, and Roma threw something fast in Juliette's direction: something soft and squarish, balled up into a mass of fabric so that it could volley through the air and into her palm. A large handkerchief. The sudden projectile made it easy for Juliette to pretend her stifled gasp was in surprise over having to catch the fabric and not because Roma had then stepped close, almost brushing her shoulder.

"To cover your face," he explained. There was another in his hands too, for the same purpose. "Since we are the executioners—*oh*."

Benedikt and Marshall went on alert, both stiffening in anticipation of a threat. But there was no threat, at least not here. Roma had merely spotted the dead woman.

"How did she get here?" Benedikt muttered.

"She had to have been an employee," Marshall replied, jerking his thumb at the bright walls of the office building. "Better be careful. There might be an outbreak coming."

Roma made a disgusted noise at the back of his throat but did not add anything more.

Perhaps it was a little sadistic of Juliette, leading them all to meet here, three feet away from a corpse. But they needed to see this before they went in. They needed to remember exactly what was at stake.

One guilty life for countless innocent ones. One guilty life to save the city.

Perhaps this was the choice that should have been made four years ago. If only Juliette had had more guilt on her soul back then. It would have made her death worthy.

Stop, she chided herself. Her pulse was thudding a symphony in her ears. She was a little afraid that the others could hear it. She wondered if each time she opened her mouth, the sound would travel from her chest and through her throat, making its way to the outside world.

Juliette pushed past her nerves. She had conquered much fiercer opponents than a loud heartbeat.

Now or never.

Juliette cleared her throat. "This is how we will proceed," she started. "We need guards at the back. Zhang Gutai's office has a window he may jump from."

Roma nodded at Benedikt and Marshall. Wordlessly, they hurried off to the back of the building.

"Kathleen."

Kathleen snapped to attention.

"I need you to cause some sort of evacuation on the first floor. Enough commotion that no one will stop us from approaching the second level and entering Zhang Gutai's office."

Kathleen pulled her pistol, readying it in her two hands. A slow exhale. A nod.

"Listen for my signal," she said. "I hope you know what you're doing, Juliette." Kathleen ducked out from underneath the vines.

Dear God, I hope so too.

"As for us——" Juliette turned to Roma. Tied the handkerchief around the lower half her face. "Ready?"

"Ready."

A thunderous gunshot echoed out from the office building. Three more pops followed in close succession. Glass shattering. Shouts of confusion.

"Let's go."

They hurried for the front doors, merging into the commotion without notice. Kathleen wasn't anywhere to be seen, but that only meant she had been fast at getting herself out of there. She had left behind a scene of general bewilderment, but no panic—people were too concerned with muttering over what they should do, to notice Roma and Juliette hurrying up the stairs. This was more a simple assassination mission than it was a direct confrontation. The faster they could get in and get out, the better it was.

Unfortunately, there were people on the second floor too: two men standing outside Zhang Gutai's office door. Perhaps they had been asked to guard it. Perhaps Zhang Gutai knew his assassination was coming.

"No," Roma hissed before Juliette could start forward. "We cannot kill them."

"Announce your business!" one of the men by the door called lazily.

"They are *in the way*," Juliette hissed back to Roma.

The two men by the door were growing alert now. If the cloths over Roma's and Juliette's faces weren't enough to rouse suspicion, the pistols in their hands certainly were. The men started forward fast.

"Leg," Roma mediated.

"Stomach."

"*Juliette.*"

"Fine!"

Juliette aimed and blew holes in the men's upper thighs. Merciless. They yelled out, collapsed to the ground, and she charged forward. When she struck her palm against the office door, it flew back hard enough to put a dent in the wall.

"Watch out!"

Roma pulled her aside roughly, muttering a prayer under his breath. A red-hot bullet struck the doorjamb where Juliette's head would have been.

Zhang Gutai stood behind his desk, aiming his gun again. His grip was unsteady. He had beads of sweat dripping down his face, eyes turned to saucers. Caught at last.

"What have I done to you?" Zhang Gutai demanded. He recognized them. Of course he did. It took more than one flimsy cloth to disguise Juliette Cai. "What is your issue here?"

"I have issue with your madness," Juliette answered, thunderous.

"I do not know what it is you speak of!" Zhang Gutai yelled. "I have nothing to do with—"

Juliette fired. Zhang Gutai looked down, looked at the blotch of red blooming on his white shirt.

"Don't," he whispered. His gun fell from his weak grasp. Instead of trying to pick it back up, his hand flopped onto his desk. He closed his hands around a framed photograph of an elderly woman. His mother. "Don't—you have no quarrel with me."

"The Larkspur told us everything," Roma said tightly. His eyes were on the photograph in Zhang Gutai's hands. "We're sorry it has to be this way. But it must."

"The Larkspur?" Zhang Gutai wheezed. Blood loss sent him crashing onto the floor. He swayed, barely holding on to enough life to remain sitting. "That . . . charlatan? What does . . . *he* have to . . . say—"

Juliette fired again, and the Communist slumped over. His blood soaked the photograph beneath him completely, until his mother's stoic expression was covered with a sheen of red.

Slowly, Juliette walked over, then nudged his shoulder with her toe to roll him onto his back. His eyes had already glazed over. Juliette turned away, putting her pistol into her pocket. It felt like the moment needed more ceremony, perhaps a solemn air, but all that was present in this room was the cold stink of blood, and Juliette wanted to get away from it as soon as possible.

She would be a callous killer for as long as she was doing something right. She cared for little else.

"Someone's coming," Roma warned. He had his head tilted toward the door, listening for the rustle of footsteps bounding up the staircase. "Climb through the window."

Juliette did as she was told. She clambered one leg out the glass pane and yelled a warning down to Marshall and Benedikt, who startled to see her appear, her neck splattered with dots of red. They were even more startled when she said, "Marshall Seo, catch me," and dropped down, leaving Marshall a split second to quickly open his arms. Juliette landed with a neat, polite bounce.

"Thank you."

An alarm started to blare from within the building. On the first sharp note, Roma quickly lowered himself through the window until he was hanging from the ledge by his fingers. When he let go, he managed to land with a firm *plop* upon the grass.

"Did you do it?" Benedikt asked immediately. "Is the monster dead?"

Just as Roma was about to nod, Kathleen burst around the corner, her breath coming fast.

"Why didn't you kill him?" she demanded. "I saw you make it to the second floor!"

Juliette blinked. Under the bleary sunlight, her hands were still stained with the evidence of her crime. "What do you mean?" she asked. "I did."

Kathleen jerked back. She swore softly.

"Then it didn't work," she breathed. "The madness. *Listen.*"

A short, sharp scream. A chorus of rough shrieking. Gunshots, in quick successions.

"No," Juliette breathed. "Impossible."

She sprinted forward. Someone called out after her and someone else made a grab for her elbow, but Juliette shook them off, coming around the building and returning to the scene of her crime. She didn't have to push the front doors, nor as much as reach for them. Through the panel of glass running vertical down the wood, she saw three workers inside tear at their throats, falling in utter synchrony.

"No," Juliette muttered in horror. "No, no, *no—*" She kicked the nearby wall. Her shoe scuffed a dirty mark onto the pristine white.

It hadn't worked.

"Juliette, come on!" Kathleen grabbed her wrist and hauled her back, hauled her to the side of the building once again, right before the doors burst open and those who were yet uninfected ran for safety. Her cousin must have intended for them to keep moving, but Juliette couldn't do it. Out of the corner of her eye, she could see that the White Flowers were looking at her, were watching to see how she would react, and still she could not hold her strength. Her knees grew weak. She gave in to the fatigue without resistance and sank to the soft grass, digging her fingers into the dirt and scrunching, until the cool soil was squirming into her nails.

"Hey!"

Police whistles. Someone must have signaled them upon hearing gunshots. Or a worker inside, having made the call to the nearest station, begging for help. When the uniformed men came into view, however, it was no surprise that they would instead focus on the five gangsters lurking by the building and begin heading over.

On a day like this, as revolution stirred all around the city, the police were itching to make arrests.

"Go," Roma muttered under his breath to Benedikt and Marshall. "Merge into the alleys until they lose you. We will reconvene on the rooftop of Jade Dragon."

Jade Dragon was the restaurant not two blocks away from here, easily the tallest building on its street and constantly packed with customers and patrons. The sheer chaos of large restaurants meant that gangsters could often slip in and out of its tall staircases whenever they pleased, climbing to the rooftops and using them for lookouts. Benedikt and Marshall shot off to the west; Kathleen said, "Juliette, come *on*," but Juliette refused.

"You go too, Kathleen," Juliette intoned. "Follow the same plan."

"What about you—"

"They can arrest you, but they cannot arrest me. They would not dare."

Kathleen sucked in her cheeks, eyeing Juliette warily, and then Roma, who yet remained, his arms folded. "Be careful," she whispered, before the three policemen approached and she darted away, gone in a blink.

"Under the jurisdiction of—"

"Scram," Roma interrupted in Russian. The policemen did not understand him. They did not need to. They only needed to hear the Russian and eye his clothing before realizing that this was the heir of the White Flowers. Then their jaws grew clenched, exchanging terse looks. Then they were forced to back away without another word, hurrying off in the direction Benedikt and Marshall had run in the hopes that an arrest was not entirely lost.

"Juliette," Roma said when the policemen disappeared. "You have to get up."

She could not. She would not. She had surpassed anger and rage, moved into numbness instead. She had been stoking the fire in her chest for so long that she had not noticed how intently she had been burning, but now the blaze was extinguished, and she found that nothing remained there except a charred space, hollow where her heart was supposed to be.

"Why should I?" she asked. "The Larkspur tricked us. He tricked us into doing his dirty work."

With a sigh, Roma dropped to a crouch. He leveled himself with her fallen state. "Juliette . . ."

"Zhang Gutai was never guilty, yet I *executed* him," Juliette went on, hardly listening to Roma. "What did we even achieve? Only more bloodshed—"

"Don't you dare," Roma said. "Don't you dare fall apart now, dorogaya."

Juliette's head jerked up. Her breath snagged in her throat, twisting her whole esophagus sour. What did he think he was *doing*? She was already down. He may as well kick her a few times just to make sure she was dead.

"I shot him," Juliette told Roma, as if he had not noticed, "in cold blood. He was not hurting me. He begged for his life."

"We took a calculated risk to save millions. You fired for Alisa. For the smallest chance of saving an innocent life. Get it together. *Now*."

Juliette breathed in. She breathed in and in and in. How many more times could she do this? How many more faux monsters would be torn down with unbidden violence in their path toward finding the real one? How was she any *different* from the killers that lurked in this city—the ones that she was trying to stop?

She didn't realize she was crying until her tears hit her hand. She didn't realize that teardrops had started running down her face faster than the pace of her rapid heartbeat until Roma's stiff posture soft-ened and his hard eyes grew worried.

He reached for her.

"Don't," Juliette managed, her breath hitching, her hand rising to knock his fingers back. "I don't . . . need your pity."

Slowly, Roma lowered himself onto the ground until he, too, was kneeling. "It is not my pity you have," he said. "You made the right choice, Juliette."

"We hunt the monster to stop it from bringing devastation to this city." Juliette held her bloody hands out. "But this—this *is* monstrosity."

Roma reached for her again. This time Juliette did not stop him. This time he smoothed his thumbs across her cheeks to dry her tears and she leaned into him, her head resting on his chest and his arms wrapping around her—familiar, foreign, *fitting*.

"A monster," he said against her hair, "does not mourn."

"Did you mourn?" Juliette asked, barely audible. She did not need to clarify what she meant. They both saw it in their minds: the explosion, the damage, the blood and the lives and the burning, burning red.

"I mourned," Roma said just as softly. "I mourned for months, *years* outside the gates of the cemetery. Yet I don't regret choosing you. No matter how cruel you think yourself, your heart beats for your people. That's why you shot him. That's why you took the chance. Not because you are merciless. Because you have *hope*."

Juliette looked up. If Roma turned, even the slightest, they would be nose to nose.

"I regret that I was ever put in the position to choose," Roma continued. His words were faint, whispered into the world while the streets roared with sirens, the building beside them teemed with chaos, and policemen along every street corner screamed for order. But Juliette heard him perfectly. "I hate that the blood feud forced my hand, but I can't—I did what I had to do and you may think me monstrous for it. The feud keeps taking and hurting and killing and still I couldn't stop loving you even when I thought I hated you."

Love. Loved.

Hated. Love.

Juliette pulled away, but only to look Roma in the eye, her pulse beating its crescendo. He did not flinch. He met her gaze, steady, unwavering.

In that moment, all Juliette could think was: *Please, please, please. Please don't break me again.*

"So you," Roma went on, "cannot fool me any longer. You are the same indomitable girl I would have laid my life down to save. I made my choice to believe in you—now you make yours. Will you keep fighting, or will you crumble?"

She had spent a lifetime doing both. She could hardly tell the difference between the times when she was fighting and the times when she was barely holding herself together, crumbled pieces staggering forward step-by-step. Maybe those two were one and the same.

"Answer me something first," she responded with a whisper.

Roma seemed to brace. He knew. He knew what she was going to ask.

"Do you still love me?"

Roma's eyes shuttered closed. A long second passed. It seemed that Juliette had misspoken, had come across a crevasse and misjudged her leap, spiriting down, down an endless dark rip—

"Do you not listen to me when I speak?" he answered shakily, his lip quirking up. "I love you. I have always loved you."

Juliette had thought her heart hollow, but now it was encased with gold. And it seemed certain then that her heart remained functional after all, because now it was bursting, bursting—

"Roma Montagov," she said fiercely.

Roma seemed to startle at her tone. His eyes grew wide, bordering on concerned. "What?"

"I'm going to kiss you now."

And on the patch of grass behind a Communist stronghold, swarmed with police from every settlement, below the crisscrossed telephone wires and bloody glass windows, Juliette reached for Roma. She took his face between her hands and shifted forward to meet his lips, kissing him with all the intensity of their lost years. Roma responded in kind, his arm coming around her waist and holding her—holding her like she was precious, a sprite snagged out of the wind.

"Forgive me," he breathed when they broke apart. "Forgive me, Juliette."

She was tired of hatred and blood and vengeance. All she wanted was this.

Juliette twined her arms around him and pressed her chin to his shoulder, holding him as close as she dared. It was a reacquaintance, a homecoming. It was her mind whispering, *Oh, we are here again— at last.*

"I forgive you," she said softly. "And when this is over, when the monster is dead and the city is ours again, we're going to have a proper chat."

Roma managed a laugh. He pressed a kiss to the side of her neck. "Okay. That's fine by me."

"For now"—Juliette released him, extended her hand—"I suppose we have a monster to find."

Thirty-Four

Alight rain starts over the city. The people on the streets run for shelter, hastening to draw their bāozi stalls off the pavement. They snap at their children to hurry, to get inside before the skies fall . . . and before the roar of sound echoes up from the south.

By now everyone has heard the rumors. A Communist revolt plots to stir today in Nanshi. At first they planned a slow uprising, factory after factory, following each other's example in a precise domino effect. Now they hurry. They have heard about the murder of their Secretary-General. They worry that there is an assassin after the Party. They scream in vengeance and vow to rise with the workers of the city all at once, before any one segment can be cut down.

The rain trickles on. Upon a rooftop, five young gangsters are one of the few still spots in this city, unbothered by the gray weather. They sit scattered on the concrete tiling—two side by side in equal concentration, two close together, and one facing the city, her face turned to the wind, letting the beads of water soak into her hair.

They simmer in misery. Their attempts at saving a beloved little blond girl in the hospital may have sped up her demise instead. If chaos truly erupts today, then death is soon to follow.

They can only pray and pray that a rumor is a rumor. They can only hold on to their belief that whispers in this city mutate faster than disease and hope for once they are correct.

The wind blows. A bird squawks.

"Perhaps we should run away. The madness is bound to spread to every corner of this city at some point."

"Where would we go?"

"They have started calling America *the land of dreams.*"

A snort floats up into the clouds. It is a sound that exists incongruous with the rest of the anxiety seeping along this city's arteries. It is the only sound that epitomizes the land in question, somehow both charming and terrible, both dismissive and weighted down. *The land of dreams.* Where men and women in white hoods roam the streets to murder Black folks. Where written laws prohibit the Chinese from stepping upon its shores. Where immigrant children are separated from immigrant mothers on Ellis Island, never to be seen again.

Even the land of dreams needs to wake up sometimes. And though there may be beauty beneath its core rot, though it is big and open and plentiful, hiding those who want to be hidden and shining on those who wish to be remembered, it is elsewhere.

"This is where we belong, Roma. This is where we will always belong."

The voice quavers even with the surety of such words. They fool themselves. These heirs think themselves kings and queens, sitting on a throne of gold and overlooking a glittering, wealthy empire.

They are not. They are criminals—criminals at the top of an empire of thieves and drug lords and pimps, preparing to inherit a broken, terrible, defeated thing that looks upon them in sadness.

Shanghai knows. It has always known.

This whole damn place is about to fall apart.

"We waste time hiding out up here," Marshall said. He was sitting with heavy impatience, constantly shuffling forward or toeing his shoes along the lines in the concrete.

"What would you have us do?" Juliette asked, tipping her head back. She resisted leaning right onto Roma, if only because that would look rather horrifying from Kathleen's point of view. "If the Larkspur has some role in this, he has moved locations since our last visit and erased every trace of his physical existence. If the Larkspur has no role in this and lied to us about Zhang Gutai's guilt only so we would kill him, then that's it." Juliette splayed her hands. "Dead end."

"Impossible," Kathleen muttered beneath her breath. "In a city so big, how can nobody else know anything?"

"It's not a matter of whether someone else knows anything," Benedikt said. "It's the time we have left. We cannot move Alisa from her machines at the hospital without endangering her. We also cannot leave her there when the factory next door rises up in revolt."

"They may not rise for weeks," Marshall said. "The numbers at their meetings are still low. Their force has not grown quite so mighty yet."

Roma shook his head. The movement trembled his frame. "Their force is not mighty," he said, "but everybody else is weak. This madness has taken too many. If not in body, then in mind. Those who remain alive do not remain loyal."

"A matter of time," Kathleen echoed.

Benedikt sighed fiercely. "None of this makes any *sense*."

Marshall muttered something quietly to him and he hissed something back. Noting the conversations to have split and Kathleen to be deep in thought, Juliette craned her head back to Roma, clicking her tongue for his attention.

"We'll figure it out," Juliette said when Roma looked down. "She is not lost."

"For now she is not," he replied, his voice low. "But they will kill her. They will slit her throat while she sleeps. She will die as my mother did."

Juliette blinked. She straightened up, turning to face him properly.

"Your mother died of illness."

A raindrop landed on Roma's cheek. He wiped it off, the motion looking exactly as it would if he had brushed aside a teardrop instead. When their gazes met, there was no confusion on Roma's part, no puzzlement over why Juliette would believe such to be the case. There was only a soft, flinching . . . sadness.

"Wasn't it?" Juliette prompted. For whatever reason, the insides of her wrists began to sweat. "How could your mother's throat have been slit from illness?"

Roma shook his head. He said gently, like a caress, "It was a Scarlet hit, dorogaya."

Suddenly Juliette could not breathe. Her vision became invaded by terrible violet dots. Her head grew light. It took all her effort to remain still—remain outwardly unaffected.

"But the blood feud is the blood feud. Don't think much on it. Don't dwell. It's not your fault."

"I thought it was illness," Juliette barely managed. "They said it was illness."

Lady Montagova had died two weeks after Juliette left Shanghai. Two weeks after the attack on the Scarlet house that had killed all their servants.

Oh God. Oh God oh God oh God—

"The White Flowers only maintained that not to lose face," Roma said. "She was found with a red rose forced into her hand."

"Wait!"

The sudden exclamation came from Benedikt, and Juliette startled to attention with a solid jerk forward, drawing a strange glance from Roma. He placed a reassuring hand on her back, all the gestures of their past remembered again with no need for formal reintroduction.

But Juliette barely registered it. Her mind was racing.

You have to tell him. He has to know.

He'll never forgive me.

Juliette shook her head quickly, clearing her thoughts. This was a matter to address later. It did no good to think on it now.

"What did the Larkspur say to you?" Benedikt demanded now. "Give it to me word for word."

"Benedikt, we already told you earlier—"

"Again," he said sharply. "Something is very familiar about this."

Roma and Juliette exchanged a curious glance.

"He said," Roma replied, "*Zhang Gutai is turning himself into a monster. I am making the vaccine using information he is giving me.*"

Benedikt's hand rocketed out to grip Marshall's shoulder. "Before that?"

"It is a little irrelevant," Juliette replied, wrinkling her nose.

"If you told me before, *tell me again.*"

"He asked, '*You wish to know my business with Zhang Gutai?*'" Roma replied. "Benedikt, what is it?"

Benedikt's frown deepened and deepened. Kathleen crept forward, as if it wasn't enough for the five of them to be dispersed across the small rooftop anymore—they had to draw tighter and tighter, making a circle to prevent the information between them from escaping.

"When we were staking out Zhang Gutai's apartment," Benedikt said slowly, "we saw foreigner after foreigner come in to speak with his personal assistant. They attempted to talk politics but left within minutes."

A fat droplet of rain came down on his forehead.

"Is this about the Frenchman you chased after?" Marshall asked.

Benedikt nodded. "I tried to threaten him into telling me what he was doing there," he said, "but he only insisted that his business with Zhang Gutai was none of mine. At the time I did not think it so strange, but . . ." Benedikt frowned. "Why would he speak on his business with Zhang Gutai so specifically if it was his assistant whom he was meeting with?"

The facts began to line up in Juliette's head too, one by one. *Perhaps the Larkspur was under a false impression.*

"Zhang Gutai's personal assistant," Juliette said. "I don't suppose he is also Zhang Gutai's professional assistant at *Labor Daily?*"

"Yes, he is," Kathleen answered confidently. "Qi Ren. He is his notetaker at Communist meetings. He must also be his transcriber at work."

The empty desk with the memo for Zhang Gutai. The drawings of the monster. The shuddering back door, as if somebody had *just* vacated their desk in feeling the onslaught of a transformation, hurrying outside so nobody would see . . .

She recalled Qi Ren's attempt at introducing himself as Zhang Gutai when she and Roma had showed up at his door. She recalled his easy answer, as if he was used to doing so, as if his job was to take the meetings Zhang Gutai did not wish to waste time with. As if he was used to impersonating his superior, acting on his behalf to the clueless foreigners who came knocking for meetings.

"Maybe the Larkspur did not lie," Juliette said quietly. "Maybe he *thought* he was telling the truth in revealing Zhang Gutai to be the monster."

Which would mean Zhang Gutai was never the monster of Shanghai.

Qi Ren was.

Without warning, the building beneath their feet rocked with a hard jolt. The five of them shot up, bracing for attack. Nothing immediately came. But as shouting started from the streets below and the sensation of heat blew into the rain, they realized something was very, very wrong.

Their vantage point up on the rooftop allowed their sights to extend two or three streets in each direction. To the west, a fire was roaring in the yard of a police station. There had been an explosion— that had been the impact felt underneath their feet. It had shaken all the rickety, neighboring buildings, unsettling a fine layer of dust and grit that floated down to the pavements.

And in such dust, *workers* were pouring into the police station like a colony of ants, all with red rags tied around their right arms, as bright as beacons.

This was not the clean-cut uniform of a foreign army. These were the rags of the people, rising up from within.

"It's starting *here*," Juliette murmured in disbelief. "The protests are starting in the city itself."

It was genius. There would be too much havoc to put a quick stop to urban protests. The chaos in the city would galvanize those in the outskirts, would incite them to rise up with steel-backed urgency and roaring mayhem.

It is starting.

"The hospital," Roma gasped. "Benedikt. Marshall. Get to the hospital. Protect Alisa."

Protect her until they could kill the monster.

"Go home," Juliette, meanwhile, commanded Kathleen. "Grab all the messengers. Have them warn the factory owners to flee immediately."

They surely had been warned already to be cautious about an uprising, warned against the mass meetings screaming for an end to gangster rule. But no one could have known it would start with such intensity. They would not be expecting such vigor. They would pay for the miscalculation with their heads.

Kathleen, Benedikt, and Marshall hurried off, sparing no time. Only Roma and Juliette were left for a beat longer on that rooftop, surrounded by fire and bedlam.

"Once more," Juliette promised. "This time we do it right."

Thirty-Five

Roma and Juliette thundered up the steps to Zhang Gutai's apartment, where Qi Ren would be waiting. At some point, Juliette noticed blood still drying in the lines between her fingers. It created handprints on the railings she grasped as they climbed flights and flights of stairs without pause.

When they came upon the top floor, Juliette stopped just short of Zhang Gutai's door.

"How do we do this?" she asked.

"Like this."

Roma kicked down the door.

Zhang Gutai's apartment was a mess. As Roma and Juliette stepped in warily, their shoes sank right into water, which drew a gasp from Juliette and a curse from Roma. The hardwood tiles had flooded from a running water source that sounded like it was coming from the kitchen. The water rose all the way up to their ankles and was only rising more with every second. If not for the high ledge of the door-frame, they would have flooded the rest of the building upon opening the apartment door.

Something was not sitting right with Juliette. She dropped to a crouch and dipped a hand into the water, frowning as the cold seeped into her fingers. The water swirled, danced, lapped. It reminded her of the Huangpu, of the way the current always moved in a dozen different directions, carrying away whatever floated into its tide, carrying away all the dead that collapsed by its side. The gangster clash at the ports. The Russians on their ship.

The first victims of each wave of madness . . ., Juliette thought suddenly, *were they all by the Huangpu River?*

"Juliette," Roma called quietly, summoning her attention. "It appears that there was a fight."

Juliette stood again, shaking the water off her hand. Deeper into the apartment, there were papers scattered everywhere: thin leaflets of propaganda and thicker sheets of accounts—numbers and letters and characters all bleeding together in the water. As she moved about, Juliette peered over the kitchen counter, finding pots and pans turned upside down, not only floating in the overflowing sink but lying *dented* on the tables, as if someone had taken the saucepan and repeatedly struck it against something.

"Where is he?" Juliette whispered. The state of this apartment only furthered her confusion. Why would an old man, an assistant of a Communist, turn himself into a monster? Why flood the floors and dent all the kitchen equipment?

"He's not here," Roma said. His eyes were latched on something over her shoulder. "But someone else is."

Juliette looked to where Roma pointed and saw the slumped figure in the corner of the living room. She and Roma had sat there once while Qi Ren served them tea. Now the chairs were overturned and the radio was smashed in pieces atop the rug, where another young man was collapsed. His legs were splayed in an awkward V-shape under the water while his back leaned against the wall. His neck lolled forward so severely that all that was visible was the top of his head—blood-matted, dark-blond hair.

Juliette's eyes widened. "My God. That's Paul Dexter."

"Paul Dexter?" Roma echoed. "What's he doing here?"

"That's what I'd like to know," Juliette muttered. She rushed forward, sinking her knees into the shallow water before she shook Paul's shoulder vigorously. There was a deep scratch on his forehead and what looked like four claw marks on his neck, marring his pale skin with red gouges.

Juliette shook him harder. "Paul. Paul, wake up."

Slowly, Paul's eyelids fluttered. The third time Juliette called his name, Paul's eyes finally opened fully and focused on her. He frowned.

"Miss Cai?" Paul rasped. "What are you doing here?"

"You answer first," Juliette replied wryly.

Paul coughed. It came out as a wheeze, one that sounded like there was no liquid left in his throat.

"The Larkspur sent me," he said slowly. He looked around, patting his hands about the space beside him, and seemed to relax when he found his briefcase, which had been floating in the water.

"What are you doing on the floor?" Roma asked.

Paul suddenly stiffened, as if his memory was returning piece by piece, triggered by the question. Wincing beneath his breath, he worked to adjust his position and pull himself higher along the wall, until he was sitting well enough to place his briefcase back onto his lap.

"The monster . . ." Paul exhaled. "It attacked me."

"It attacked you *here*?" Juliette demanded. She stood and spun in a circle, sloshing water as she surveyed the living room. "Where is it now?"

"I—I don't know," Paul answered. His eyes lowered while he opened his briefcase and checked on the contents. He placed something into his pocket. "Heck, it could still be here. Could you help me up, Miss Cai?"

With a glance over her shoulder, eyeing the rising water levels and still finding *something* off about that fact, Juliette extended a hand, biting back a haughty retort at Paul Dexter's uselessness.

It was her fault for underestimating him. As his hand clasped on to hers and he pulled himself to his feet, he was also pulling the tip off a syringe in his other hand. Juliette's arm straightened in her effort to haul him up . . . and then Paul was plunging a needle into the exposed veins at the crook of her elbow.

Juliette gasped; the needle glinted. Before she could pull her arm away, Paul was pushing down on the syringe, and the vial of blue emptied into her bloodstream.

Too late, Juliette hurled herself backward, clutching her elbow. Roma managed to catch her before she tumbled into the water in her shock.

"Did he hurt you?" Roma demanded.

"No," Juliette replied. She slowly removed her hand from her inner elbow, finding a pinprick of red. "He *vaccinated* me."

Paul straightened to his full height then, dropping the used syringe and all his pretense into the water.

"I'm only trying to help you, Juliette," he said. "I don't want you to die. I love you."

Juliette let out a single laugh.

"No, you really don't," she croaked. "That is not what love is."

Paul's face thundered. He jabbed a finger toward Roma, who still had his arms around Juliette. "And that is? Love, tainted with the blood of all your dead kinsmen?"

Juliette's breath caught in her throat. It wasn't at Paul's insult—she had barely heard his words. It was at the low growl of his voice and the sudden realization where else she had heard it before.

"You want to talk about my dead kinsmen?" Juliette seethed. "Let's talk, *Larkspur*."

Roma inhaled sharply. Paul only smiled. He did not attempt to deny it. Instead, he tilted his head in a bastardized, cherubic manner and said, "I've been wanting to tell you, Juliette. I must admit, when I imagined this revelation coming to light, I envisioned you more impressed than you presently seem to be."

"Impressed?" Juliette repeated. She was perhaps three decibels away from screeching. "What part of this is *impressive* to you?"

"The part where I have the whole city dancing on my puppet strings?" Paul reached into his coat pocket and Juliette braced, her hands inching toward her pistol, but he was only retrieving another blue vial, holding it up into the light. It refracted little crystals onto the beige walls, lapis lazuli marks dancing in tandem to one another. "The part where I unleashed the solution to my father's suffering? Tell me, Juliette, is it not a child's wish for their parents to live as happily as possible?"

Juliette raised her pistol. Hesitant fright registered in Roma's expression, and though Juliette was perfectly aware that it was dangerous to provoke Paul before they knew what more he had up his sleeve, she had too much anger raging within her to keep herself temperate to Paul's standards.

"All the gangsters and merchants who were targeted along the river," Juliette said. "I thought it was the Communists. I thought it was them eliminating their capitalist threats." She laughed bitterly. "But it was *you*. It was you clearing the market for your business to thrive. It was you clearing your threats so the Larkspur couldn't be questioned."

Paul smiled brightly, rows of white teeth flashing. "Brilliant, no? And to think it all started when I found an itsy-bitsy bug in England."

"You fool," Juliette hissed. "How dare you—"

"It started as a *favor* to this city," Paul cut in, his eyes darkening. He was starting to take offense at Juliette's anger. He had never before seen this irate side of her. "Had you not read the papers? Heard the whispers? Everyone was talking about how capitalist ventures in this city would be threatened if legitimate politics entered Shanghai, and the Communists were looking to be the most likely contenders. I was going to help. I meant to kill the Communists. Surely you cannot disapprove of that."

Juliette disapproved mightily. But this was not the time to vocalize such an argument.

"You wanted to infect Zhang Gutai first," she guessed. She spared a glance around the living room, at the overturned chairs, her inspection sharpening. Instead of merely one syringe lying by his feet, she saw two. Where had that second one come from? More important, what had it been used for? "You didn't realize you were speaking to his assistant."

"But it didn't matter, did it?" Paul took a step forward; Roma and Juliette took one step back. "I thought that the first insect would simply jump from one host to another and kill the Communists individually. Imagine my *surprise* when the old man transforms into a *monster*! Imagine my surprise when he becomes the mother host and releases *thousands* of replicate insects capable of driving everyone in this city *mad*!"

In her anger, Juliette's arm started to shake. Roma placed a hand on her elbow, but it did nothing to persuade her to lower her weapon.

"The water," Juliette whispered, half a question, half an answer that she already knew. She swished a foot, disturbing the liquid that was rising all around them. It had reached the middle of her calf now. Paul had meant to kill the Communists, but his plan evolved once the monster only ever appeared along the Huangpu River. That river was the beating heart of this city; an infection starting there meant the madness would sweep through the gangsters working at the ports, through the merchants taking meetings.

They weren't even true *targets*. It just so happened that it was the gangsters and merchants who spent the most time by the Huangpu River, and that was where the monster went to release its insects.

And with every wave, suddenly Walter Dexter's business was booming again. Suddenly the Larkspur was sweeping in with a vaccine that earned more money than an ordinary merchant could ever imagine. A vaccine that the workers couldn't afford but bought anyway. A vaccine that other merchants *could* afford, only to be given a saline solution that would offer false assurance and then their death, dropping like fruit flies to clear the market for Walter Dexter to shine.

"Water," Paul echoed. "How fortunate for the city above the sea."

Juliette could take this no longer. She pulled the safety on her pistol. "You disgust me."

Paul took another step forward. "My father gave up everything to find a fortune in this country."

"Oh, your father experienced being a little *poor*," Juliette sneered. "Was it worth it? Was his sense of success as a merchant worth the lives of all my people?"

Paul sighed and wrung his hands, like he was finally experiencing some guilt.

"If you really wish," he said, as if he were doing her a grand gesture out of the good of his heart, "I'll mass-produce the vaccine to the Scarlet Gang—"

"You don't get it," Juliette interrupted. "I don't want your vaccine. I want the madness stopped. I want the monster dead."

Paul became still, the hopeful lift of his brow lowering. He became who he had always been, the mask shed.

"Would you complain if the madness was only killing White Flowers?" Paul asked coldly.

Spittle flew from Juliette's mouth in her vehemence. "Yes."

"Because of him, right?" Paul tipped his chin at Roma. Ten thousand pinpricks of loathing passed in that one motion. "Well, I apologize, Juliette, but you cannot kill Qi Ren. I won't allow it."

"You cannot stop me," Juliette said. "More apt men have tried and failed. Now, where is he, Paul?"

Paul smiled. That smile was the city's damnation, planting rancor into its layers. And Juliette—Juliette felt possessed by her terror, goose bumps breaking out on every inch of skin, a shudder sweeping from head to toe.

The water in the apartment hallway sloshed quietly. Someone was coming out from the bedrooms.

Roma and Juliette swiveled around. A shaky inhale filled the room. A breathless exhale.

A creature emerged into the sunlight, shaking with its own effort. Qi Ren was in there somewhere. Juliette could see it in the tired slouch of the monster's shoulders and the constant squinting, as if the old man's eyesight had transferred into this other form. But that was where the resemblance ended. For the monster's eyes had turned wholly opaque with a sheen of silver, slimy with the same texture as seaweed. From head to toe, it was built of wiry, blue-green muscle, hosting scales along the chest and suction-cup circles along the arms.

With a pitiful hiss from its loose, gray lips, the monster emitted a noise that could have been one of pain. It pressed a webbed hand to its stomach and doubled over, gasping for breath. The triangular horns studded along its spine shook vigorously. Seconds later, they all disappeared, receding *into* the monster and leaving diamond-shaped holes in their wake.

Juliette felt Roma grab her hand. He gave her a sharp tug, trying to pull her back.

"No," Juliette said, her voice hardly audible. "No, it only releases in the river. It hasn't released its insects outside the river before."

Right?

Paul snorted. He had heard her hesitance.

"The thing is, Juliette"—Paul straightened his sleeve cuffs—"it's rather irritating that Qi Ren has to transform back as soon as all the insects come out. So I did some fiddling around. I made some . . . alterations, so to speak."

The second syringe.

An insect dropped out from the monster's spine. Then another. They came slowly, like the trickle of a single bead of water, creeping down a slope of dry asphalt.

"Run free!" Paul commanded. He threw open the sliding doors to the mini balcony, letting in a burst of wind and a burst of sound, and without wasting a beat, the monster charged for the balcony, crashing through so fiercely that it chipped off a chunk of the drywall and shattered every potted plant placed outside.

And as it hovered on the edge of the balcony, poised to jump, the insects started to *pour*.

"No!" Juliette yelled, lunging forward.

It was too late. The monster leaped from the balcony and crashed upon the street below, insects pouring and pouring, landing on the ground and dispersing outward. An infection like this would be colossal. If the monster ran through the city, ran through the crowds—the *riots*—at this time of day, the casualties would be devastating.

Juliette aimed her gun and fired—again and again and again in hopes that it could kill the monster or, at the very *least*, slow it down—but the bullets bounced off its back like she had shot at steel. The monster began to move, began to lumber down the street, its speed steadily increasing.

"There's no use, Juliette."

With a scream, Juliette spun around and fired into the apartment. Her aim went wide in her anger; Paul swerved and jerked out of the way. Her bullet merely grazed his arm, but he winced, backing up against the wall with his fingers pressed to the wound.

"How do we stop it?" Roma demanded. He crossed the length of the room in two strides, grabbing Paul by the collar and giving him a shake. "*How* do we stop it?"

"You can't," Paul rasped, grinning. "You can't stop the monster. And you can't stop *me*." In a flash, he gripped Roma's arm too, twisting until Roma let go with a startled breath. Paul ducked, and though Juliette aimed again in an attempt to shoot, he was too fast.

Three bullets embedded into the wall along a straight line. Paul Dexter swooped his briefcase from the water, hugged it to his chest, and fled out the door of the apartment.

"Dammit, dammit," Roma muttered. "I'm going after him."

"No!" Juliette searched the view from the balcony again, her breath coming fast. "The monster—it's heading due east. I think it's going back to the Huangpu River."

If the monster was going to the river, then it had to cut through the whole French Concession first. Juliette could hardly swallow past the lump in her throat, a sourness building behind her nose, her eyes. The monster had to pass all the open storefronts, all the little kids that ate their red bean buns on the steps of the shops. It had to merge into the city central, into the clusters of students walking out of their classrooms to protest, into the elderly doing their regular afternoon strolls.

Juliette grabbed the balcony curtain, tearing it right off its rod. "Go, Roma," she exclaimed. "Get to the river before it does. Clear the people out."

"And you?"

Juliette twisted the curtain until it was a solid rope, until it was a swath of fabric thick enough to hold her weight. The riots tearing through the city were on the move, dispersed across different areas regardless of which country owned the sidewalks they marched on. They would not know the monster was coming until the insects were crawling deep into their skulls.

"I need to warn everyone on its route to get the hell inside," Juliette breathed. She stepped onto the balcony, her shoes crunching down on the broken potted plants. She glanced over her shoulder. "I'll meet you at the Bund."

Roma nodded. It seemed he wanted to say more, but time was of the essence, so he simply settled for a look that felt to Juliette like a soft embrace. Then he pivoted on his heel, sprinting out of the apartment.

Juliette gritted her teeth. "Okay," she said. "Let's do this."

Her eyes landed upon the pipe running down the exterior wall, right by the edge of the balcony. She pulled herself up on the railing and leaned against the wall for balance, her gaze darting down to the street every few seconds to keep track of the monster ambling for the east. It would disappear down the long street in mere seconds. She had to hurry.

"Please don't snap," she prayed, pushing one end of the curtain between the pipe and the wall. "Please, please, please—" She pulled the other end out, and with the two ends of the curtain looped around the pipe, she held the fabric as if she were noosing a tie.

Juliette leaped off the balcony. The fall was fast and bumpy; by the time she landed on the streets, the curtain had almost frayed into two pieces from friction, but it didn't matter—she took off running, her pistol aimed up at the sky.

"Get inside, get inside!" she screamed. She fired, the sound startling those who were not near enough to hear her call. By the time she was racing to catch up with the monster, chaos had already erupted in its wake, leaving insects scrambling upon street stalls and civilians clawing at their throats. Others—those who had not been infected—only stood by, unable to believe the sight that had passed them in broad daylight.

"Go!" Juliette shouted. "Move!"

Those who had frozen snapped out of it and scampered back inside.

Juliette kept yelling, moving without pause, her lungs burning both from exertion and from hollering so loudly. Onward and onward she persisted, and yet no matter how fast Juliette ran, she could not catch up to the lumbering monster.

In absolute horror, she watched it enter the Chinese part of the city. She watched it charge right through the crowds that were congregated here, watched it penetrate the clusters of protesters so swiftly that none of them realized what was happening until those first infected by the insects started to drop. Then the rioters stopped pumping their fists. Then they looked around, noticed Juliette approaching in their periphery with her arms waving frantically, and if it wasn't too late, finally dispersed, taking shelter.

This city was bigger than a world unto itself. No matter how loudly Juliette yelled, the people one street over would be oblivious to the panic until the insects crawled over, burrowing into their heads. No matter how much she shouted, the crowds that raised their red rags did not care to listen until the monster barreled right by and their hands flew to their throat. They would drop—one by one by one. They were fighting for their right to live, but this city had not even promised their right to *survive*.

There were so *many*. So many goddamn crowds on the streets.

"Please!" Juliette cried. She crossed into the next street briefly, almost skidding right upon the tram tracks. "Get inside! This isn't the time!"

The rioters paid her no heed. Rich gangsters were always going to tell them that it was not the time—why was this instance any different? Why should they ever listen?

Juliette could hardly blame them. And yet this meant death. This meant the pavement stacking up with bodies, piled atop one another, staining the whole city red.

The monster was rapidly disappearing up the other street. If they just looked, if they just walked over a few steps and looked, the rioters would see the path of destruction, would see the twitching bodies and the frantic bodies, the bodies hurrying away by stepping on the bodies collapsed.

Juliette tightened her fists, tightened her grip on her gun. She forced back the maddening tears threatening her eyes and cleared her throat, forcing the hoarseness away. Then she fired into the air once more and surged after the monster again.

It felt like a lost cause.

But no matter what, she still had to try.

Roma had hijacked a car.

To be fair, he really had no choice. And when the heir of the White

Flowers marched toward you with a pistol in his hand, demanding you get out your car, it did not matter what important position you held in the Municipal Administrative Council—you got the hell out of the car.

"Faster," he told the chauffeur. "I really do mean it, as fast as you can possible go—"

"You want us to drive over the people?" the driver asked. "Is that what you want?"

Roma reached over. He pushed on the horn and did not let go. The clumps of rioters that they passed by were forced to scatter, lest they be run over. *"Drive!"*

They tore through the Concession, taking as direct a path as possible. It was hard to gauge how much time was passing, how fast they were going in comparison to the running monster. He didn't know if Juliette was managing to keep up.

But the chaos was starting.

Outside the car's window, if it was not groups of angry laborers with red rags tied around their arms, it was ordinary civilians trying to get a meal in before the whole city was turned over by the Communists. Yet everywhere Roma looked, people were moving fast, running up to loved ones and telling them to hurry, ushering children into corners and peering over their shoulders, tasting the bitter sharpness in the air. The sharpness that warned of disaster coming.

"Up there, up there," Roma said quickly. "Right to the edge of the Bund. Merge into the lane."

The car came to a halt outside a foreign bank and Roma tumbled out, searching the scene before him for any sign of the monster. It wasn't here yet. Nor were the protesters.

Good.

Roma aimed his pistol at the sky. He shot: three bullets in succession.

"Evacuate!" he called when the workers by the water glanced over, when the fishermen pulled in their lines, when the men chomping on toothpicks at the helm of their ships peered down at him. "Evacuate *now* if you want to live. Move north!"

"Hey, come on, enough with the shouting!" A White Flower leaned over his ship railing. "What could possibly be—"

Roma aimed his gun, his stomach twisting hard. He fired, and when the bullet studded itself into the White Flower's shoulder, the White Flower could only spit out his toothpick, his jaw dropping at Roma. Roma never missed.

"I mean it," he said coldly. "Get yourself to the hospital. Everyone else—*move*, or I'll force you into the nearest hospital too."

They hurried. He wished they would move faster. He wished it didn't take the threat of violence for them to do it.

A scream echoed through the Bund.

Roma whirled around, raising his gun immediately. "Get into the buildings!" he roared. All the ladies taking strolls by the Bund, the foreigners with the parasols, they stared at him with wide, frightened eyes, but they did not hesitate. The screaming was a signal of a real threat. Roma's manner was confirmation of something incoming. The crowds surged inward, away from the water, and Roma searched desperately from where he stood—eyes scanning the multiple streets that fed into the Bund, tensing for the appearance of the monster.

"Move! Move!"

Juliette. He'd recognize her voice anywhere. And it was coming from the far road.

Roma ran, darting right onto the road and signaling for the cars to go backward. It didn't matter if they honked and narrowly ran him over. He waved his gun and those at the front immediately tried to back up with a loud *bang* of their engines, creating a block as the cars behind tried to creep forward.

Satisfied with the gridlock, Roma turned his attention elsewhere. There was only one road between the water and the mouth of the intersecting street—one road and one long wharf, depending on which way the monster wanted to run, depending on if it would dive into the shallows where the fishermen's boats were docked, or if it would move down the wharf toward the deep end. Roma strode backward, coming to a halt at the head of the wharf. Down the street, a blur of movement came barreling along the tram lines, dispersing dots of black wherever it went.

The monster.

"Okay," he muttered. He lifted his gun. Aimed. Even if bullets did not penetrate its back, its front was still soft in the way humans were. "Enough is enough."

Roma pulled the trigger.

The gun kicked back . . . but nothing came out.

He had no bullets left.

"Dammit!"

Roma tossed the gun aside, reaching into his jacket for his spare. A flash of movement to his side. Before he could retrieve anything, Roma turned just in time to sight Paul Dexter with his pistol raised.

On pure instinct, Roma ducked fast, barely avoiding a bullet to the head. He pressed his palms into the hard ground, looking around his immediate surroundings.

"Give up," Paul hissed. In one hand he had his weapon, and in the other, a briefcase.

Roma didn't humor him. He swooped for the nearest object—a wooden box—and threw it, aiming right for the face. With a yelp, Paul was forced to drop his briefcase, forced to almost lose his grip on his pistol. By the time he recovered, Roma had already reached into his jacket and pulled out his second gun.

Roma's finger hovered on the trigger. He would have shot Paul, then and there, if the ground had not started trembling. If the world around him hadn't suddenly started teeming with a flood of deadly specks rushing toward him en masse.

"No," Roma whispered.

The monster had arrived.

"Move, move!"

Juliette pushed the woman down, narrowly saving her from the arc of insects that crawled by her food cart, panting hard. A group of people not three steps away collapsed in unison. The woman whimpered, her eyes wide.

"Stay there," Juliette snapped. "Stay low, keep your eyes on the ground, and *move* when you see the insects, understood?"

The woman nodded, the motion fitful. Juliette bolted back up, searching for the monster once again. They had almost neared the Huangpu River, neared the final destruction that marked the end of a bloody, gruesome trail—or at least what Juliette hoped would be the end. The Bund was right ahead, upon the next intersection.

"No." Juliette's eyes landed on two figures right by the water, grappling with each other. Her eyes tracked the monster, tracked its trailing insects as they whipped in the direction of any victim it could find.

"Roma!" she screamed. "Roma, get down!"

Roma whirled around, his eyes wide. He acted immediately, throwing himself away from the monster as it thundered upon the wharf, avoiding a clump of insects as they fell upon the ground and ran along Paul's shoes before dispersing. Paul did not need to move. He was immune.

Juliette supposed that was why he was not at all worried when the monster dove into the water.

A loud, loud splash echoed through the near silent Bund.

She shouldn't have asked Roma to get to the river first. She should have switched roles with him.

"Roma, run!" she screamed, sprinting as fast as she could. "It's going to—"

An eruption. Just as Juliette finally arrived by the wharf, the water burst with spots of black, rocketing ten feet into the air before descending upon the ports. The insects skittered far and wide, finding every nook to burrow into, every surface to latch upon. There was no time to take cover. They rained down—on Paul, on Juliette, on Roma.

Juliette had never been so disgusted in her entire life. Hundreds of legs were crawling over her, burrowing into the lines of her clothes and taking bites of her pores as they tested where to land. Her skin had never itched to this extent; she had never experienced such repugnance that she wanted to throw up at the sensation.

But the insects, even as they landed upon her, slid off within seconds. The insects rained from the water then glided right off the arms that Juliette and Paul had thrown into the air, for the vaccine ran blue in their veins, fending off the attack.

The last of the eruption hit the ground. The air cleared. The insects skittered outward on the pavement.

Juliette, gasping, lowered her arms.

"Roma," she cried.

Thirty-Six

Roma's hands launched to his throat.

Thirty-Seven

The madness would not have come so quickly upon ordinary victims, who received only one insect to begin the infection. One would turn to ten over time, and ten to a hundred, until enough had multiplied within the victim to take control. But Roma—Roma was receiving them all at once, and at once they were overriding his nerves, driving him to gouge for blood.

Juliette furiously brushed the few stubborn insects off her arms and steadied her grip on her pistol. There was only one way to save him, only one way to put a stop to this all. She ran up to the end of the wharf and searched for the monster, thinking of nothing except *finding* the blasted thing and—

She should have paid more attention to the danger behind.

Her head slammed into the wooden boards of the wharf.

"I really cannot let you do that, Juliette." Paul grunted. "Why don't we just . . . ?"

Before Juliette could get her bearings, could even think to get back up and aim again, Paul kicked her hard in the stomach. Juliette fell off the main wharf, her whole body slamming onto the smaller platform below, which floated right above water. Her lungs rattled. With laborious effort, she tried to raise her weapon, tried to push past her spinning head, but then Paul jumped and landed on his feet beside her and kicked the gun out of her hands with a pitiful flop.

"I'm sorry, Juliette."

He grabbed a fistful of her hair and stuck her head into the water.

Juliette nearly gasped, except opening her mouth meant swallowing the dirty river water, so she kept her lips pinched tightly together. She struggled to writhe out of Paul's grip, forcing herself to keep her eyes open even as the water swirled with the horrendous black of swimming insects. Paul's grip was far stronger than his lanky frame would let on. His fingers upon her head were a steel claw.

"This is for the best." Juliette could barely hear him though he was kneeling by her side. Her ears were blocked with water, with merciless insects. "I don't want to hurt you, but you've given me no choice. I tried to *save* you, Juliette. I really tried."

Juliette bucked and kicked, harder and harder to no avail. She should have shot Paul when she had the chance. He was not only trying to kill her now, but he was trying to kill her *slowly*, so she would die with the knowledge that Roma had been within saving. So she would die with the knowledge that she had failed. Roma was strong, but he couldn't stay in control forever.

Perhaps he had succumbed, digging his fingers into his neck. Perhaps he was already dead.

Her struggling was useless. Paul's blue vial had saved her from a death to the madness. Now Paul had decided that she was to be discarded anyway, into a watery grave.

The blue vial, Juliette suddenly remembered. Paul had had another in his coat pocket. And if he had a blue vial in there, was there a chance that he kept around another syringe too?

Juliette reached her hand out, groping blindly for the edges of Paul's coat. It was almost laughable how easily she found it—how easily her hand shoved right into the wide opening of his pocket.

Frantic, on the very last gasp of air in her lungs, Juliette pulled the syringe out, and stabbed the needle into Paul's wrist.

With a roar, Paul loosened his grip, his hand flexing in pain. Juliette sat up quickly, gasping for breath, barely pausing to get ahold of herself, barely pausing to glance up at the wharf and cry at the sight of Roma struggling against his own hands as they dug deeper into his throat. She was scrambling onto her knees, diving for Paul before he could secure his grip on his gun, tackling him around the waist and pushing both of them into the water.

The river hit her with a shock, but Juliette was the one in control now. Juliette was the one hovering above Paul as they sank deeper, one of her arms still looped around his waist, the other firmly on his wrist, and as the foam around them cleared, as Paul's eyes snapped open to find Juliette hovering before him like some vengeful demigod, she plucked the gun from his hand.

No, his mouth formed. There was utter horror in his expression. *Juliette.*

She kicked him in the chest; he flailed backward. She put both her hands around the gun, pointed to his forehead, and merely inches away, she pulled the trigger.

The water muffled most of the sound. The water did not muffle the blood.

Paul Dexter went into death with three eyes open—the third eye a weeping bullet wound. The water turned red and Juliette surged up, coughing as she broke to the surface, her gaze wild as she searched for her next order of business.

She found the monster immediately, for he had already returned upon the main wharf.

Yet he was not quite a monster anymore. He was transforming back, the process incomplete. His face had returned, but the lower half of his body was still strange and changed and green, and as the old man knelt there, it seemed he had already given up.

Juliette pulled herself up onto the smaller platform. Then, the pistol in her hands, she scrambled back onto the wharf.

"Qi Ren," she called.

The unwilling monster of Shanghai turned to face her. The old man had a horror marring his tired features too, but a sort different to the one that had paralyzed Paul in his final moments. This was a horror at himself—at all he had been made to do and all he wanted to be rid of. He nodded at her. Juliette raised the pistol. Her hands were shaking.

"I'm sorry," she said.

Once again, she pulled the trigger.

The bullet struck his heart. The bullet was as loud as the bang at the end of the world.

But Qi Ren's sigh was soft. His hand came up to his chest gingerly, as if the bullet were nothing but a heartfelt compliment. Rivulets of red ran down his fingers and onto the wharf, tinting his surroundings a deep color.

Juliette inched closer. Qi Ren had become still, but he had not pitched over. Something was happening inside him. Something was *moving*.

A bulge appeared in his left wrist. Juliette watched it migrate from the veins amid the old man's forearm to the wiry space between his neck and shoulder. Suddenly his Adam's apple was the size of a true apple, pushing against thin, capillary-filled skin.

Qi Ren's throat split down the middle. Just like that, as if a knife had slit him apart, the flaps of his skin burst open and detonated a mess of black-red blood. Qi Ren collapsed immediately. From his throat, an insect as big as Juliette's fist flew outward, detaching from the veins and tendons it had been living off.

Screeching, Juliette fired the pistol—once, twice, three times. Her mind was panicking into overdrive, her most basic reflexes shaking violently. Two of her bullets flew wide; one grazed the insect, sending it nose-diving onto the wharf. For a moment its circular, flat body scurried about the surface of the wooden panels for something—anything—to hold on to, dozens of tiny legs that resembled microscopic hairs scrambling to meet a body. Then the insect stilled, and when it stopped twitching at last, so too did the other insects in the water.

She could feel the change. It felt like the shroud of death had lifted off this city.

"It's over," Juliette whispered. "It's really over."

She turned around slowly. She searched for life at the other end of the wharf.

"Roma?"

She was frightened that he would not respond, frightened that all she would be met with was silence. She was frightened that she would not find him at all, that he had long been taken by the waters that ran this city red.

But then her eyes landed upon where he had placed himself, found him in a curled ball up against a parked car in the middle of the wide, wide road. Slowly, he lowered his hands from his throat. Blood trickled down his neck.

She ran up to him, tossing the pistol away. She could hardly breathe even as her hands came upon his shoulders, gripped him hard to make sure he was real, that this was the truth before her and not a hallucination of the broken mind.

"I'm okay," Roma assured, his voice quavering.

He had nearly gotten there. Ten puncture marks dotted his neck, deep enough to leave his red insides on show.

But he was alive.

Juliette pulled him to her fiercely, locking them in an embrace.

"The monster is dead," she whispered.

So why did she still feel empty? Why did it feel like their roles weren't over?

"Did Paul hurt you?" Roma asked. He pulled away and ran his eyes over her to check for wounds, as if his own hands weren't still running with blood.

Juliette shook her head, and Roma sighed in relief. He glanced to the water, where Paul's body floated in those green-gray waves.

"He thought he loved you."

"It wasn't love," Juliette whispered.

Roma pressed a kiss to her temple, closing his eyes against the dampness that stuck to her hair.

"Let's go," he said. "Let's go wake Alisa."

Thirty-Eight

One by one, the insects detached from Alisa Montagova.

They writhed and screeched as the mother host bled out, gnashing their microscopic teeth at one another. When the heart that fueled them all stopped beating, they too were forced to go to their death throes, detaching from the tissues they had clutched, unhinging their jaw from the nerve they had selected. In their last moments, they started to emerge. Where their only goal had once been to bury deep, the insects now desperately tried to burrow out, thrashing and thrashing in a tangle of limp blond hair, before at last passing into death and dropping onto the white fabric of the hospital linens.

With a gasp, Alisa awoke. She bolted upright and heaved for fresh air—coughing and coughing until the pipe that had been feeding her flew out of her throat. She had risen just enough to scatter about the dozen arthropod bodies left behind on the pillowcase, already shriveling in their death. She did not dare move any more than that. She inhaled sharply and held the breath in her lungs this time, her eyes almost crossing in her attempt to look upon the barrel of the gun pointed to her forehead.

"It's okay, Alisa," someone wheezed from the corner of the room.

Alisa flicked her eyes to the voice. It did more to heighten her panic than it did to ease it: she found Benedikt, her cousin, with his hands up, two guns pointed upon him, and Marshall Seo in a similar predicament near the door.

"Welcome back to the world, Alisa Montagova," Tyler Cai said. He pressed the hard muzzle of his gun into her skin. "Sorry it has to be in this way."

The city streets remained an uproarious parade of commotion as Roma and Juliette made their way through. Everywhere Juliette looked, she saw the corpses of those who had been in the monster's path of destruction. She saw political chaos—rioters, still intent on making themselves heard even when their fellow workers were lying dead in the gutters. In her hurry, she had lost count of how many near collisions she had made with a protester, how many times she was almost hit with their flaming torches or withering signs blowing with the wind.

But when Roma and Juliette ran to the border of Nanshi, it was quiet.

"Did we take a wrong turn?" Juliette whispered.

"No," Roma said. "This is right."

The tall factories were slouching in a muted, mild manner. The roads were void of rickshaw runners, void of vendors, void of even the faintest sounds from children running amok.

That was to be expected—but in the absence of the regular humdrum, they had expected pandemonium, not *quiet*.

"Have the riots not started here yet?"

"I suppose it is to our benefit if they have not," Juliette said hesitantly. "Where is the hospital?"

Roma pointed. They ran. Each hard step of Juliette's heel coming down threw shocks into her legs, until she was hurrying up the steps of the hospital with her calves throbbing and her teeth chattering. The anxiety coursing through her limbs had no other place to go.

"Hello?" Roma called, pushing the double doors open. There was nobody in the reception area. No nurses, no doctors.

"Listen, Roma," Juliette whispered. They stilled, under the chipping paint of an archway leading into the thin corridor. A squeak of a shoe. A low murmur.

An angry shout.

"Get *off* me—"

"That's Marshall," Roma breathed. He shot off in a sprint. "Marshall!"

"Wait, Roma," Juliette snapped. "Roma!"

She raced after him, hands on her pistol, finger curled about the trigger. But by the time she arrived, weapon outstretched and aimed, it was too late to gain the upper hand. Roma had already skidded into the room and walked right into an ambush, forced to place his hands over his head as three Scarlets leveled their guns at him.

"Would you look at that?" Tyler clicked his tongue. Alisa whimpered. "At once, the big fish all come swimming in."

"Tyler," Juliette hissed.

Tyler shook his head before she could say anything more. Every move coming from him was a slow moment of carefully contained fury—except his arm, steady as ever while he kept his weapon pointed at Alisa. "Tell me, tángjiě. Who are you aiming at right now?"

Juliette did not know. She had raised her gun for the sake of raising it, for the sake of having something to do if events erred sideways, but she supposed it already had, and it had been erring for a long, long time. Slowly, Juliette lowered her weapon, her hands shaking.

The Scarlets in the room looked upon her in disdain. She understood. Tyler had discovered the truth of her alliance with the White Flowers and had come to enact his revenge. He had turned the Scarlets against her, had painted a picture of her betrayal. Their eyes flickered between her and Roma, and in that moment, with startling clarity, Juliette realized her mistake. It was her fault for believing. For hoping.

A love like theirs was never going to survive in a city divided by hatred.

This would be the death of them all.

Unless Juliette could save them.

Breathe. She was not merely the heiress who had come from the West, a caricature ripe for their rumors, ripe to be painted as easily swayed, easily manipulated, her heartstrings open to pluck at a moment's notice.

Smile. She was a monster in her own right.

"What do you think you're doing?" Juliette asked. Her voice came out level, edging on dull.

"Redeeming your lack of judgment. You've betrayed us, Juliette. Pulled us back miles in this feud." Tyler shook his head. "I'll make up for it. Worry not."

His finger tightened on the trigger.

"*Stop*," Juliette snapped. "You absolute idiot. You think I betrayed you? You think you're doing us a favor by killing all the Montagovs? It's a *trick*, Tyler. All you shall invite with their deaths is retribution upon our family."

Tyler laughed harshly. "Don't try fooling your way out of this—"

"I tell the *truth*—"

"But you have always been a liar."

A sudden shot rang through the room then, tearing a startled cry from Juliette's throat. Only it was not from Tyler's gun. It came from the pistol that Marshall suddenly wrenched from the Scarlet nearest to him, turned against its owner. The Scarlet dropped to the floor. Marshall lunged forward—hoping to save Alisa, hoping for one frantic shot to move Tyler out of the way.

Then Tyler whipped his pistol up and fired first. Marshall sank to the ground. His hand went to his ribs, where a blotch of red bloomed.

"Mars!" Benedikt roared.

"Don't you dare," a Scarlet hissed immediately. He jammed his gun hard into Benedikt's temple. It stopped Benedikt dead in his tracks, unable to move a single step toward Marshall lest he be shot too. The Scarlets would find any reason to shoot. Juliette knew they would.

"You are all mad," Marshall managed from the floor. He winced. The blood started to pour through his fingers, making a mess that dripped and dripped onto the floor. "You are all cursed. Montagovs and Cais alike. There's a plague on both your damn houses."

Tyler raised his gun again.

"Stop," Juliette demanded. "Stop—"

Another gunshot. This one from Roma. He had sidestepped one of the men, managed to fire once in the time it took them to get him under control again. His bullet merely skimmed Tyler's shoulder, sending Tyler back a step, hissing in pain.

"STOP!"

The room stilled. Guns upon guns upon guns. That was how it would always be.

"Do you hear that?" Juliette hissed. She held up a finger near her ear, demanding the men in the room *listen*. The united roar of noise. The united stomping of feet and chanting of slogans, coming from afar and coming ever closer.

"When they get here," Juliette seethed, "they will kill us all. White Flower or Scarlet Gang, it does not matter. They have machine guns and machetes and what do we have? *Money?*"

She turned to her side. The Scarlet gangster that Marshall had shot was dead on the ground. The bullet was in his neck. His eyes were glazed, staring up at the ceiling. She had not even known his name.

Marshall's torso, too, was dripping red. Tyler would not let the White Flowers leave in time to save Marshall. Tyler was not so kind. He needed to register at least one sacrifice in order to be appeased.

One sacrifice had to be made for the White Flowers to escape. For Alisa to live.

Her throat tight, Juliette stuck her hand into her pocket. She wished there existed something up her sleeve that would defuse the situation, but there was nothing. There was only the blood feud.

"We must leave before it is too late."

"Have you no honor?" Tyler hissed.

"Honor?" Juliette echoed harshly. Her voice was terrible in the reverberant quiet of the hospital room. "Who cares about honor when we will be *dead* should we remain any longer?"

"I will not be the first to leave this room, Juliette," Tyler said coldly. "I wish not to be shot in the back—"

"Then they leave first," Juliette proposed, squaring her shoulders. "Lex talionis, Tyler. An eye for an eye. That's how this feud works." She pointed a finger to Marshall. She forced it not to shake. "Let go of your deluded revenge plan. We only kill *him*, for the Scarlet lost. The others go free."

"No," Roma and Benedikt snapped in unison.

Juliette's stomach was ice-cold when she looked Roma straight in the eye. "You are not exactly in the position to be bargaining right now."

"It's not going to work, Juliette," Roma said firmly. "If Tyler wants a fair fight, let us have a fair fight. Do not lie to have us retreat."

Did he not realize she was saving him? Did he not realize that an armed uprising was occurring outside, mobs upon mobs seeking to kill all whom they recognized as part of the elite? Did he not realize that cutting off ties between them was the only way they could all walk out alive, that if Tyler even faintly suspected Juliette of being Roma Montagov's lover, then Roma was already half lowered into his grave?

He does realize, a little voice whispered. *He stays for you. He will not walk away from you. Not a second time. He would rather die.*

Juliette supposed it was her turn to walk away. The lover and the liar, the liar and the lover. They switched those roles between themselves like it was a game.

"I tell the truth," Juliette said again. Each word was a blade that sliced through her tongue, cutting her twice as deep as the harm she put out into the world. "Wake up. This entire dalliance between us has been an extraction of information."

"Juliette, don't say such—"

"Mybergh Road," Juliette interrupted.

Roma stopped. He simply . . . stopped. He recognized the address. It was his mother's safe house. The one that no one knew about.

The blood feud is the blood feud. Don't think much on it. Don't dwell. It's not your fault.

Oh, but it was. *It was.*

Lady Montagova had died two weeks after Juliette left Shanghai. Two weeks after the attack on the Scarlet house that had killed all their servants.

Because after the attack, Juliette had lost her temper at the two Scarlet men escorting her onto the boat to New York. Her parents were too busy to even send her off. The Scarlets had thought the task beneath them; one had snapped for her to shut up, that she was merely a child who knew nothing about this city, who wasn't needed here.

Because that day, Juliette had stomped her foot down in a fit of childish anger and, to prove herself, told the two Scarlet men everything she knew about the White Flowers in one long breath, including the safe house location of Lady Montagova. She had gotten the address on an off chance, one lazy afternoon when she had gone into White Flower territory to surprise Roma and overheard him talking to his father.

The Scarlet men hadn't asked questions about how she knew such information. They had brushed her off. She thought they hadn't taken her seriously. She had felt sick to her stomach once she boarded the boat, but she told herself that Roma betrayed her *first*. That the Scarlet Gang could do what they pleased with the information she gave them and it would serve him right.

She never could have thought that they would hunt down his mother.

"I knew," Juliette said. "I always knew. Your mother's death is my doing."

From her bed, Alisa had started to shake. She was looking at Juliette with wide, wide eyes.

"No." Roma could barely get the word out. "You didn't."

Outside, the sounds of the workers' protests rang in stark closeness. Metal struck the other side of the hospital walls in frenzy and hysteria.

Roma was having trouble breathing. He suddenly could not see clearly, could see only blurs of colors, vague figments of shapes, the barest glitter of a person who opened her mouth and spat, "I was raised in hatred, Roma. I could never be your lover, only your killer."

Juliette Cai strode forward, directly in front of Marshall. She knelt down callously, pulled his hand away from his wound, inspecting him as if he were nothing more than a piece of trash tossed before her feet.

"An eye for an eye," Juliette said.

She struck Marshall hard across the face. He was sent skittering, his body colliding with the hard, cold floor, both his arms winding around his head, a hand in front of his face as if to protect himself. Blood. So much blood beneath him.

Juliette put both her hands around her weapon. She made a twisting motion to her pistol, securing her grip. Then:

"A life for a life."

Bang.

"No!" Benedikt roared.

Marshall's head lolled back. He was motionless.

Motionless.

Roma couldn't breathe.

"Marshall, get up," Benedikt spat. "Get up!"

Juliette made a flippant, waving motion to the Scarlets holding Benedikt captive. "Let him go," she said. "Let him see for himself."

And the Scarlets listened. They eased up on their guns just enough so that Benedikt could move away, but not so much that they could not shoot should he suddenly attack. Juliette had pulled herself up to the top again. She was slotted back above Tyler, and there she would remain, so long as she was terrible.

Benedikt walked to Marshall. Appearing utterly, utterly devoid of anything, anything—he put his hand to Marshall's throat and kept it there, waiting.

A terrible noise tore forward from his cousin. Roma would hear that sound in his head forever.

"Wake up," Benedikt demanded roughly. He shook Marshall's shoulders. Marshall was unresponsive. Only a corpse, limp as a marionette. "Wake up!"

He would not wake up.

Juliette did not react to the scene before her. She looked at the body and the mourner like they meant nothing to her—and Roma supposed they didn't.

"Go," Juliette said to him. She aimed her gun at Alisa. "Go before we kill you all."

Roma had no choice. He staggered to Alisa, held out his hand for her to take.

And the White Flowers retreated.

Juliette watched them leave. She burned the image into her mind, burned in the relief that flooded through her veins and tasted like sweetness on her tongue. She forced herself to remember this moment. This was what monstrosity achieved. Perhaps Paul Dexter was onto something after all. Perhaps there was something to terror and lies.

A cacophony of voices burst into the hospital. It echoed through the long corridors, calling for workers to fan out and sack the place, to enact as much destruction as possible.

"I'll deal with him," Juliette said, nodding to the body she was kneeling over. "Go, Tyler. Take your men. There's a back door."

For a long moment, it seemed that Tyler would not accede. Then, as a loud clang of metal against metal rang through the hospital, he nodded and waved for his men to follow him.

Only Juliette remained, settling her hand on a cooling body.

Only Juliette remained, living with the weight of her sins.

Epilogue

The workers' strike was a failure," the maid said, "but that is to be expected."

Juliette gritted her teeth, placing the food she had gathered from the kitchen into the basket she had set out. The sky had turned dark and she had long scrubbed the blood that stained her hands from the events earlier in the day. When she had returned to her house, her relatives had not even known where she had gone—had not even known she had narrowly been caught in the riots that decimated Nanshi.

The riots had not lasted long after Juliette vacated. As soon as the police forces came barreling through, aided by the gangsters in mass numbers, it was not a fair fight at all. The workers would return to their factory jobs tomorrow morning. Those who had killed their bosses would receive a jail term.

That was that.

Juliette had a feeling the Communists would not be deterred so easily. This was only the beginning of their revolts.

"Anyway," the maid said gingerly. "Your parents are asking if you will be at dinner. They seek Miss Kathleen and Miss Rosalind too."

Juliette shook her head. "I have an errand to run. I'll be back within the hour. Let my parents know, would you?"

The maid nodded. "And your cousins?"

"I sent Kathleen out on a task. She's to be excused too."

Perhaps Juliette had said it in a tone that revealed her confusion, or perhaps the words themselves were enough to incite curiosity. The maid tilted her head, noted the sole name, and asked, "What about Miss Rosalind?"

Juliette shook her head with a shrug. "Kathleen said she didn't want Rosalind going with her, so Rosalind is still up in her room. You may wish to ask her yourself."

"Very well." The maid bobbed her head and hurried to her task.

Juliette, sighing, closed her basket tightly and set off too.

Kathleen wrinkled her nose, surveying the state of the Bund. She had been warned about the corpse, about the insects floating in the water and the bullet holes studded in the most bizarre places, but seeing it for herself was another matter. What a *mess*.

Kathleen spun in a slow circle, grimacing as her shoe came down on the insects lying dead on the pavement.

"She said it should be where the dead man is," Kathleen called, waving her arm to direct the group of Scarlet men Juliette had assigned to help her. "Get looking."

Their task? Juliette wanted a fist-size insect, one that she said remained upon a wharf along the Huangpu River. For the sake of science, Juliette had claimed. Really, Kathleen wondered if it was so her cousin had something concrete in front of her, something that confirmed this madness was over and Juliette had done what she had needed to do and it had been worth it.

"Should we, er . . . move the corpse first?"

Kathleen grimaced. She peered down at the wharf, at Qi Ren in his slumped form, wholly human now and very, very dead.

"Leave him be for now," Kathleen said quietly. "Start searching."

The men nodded. Kathleen helped, toeing around the wharf and kicking some of the smaller insects down into the water. The insects floated. All their little dead bodies and exterior shells lumped together on the river, drifting about in groups, resembling oil atop cold soup.

"Miss Kathleen," one of the men called. "Are you sure it's this wharf?"

A giant insect was not something that should have been hard to spot. But it was nowhere to be found.

"She said it was the one with the corpse," Kathleen replied. "I don't see any other corpse on any other wharf."

"Perhaps Miss Juliette was mistaken?" another Scarlet tried.

"How could she mistake the retrieval of a giant insect?" Kathleen muttered, perplexed. Still, there was no use searching any further if it was not here. Perhaps it had been crushed underfoot, so harshly that it was nothing more than specks of dust now, invisible to their searching eye.

Kathleen sighed. "Never mind," she said. She pointed to the corpse. "Move him out?"

The men hurried to comply. Left to her own devices, Kathleen took one last inventory of the scene, eyeing the bloodstains where the wharf started. She nearly missed it, but under an overturned wooden box, she spotted a briefcase lying atop yet another small clump of dead insects.

"Let's have a look at you," Kathleen muttered, pulling the briefcase free. Without thinking, she clicked it open, but she clicked it the wrong way, causing the lid to immediately flop in the other direction and spill forth its contents. The items hit the floor with a *thud*, drawing a concerned shout from the Scarlets nearby.

"Don't worry!" Kathleen called quickly. She dropped to a crouch and hurried to clean up the clutter. "I am clumsy."

She shuffled through the papers, snagging them before they could blow away with the wind. But before she could slot them back into the briefcase, her eye caught on the letter at the very top, one that was postmarked with COPY, signaling the paper to be a receipt of something that Paul had sent out. In the top corner, the address of the sendee placed the destination of this letter in the French Concession.

Kathleen scanned the short message.

And at once, in utter and abject horror, she dropped everything in her arms again.

The basket dangling on her arm, Juliette knocked on the door to the Scarlet safe house, glancing over her shoulder. She felt assured that she had not been followed—she had checked every three steps on her way here—but still, she turned anyway, ruling out any chance.

Shuffling came from within the apartment. The sound was loud, the motion immediately drifting in Juliette's direction due to the tiny size of the apartment and the low, squat ceiling.

"Hurry up," Juliette called, banging on the door again. "I don't have all day."

The door swung open. Marshall Seo raised an eyebrow. "Don't you?"

"I'm a busy person," Juliette said firmly. She motioned for him to step back so she could enter and shut the door firmly behind her. This was a safe house rarely used, so rarely—given its location in the poorest parts of the city—that it did not have running water, nor any amenities past a bed. It did, however, have a dead bolt on the door and a convenient window for jumping, should the occasion rise. It did provide a place where no one would come looking.

"Did you bring me water?" Marshall asked. "I've been so damn thirsty, Juliette—"

Juliette brought out the giant canister of water, tossing it onto the table so that it made an unsavory clatter, daring Marshall to say anything more. He grinned.

"I also brought food," Juliette said. "Because I do not wish for you to starve to death."

Marshall peered into the basket, inspecting the little bags. "Only oranges? I prefer apples."

Juliette sighed. "For a dead man," she muttered, "you sure are annoying."

"Speaking of which . . ." Marshall wandered off, then plopped down on a rickety chair by the wall. He folded his arms across his chest, wincing imperceptibly when it pulled at his fresh wound. "When can I resurrect?"

It had been a gamble on Juliette's part. A matter of timing, a matter of trust—in Marshall, that he would know what she was trying to have him do, and in Lourens, in believing the serum she had stolen would really work as he said. It had been a matter of framing her sleight of hand when she pulled that jar from her pocket, when she tugged Marshall's hand away from his bullet wound and shoved the jar into his palm with the lid off. A matter of hitting him so he could collapse with his arms over his face, unseen while he drank it. A matter of taking the bullets out of her pistol so it fired only with the sound, stopping the barrel from pushing a second bullet into Marshall.

Then it had been a matter of pure luck. Of Juliette running into the main office and finding one doctor who had not evacuated, who was sorting through her filing cabinet with no concern about the workers flooding the hallways. Of Juliette convincing the doctor to operate on Marshall despite his lack of heartbeat, hauling his body into the surgery room right before the protestors spotted them in the adjacent corridor, and chaining down those doors until the workers got tired and left that wing of the hospital. The bullet that Tyler fired came out quickly—having only embedded itself shallowly at the skin of Marshall's ribs—and the doctor stitched Marshall up. Juliette had promised her money to keep her quiet, but the doctor had wrinkled her nose, not even knowing who Juliette was.

"Give me some time," Juliette said quietly. "Lie low until I can figure out what to do with Tyler. Until he believes entirely that I was merely tricking Roma."

Marshall narrowed his eyes then. "How much of it *was* a trick?"

Juliette looked away. "Is this really the time for defending your fellow brother-in-arms?"

"I'm a dead man, darling. What's the harm in answering the question?"

What was the harm? Only her dignity.

"None of it, Marshall Seo," Juliette said. She wiped her eye quickly. "I didn't have to save you. I could have shot you right through the head."

"But you saved me," Marshall said. "Because you love him."

Juliette made a frustrated noise at the back of her throat. "Don't say it like that. Don't be so loud."

Marshall gestured around, as if to demand, *Who is listening?* Nobody. Nobody was listening. Nobody would hear this confession of Juliette's except a dead man walking who could take it nowhere.

"And you love him enough to have him hate you."

"He *should* hate me," Juliette replied tiredly. "I killed his mother."

"Personally?" Marshall asked, knowing the answer.

"No." Juliette looked down at her hands. There was a scratch at the side of her wrist. She had no idea how it got there. "But I gave them her location with malice. I may as well have held the knife."

Marshall stared forward at her, unspeaking for a long while. There was pity in his gaze, but Juliette found that she did not quite mind. Pity from Marshall Seo did not feel prickly. It felt a little warm, a little kind.

"Before you leave me again," Marshall said after a pause, "in such a rush as you did earlier while I was still bleeding through my bandages, I have one request."

It might have been her imagination, but she thought his voice grew a little fainter. Juliette frowned.

"Go on."

Marshall Seo's gaze flicked away. "Benedikt."

"You can't," Juliette replied immediately, knowing what the request was without need for elaboration. It hadn't been her imagination after all. "Just one more person in on the secret makes this a hundred times more dangerous."

Juliette imagined Tyler finding out that Marshall was alive. She imagined him going on a crusade to figure out where Marshall was, hurting everyone who might hold the location. She didn't think Benedikt liked her very much, but she would not let Tyler hurt him.

"I may have to hide for months," Marshall said, his arms coming around his middle. "He will have to believe I am dead for *months*."

Juliette's heart clenched. "I'm sorry," she whispered. "But as a favor to me, please, let Benedikt Montagov believe it. He must."

The floorboards groaned. The walls and ceiling blocks creaked, shifting with the howl of the wind outside. A small eternity passed with Juliette's breath held before Marshall finally nodded, his lips thinned.

"It won't be long," Juliette assured him, pushing the basket of food forward. "I promise."

Marshall nodded again, this one to show his acknowledgment of her promise. When she left him, shutting the door after her with a quiet click, Marshall was staring pensively out the window, squinting through a crack in the weakly boarded up glass.

Juliette returned to the streets, to the hustle and the bustle and the loud, loud anarchy. The sky was dark and the day had been long, but the city central had already returned to business per usual, to vendors selling their wares and merchants screaming their prices, like a monster had not torn a warpath through it hours ago.

And to gangsters. Gangsters, lurking in each corner, their eyes pinned to Juliette as she walked by.

"Miss Cai! Miss Cai!"

With a frown, Juliette paused and turned, finding a messenger running toward her. He appeared vaguely familiar as he approached, but it was not until he handed her a note with Kathleen's handwriting that she recognized him as one of the men she had sent to the Bund.

"Did you find what I asked for?" Juliette asked.

"There was no giant insect," the messenger reported. "But Miss Kathleen said to get you this as fast as possible."

Frowning, Juliette took the note and flipped it open. It was not a note *from* Kathleen, but rather what appeared to be the copy of a letter, marked as sent by Paul Dexter and addressed somewhere Juliette did not immediately recognize, identified only within the French Concession.

Juliette read the one-lined scrawl, squinting to decipher the spindly, long handwriting perfectly fitting for Paul Dexter.

She almost wished she hadn't.

In the event of my death, release them all.

The cold sweat that swept through her body was immediate. From her fingertips to her spine, she became possessed by a bone-deep terror, turning her wholly numb.

"What is this?" Juliette demanded. "What the *hell* is this?"

The messenger blinked at her, stunned. "Miss Kathleen just said to give it to you—"

Juliette shoved the note back at him. The messenger did not react fast enough to take it before the slip of paper fluttered to the ground, dropping onto the gravel like a softly landed butterfly. It was crushed underfoot at once as Juliette took a step forward, as she wheezed an inhale into her throat and searched her surroundings desperately, trying to think, think, think. . . .

"No," she whispered hoarsely. "No, he couldn't have."

The bells along the streets began to ring, seven times for the hour.

And in the distance, a chorus of screaming tore through the city.

TO BE CONTINUED . . .

Acknowledgments

When I was a teen reader, I almost never read the acknowledgments section unless it was to browse for a famous person's name, and I know there are a lot of you out there who are exactly the same. So before I start, I just want to declare that I'm Not Like Other Acknowledgments, by which I mean I'm *exactly* like other acknowledgments, just more obnoxious, so you who are about to close the book should probably read me.

Thank you to Laura Crockett, for your belief in this book, and in me. I hope you know that after our every e-mail exchange, no matter how mundane, I have to happily stare off into space for a few minutes to handle my appreciation for you. You saw my wild concept of Romeo and Juliet killing a monster in 1920s gangster-run Shanghai, plucked it out of your slush pile, and championed it with such brilliance that I felt assured every step of the way. I am so, so lucky to have you in my corner. Thank you also to Uwe Stender, for founding the magic that is Triada US, and thank you to Brent Taylor and the entire team at the agency for their wonderful work.

Thank you to Tricia Lin, for your editorial genius that absolutely bowls me over. From the moment we first spoke on the phone, I knew that you saw exactly what I wanted this book to be, and your vision and guidance transformed it from a cute little bud to a fully blooming rose bush. I couldn't be more grateful. Thank you also to Sarah McCabe for taking me in with so much care and enthusiasm. Thank you to Mara Anastas, and everyone at Simon Pulse for their passion and hard work: Chriscynethia Floyd, Sarah Creech, Katherine Devendorf, Elizabeth Mims, Sara Berko, Lauren Hoffman, Caitlin Sweeny, Alissa Nigro, Anna Jarzab, Emily Ritter, Annika Voss, Savannah Breckenridge, Christina Pecorale, and the rest of the Simon & Schuster sales team, Michele Leo and her education/library team, Nicole Russo, Cassie Malmo, Jenny Lu and Ian Reilly. Thank you to Billelis for such beautiful cover art that I physically had to lie down after first seeing it. And the biggest thank-you to Deborah Oliveira and Tessera Editorial for the thoughtful read and notes.

Thank you to Māma and Bàba for supporting me unconditionally. In every step of life, you have both always pushed me to be the best I can be and provided me with the best you could. It was your stories at the dinner table, your random anecdotes on long car drives, and the very way you raised me that sowed my love for the city above the sea. I'm glad I got mushed with your genes. Also yes, I *do* regret quitting my Chinese lessons ten years ago. Thank you for not rubbing my face in it *that* much, and thank you for translating the historical documents I send, for looking up things I can't find on English websites, and for making sure my pinyin isn't wildly off-tone. Also thank you to my fellow gene-sharers, Eugene and Oriana, who have to keep up with my weird requests on the family WeChat group.

Thank you to Hawa Lee, my best friend. From our days as annoying Year Sevens singing Selena Gomez at the back of the classroom to now, you have always been my number one hypewoman and I adore you until the end of time. You read the very, very first version of this book and said that my words play in your head like a movie: it warmed my heart then and it warms my heart now. Thank you to Aniket Chawla, also my best friend. As I'm writing this, you're finally reading this book after sending my earlier drafts to spam, but I'll forgive you because you're a kind soul who tried to teach me math in Year Eleven and I'll also adore you until the end of time. Thank you to Sherry Zhang, who I fondly call Sherry Berry, for offering me the sagest advice in my most panicked times. You were a literal saint while I was pacing up and down our tiny hotel room in Wellington trying to figure out my entire career. I'll always be cheering you on too. Thank you to Emily Ting, a ray of sunshine, for being excited about my writing from the very beginning (aka Year Nine science class) even when I was a pretentious potato.

Thank you to Mr. Randal for being such an amazing English teacher and having so much passion for teaching Shakespeare. I completely owe my love of language to those class lessons in Year Twelve and Thirteen analyzing metaphor and symbolism and imagery, and I hope all your future students realize how lucky they are to have you as a teacher. Thank you also to Ms. Black and Ms. Parkinson for being so encouraging with supporting my little NaNoWriMo club, and for being wonderful in the English department.

Thank you to Professor Chi-ming Yang for agreeing to oversee my research project alongside this book, listening to my unending thoughts about the Young Adult category, and helping me focus it all into a productive study. Thank you also to Professor Josephine Park for being the best when all my student hurdles started popping up, and walking me through everything so patiently.

Thank you to João Campos for reading the messy early draft of this book with enthusiasm, and for your notes and amazing suggestions that made these characters so much better. Also for being the best hugger. Thank you to Ryan Foo, for always thinking the best of this book and giving me joy. Thanks for promising to be my defense attorney if I ever murder a man one day. I'm holding you to that. Thank you to Andrew Noh, for supplying me with metaphorical tea and entertaining me while I was dying over edits on this book, and checking my French. Thank you to Kushal Modi, also for checking my

French to make sure I don't sound like a fifth grader, and for keeping me company whenever I hole up in my room to write. And of course, thank you to Jackie Sussman, for always listening to me brainstorm plots and putting up with me sticky-taping our room full of character webs, and not jumping in fright every time I exclaim aloud because I worked something out. Thank you to Rebecca Jiang and Ennie Gantulga, for being amazing friends and amazing roommates, and for making our apartment a place of laughter. Thank you to Anastasia Shabalov for your wonderful notes on this book's early draft, our long conversations about the publishing industry, and also for checking my Russian to make sure no one was calling anyone a little rat.

Thank you to my early readers, also known as the friends I gathered from the internet. To Rachel Kellis—one of my favorite people ever. Our chats range from so-hilarious-I-literally-can't-breathe commentary to serious feedback on our writing, to proofreading each other's e-mails for tone and appropriate amounts of exclamation marks, and I appreciate them—and you—to the ends of the earth. To Daisy Hsu—you were my first friend from the internet, which is wild since we actually have real-life mutual friends. It's because of your genius suggestions that I stopped pulling my punches in this book and leaned into the angst. To Tori Bovalino—the queen of dark stories, and my favorite person to complain about bad books with. I enjoy our bitterness very much, and I can always count on you to be equally as flabbergasted as I am over the most . . . peculiar decisions made on the internet. To Eunice Kim—the nicest person alive and a wizard at helping me summarize things. You know I'm the biggest fan of your GIF selections. Sorry for hurting your sinnamon rolls . . . or am I? To Miranda Sun—my fellow salty Gen Z'er. I don't know how we constantly have so many opinions on everything, but at this rate we have definitely written the equivalent of at least ten novels in our DMs with our hot takes. Here's to a million more DM novels filled with hot takes. To Tashie Bhuiyan—who I'm always screeching with. I can't believe we became friends because I saw someone who looked like Gansey and I started sending you live updates, but it's pretty representative of us. I don't know what I would do if I didn't have you to send all my "what-fresh-hell-is-this" screenshots to. To Alina Khawaja—I'm in awe by the power of your memes and the strength of your meme collection. This book's meme page is singlehandedly run by your will-power. And when the power of will fades, there will always be the power of thirst. To Molly Chang—my one-woman hype parade and the one who is always encouraging me to channel my inner Juliette (by which I hope you mean I should be more tough with the world, not that I should go out and pick a fistfight). To Grace Li—for saying such nice things about this book, and inspiring me with how much beautiful pain your words cause. To Zoulfa Katouh—queen of the funniest reaction images I've ever seen, queen of making people cry, and queen of everything, actually. To Meryn Lobb—you could liter-ally slap me across the face (and metaphorically, with your feedback) and I would thank you for it.

Thank you to the lovely people in the publishing industry who are kind to me for no reason other than to be kind. Thank you to Tasha Suri for answering the many, many questions in my e-mails. Thank you to Morgan Al-Moor for reading this book and making me the coolest aesthetic I've ever seen in my entire life. Thank you to Faridah Àbíké-Íyímídé, for being a wonderful person in general, and for assembling the Avengers of Colour mentorship program, which filled me with such joy. Thank you to everyone in the Roaring Twen-ties Debut group, the most wonderful community. Here's to us push-ing through one of the most difficult debut years, y'all.

Thank you to the bloggers who were hyping me up before there was even anything publicly available about this book other than a one-line pitch. Thank you to the people I adore on Twitter who send me eye emojis in excitement. Thank you to those who go out of their way to include me. Thank you to CW and all the friends at The Quiet

ACKNOWLEDGMENTS

Pond, Shealea, Danielle Cueco, Lily @ Sprinkles of Dreams, Noémie @ Tempest of Books, Karina @ Afire Pages, Tiffany @ Read by Tiffany, Laura @ Green Tea and Paperbacks, Kate @ Your Tita Kate, Fadwa @ Word Wonders, and so, so many more that I know I must be forgetting. And because I can, thank you to Halsey's *Hopeless Fountain Kingdom* album, which played on repeat while I drafted this book.

Thank you to my earliest, *earliest* readers, who read this book (and technically, its sequel!) when it was all one big manuscript posted online in installments. It's almost unrecognizable now except for the character names, but your feedback was critical to molding it into what it is now. To Kelly Ge—you were the very, very first person to hear about the conception of this book as an idea, and encouraged me forward. To Paige Kubenka—your regular comments kept me going and meant the world to me. To Gabrielle, Kamilia, Clairene, Hala, Aubry, Ejay, Tanvi—I don't know your last names and I don't know if you know that the story you read got published, but if you're out there, and you happen to pick up this book again, thank you. The reason why I kept writing all these years was because I knew there was someone out there treasuring my words. Growing up, no matter how shaky my craft was when I first started, I never once doubted the value of my stories because I had readers who spoke up about what they enjoyed. For as long as I have my readers, I can never stop being a writer. Without my readers, I am no writer at all.

So thank *you*, reader. Thank you for picking up this book.

Author's Note

Shanghai in the 1920s was a vibrant, divided place, and though much has been made up in *These Violent Delights*, the atmosphere is as true to history as I could possibly capture. This was a time of political turmoil and factionalism, Nationalist against Communist, and the whole city on a tight string that was only moments away from snapping. Though there was no blood feud, Shanghai really was split: among foreigners, who gained control through unfair treaty terms after China's loss in the Opium Wars; the French had ahold of the French Concession; the British, Japanese, and Americans were in the International Settlement; and all the injustices that Juliette mentions are pulled right from the history books. Foreigners built parks and demanded the Chinese keep out. They poured funds into the city, and though China was never formally a colony, that was precisely what was going on in Shanghai: segment after segment being colonized.

So Shanghai grew lawless in this climate, and yes—it really was ruled by gangsters! Because each foreign territory was controlled by the country in charge, there were different laws operating in different parts of Shanghai. Add in the rules of extraterritoriality for non-Chinese citizens—meaning foreign citizens could not be persecuted by Chinese law, only the law of their home territory—and it was almost impossible to govern Shanghai as one city. While the Scarlet

Gang did not exist, the Scarlets are based on the very real Green Gang (青帮; Qīng Bāng), who were said to have involvement with any crime that occurred in the city. They were unofficially a governing force, and one of the major gangsters—think someone of Lord Cai's stature— was also working as a detective in the French Concession police. The White Flowers did not exist either, but in this decade, the Russian population in Shanghai had grown large enough to constitute a huge portion of civilians. Shanghai was a free port, so those fleeing the Russian Civil War could easily enter the city, not needing visas or work permits. They were treated terribly by the Western Europeans, and worked the smaller jobs like garbagemen, or poorly paid jobs like club dancers. In my reimagining, there is a reason why the Scarlet Gang and the White Flowers are the ones on an equal playing field, grappling for what was left of the city while the foreigners ate it up in big, casual gulps.

Suffice to say, the characters that appear in *These Violent Delights* are figments of my imagination. Real Nationalists and gangsters collaborated often, true, but all specific names and personalities have been made up. There was indeed a Secretary-General of the Communist Party, but Zhang Gutai was not a real person. That being said, because of later civil warfare, there are huge gaps in the records regarding who held the position of Secretary-General and other various roles, so who's to say what *really* went on at this time? Even true history is not entirely sure about itself sometimes: memories are lost, evidence destroyed, logs purposely erased.

What *is* certain is that there was no monster spreading a contagious throat-tearing epidemic through Shanghai. However, there was hunger and wage depreciation and terrible working conditions, and in real history that was enough to incite hundreds of strikes involving hundreds of thousands of workers in 1926 alone. If I had adhered to a true historical time line and included them all instead of just the one that unfolds at the very end of this book, there would be disruption in every chapter. In the world of *These Violent Delights*, it was people dropping dead because of madness that intensified the anger and incited revolt. In truth? Even without a rampaging monster, it was bad enough that the labor unions were rising up against foreigners and gangsters alike in an attempt to change the workers' way of life. As for how it all went down from there, I'll leave the rest for the author's note at the back of the sequel. . . .

There was a secret nook behind one of the gravestones in Shantung Road Cemetery, where fifteen-year-olds Roma Montagov and Juliette Cai used messengers to drop off and retrieve letters. The following includes letters from Roma that Juliette kept, as well as undelivered letters that still remain at the bottom of Roma's desk drawer, locked away and collecting dust.

1922.11.13   DELIVERED

J,

    May we meet at that other place with the statue instead of the usual today? There were some rumblings in the house about an ambush at the Bund, so it may be safer to avoid the area. I write vaguely on the off chance that this message is intercepted from the runner I am sending it with . . . but I suppose there is more to worry about than the message itself if they find out who it is going to.

    While I have your attention, you will never guess what I saw today. A . . . I am momentarily forgetting what it is called in English. The white bird that is everywhere in the French Concession. Annoyingly red feet. 鴿子? I saw one sitting outside my house today—sitting!!! I did not know birds could sit. I wish I could have taken a picture and shown it to you, but we do not yet have a camera for personal use. "Too unnecessary," my father says.

    Returning to my initial point, do write back to confirm. I will be waiting.

—R

P.S. A pigeon. I just remembered it is called a pigeon.

J,

    I write with news on the dumpling store. It has closed, as have all my hopes and dreams with the knowledge that we will never get their 小籠包 again. I suppose I will see you at the Bund tomorrow without a pit stop first. We can mourn together the loss upon the world.

    I am only half joking.

—R

J,

How do you feel about Chinese opera? Hear me out before you toss away this letter. They are showing "Yang Naiwu and Xiao Bai Cai" at Great World this weekend, which has all the torture and tragedy you enjoy. Early paper reviews say they might even splatter some fake blood into the front row seats. And I <u>know</u> you are intrigued by that thought. For someone with a face so pretty, you really have the interests of an elderly mad scientist, you know that? And before you kick me, I am not complaining, I am merely putting all my persuasive arguments on the table so that you are willing to come to the opera to me.

So . . . Friday? Or we could do something else, if the opera does truly sound terrible to you. My feelings will not be hurt—you may speak your truth. (Okay, a little hurt. You will have to say some nice things about me to smooth it over.) I am simply in the hope that we expand our entertainment beyond the Bund, for some versatility. You can throw marbles at my head in other parts of the city too. It will be fun.

—R

J,

    I thought I saw you along Nanjing Road today and almost had a heart attack. The White Flower presence was rather plentiful nearby, so I do not exaggerate when I say I broke out in an immediate cold sweat. Then the girl turned around and I realized it was only a fur coat similar to yours, that her hair was longer, and her smile nowhere near as radiant.

    On that thought, however, may we meet on Nanjing Road this evening, to stroll Wing On? Contrary to how I opened this letter, there will be no White Flowers running patrol there, I promise. Their routes will have moved north by nightfall.

    I owe you a present after my last five marble victories. I must restore <u>some</u> balance to the world, after all.

—R

P.S. Do you have plans on Christmas? I was wondering if you would perhaps like to meet that day?

Juliette,

Though our families are at war, I want no part in their meaningless fight. I am in love with you. I will not sit upon it a second longer. Scarlet or White Flower, none of it matters. Allegiances and territory lines are meaningless constructions, as is the idea of hatred passed on by blood. It will never be hatred for me. It is love. It is your smile when you think no one is watching. It is you, all you, lifting your shoulders up to your ears when you are cold. It cannot be that you do not feel it too: that which passes between us as easily as a spark of light. You are half of my living spirit, my kindred soul

This is so ridiculous. Why am I writing this in a letter? Do not be a COWARD.

Okay. Okay. I shall say it. With words. Spoken. Out loud. Боже мой.

1922.12.26   DELIVERED

J,

    You looked beautiful yesterday. Just wanted to let you
know. Can I see you more often now? Everything I said
was true. I promise to court you properly, blood feud be
damned.

—R

Dear Juliette,

    I am no longer writing short, vacuous missives that go unsigned and unaddressed in the fear that we will be caught. Let them catch us—let us wage war if they are to stop us. Let them hear me when I speak theatrics from the rooftops. The city already writes poetry of your eyes and lips; it is hardly fair to punish me for joining the masses. I want them to know: That when a raven flies by, I think of your hair. That when the sun sets over the river, it is nothing compared to your grin, it pales even to your feigned glares, to the valiant effort you make at looking angry when you scrunch your nose at me.

    Meet me by the statue today. I have far more to say, but only once you are in my arms, bundled close against the cold. You can laugh me off all you like, I don't mind. I will speak the most outrageous nothings until I grow hoarse. You make me brave. Ты – моя родная душа.

    Yours, for as long as the stars burn,
    Roma

Dear Juliette,

    Juliette. Juliette. Was there ever a name so sweet? I do not think I could ever tire of it, of murmuring it again and again in the silence of the night. The city is always terrifying, always loud, but the mere thought of you puts it all at ease.

    I do not recall what I was initially writing about. I will send another letter when I do remember. Poor messenger is going to hate me for sending him back and forth so often.

Yours,

Roma

1923.02.16   DELIVERED

Dear Juliette,

    Much to my dejection, I will not be able to meet this week. There are a strange amount of White Flowers posted around the house and I cannot sneak out.

    My father is knocking on my door now in summons, so forgive me for the haste in which this letter is written. I will write again when the coast is clear.

Yours,

Roma

1923.02.24   <u>**UNDELIVERED**</u>

Dear Juliette,

I don't expect you to forgive me. I don't expect you to
ever receive this letter, nor any of its contents, so perhaps
all I ask forgiveness for is writing to you to make myself feel
better, like some fool pretending I still have you.

I had no choice. It was either to

I'm sorry. I'm sorry. Я тебя люблю. 我愛你.
為了愛我願意做這一切.

Yours forever,

Roma

1923.04.02   <u>UNDELIVERED</u>

Dear Juliette,

    I promised myself I would stop writing. I promised myself I would let you go, out of sight and out of mind, now that you are an ocean away. But I still dream of you. Too many nights I wake up in a start because I imagined you here with me, and my first instinct is never relief, it is panic. Panic that no matter what I do, it is not enough to keep you safe.

    You never needed me to protect you from the dangers of the world, I know. There will always be the blood feud, and there will always be hate between the Cais and the Montagovs, I know. But I put you at risk of more harm. In my father's eyes, you are no longer only Juliette Cai, the enemy's daughter, but Juliette Cai, the girl I would choose over anything, anyone, even the White Flowers. It is my fault there is a target on your back, painted with the blood of my heart.

    I brought you danger, but I can fix it. It is a greater act of love to let you go. I know. I know.

Yours,

Roma

1923.05.15

Dear Juliette,

 I thought I could freeze you in time. That when you went away, you would remain as you were, as that last image I had of you with your face tilted to the wind and your eyes closed, my kiss pressed to your cheek in goodbye.

 Am I wrong to have hoped? I suppose so. I can barely see these words I am writing under this dim moonlight, but they are the last that I am putting to paper. I read in some story that we should never swear on the moon, because it is ever changing. If the moon is inconstant, so too is our promise. Bright and aglow one day, shining the way for every late hour wanderer. Gone entirely the next, shrouded in shadow and hiding from those who need it the most.

 We said we would build the world anew. One by our own rules. Perhaps we could not make it kind, but at least it would be salvageable. We swore by it. And now . . .

 They say you opened fire on innocents. That you struck a showgirl across the face and laughed. That you invite lovers into your bed and strangle them. I don't know how much is true. I don't know how much is rumor that you yourself invented.

 You are the moon, Juliette. I don't know who you are anymore. I don't know who you have become.

 I cannot fool myself any longer, nor can I continue pinning hope onto letters never sent across the sea. It is for the best if I have lost my Juliette. It makes it easier to grieve.

Roma

Turn the page for an exclusive series

of vignettes between

ROMA and JULIETTE!

"THE YEAR WAS 1922, AND NOTHING WAS IMPOSSIBLE."

I.

Juliette closed her left eye, trying to line up her shot. This was life-or-death. This had everything riding on it: the fate of the day and the fate of her reputation. . . .

She flicked her finger and the marble sped into the circle, colliding against the others with a satisfying *clink-clink-clink*. For a moment, there was a dizzying array of colors skittering in all directions. Then the red beads settled, the green beads came to a stop by the piece of string, and Juliette scrambled to her feet with a high-pitched squeal.

"Victory," she crowed, "is *mine!*"

Roma Montagov rolled his eyes, bending down to collect the marbles. He feigned annoyance, but Juliette caught him trying to suppress his smile.

"Okay, drama queen. It was a game of marbles, not a cage fight."

"I would win that too."

Juliette stopped a still-rolling marble with her shoe and kicked it over to him to help with the tidying efforts. She had struck her last shot so hard that the marbles had scattered everywhere in the alley, one hiding behind a half-rotting trash bag damp with rainwater. With a grimace, Juliette pushed her dress sleeve up, folding the fur around her wrist so it wouldn't get dirtied when she nudged aside the trash. These alleys were cramped, soggy, and vaguely dark, even with the morning sun hovering somewhere along the winter horizon.

Nevertheless, it was where they came to hang around, because it was the place with the fewest prying eyes.

Juliette finally rolled the marble out, huffing a breath as she stood and nudged it again with her shoe. It was then that a sudden pressure struck against her temple, like something had fallen from the sky. Juliette reared back, blinking in shock as her hand flew to cup her head. By the time she realized it was not the heavy sky pelting miniature rocks at her, but *Roma* plucking marbles from his palm one by one and shooting them at her with deadly aim, another had struck the back of her hand and bounced to the ground.

"Hey!" she whined.

"What?"

"What do you mean, *what*?" Juliette dodged the next marble. "Quit it!"

"Make me."

The sea breeze blew in, salty and cold and wicked. It seemed to liven Roma up further as he grinned. Even at fifteen, he was a better marksman than half the gangsters in the city, though not for any notorious reason. Money simply bought the best tutors and teachers. He was good . . . but Juliette was better.

She caught the next one he threw, right out of midair, and hurled it back at him.

It struck his shoulder. Roma gave a short yell, all the marbles in his hand falling to the ground loudly. The Bund was nearby, making a constant ruckus from the ship workers and crew men as they bellowed and made haste, trying to get home earlier and earlier in the day as the end of the year approached. Juliette didn't hear Roma emit any other noise of pain after his first yell, but she saw his lips part as he staggered against the wall, his head lolling down.

Juliette blinked. "Ro—"

She cut herself short. It had been a month since they first met by the Bund, a month of coming here to play with marbles, but they had not yet acknowledged who the other person was. There was no doubt that Roma knew—he knew she was Juliette Cai, heir to the Scarlet Gang, heir of the group that was his greatest enemy. All the same, they did not speak of it.

"Hey," Juliette tried again, stepping closer. "Are you okay?"

No response. Roma was looking to his feet, his hair fallen into his eyes, hand clutched around his shoulder. She didn't *think* she had thrown that hard. What could it be? Paralysis in the nerves? Internal bleeding? Those involved in the blood feud would be awfully happy if she had accidentally killed the White Flower heir.

Juliette reached out with her hand. And in the blink of an eye, Roma grabbed her wrist, hauling her up against the wall until her back was to it and he had her boxed in, both of her hands pinned above her head. They were pressed close enough that it would be a scandal between any two kids in this city—and even more so that it was the two of *them*—but Juliette only loosed an irritated breath, vexed to have been caught out in his charade.

"Still winning that cage fight?" Roma asked cheerily.

"Ugh!" Juliette tried to kick with her feet, but he only side-stepped, avoiding each strike. "You are such a sore loser."

"It doesn't look like I am losing."

"At *marbles*, you wet blanket."

Roma laughed, the sound so warm, so all-encompassing that it trembled throughout his whole body. Juliette couldn't help the grin that slipped onto her face too—that sudden flood of happiness, rare in a city slick with blood.

"Now look at that." Roma released one of her hands from his grip, only so his own was free to grasp her chin lightly. "I count this as a victory."

His touch was soft, and yet she felt it like a divine burning, like taking a drink directly from the sun. Juliette didn't know what to make of any of that, so she simply wiped off her grin and batted at him with her free hand until he stepped away. There was a sigh in the wind, like the sigh of the world, displeased that this was how Juliette would choose to respond. But there was nothing it could do except blow a strong breeze that whirled around the two, darting through Roma's shirt collar and ruffling it against the hollow of his neck, darting in and out of the pomade in Juliette's hair, yanking just one strand loose from her finger waves. The two heirs stood there in stillness, simply looking at one another in curiosity, until the wind died down and the moment passed. Juliette picked up one of the fallen marbles. "Shall we play again?"

11.

Roma leaned against the bookshelves, his book resting against his knees. The cold tiling of the floor sunk into his bones, but he didn't shift around, afraid that if he fidgeted it would make Alisa fidget as well, and she had only just gotten comfortable, reading from the book of world maps that he had picked out for her. With December rolling around and the start of the Western holiday season approaching, their foreign tutors had already stopped coming in to teach lessons. It had left Alisa bored around the house this week, so Roma took it upon himself to start hauling her around the city with him. When Roma was eight, as Alisa was now, he and Benedikt were already running about the borders of White Flower territory, slinking around the corners to investigate where the shootouts were happening. Give it a year or two and he was sure that Alisa was going to stop humoring him and find her own ways to spend an afternoon too.

The library suddenly boomed with sound, ringing with the echo of the heavy front doors slamming closed. Someone had entered, and the library was small enough—only ten or so shelves extending past the librarian's front desk—that her heels clicked loudly on the marble. Roma could mark her progress as she walked, could mark where she hurried and where she paused, slowing to inspect the chandeliers dangling from the tall ceiling and the little jade statues decorating the hollows of the walls.

The footsteps finally approached the back of the library. Juliette Cai turned around the corner, offering no smile in greeting but instead a click of her tongue and a wink, which was somehow better.

"Hello, darling," she said.

Roma blinked, heat rushing to his cheeks. A prolonged second passed, his heart pounding in his chest, before he realized with a jolt that Juliette was talking to his little sister, not him. In fact, Juliette's attention was only on Alisa, head ducked to coo at the little girl before she passed her a vegetable bun.

"Xièxiè!" Alisa shrieked gleefully, snatching the bag. She ran off immediately, scurrying like an attic mouse to go eat elsewhere. Alisa never ate in front of people. It was such a strange quirk.

Juliette watched Alisa go with a glint in her eyes, folding her gloved hands in front of her.

"Do you think she's going to remember in a few years how well I fed her?"

"Only if you keep feeding her," Roma replied evenly. He was quite impressed that he kept his voice level, setting his book down next to him and calmly gesturing for Juliette to come sit. "She already calls you Bun Girl."

Juliette snorted, closing the distance between them and dropping onto the floor too, so that she was seated beside Roma but facing him, her knees pulled up and pressed to the shelves. She was graceful even with such abrupt movements.

"I offer her a bun three days in a row and suddenly I am Bun Girl."

"Well—"Roma couldn't help himself. He reached out and ran a finger along the edge of her glove, fascinated by the lace hem, the delicate pattern pressed to smooth skin "—shall I give her your real name?"

Juliette tensed. She tried not to show it, tried not to react, but it was the subtlest change in the air, the darting of her eyes to his face, moving from relaxed to alert.

"And what would you tell her?" Juliette asked, testing him.

The truth was that Roma had known since the very first moment. He knew Juliette had discovered it sometime later, after their first meeting, perhaps their second. She had made the active decision to come back and keep seeing him, but he had been looking for her from the beginning. Juliette Cai, heir of the Scarlet Gang, the terrible thing with bloodlust in her veins, raised in the West to be as ruthless as a snake. Then he had rolled his marble at her, and she had merely raised an eyebrow, a picture of stillness as the rest of the Bund hurried and bustled, and all Roma could think was *Hello, kindred soul.*

"Princess of Shanghai, of course." He withdrew his hand. "Nothing else would be worthy."

Juliette's posture eased. Just as Roma was pulling back, she leaned forward, setting her gloved hand on his shoulder. He felt the smoothness of the silk brush against his jacket, as starkly as if it were skin-to-skin.

"As ruler of this kingdom," she intoned, "I hereby dub thee Sir Barnacles, Lord of the Garbagelands."

Roma's hand came up immediately, laid atop hers. "I heard they were in search of a Lady Barnacles too. Interested?"

Juliette's lips parted, her eyes narrowing for a beat as she seemed to decide whether or not Roma was joking. A moment passed. Then another. Though the library remained humming around them, though the old antique clocks were ticking to mark time, though the first droplets of rain pressed against the stained windows outside, it was all distant and far away, of another world separate to the one only Roma and Juliette occupied.

Then there was a loud thud behind them and Juliette jumped, yanking her hand back. Roma, too, swiveled around, squinting through the gaps of the shelves with his heart at his throat.

"Hello."

It was only Alisa, who had climbed a shelf and was now waving from the top, having thrown one of the books onto the floor.

"*Christ*, Alisochka," Roma chided. "Get down from there, would you?"

Alisa squeed, running along the top. With a soft exhalation, Juliette got to her feet.

"I'll get her."

III.

Juliette held a hand up, trying to shield her eyes from the sun. It was mid-December, so it was strange for the day to be so bright, and for it to be rather warm too. The collar of her coat felt too snug around her neck while she lay on the grass. She would be collecting stains on her clothes and gathering dust in her carefully curled hair, but she had no interest in leaving the park and going back home either. Under the beating sun, she closed her eyes hoping that a cloud would come eventually.

Her etiquette tutor had dismissed her for the day. Juliette had learned the lesson at record speed, and there was little use for sitting around the kitchen table wasting more time while Nurse lingered around her asking if she was hungry. It only stressed Nurse out when Juliette was sitting idle—but Juliette liked sitting idle, even if that seemed to be taboo in the Cai mansion, where everything was always moving, where *something* had to be happening. She liked observing, and thinking, and watching. She liked being a menace too and driving Nurse up the walls when the woman tried to shove more food into her, and all Juliette would do was put her nose in front of the bowl of rice and heave in a deep, peaceful inhale.

Poor Nurse.

"What are you smiling about?"

Juliette cracked one eye open, turning her head to the left. The grass under her head bristled, the stout, green blades tucking around her cheek. While she was flat on the cold ground, Roma was sitting against the tree, sharpening a pocketknife against a rock. The light hit him perfectly, so that his dark hair glowed slightly golden at the edges.

"The sweet, sweet sound of you sharpening that blade," Juliette teased, sitting and propping herself up with one hand behind her. She tried to smooth out her hair, but the back was beyond saving. "Like music to my ears."

Roma quirked a brow. He held the blade up, its edges glinting.

"A gift, then," Roma said. "For you."

Juliette rolled her eyes, pushing his hands back before he could give her the pocketknife. "Don't be ridiculous. Only White Flowers carry pocketknives."

If Roma hadn't known about the Scarlet aversion to pocketknives, he didn't show it. Or perhaps he did know, and had expected to have been declined anyway, offering for the sake of playing pretend.

"Some other day then," he said, "I will commission the best dagger in the city instead and carve your name upon it."

Juliette winced. He had been doing this a lot lately. Inching closer and closer to their identities. Pushing through the bubble between them that contained only Roma and Juliette, letting in the shards and pieces that read Montagov and Cai instead.

A rustle came from afar, interrupting Juliette just as she opened her mouth. She would have tried to change the subject anyway, but her reaction now was genuine, her head whipping to the sound of intrusion. She had passed a construction team around a gazebo earlier, all of them hurrying onto their ladders and passing buckets up. It had looked important from afar, as if something on the gazebo was coming loose, only when Juliette walked closer, she saw that the buckets were filled with tinsel and the construction workers were merely decorating for Christmas. They had enough tinsel among them that the whole park would soon be covered in it, but Juliette didn't think they would come into *this* area. It was usually unoccupied, surrounded by a dense cluster of trees. There was a pond that ran somewhere to the west, and a path that curved around the trees. No one came by unless it was a local nanny taking her foreign charges on walks, which was why Roma and Juliette came often, even when the grass was hard with frozen ice.

Juliette strained her ears. Now that she was paying attention, it didn't sound like Englishmen installing tinsel at all.

"Are they speaking Russian?" Roma asked, listening too.

"It appears so."

The more she concentrated, the easier it became to decipher the voices, until she realized it wasn't because she was particularly good at focusing, but because they were getting nearer and nearer. Whoever was coming, they were directly upon the path that would wind into the clearing.

"We need to hide."

"What?" Roma exclaimed. He folded his pocketknife, putting it away. "There would not be White Flowers on foreign territory like this—"

"I don't think they are White Flowers."

Juliette gave him a push without waiting for a response, sending him sprawling to the other side of the tree. Before Roma could complain or yelp in indignation, Juliette flopped right onto him and slapped her hand over his mouth.

"Bolsheviks," she explained, her eyes wide. "I think they are Bolsheviks."

They stilled, listening again. It was two men, discussing something about the Communist Party, which had only formed last year. Juliette had heard bits and pieces from within her own house, but certainly not enough to think it any big matter.

Roma squirmed, shaking her hand off his mouth.

"Dorogaya," he hissed. "Can you let me *see?*"

Juliette gave him a pointed look, warning him not to be so loud. She relented, however, and eased her elbow off his chest, letting him twist just enough to peer around the other side of the tree. The two men came into view, dressed in Western suits. The style was similar to the sort Roma wore, but where Roma never had his jacket on, the front buttons of his shirts always undone, these men were stiff in their getups.

"...*Voitinsky?* ... *Comintern* ...*cannot next* ...*week.*"

They faded from view, disappearing through the trees.

"Did you catch any complete sentences?" Juliette asked. She wasn't sure if it was her vocabulary that was lacking, or if they hadn't spoken very clearly.

"Something about the Party," Roma replied. "I doubt it is anything we have to worry about."

"Yes, well . . ." Juliette bit down on the inside of her cheeks, still running through what they had picked up. "I am worried nonetheless."

"I know. You shoved me so hard that I am going to bruise."

Juliette frowned, plonking her palm flat on Roma's face. It was a light smack—a teasing one, if anything—but Roma still feigned pain, scowling. His hands came to her waist, fit snug around each side.

"I shall throw you off now."

"Don't you dare."

"One, two—"

"No!"

"*Three!*"

He tightened his grip, his fingers pressing into the thick fabric of her coat. Juliette tensed, squeezing her eyes shut and bracing to be tossed right off and onto the grass, but nothing happened. When a few seconds passed and she still remained sprawled atop him, Juliette opened her eyes slowly, cautiously.

Roma looked entirely too gleeful. "Scared you, didn't I?"

Juliette smacked him again, this time with both her hands on his chest, and with much more vigor. "*Clown.*"

IV.

Roma paced the length of his room, the letter scrunched in his hands. It was too sappy. Too orchestrated. Juliette would laugh at him if he gave her this.

With a huff, Roma stopped in the middle of his carpet, glancing at the letter again. It was Christmas Eve today, and the streets outside were abuzz with noise. Though few locals in Shanghai celebrated such a holiday, it was prime time for the foreigners to be throwing money around, and so the shops were pulling out all the stops, the markets slashing down their prices. He could hear the street-level bartering and bantering from here, albeit faintly as he stood surrounded by the uproar of his own thoughts.

Juliette, the letter started with. *Though our families are at war, I—*

Roma folded the paper up roughly, uncaring when the edges creased. He shoved his hair out of his eyes then turned a fast pivot on his heel, facing his mirror as if the other figure in the glass were Juliette.

"I am in love with you," he declared.

It was only for practice, yet his face turned red nonetheless. This was ridiculous. He was fifteen. He could be more suave than this. Roma didn't know much, but he knew that he had fallen too hard and had fallen too fast. If he didn't speak now, he might never have a chance, because this city was brutal to dazzling things walking its streets, and Juliette was the most dazzling of them all.

"Maybe that is coming on a little too strong," he muttered under his breath, bracing his two hands on his desk and leaning closer to the mirror. It wasn't as if Juliette had ever indicated she felt the same. *She* was the suave one, the one who gazed back coolly anytime he was caught staring at her over a game of cards. *She* was the one who always held her composure when they smuggled bottles of champagne up to their rooftop meetings while Roma's world turned bright and glittering, unable to stop gravitating around her.

Roma pushed away from the desk, blowing out a breath.

All the same, Juliette looked at him more fondly than anyone. Not his mother, and certainly not his father—although it wasn't the sort of fondness that he would expect from his parents either. It was . . .

A light tapping sounded from his window. Roma jumped, thinking that it would be Alisa catching him fretting over the letter in his hands. Their bedrooms were high up on the fourth floor of White Flower headquarters, but his sister was prone to climbing the outside of the house, shuffling along a water pipe that ran just under the windows.

However, it was not Alisa sliding along the pipe and tapping to be let in.

It was Juliette.

Roma had to be hallucinating.

"Let me in!" Juliette whispered, her voice muffled by the glass. She wasn't hanging from the walls like Alisa would but leaning out from the window of the neighboring building. The apartments were built closely enough that when Roma came to open his window, Juliette clambered onto the windowsill of the other building and climbed over, hopping the space between two buildings easily like she wasn't minding a gap from four stories high.

"What are you doing here?" Roma asked, flabbergasted. He offered a hand and Juliette took it, landing softly on his carpet. "I thought we were meeting *tomorrow*."

Juliette straightened, tossing her head so that her hat shifted back into place. "I was in the area."

"You were in the area?" Roma echoed. "And you decided to enter enemy territory?"

Juliette wrinkled her nose. She never liked it when he reminded her that they were supposed to be enemies, as if he were manifesting the thought by speaking it too many times and that it might come true one day.

"You don't want me dropping in?"

"I never said that."

"Hmm . . . " Juliette wandered about his room, peering at his bookshelves and the photo frames on the painted white walls. Roma still had not entirely grasped the situation. Juliette. Here. In his house. In his bedroom. Juliette. Here. Now. Plopping onto his bed.

"I am serious," Roma said. Juliette had collapsed like a marionette doll, her shoes planted on the floor but the rest of her upper body splayed to the side, so he approached her and crouched too, bringing their faces near. "What are you doing here?"

Juliette propped her head up on one hand.

"My house got too loud," she said quietly. "So many foreigners invited over for their little Christmas party. I could hardly hear myself think."

Roma breathed a soft sigh, his heart twisting in his chest. Panicked as he was—over Juliette being here, over Juliette in general—he hardly hesitated before reaching out and smoothing a thumb along the curve of her cheek. Juliette immediately held open her arms, squirming against him until her chin settled in the crook where his shoulder met his neck, locking him into an embrace. No matter what they were, no matter what it was between them, they were comfortable enough for this at least: for a safe place to land and a shoulder to lean on.

A few moments passed. Roma wanted to close his eyes and stay like this forever. But, because this was a serious matter:

"There are other quiet spots in the city," he said against her hair. "Quiet, *safe* spots. The parks. The riverside. Anywhere but the White Flower central building."

"I know," Juliette replied, her words equally soft. "Maybe I just missed you."

Roma was going to start bawling, right here and right now. He wasn't built for so many feelings.

Fortunately, before he could, Juliette pulled out of his arms, then frowned, tilting her head.

"What is that in your hand?"

"Nothing," Roma answered, at the same time that a sudden knock came on his door. The sound drove such alarm into him that he bolted to his feet, all the blood rushing from his head. His vision flashed white for a second as he shoved the letter into his pocket and marched to the door, stepping directly in front of it in case someone was about to open it and find Juliette Cai in his room.

"Who is it?"

"Me," a voice that sounded like Marshall said. "Come on, we need to go."

"Go?" Roma echoed. "Go where?"

"Can you open the door?" another voice asked. His cousin, Benedikt. "We are needed downstairs."

Roma spun fast on his heel.

"I hate to do this," he whispered to Juliette, "but you must leave."

Juliette folded her arms. She was feigning annoyance, but there was also amusement sparkling in her eyes, her shoulders too relaxed to have any true irritation. "You will toss me out on the streets?"

"*Yes*, it is a better option than getting caught here."

A huff, then Juliette hopping to her feet. "Fine, fine."

While Roma reached into his wardrobe, finding a new jacket so it didn't seem like he was keeping his friends outside for no reason, Juliette walked to the windowsill again, clambering up and readying to duck back out.

"Wait! Roma!"

Roma startled. This was the first time he had ever heard his name from her lips. It was beautiful. He never wanted to be called anything else again. Not Roman, not Montagov. Just Roma.

"What?" he asked, his pulse rocketing. Was there something he had forgotten to hide? He didn't know what he could possibly have in his room that would give away his friendship with the Scarlet heiress, but still he searched in a panic, glancing around at his feet.

"No, come *here*," Juliette hissed, still balanced precariously on the window ledge, her hands clutching the frame.

"What?" Roma asked again. He rushed in front of her. "What is it?"

Juliette brightened suddenly with a grin and leaned in, her hand touching his face and her lips pressing a kiss to his cheek. It was so quick he might have imagined it; he would have thought so if the spot weren't humming with sensation, the imprint of her mouth buzzing like an electric shock.

"You are trying to get me killed," Roma whispered, breathless.

Juliette didn't respond—she merely blinked innocently, and then she was gone, hopping the gap again and climbing through the other window. Soon as she disappeared, Roma drew his curtain tight, afraid that he had somehow left evidence all over the glass, and with his heart thudding in his chest, he went to open his bedroom door.

"Okay, we may go," he said. "I needed my jacket."

Marshall turned on his heel immediately, starting down the hallway. Benedikt, meanwhile, stared at Roma a second longer.

"What is that on your face?" his cousin asked, frowning.

Roma touched his cheek. It came back smeared with red.

"Blood," he lied without hesitation.

V.

J uliette was freezing cold, but she was the one who had set their meeting place today, so she only had herself to blame as she hovered around the alley, trying to burrow her neck into the fur of her coat. She had given Roma enough grief yesterday by showing up to his house, she figured she wouldn't wander around now in case he couldn't find her when he arrived.

The air was so frigid that it hurt a little to breathe. The foreigners in the Concessions were in peak festive mode, so the streets echoed with ringing bells, the nearby churches pealing with sound on the hour. Every storefront she passed had been decorated with wreathes and mistletoes, over-decorated if you asked her. She hadn't celebrated

Christmas even when she was in New York, so she certainly would not start in Shanghai, even if the whole city seemed to be caught up in the fervor today.

She didn't think Roma celebrated either, until she turned around and saw him approaching, a gift box in his hands.

"What is that?" Juliette asked, her voice accusatory. "You didn't say we were getting Christmas gifts! I would have gotten—"

"It is not a Christmas gift," Roma interrupted before Juliette could start prattling all the various items she knew Roma would like. "It is a birthday gift."

Juliette blinked. "My birthday was October 15th."

"Your Lunar calendar birthday. I calculated. It is today, is it not?"

Juliette thought for a second. "Oh. Oh, it is."

Roma was already opening the gift box for her, revealing a string of pearls. Before Juliette could speak on how beautiful they were, he had already looped them around her neck, pulling the clasp tight and then stepping in front of her again, adjusting her coat so the pearls fell inside, protected from the cold.

Juliette stared at him, her jaw agape. She needed to crane her neck ever so slightly because Roma was taller, but Juliette was sure she would catch up—Nurse kept saying she had yet to hit her growth spurt.

"What?" Roma asked, catching her staring.

"Thank you," Juliette replied, her eyes wide. "You didn't have to—"

"We are not finished celebrating yet." He grabbed her hand, pulling her along. "Come on, I have just the place."

Juliette followed wordlessly, at a loss for what to say. They ran through the streets, bursting into laughter when a tram pulled up fast ahead of them and drove into a puddle, almost dousing Roma in dirty water before Juliette yanked him quickly onto the pavement. Another few streets later, a rickshaw driver almost collided with

Juliette when she dashed into the road too fast, but Roma picked her up just in time, plonking her back on the sidewalk while Juliette gave an adrenaline-filled screech.

Eventually, they arrived before a jazz club, but they didn't enter through the front. Roma eyed the building carefully, then when the patrons around the door all disappeared inside, he tugged on Juliette's hand and pulled them around the side, entering through a tinsel-covered back door and trudging up a set of stairs before anyone could see them.

"Are you cold?" Roma asked, holding the rooftop door open for Juliette.

Juliette stepped through, feeling the wind slap against her face. Strangely, she was not. "I'm okay. How did you find this place?"

The walls of the rooftop were low, only raising up to her knees when she wandered over to look out at the city. From below, the music of the jazz club was loud enough that every beat was audible: the twang of the strings and the dizzying rhythm of the piano. This wasn't like any of the other rooftops they had hidden out on. This one had some strange quality to it: the flooring was a little too clean, the view a little too nice. The city stretched on before them, twinkling with daytime lights as people spilled onto the streets with hot drinks in their hands and others hurried home with shopping bags overfilled in their arms.

"Asked around. Did some research."

Juliette turned around, arching a brow at Roma. He sounded rather cryptic, but he was grinning.

"Research? Of what kind?"

Roma waved her off, then held his hand out.

"Dance with me?"

A little white fleck settled onto his palm. Juliette looked up, and suddenly found more to be falling from the skies, drifting hazily down on them. It was snowing. It was snowing, and the music beneath their feet roared even louder, not fit for the slow sort of dancing, but Juliette didn't care. She took Roma's hand and let him draw her close.

"You may confess now," Juliette said. "How long have you been planning this?"

Roma's grin only grew, letting them sway utterly off-beat with the string tunes and rapid tapping rhythm.

"I missed your October birthday."

"We hadn't met yet."

"Nevertheless. It was inexcusable to let that slide."

"Meaning . . . ?"

"A while, dear Juliette," Roma finally answered, his eyes crinkling. "I have been planning a while."

Juliette felt her breath catch in her throat. She didn't know how to express the emotion that swept through her. It was only that she looked up at Roma and could feel time shudder to a halt around them. It was only that every time she looked at Roma, she didn't want to stop looking; she wanted to sit down beside him and bid him never to leave her, to listen to him talk forever and ever and ever.

The music suddenly hit a lull below, the instruments falling quiet. The two of them followed suit, their swaying paused, but Juliette did not step away. Roma brought his hand up from her waist. While Juliette watched him, he brushed a finger along her cheek—slowly, so slowly that Juliette's heart started to pound before he showed her the eyelash that he had retrieved, and Juliette sighed a soft "oh," not sure why she was disappointed.

He had been so close. She had thought . . .

"Make a wish," Roma said.

Juliette smiled, trying to cover her momentary dejection. "A birthday wish or an eyelash wish?"

"Both. Why not?"

"Okay." Juliette inclined her head up at the skies. She couldn't see any part of the blue afternoon under the heavy cover of the clouds, but she imagined the falling snow to be falling stars instead, burning white-hot onto the world. "I wish—"

She didn't finish her sentence. Because then Roma was kissing her, his lips softly captured over hers, his hands to either side of her face. Juliette rose up on her toes immediately, her eyes closing and her arms twining around his neck. She could feel the snow landing between them, falling in little cold droplets on her hair, on her hands, on her coat. It didn't matter. Nothing mattered in that moment except the feeling of Roma's mouth on hers, keeping her warm from her very soul.

They broke apart slowly. A breath passed between them, a secret missive that revealed everything left unsaid, though there was hardly anything to be said when a kiss fulfilled it all.

"Are *you* cold?" Juliette whispered, her eyes fluttering open again. Roma was already looking at her, his gaze wide and reverent.

"Why do you ask?" he replied. A snowflake landed on the bridge of his nose, melting as delicately as artwork.

Juliette touched her fingers to his, to the soft grip he had upon her. She couldn't hold back her quiet laugh. "You're trembling."

He tried to still his hands. It did not work. It only delighted Juliette more when he could not stop trembling, so Roma gave up pretending to be dignified, wrapping his arms around her instead and spinning her around until they were both dizzy and delirious and giggling.

They came to a stop. Juliette cupped a palm to his face, right on the red flush that had risen.

"I'm sorry," Roma said breathlessly. "I interrupted your wish before."

"No, you didn't," Juliette replied. She gave a pleased sigh, then leaned in again. "You finished it perfectly."

Keep reading for a sneak peek
at the captivating sequel!

The New Year in Shanghai passed with such fanfare that a sense of party still permeated the city a week later. It was the way the people moved about—the extra bounce in their toes and the twinkle in their eye as they leaned over the seats of the Grand Theatre to whisper to their companion. It was loud jazz music audible from the cabaret across the street, the cool air of handheld bamboo fans waving about in rapid color, the smell of something fried smuggled into the viewing room despite Screen One's strict rules. Marking the first day of the Gregorian calendar as a time for celebration was a Western matter, but the West had long stuck its roots into this city.

The madness in Shanghai was gone. The streets had been lulled back into uproarious decadence and nights that went on and on—like this one, where theatergoers could watch a picture and then saunter along the Huangpu River until sunrise. After all, there was no monster lurking in the waters anymore. It had been four months since the monster of Shanghai died, shot to death and left to rot on a wharf by the Bund. Now the only thing civilians needed to worry about were gangsters . . . and the increasing number of bullet-hole-ridden corpses showing up on the streets.

Juliette Cai peered over the railing, squinting down at the ground level of Screen One. From her vantage point, she could see almost everything below, could pick out every minuscule detail among the chaos broiling under the golden light fixtures. Unfortunately, it would have been more useful if she were actually down there herself, mingling with the merchant she had been sent here for, rather than staring at him from high above. Their seats tonight were the best that she could do; the assignment had been given far too last minute for Juliette to finagle something good in the thick of the socializing sphere.

"Are you going to be pulling that face all night?"

Juliette swiveled around, narrowing her eyes at her cousin. Kathleen Lang was trailing close, her mouth set in a grimace while the people around them searched for their seats before the picture started.

"Yes," Juliette grumbled. "I have so many better things to be doing right now."

Kathleen rolled her eyes, then wordlessly pointed ahead, having spotted the seats marked on their tickets. The stubs in her hands were ripped poorly after the uniformed ticket boy at the door got his top hat knocked into his eyes by the crowd surging into the portico. He had hardly a moment to recover before more tickets were waved in his face, foreigners and rich Chinese alike sniffing their noses at the slow speed. In places like these, better service was expected. Ticket prices were sky-high to make the Grand Theatre an *experience*, what with its arched ceiling beams and wrought-iron railings, its Italian marble and delicate doorway lettering—only in English, no Chinese to be found.

"What could possibly be more important than this?" Kathleen asked. They took their seats: the front-most row by the second-level railing, a perfect view of both the screen and all the people beneath. "Staring angrily at your bedroom wall, as you have been doing these few months?"

Juliette frowned. "I have *not* been doing merely that."

"Oh, pardon me. How could I forget screaming at politicians?"

Huffing, Juliette leaned back into her seat. She crossed her arms tightly over her chest, the beads along her sleeves clinking loudly against the beads dangling from her front. Grating as the sound was, it contributed only a small fraction to the general bedlam of the theater.

"Bàba is already giving me enough grief for upsetting that Nationalist," Juliette grumbled. She started to take inventory of the crowd below, mentally assigning names to faces and keeping track of who might notice that she was here. "Don't you get on my case too."

Kathleen tutted, setting her elbow onto the armrest between them. "I'm only concerned, biǎomèi."

"Concerned about what? I'm always screaming at people."

"Lord Cai doesn't reprimand you often. I think that might be an indicator of—"

Juliette lurched forward. Out of sheer instinct, a gasp rose in her throat, but she refused to let it out, and instead the sound lodged itself tightly in place, an ice-cold sensation pressed up against the back of her tongue. Kathleen immediately jerked to attention too, searching the floor below for whatever it was that had drained Juliette's face utterly of blood.

"What?" Kathleen demanded. "What is it? Do I call for backup?"

"No," Juliette whispered, swallowing hard. The theater dimmed. Taking their cue, the ticket boys started to walk the aisles, forcing the crowd to settle for the picture. "It is only a small hiccup."

Her cousin's brows were furrowed, still searching. "What *is* it?" Kathleen repeated.

Juliette simply pointed. She watched as Kathleen followed the direction in which she was indicating, watched as the realization set in when they were both looking at one figure pushing his way through the crowd.

"It would appear we were not the only ones sent here for a task."

Because down on the ground level, looking like he had not a care in the world, Roma Montagov smiled and stopped in front of the merchant they were after, extending his hand for the merchant to shake.

Juliette curled her fists tightly into her lap.

She had not seen Roma since October, since the first protests in Nanshi shook the city and set the precedent for those that were to follow when winter swept into Shanghai. She had not seen his physical person, but she had felt his presence everywhere: in the corpses littered across the city with lily-white flowers clutched in their stiff hands; in the business partners disappearing out of the blue with nary a message or explanation; in the blood feud making its mark. Ever since the city caught wind of a confrontation between Roma Montagov and Tyler Cai, the blood feud had shot back into its most terrible heights. Neither gang needed to worry about their numbers being picked off by the madness anymore. Instead their thoughts circled retribution, and honor, and as different mouths ran different accounts of what had happened between the inner circles of the Scarlet Gang and the White Flowers that day, the only definitive truths that came out were this: in a tiny hospital along the edges of Shanghai, Roma Montagov had shot at Tyler Cai, and to protect her cousin, Juliette Cai had killed Marshall Seo in cold blood.

Now both sides were vengeful. Now the White Flowers were pressing down on the Scarlet Gang with a renewed urgency, and the Scarlet Gang were fighting back just as hard. They had to. No matter how carefully the Scarlets cooperated with the Nationalists, every single person in this city could feel something shifting, could see the gatherings grow larger and larger each time the Communists attempted a strike. The political landscape was soon to change, soon to swallow up this way of lawlessness, and for both gangs currently ruling this city with an iron fist, it was either to be violent now and secure their holdings, or regret it later should a greater power swoop in when there was no way to win territory back.

"Juliette," Kathleen said softly. Her cousin's eyes shifted back and forth between her and Roma. "What happened between you two?"

Juliette didn't have an answer to give, just as she hadn't had an answer all the other times she was asked this question. Kathleen deserved a better explanation, deserved to know why the city was saying Juliette had shot Marshall Seo point-blank when she had once been so friendly with him, why Roma Montagov was dropping flowers everywhere he went in mockery of the feud's victims when he had once been so gentle with Juliette. But one more person in on the secret was one more person dragged down into the mess. One more target for Tyler's scrutiny—one more target for Tyler's gun.

Better to speak none of it. Better to pretend and pretend until maybe, just maybe, there came some chance to salvage the fractured state this city had fallen into.

"The picture is starting," Juliette said in lieu of a reply.

"Juliette," Kathleen insisted.

Juliette gritted her teeth hard. She wondered if her tone still fooled anyone. In New York, she had been so good at lying, so good at playing pretend as an utterly different person. These last months had been wearing her down until there was nothing left of her but . . . her.

"He's not doing anything. Look, he's taking his seat."

Indeed, Roma appeared to be walking away from the merchant after a mere greeting, settling into an end seat two rows behind. This did not have to be a big deal. They did not need to engage in a confrontation. Juliette could quietly keep an eye on him from where she sat and make sure she approached the merchant first when intermission came. It was a surprise that she had even been sent after a merchant. The Scarlet Gang rarely chased after new clientele; they waited for clientele to come to *them*. But this merchant did not dabble in drugs like the rest of them. He had sailed into Shanghai last week carrying British technology—heavens knew what kind; her parents had not been specific in their briefing, save that it was some sort of weaponry and the Scarlet Gang wanted to acquire his inventory.

If the White Flowers were trying to get in on it too, then it had to be something big. Juliette made a note to ask for details as soon as she got home.

The lights went dark. Kathleen glanced over her shoulder, fingers twisting into the loose sleeves of her coat.

"Relax," Juliette whispered. "What you're about to watch came directly from its premiere in Manhattan. Quality entertainment."

The picture started. Screen One was the largest viewing room in the whole Grand Theatre, its orchestral sound booming from all sides. Each seat was equipped with its own translation system, reading out the text that appeared alongside the silent film. The couple to Juliette's left were wearing their earpieces, murmuring excitedly to each other as the lines filtered through in Chinese. Juliette didn't need her earpiece, not just because she could read English, but because she wasn't really watching the film. Her eyes, no matter how much she tried, kept wandering down.

Don't be a fool, Juliette scolded herself. She had tipped herself into this situation at full speed. She would not regret it. It was what had needed to be done.

But still, she couldn't stop looking.

It had been only three months, but Roma had changed. She already knew that, of course, from the reports that came back to her about dead gangsters with Korean characters slashed in blood beside them. From the bodies piling up farther and farther inward into Scarlet territory lines, as if the White Flowers were testing the limits they could encroach upon. It was unlikely that Roma had sought out Scarlets specifically for vengeance killings—he didn't have it in him to go *that* far—but each time a conflict erupted, the message left behind was clear: *This is your doing, Juliette.*

It was Juliette who had escalated the feud, who had pulled the trigger on Marshall Seo and told Roma to his face that whatever happened between them had been nothing but a lie. So now all the blood left in his wake was his revenge.

He looked the part too. At some point, he had traded his dark suits for lighter colors: for a cream jacket and a golden tie, for cuff links that caught the light each time the screen flashed white. His posture was sharp, no more slouching to feign casual, no more stretching his legs long so he could slump into the chair and avoid being seen by anyone giving the room a cursory glance.

Roma Montagov wasn't the heir scheming in the shadows anymore. It seemed that he was sick of the city seeing him as the one slitting throats in the dark, the one with a heart of coal and the clothing to match.

He looked like a White Flower. He looked like his father.

A flash of movement blurred in Juliette's peripheral vision. She blinked, pulling her gaze away from Roma and searching the seats across his aisle. For a moment, she was certain she had merely been mistaken, that perhaps a lock of hair had come undone from her front curl and fallen into her eyes. Then the screen flashed white again as a shrieking train derailed in the Wild West, and Juliette saw the figure in the audience rise.

The man's face was cast in shadow, but the gun in his hand was very, very illuminated.

And it was pointed right at the merchant in the front row, who Juliette still needed to speak to.

"Absolutely *not*," she muttered angrily, reaching for the pistol strapped to her thigh.

The screen dropped into shadows, but Juliette took aim anyway. In the second before the man could act, she pulled the trigger first with a loud *bang*.

Her pistol kicked. Juliette pressed back into her seat, her jaw hard as the man below dropped his weapon, his shoulder wounded. Her gunshot had hardly drawn any notice, not when there was a shootout going on in the picture, too, drowning out the scream coming from the man's mouth and covering up the smoke wafting from the barrel of her pistol. Though the picture had no dialogue sound, the orchestral backing track had an uproarious cymbal banging in the background, and the theatergoers all assumed the gunshot a product of the film.

All except for Roma, who immediately swiveled around and looked up, eyes searching for the source of the gunshot.

And he found it.

Their gazes locked, the *click* of mutual recognition so forceful that Juliette felt a physical shift in her spine, like her body was finally righting itself into alignment after months out of configuration. She was frozen, breath caught in her throat, eyes pulled wide.

Until Roma reached into his jacket pocket and drew his gun, and Juliette had no choice but to jolt herself out of her daze. Instead of combating the would-be assassin, he had decided to shoot at *her*.

Three bullets whizzed by her ear. Gasping, Juliette struck the floor, her knees grazing the carpet hard as she threw herself down. The couple to her left started screaming.

The theatergoers had realized the gunshots were not a part of the soundtrack.

"Okay," Juliette said under her breath. "He's still mad at me."

"What *was* that?" Kathleen demanded. Her cousin dropped quickly too, using the railing of the second level for cover. "Did you shoot into the seats? Was that Roma Montagov shooting back?"

Juliette grimaced. "Yes."

It sounded like a stampede was starting on the floor below. The people on the upper level were certainly starting to panic too, hurtling out of their seats and rushing for the exit, but the two doors on either side of the theater—marked EVEN and ODD for the seat arrangements—were rather thin, and all they managed to achieve was a bottleneck situation.

Kathleen made an indecipherable noise. *"He's not doing any-thing . . . he's taking his seat!"*

"Oh, don't mock me!" Juliette hissed.

This situation was not ideal. But she would salvage it.

She scrambled to her feet.

"Someone was trying to shoot the merchant." Juliette made a quick glance over the railing. She didn't see Roma anymore. She did see the merchant pulling his suit jacket tightly around his middle and securing his straw hat, trying to follow the crowds out of the theater.

"Go find who it was," Kathleen huffed. "Your father will have your head if the merchant is killed."

"I know you're joking," Juliette muttered, "but you might be right." She pressed her pistol into her cousin's hand and took off, calling over her shoulder, "Talk to the merchant for me! Merci!"

By now the bottleneck at the door had thinned enough that Juliette could push through, merging into the main anteroom outside the second floor of Screen One. Ladies dressed in silk qipao were screaming inconsolably at one another, and British officers were clumped together in the corner to hiss hysterics about what was going on. Juliette ignored it all, pushing and pushing to get to the stairs, to get down to the ground floor, where the merchant would be emerging.

She skidded to a stop. The main staircase was far too crowded. Her eyes darted to the side, to the maintenance stairs, and she tore the door open without a second thought, barreling right through. Juliette was familiar with this theater; it was Scarlet territory, and she had spent parts of her early childhood wandering around this building, peering into the different screening rooms when Nurse was distracted. Where the main staircase was a grandiose structure of polished flooring and arched, wooden banisters, the maintenance stairs were made of cement and void of natural light, relying on naught but a small bulb dangling at the middle landing.

Her heels clacked loudly, turning the corner of the landing. She stopped short.

Waiting there, by the door into the main lobby, was Roma, his gun raised.

Juliette supposed she had grown predictable.

"You were three paces away from the merchant," she said. She was surprised her voice remained level. Tā mā de. There was one knife strapped to her leg, but in the time it would take to reach for it, she would be giving Roma plenty of time to shoot. "You left him just to find me? I'm flattered—"

Juliette swerved with a hiss. Her cheek radiated heat, swelling from the harrowingly close contact of the bullets that flew by her head. Before Roma could think to aim again, Juliette ran the quickest survey of her options, then dove through the door behind her, surging into the storage unit.

She wasn't trying to escape. This was a dead end, a thin room crowded with stacked chairs and cobwebs. She only needed . . .

Another bullet whizzed by her arm.

"You're going to blow this place up," Juliette snapped, spinning around. She had come to the very end of the storage space, her back pressed to the thick pipes that ran along the walls. "Some of these pipes carry gas—put a hole in one and the whole theater bursts into flames."

Roma was hardly threatened. It was as if he could not hear her. His eyes were narrowed, his expression scrunched. He looked unfamiliar—properly foreign, like a boy who had pulled on a costume and hadn't expected how well it would fit. Even under the dim lights, the gold of his clothes glimmered, as bright as the twinkling billboards outside the theater.

Juliette wanted to scream, seeing what he had been made into. She could hardly catch her breath, and she would be lying if she said it was only because of her current physical exertion.

"Did you hear what I said?" Juliette eyed the distance between them. "Put that gun away—"

"Do you hear *yourself*?" Roma interrupted. In three strides, he was close enough to point his gun right in Juliette's face. She could feel the heat of the barrel, hot steel an inch away from her skin. "You killed Marshall. You killed him, and it's been months, and I haven't heard a word of explanation from you—"

"There is no explanation."

He thought her a monster. He thought she had hated him the whole time, so viciously that she would destroy everything he loved, and he *had* to think that if he was to keep his life. Juliette refused to drag him down just because *she* was weak-willed.

"I killed him because he needed to die," Juliette said. Her arm whipped up. She twisted Roma's gun away, letting it clatter at their feet. "Just as I will kill you. Just as I will not stop until you kill me—"

He slammed her into the pipes.

The effort was so forceful that Juliette tasted blood inside her lip, sliced by her own sharp teeth. She stifled a gasp and then another when Roma's hand tightened around her throat, his eyes murderous.

Juliette was not frightened. If anything, she was only resentful— not at Roma, but at herself. At wanting to lean in even while Roma was actively trying to kill her. At this distance between them that she had willingly manufactured, because they had been born into two families at war, and she would rather die at Roma's hand than be the cause of his death.

No one else is dying to protect me. Roma had blown up a whole house of people to keep Juliette safe. Tyler and his Scarlet men would go on a rampage in the name of defending Juliette, even if they too wanted her dead. It was all one and the same. It was this city, divided by names and colors and turfs, but somehow bleeding the exact same shade of violence.

"Go on," Juliette said with effort.

She didn't mean it. She knew Roma Montagov. He thought he wanted her dead, but the fact of the matter was that he never missed, and yet he had—all those bullets, embedded into the walls instead of Juliette's head. The fact of the matter was that he had his hands around her throat and yet she could still breathe, could still inhale past the rot and the hate that his fingers tried to press into her skin.

Juliette finally reached for her blade. Just as Roma shifted forward, perhaps intent on his kill, her hand closed around the sheath beneath her dress and she pulled the weapon free, slicing down on whatever she came in contact with first. Roma hissed, releasing his hold. It was only a surface cut, but he cradled his arm to his chest, and Juliette followed close, leveling the blade to his throat.

"This is Scarlet territory." Her words were even, but it took everything in her to keep them that way. "You forget yourself."

Roma grew still. He stared at her, utterly unreadable as the moment drew long—long enough that Juliette almost thought he would surrender.

Only then Roma leaned into the blade instead, until the metal was pressed right into his neck, one hairsbreadth away from breaking skin and drawing blood.

"Then do it," Roma hissed. He sounded angry. . . . He sounded *pained*. "Kill me."

Juliette did not move. She must have hesitated for a fraction too long, because Roma's expression morphed into a sneer.

"Why do you pause?" he taunted.

The taste of blood was still pungent inside her mouth. In a blur, Juliette flipped the blade onto its blunt end and slammed the handle to Roma's temple. He blinked and dropped like a rock, but Juliette threw the weapon away and lunged to break his fall. As soon as her hands slid around him, she let out a small exhale of relief, stopping Roma just before his head could hit the hard floor.

Juliette sighed. In her arms, he felt so solid, more real than ever. His safety was an abstract concept when he was at a distance, far from the threats that her Scarlets posed to him. But here, with his pulse thudding through his chest and beating an even rhythm onto hers, he was just a boy, just a bloody, beating heart that could be cut out at any moment by any blade sharp enough.

"Why do you pause?" Juliette mimicked bitterly. Softly, she set him down, brushing his mussed hair out of his face. "Because even if you hate me, Roma Montagov, I still love you."